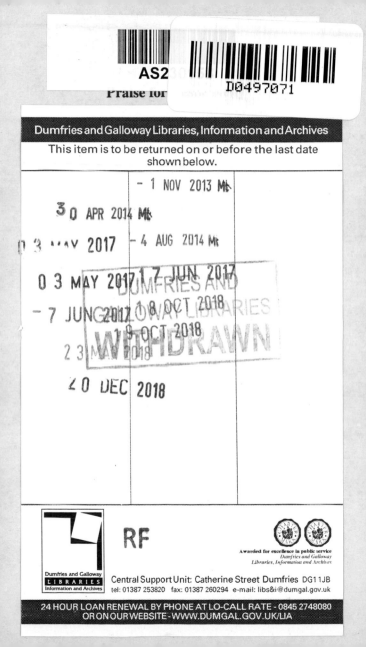

AS2 D0497071

LYING IN YOUR ARMS

BY
LESLIE KELLY

First published in Great Britain 2013
by Mills & Boon, an imprint of Harlequin (UK) Limited,
Eton House, 18-24 Paradise Road, Richmond, Surrey TW9 1SR

© Leslie A. Kelly 2013

ISBN: 978 0 263 90327 0
ebook ISBN: 978 1 408 99704 8

14-1013

Harlequin (UK) policy is to use papers that are natural, renewable and recyclable products and made from wood grown in sustainable forests. The logging and manufacturing processes conform to the legal environmental regulations of the country of origin.

Printed and bound in Spain
by Blackprint CPI, Barcelona

Leslie Kelly has written dozens of books and novellas for Mills & Boon Blaze. Known for her sparkling dialogue, fun characters and steamy sensuality, she has been honored with numerous awards, including a National Reader's Choice Award, a Colorado Award of Excellence, a Golden Quill and an *RT Book Reviews* Career Achievement Award in Series Romance. Leslie has also been nominated four times for the highest award in romance fiction, the RWA RITA® Award.

Leslie lives in Maryland with her own romantic hero, Bruce, and their daughters. Visit her online at www.lesliekelly.com or at her blog, www.plotmonkeys.com.

To my sisters, Lynn, Donna, Karen and Cheri.
You are all always in my heart.

Prologue

The Hollywood Tattler—
Shane Going NC-17?

WELL, LADIES, GET ready to indulge in a sexy lovefest with *superhot movie star Tommy Shane. Word is circulating that Shane's fiancée, screenwriter Madison Reid, is on the verge of selling her naughtily-ever-after screenplay and her hubby-to-be is going to star in it!*

Shane, who regularly lands on everyone's sexiest men alive lists, has played action heroes, romantic leads and innocent soldiers. But my sources tell me this next role—as a mysterious, dangerous man who lures an innocent young woman into his dark sexual fantasies—will be the edgiest, hottest performance of his career.

As if women all over the world didn't already have enough to fantasize about when it came to this golden-haired Adonis.

Soon, fantasizing will be all other women can do. Because we're also hearing rumors that Tommy and his fiancée have finally started making wedding plans for next year. Although Shane and Reid—his childhood sweetheart—live in a swanky beachside house in Laguna, they're heading to the other coast for the nuptial celebration. They will reportedly be having a small, private ceremony with their families in Florida, where they grew up as next-door neighbors.

Can you imagine Thomas Superstud Shane being the boy next door? Be still my heart.

We don't know a whole lot about the beautiful Miss Reid. But we suspect millions of women around the world would give anything and everything to be in her shoes. Or at least in her bed. I mean, who doesn't want to know just how much of her sultry screenplay is based on her real-life adventures with Tommy!

Congratulations and good luck you gorgeous lovebirds. I'll be watching the mail for my invitation.

1

"WAIT, ARE YOU SAYING you *want* me to break up with you?"

Not sure she'd correctly heard the drop-dead gorgeous man sitting across from her, Madison waited for a response from Tommy Shane. Aka her fiancé, aka the handsomest man alive, aka Superstud, aka Academy Award nominee.

Aka the man who wanted *her* to dump *him* right after they'd intentionally leaked details about their hush-hush wedding.

Aka...WTF?

"Yeah, Mad. I do."

She didn't get angry, the way most fiancées probably would. She wasn't the typical fiancée and theirs wasn't a typical relationship. Not by a long shot. If they knew the truth, most people would say she and Tommy put the "dys" in dysfunctional.

So, no, she wasn't angry. She was just confused, not sure what was going on. "You're the one who wanted this engagement."

"I know."

"You're the one who leaked the wedding date to the press."

"I know that, too."

"You're the one who played up the childhood-sweethearts-going-home-to-Florida-to-get-married angle."

"Yes."

"You convinced me to leave New York and move out here."

He shook his head. "But you're glad about that, aren't you? Look how well you're doing. Any day now, you're going to get a call that one of the big studios is going to produce your screenplay."

She wished she could be as sure. Madison had confidence in the story she'd crafted and pitched to the studios, with Tommy's help. But that didn't make it a done deal, even with his name attached to it as the star. Although, that sure didn't hurt.

She hadn't written it with him in mind. She'd seen her possibly murderous hero being someone much more dark and twisted. But he'd read the script, loved it and asked for the role. Who was she to turn down Hollywood's number one box office draw?

"This isn't simply cold feet, is it?" she asked, glancing down at the feet in question. "Make that cold ginormous feet."

"They're warm and toasty," he said with a flirtatious grin that would melt the underwear off any woman. Well, any woman who didn't know him well. "And you know what they say, big feet…"

"Big, fat ego," she said with a definite eye roll. Tommy Shane had long ago lost the ability to flirt his way around her common sense. She liked him—loved him, in fact—but she was wise to his antics and not susceptible to his looks or his charm.

"So, what do you say? Will you dump me, ASAP, preferably in as public a manner as possible?"

"Dude, seriously? I'd be happy to dump you on your ass so hard your butt cheeks will look like pancakes," she said, feeling far more relieved than a supposedly blushing bride should. "But I have two questions. First, will anybody buy it?"

"Huh?"

"I mean, why would any woman ever break up with you?"

"Well, I'm gay."

There was that.

Tommy's legion of worldwide fans wouldn't believe it, but his sexuality hadn't been a secret to her, not for a long time. He might play the part of sex symbol to every woman on the planet, but in his private life, Tommy Shane was strictly attracted to men—lately one particular man—and was very happy about it.

"Yeah, but nobody knows about that. Wasn't your in-the-closet-ness the reason we got engaged in the first place?"

"Of course."

"And haven't we been playing lovebirds to the press to cement your cover story so you can keep those sexy-leading-man roles coming your way?"

He smirked. "Well, it wasn't for your smoking-hot bod."

Chuckling, she placed a hand against her smoking-hot hip, knowing she held as much sex appeal for him as a beach ball. The one time she'd tried to kiss him romantically—when they were in middle school—she'd known they lacked any chemistry. It hadn't taken her long to figure out why. Hell, she should have figured it out in elementary school when the two of them would always fight over who got to be Buttercup when they played Powerpuff Girls.

Although the story they'd fed to the press had been fairy-tale nonsense, there had been some truth in it. They had known each other from childhood. She, Tommy and her twin sister Candace—who'd always played Bubbles to their Buttercup during *The Powerpuff Girls* days—had been inseparable growing up. He'd climbed into their window for secret sleepovers, had spent long summer days with them at the beach. He had taught Candace how to dance, and Madison how to give a blow job…using a banana, of course. He'd always loved to perform, but had also been strong—he even punched a guy once who'd groped Madison at a concert. Heck, he'd been the one who'd bought a pregnancy test kit for her when she'd had a late-period scare in high school. He'd even offered to marry her if the stick turned blue!

He was a wonderful, loyal, devoted friend. Which was why she had stepped in and agreed to get engaged to him in his time of need…after her sister, who was *supposed* to be the false fiancée, had gone and fallen in love with her dream man.

No, the engagement wasn't supposed to culminate in a real marriage, but their planned breakup was a long way off. They'd scheduled everything, figuring in shooting schedules and premieres, knowing how long they needed to keep up the pretense. They'd discussed how to pull off a gradual, *friendly* breakup once both of them were in good enough career positions to come out of it unscathed. And now he wanted to ditch all that in favor of an impromptu dumping, before they'd even had a chance to stage a public disagreement?

"Nobody'll buy it. You're the biggest fish in the ocean. What woman in her right mind would let you slip off her hook?"

"They'll believe it once the world knows what a cheating mackerel I am," he said with a simple shrug.

She gaped. "Tell me you're joking. You did not cheat!"

She didn't add *on me*. How could he cheat on her when they weren't involved? Even if the big rock on her finger said otherwise.

But there was someone else he could have cheated on, which would break Madison's heart. Tommy's new guy was wonderful.

"You didn't betray Simon, did you?"

"No, of course not," he insisted, looking horrified.

That made her feel a little better. Tommy wasn't the most reliable sort when it came to his romantic life. If he was stupid enough to screw up this new relationship, she'd personally whack him upside the head with his own SAG Award.

"So you two are still okay?"

"Fine." Tommy smiled wistfully. "He's great, isn't he?"

"More than great." Simon, a neurosurgeon, made her friend happier than she'd seen him in years. "So who'd you cheat on?"

"You."

"You're saying you have another best-friend-turned-fake-fiancée…besides Candace? I mean, I've always forgiven you for cheating on me with my sister, even when we were in third grade and you always picked her first for kick ball."

"Not Candace," he said. "I meant, you tell the world I cheated on you. Since I'm turning over an open-and-honest leaf, you don't even have to say it was with a woman. That'll just be what people will think. Who wouldn't dump me for cheating?"

Huh. He had a point. Technically, that was true.

"People will buy it. We'll be all Rob-and-Kristen-like."

She caught the reference. Madison wasn't a Hollywood insider, despite her engagement to a crown prince of Tinseltown, but who hadn't heard of the scandal surrounding one of Hollywood's "It" couples during the whole *Twilight* craze?

"Okay, so they probably would believe that. People have been wondering how on earth I caught you in the first place."

"Don't sell yourself short, gorgeous."

She shrugged. Attractive? Yeah, she'd cop to that. But gorgeous? No way. She had never felt more inept and lacking as a woman than when she'd attended some of these L.A. parties packed wall-to-wall with women who were pretzel-stick thin, cover-girl perfect and runway model clothed. Oh, and saber-toothed-tiger clawed. Sheesh, the competition out here was insane.

"But even if it works, *why* should we do it now rather than sticking to our long engagement, slow-breakup plan?"

He thrust a hand through his thick, sun-streaked hair, looking boyishly adorable. If there'd been an audience, all the women would just have sighed, every one of them dying to smooth that soft hair back into place. Madison just grunted.

Melodrama over, he said, "It's because of Simon."

"He asked you to do this?"

"No. We've been talking about how important it is to be honest. Me living a lie with you—no matter how good the reason or the fact that you're fine with it—won't convince him I'm growing and becoming true to myself."

"Simon would never want you to sabotage your career."

"I know. But this is a step toward the kind of life I want, and the kind of man I want to be. One who isn't afraid, who doesn't go to crazy lengths to hide who he is."

She rarely heard Tommy talk this way. His blue eyes didn't sparkle with mischief. He didn't appear to be acting. He was just being the sweet boy next door she'd always known, telling her what he really wanted, all the pretense stripped away, all the trappings of his life-style shoved into the background. Just Tommy. Just her friend. Her friend who needed her.

She'd always been there when he needed her, and vice versa.

"Besides, you're not being true to yourself, either," he added. "You aren't like Candace. I knew it wouldn't be a hardship for her to go without sex for a while. You, though... I know you're horny enough to climb out of your own skin."

She couldn't deny that; Tommy knew her well. She'd been the first one of the three of them to lose her virginity—at sixteen—and had probably had more lovers than the other two combined. The six months of their engagement had been the longest she'd gone without sex in *years,* and her biggest, naughtiest toys just weren't filling the gap anymore. So to speak.

"You've been a great fiancée. Now you can be off the hook and go out there and *get* some."

"Sure, I'll just find a hot guy and say, 'Do me, baby.'"

"Yep."

"Not so easy."

"Not so hard, either. So, will you dump me? Free us both?"

Hell, she'd gotten engaged to him out of love, hadn't she? Of course she could dump the man for the same reason.

But, she suddenly realized, dumping him might not be in his best interest. Because here was the thing about movie star breakup scandals. It was always the cheater who got slammed, not the cheatee. Frankly, Madison didn't need public approval. They wouldn't pay one moment's attention to a wannabe screenwriter who'd had a fling.

But Tommy Shane? Every woman's fantasy man, every kid's comic book hero, every man's wanna-be-him guy? Well, hell. Tommy Shane couldn't be a cheater. It would be like…like John Wayne turning out to be a secret communist or something.

"We can do this," she told him, slowly thinking it out. "But I have a condition of my own."

"I'll still pay you half of everything I made this year."

"Forget the money." She'd never take another dime from him. Tommy had supported her while she'd finished her screenplay. He'd helped her pay her student loans. And she'd let him, figuring if she was going to give up her life, her job, her home and any other man for the duration of their engagement, she would earn it. She was not coming out of this relationship grasping the short end of the stick.

But she was almost free now. That was worth more than money. She'd gone into this with her eyes open, and didn't regret it, but she couldn't deny a big part of her was ready to be just Madison Reid, writer, not Tommy Shane's fiancée.

And, though she wouldn't admit it, getting to have sex again was a pretty darned big perk, too.

"So what's your condition?" he asked.

"The condition is…I take the heat."

"Huh?"

"I'm the cheater. I'm the bitch. And you break up with me."

He sputtered. "No, you can't do that."

She put a hand up, cutting off his arguments. "Tommy Shane can't be a cheating dog. I can. Nobody'll give a damn."

"You don't know that," he said. "The press can be nasty."

"Why would they? They'll say I'm an idiot for letting you get away and that'll be the end of it."

"What if it's not?"

"Well, then, I'll...take a vacation. You send me somewhere tropical and I'll hide out until they forget all about me."

"You should do that anyway. Find a nice, hunky beach bum to shack up with for a little while," he said with an eyebrow wag.

"I'll think about it. So we're agreed?"

He frowned, clearly not liking the idea, but she wasn't going to change her mind. Tommy would never get through a scandal unscathed, but she would. Who cared about Madison Reid? She could take whatever heat anybody wanted to dish out because it wouldn't last for long.

And if it did? Well...there was always the somewhere-tropical-with-a-hunky-beach-bum idea.

2

"IT'S GOING TO BE one hell of a honeymoon."

Although the driver of the cab looked confused, considering Leo Santori was sitting alone in the backseat, he didn't reply. And it wasn't just because this was Costa Rica and Leo didn't speak Spanish. The driver spoke English, or something very much like it. No, he just seemed to be abiding by the code that said Americans on vacation in tropical paradises could be as strange as they wanted to be. It was all good. No problem.

"All good. No problem," Leo muttered.

All good that he was honeymooning alone.

No problem that he'd been betrayed.

It's really all good that my fiancée cheated on me six months ago so we canceled the wedding, which was supposed to have taken place yesterday. No problem that she kept the ring, the apartment, her yappy bichon frise—which really was *no problem—and the new KitchenAid mixer, and I kept the nonrefundable honeymoon.*

She'd also kept the best man. The one she'd cheated with.

No problem.

Still, it certainly was not a conversation he wanted to have with anyone. Especially not now that he was here in Central America, ready to embark on some to-hell-with-it adventures. Those would definitely include surfing and zip lining. Good drinks, beautiful beaches, exotic foods.

They also might include getting laid. *If* he happened to meet a woman who was interested in a rebound-sex-fest with a Chicago firefighter who had a slight chip on his shoulder and a honeymoon package created for two but starring only one.

"Here we are, *señor*," said the driver.

The ride from the international airport in Liberia to this west coast paradise had been comfortable. The driver had pointed out various sights that Leo felt sure he'd explore over the next several days. No doubt about it, Costa Rica was every bit as beautiful—sunny, robin's-egg-blue skies, vivid hills and jungles, perfect eighty-degree climate—as the brochures had said. An outstanding choice for a honeymoon. Even a solo one.

"Thanks, man," he said.

The driver pulled out his suitcase and handed it off to a broadly smiling doorman who quickly swept it through the entrance of the hotel, which, as advertised, looked small, tasteful and upscale. Inside, Leo glanced around, noting that every wall seemed open to the outdoors. But it was still comfortable, a soft tropical breeze blowing through, whispering along the cool tile floors and setting the potted palms in gentle motion.

A bellhop engaged him in conversation in heavily

accented English as they walked to the check-in desk. Leo only understood half of what he said, responding with smiles and nods.

The woman at the desk greeted him. "Welcome, Mr. Santori, we're so very glad to have you with us."

She smiled, obviously noting his surprise at being called by name. Then he thought about it and realized he might very well be the only person checking in today. He remembered from the research he'd done on this place that there were only twenty-four rooms on the whole property. Twenty-four bungalows each with a small, private pool and walled garden, just the thing for a romantic interlude between a new bride and groom.

Christ, what was he doing here?

The middle-aged woman, whose English was only slightly tinged with an accent, glanced past him and looked around the open lobby. "And where is Mrs. Santori?"

He grimaced. Obviously, despite his calls and his emails, word had not filtered down to the front desk that he would be traveling alone.

"Uh..."

"Oh, dear," the woman said, reading something on the screen and biting her lip in consternation. She swallowed, visibly embarrassed. "I'm so sorry, Mr. Santori, I didn't see the notation on your reservation."

Okay, so *somebody* had paid attention when he'd changed the reservation to make it clear he was no longer traveling with a companion. It had just taken her a moment to see the note. He wondered what it said.

Maybe: *attention—pathetic sap was cheated on and didn't get married.*

He doubted it happened often, but he couldn't be the first single-on-a-honeymoon vacationer they'd ever seen.

He didn't ask her to turn the screen so he could read it. His imagination was good enough. "No problem."

She smiled her appreciation. "How was your trip from the airport, sir?"

"Fine, thanks."

"Wonderful." Her fingers continued to click on her keyboard as she finished working on his check-in. "We have you in our Emerald Bungalow. It's one of our nicest on the west side of the property. Sunsets over the Pacific will make you gasp."

Yeah. He was sure he'd be doing a lot of gasping during this trip, just not for the reasons he'd expected. It sure wouldn't be out of breathlessness from the ninety-seven ways he and Ashley would have been having sex.

He pushed her name out of his head. He'd done a great job of that for the past six months, since the day he'd mistaken her phone for his and discovered the kinds of intimate sexting pictures he'd *never* want to see from a guy. Definitely not from Tim, his own old friend...and best man. Especially not when those messages were written to—and welcomed by—Leo's fiancée.

Six months had been enough to calm the anger, soften the insult, heal the heart. For the most part. It maybe hadn't been enough to kill the embarrassment, which was what he most felt these days when he thought about it. Which wasn't often.

It was only because he'd come here, to take advantage of the nonrefundable vacation he'd paid for months before the scheduled wedding date, that he was thinking of his ex. Back home in Chicago, around his big extended family, or the guys at the station or the women wanting to help him jump back into the dating game, he was able to forget there'd ever been an Ashley. Or that he'd ever been stupid enough to think he'd *really* been in love with her. If he'd *really* been in love with her, Tim wouldn't have ended up with a broken nose— he'd have ended up in traction. Or, if his great uncle Marco—supposedly mob connected—had had his way, with a pair of cement shoes.

But no. That wasn't Leo's way. No broken legs or kneecaps, definitely nothing even worse. Ashley just hadn't been worth it. When it came right down to it, he'd known his pride had been a whole lot more bruised than his heart. So he'd walked out on her without a big scene, not moved by her crocodile tears. And he'd let Tim off with a punch in the face…and a warning to watch his wallet since Ashley was a bit of a spender.

Frankly, that was why he figured she'd gone for the guy to begin with. The one place Tim had ever outdone Leo in *anything* was the wallet. Hopefully the lawyer would continue raking in the bucks to keep Ash supplied in the stupid snowmen figurines to which she was addicted. Actually, screw it. He didn't care if she never got another one, or if the freaky-faced little monsters melted. At least he didn't have to look at them anymore.

"Sir?" the desk clerk prompted.

Realizing he'd let his mind drift, he shoved away thoughts of Ashley. He was in paradise and had no room in his head for anything dark. "Sounds great, thanks."

"Here you go," she said, handing him a plastic key-card. She also gave him a map of the property. "I hope you have a wonderful time. There are so many things to do, so many people to meet."

He needed to get away from her slightly pitying expression before she mentioned that she had a single niece or something.

The bellhop approached with his suitcase and led him out of the lobby onto a path that wound through the lush grounds. He pointed out a few conveniences including, Leo thought, directions to the pool area and the beach. Or maybe he'd been pointing out a bird or an outhouse, frankly, Leo had no idea.

Finally, they came to a stop in front of a thatch-roofed cottage. "You," the man said with a big smile.

Nodding, Leo slid his key into the reader. The light didn't turn green, and he didn't hear a click as the lock disengaged.

"Is no good?" the belhop asked.

"Doesn't appear to be."

The worker took the key card, tried himself, several times. It didn't work for him, either.

"Forget it. I'll have them reprogram it," Leo said, not happy about having to trudge back to the lobby. Right now, he just wanted to strip out of his clothes and take a cool shower.

"Here," the bellhop said, pulling out his own master keycard. That would save him the lobby trip for a while, anyway.

Following the man inside, Leo glanced around the room. It was large, airy, bright and immaculate. The vaulted ceiling was lined in pale wooden planks and two fans spun lazily overhead. Sandstone tile floors, peach walls, vibrant paintings of island life…just as advertised. A small café table designed for cozy, intimate breakfasts stood in one corner near a love seat. And the enormous king-size bed looked big enough for four honeymooners. He hid a sigh and shifted his gaze.

The bellhop lifted the suitcase onto the dresser, then headed over to unlock the patio door. He pulled it open and a warm, salt-and-flower-tinged breeze wafted in, bathing Leo's skin. He wouldn't need any AC, the ocean breezes were amazing.

"Pool, is very private," the man said.

"I can see that." Naked midnight swims had sounded appealing when they'd chosen this place. "Thank you," he said, pulling some cash out of his pocket and handing it over.

The man smiled and departed. Alone, Leo walked to the sliding door, glancing outside at the small pool, which was surrounded on all sides by a tall hedge covered with bright pink flowers. The owners had really meant it when they'd promised privacy for the pool. The resort boasted a large one, with a swim-up bar and lounge chairs, but right now, wanting that coolness on every inch of his skin, he figured this smaller one would do the trick. Midnight naked swims? Hell…

with that hedge and the stone wall behind it, daytime oncs would be fine, too.

Smiling, he checked out the rest of the suite, pausing in the bathroom to strip out of his clothes and grab a towel, which he slung over one shoulder. He returned to the patio door, put one hand on the jamb and another on the slider and stood naked in the opening, letting that breeze bathe his body in coolness.

Heaven.

He was just about to step outside and let the warm late-day sun soak into his skin when he heard something very out of place. A voice. A woman's voice. Coming from right behind him...inside his room.

"Oh. My. God!"

Shocked, he swung around, instinctively yanking the towel off his shoulder and letting it dangle down the middle of his body. To cover the bits that were dangling.

A woman stood in his room, staring at him, wide-eyed and openmouthed. They stared at each other, silent, surprised, and Leo immediately noticed several things about her.

She was young—his age, maybe. Definitely not thirty.

She was uncomfortable, tired, or not feeling well. Her blouse clung to her curvy body, as if it was damp with sweat. Dark smudges cupped her red-rimmed eyes, and she'd already kicked off her shoes, which rested on the floor right by the door, as if her first desire was to get barefoot, pronto.

Oh. And she was hot. Jesus, was she ever.

Gorgeous, in fact, with honey-brown hair that fell in a long, wavy curtain over her shoulders. Although reddened, her big green eyes were sparkling, jewel-toned, heavily lashed, with gently swooping brows above. Her face was perfect—high cheekbones, pretty chin, lush mouth. That body... Well, he suddenly blessed perspiration because the way that silky blouse clung to the full curves of her breasts was enough to make his heart skip every other beat. And the tight skirt that hugged curvaceous hips and several inches of long, slim thigh—leaving the rest of her legs bare for admiring—was making it skip every one in between.

She was also something else, he suddenly realized. Shocked. Stunned. Maybe a little afraid.

"Hi," he said with a small smile. He remained where he was, not wanting to startle her.

"I... You... You're naked!"

"I am, yes."

Her green eyes moved as she shifted her attention over his body, from bare shoulders, down his chest, then toward the white towel that he clutched in his fist right at his belly. She continued staring, scraping her attention over him like a barber used a blade—close, oh so damned close, and so very edgy.

Something like comprehension washed over her face and her tensed, bunched shoulders relaxed a little bit. "Did Tommy send you?" she whispered.

"Huh?"

"Of course it was Tommy. Or Candace? But, wait, this isn't... I'm not... Look, I don't need you."

"Don't need me for what?" *To do your taxes? Cut your hair? Carry your suitcase?*

Put out your fire?

Oh, he suspected he could do that last one, and it wasn't just because of his job.

"To have sex with me. I don't need to get laid this badly."

His jaw fell open. *"What?"*

She licked her lips. "I mean, you're very attractive and all." Her gaze dropped again, and he noticed the redness in her cheeks, and the audible breaths she drew across those lush lips. "Still, I just don't do that. I couldn't."

He had no idea what she was babbling about. But he was starting to get an idea. The gentlemanly part of him wanted to tell her right away that she was in the wrong room. The *male* part demanded he wait and see what on earth this beauty would say next.

"You couldn't do what?" he asked, letting the towel drop a little bit. Oh, it still covered what he needed to cover, but he wasn't gripping it the way a spinster virgin would grip her petticoats. And when she licked her lips, eyeing the thin trail of hair that disappeared beneath the terry fabric, he couldn't resist letting it slip a little bit more.

He was no flasher. But damn, the woman made it interesting to be ogled.

Her eyes almost popped out of her head. "I couldn't, you know, uh, hire you."

He didn't ask what for. It sure wasn't to trim her hedges. At least, not any green ones. He'd begun to suspect she'd taken him for an escort...or even a gigolo. Why on earth this beautiful woman would need either one, he couldn't say. But he was having fun trying to figure it out.

"I'm not desperate. I would never, uh, have sex with a, uh, professional." Her voice falling into a mumble, she added, "Not even one with the finest male ass I have ever seen in my entire life."

Leo was torn between indignation, laughter and lust. Right now, judging by how he felt about the way her assessing eyes belied every word she said about not wanting him, lust was winning the battle.

"You wouldn't, huh?" He stepped closer, moving easily, slowly, almost gliding.

She did the same, edging closer, her bare foot sliding smoothly over the tile floor. "No. Never."

They met near the end of the bed, both stopping when they got within a couple of feet of each other. She licked her lips, shrugged her shoulders, and said, "So, thanks for the effort, it was a, um, nice surprise. But I think you should go."

"You'd like that, would you?"

Her eyes said *no*. Her lips forced out the word, "Yes."

"I can't do that," he said, his voice low, thick.

He edged closer, unable to resist lifting a hand to brush a long, drooping curl back from her face, tucking it behind her ear. She hissed a little, tilting her head, as if to curve her cheek into his palm.

"Why not?" she whispered.

His tone equally as intimate, he replied, "Because you're in my room."

She froze, eyed him, then quickly looked around. Her gaze landed on his suitcase. She turned to peer into the bathroom, obviously seeing the clothes he'd let fall to the floor. Then back at him. "Your…"

"My room," he said, a slow smile pulling his lips up.

"You mean, you're a… You're not a…"

"Right. I'm a. And I'm not a."

She groaned softly, her green eyes growing bright with moisture. Those shoulders slumped again in pure, visible weariness and her mouth twisted. She didn't look so much embarrassed as purely humiliated. Dejected.

"I'm so sorry," she muttered.

She backed up a step, obviously not realizing how close she was to the bed. Her hip banged into the wooden footboard, and she winced, jerking away and suddenly losing her balance. She tumbled to her side, toward the hard tiled floor.

Leo didn't stop to think. He lunged, diving to catch her as she fell, letting out an oomph as she landed in his arms. Her tall, slender body was pressed against his, fitting perfectly, her head tucked under his chin, her slim waist wrapped in one arm, her shoulders in the other. She didn't immediately squirm away. Instead, she stared up at him, her eyes round, her mouth rounder.

Their stares locked and he found himself trying to identify just what shade of green those beautiful eyes were. Emerald? Jade? Jungle? Something like all of the above, plus they had a tiny ring of gold near the pupil, looking like a starburst.

She said nothing, just stared at his face. The moment stretched between them, long, heavy and strange. It was as if they were communicating on a deep, elemental level, no words being necessary, saying everything two people who'd just met would usually say. Like they wanted to get the preliminaries out of the way. For what, he didn't yet know.

"Thank you," she said, breathing the words across those lush lips.

If this were a movie, his next step would be to kiss her.

If it were a steamy one, the kiss would lead to so much more. He could suddenly see himself touching her, stroking the tip of his finger down the slick column of her throat, into the V of her blouse. Flicking it open, button after button, and pulling the fabric away from her heated skin.

In a moment as long as a single heartbeat, his mind had filled in all the blanks, seeing what it would be like to touch her, make love to her, without ever even learning her name. As if she were a present who'd landed in his arms just because he deserved her.

His body reacted—how could it not react?—but the position wasn't awkward enough to make it incredibly obvious to her. But maybe she was aware, anyway. A pink flush had risen up her face and her lips had fallen apart so she could draw deep, shaky breaths. He could see the frantic racing of her pulse in her throat, and her body trembled.

Yeah. She knew. And judging by the warm, musky scent of woman that began to fill his every inhalation, he wasn't the only one affected by the shocking encounter.

There's one problem. This isn't a movie.

Right. This was real life, she was a stranger and he,

as far as he knew, was a nice guy. The woman was obviously confused, light-headed enough to fall when she moved too quickly. And she didn't look like the type to have anonymous sex with someone she'd known for five minutes.

Time to end this, he knew. Time to put her on her feet, push her out the door and hope he ran into her again this week when she was steady, healthy and fully in control of her thoughts.

God, did he hope he'd been good enough in his life to be rewarded like that.

"This is a little awkward," she finally whispered, as if realizing the cloud of lust had begun to lift from his brain and reality was returning.

"Easy for you to say. At least you have some clothes on."

A tiny gasp escaped her lips. Reflexively, she cast a quick glance down at the floor. He followed the glance, seeing the same pile of white fabric she was seeing.

His towel. He'd dropped it when he'd lunged to catch her.

Yeah. He was naked. Completely naked, aroused at the feel of hot, musky, soft woman in his arms.

A woman who looked on the verge of…

"Son of a bitch," he mumbled.

Because she was no longer on the verge of anything. The beautiful stranger had fainted.

3

MADISON HAD BEEN HAVING the strangest dream. As she slowly woke up, feeling coolness on her face, she realized she must have drifted off on the plane. The cool air had to be coming from the vent over her seat.

She shifted, but didn't open her eyes right away, liking the dream a little too much. In it, she'd already arrived at her destination—a tropical resort where she intended to hide out for a week. She'd entered her room, exhausted, sweaty, miserable and nauseous from the long cab ride—necessitated by her landing at the wrong Costa Rican airport. Just another example of how quickly she'd had to get out of the U.S., how desperate she'd been to get away.

Things hadn't gotten much better on her arrival. The doorman had been arguing with a deliveryman, the guy at the check-in desk barely spoke English and kept suggesting she wait for a woman who was apparently on break. She'd lost patience, demanding her key and dragged her own suitcase through the thickly vegetative grounds.

Arriving in her room, wanting nothing but a cold shower and bed, she'd entered, kicked off her shoes, and had been stunned to behold a naked Adonis standing with his back toward her.

That was how she knew she'd been dreaming. Men that gorgeous, that utterly perfect, didn't exist outside of dreams and fantasies. Even Tommy, admittedly one of the handsomest men alive, wasn't built like *that*.

The man's hair had been dark, almost black, short, thick and wavy. And his bare body had been a thing of art. Broad shoulders had flexed as he'd leaned in the doorway, as if wanting to soak up the outdoors. His strong back was delineated with muscle that rippled with his every movement. Smooth skin encased a slim waist and hips, and he had an unbelievably perfect butt and long, powerful legs.

He'd turned around to reveal a strong, handsome face, masculine and unforgettable. Broad of brow, with deep-set, heavily-lashed brown eyes, slashing cheekbones, jutting chin with a tiny cleft, and a sexy, half smiling mouth.

Unfortunately, her dream state hadn't left him completely uncovered in the front. Her brain had inserted a coy white towel. She wanted to dive back into the dream to see it drop. Oh, she hoped she didn't have to open her eyes before that towel dropped.

But, wait…it *had* dropped. Hadn't it? For some reason, she remembered it on the floor. But she couldn't remember if he'd let it fall as he took her into his arms to passionately kiss her or what. Stupid dream really needed to come back and fill in all the blanks. Or at least most of them. The most interesting ones. She wasn't going to let herself wake up until it did, not even if they landed and started deboarding the plane.

"Open your eyes."

She growled in her throat.

"Come on, open up. You're okay."

That voice was seriously messing with her good dream vibes. But it was, she had to concede, a nice voice. Deep, sexy, masculine. Was it a flight attendant, rousing her for landing? Or was she still dreaming about Mr. Tall, Dark and Built?

"Come on, sweetheart." Coolness brushed her temples, soft, featherlight, then her mouth. "Take a sip."

Moisture kissed her lips. Was her dream guy giving her champagne? She swallowed.

Water. Not champagne.

And that moisture on her temples was sliding down into her hairline.

And…and…this wasn't a dream.

Her eyes flew open.

Definitely not a dream.

"You," she breathed.

It had really happened. She'd arrived at the hotel, walked into her room, seen a gorgeous stranger, and, what? Fallen and hit her head or something? What other reason would there be for her to be…where was she?

It took only a second for her to gather her wits. Holy shit, she was lying flat on her back in a bed. And this handsome, bare-chested stranger was sitting right beside her, tenderly pressing a damp facecloth to her forehead, eyeing her with visible concern.

"You're okay. Take deep breaths. Drink a little more."

She obediently sipped from the water bottle he placed against her lips, trying to kick her brain back into operation.

"What happened?"

"You fainted."

"I never faint." Girlie-girls fainted, and Madison was not a girlie-girl. She'd never been the type who'd wilt like a flower, especially not in front of some man.

Some man who'd apparently picked her up, put her on the bed and taken care of her.

"There's a first time for everything."

She frowned, still having a hard time believing it.

"Why would I faint?"

"When was the last time you ate?"

"I can't remember."

"Well, that could have something to do with it."

Yes, it could.

"You don't look like you've slept much lately, either."

She couldn't remember the last time she'd had a full, uninterrupted night's sleep. "I slept on the plane. Or… maybe that was a dream of a dream. Hell, I don't know."

"You looked pretty uncomfortable when you arrived. Sick maybe."

Sick? Maybe sick at heart. Heaven knew she had reason, considering what her life had been like in recent weeks.

"Do you think you're going to be okay? Should I have the hotel call an ambulance?"

"Good heavens, no!" That was all she needed. More attention. So much for slinking unnoticed into another country and hiding from the world for a while. "I just… I was really carsick. I guess I flew into the wrong airport and it took hours to get here, with no air-conditioning and tons of twisty roads." Ugh, when she thought about all those ups, downs and hairpin turns, she felt her stomach roll over.

"You need to eat something."

It rolled again. But she knew he was right. Something light would probably be good.

She scrunched her brow, trying to recall the last time she'd sat down for a meal, and honestly couldn't remember. Crackers on the plane probably didn't count, though she'd give her right arm for some right now, if only to settle her churning stomach. Whether it was still churning from the drive here or from the fact that this gorgeous stranger was sitting close beside her on a bed, she had no idea.

"Why don't I order something from room service?"

"You don't have to do that."

"You know what they say, save someone's life and they become your responsibility."

She rolled her eyes. "Saved my life, huh?"

He smiled and a tiny dimple appeared in one cheek, taking that dish of handsome and adding a big heaping helping of freaking adorable on top.

"If I hadn't caught you, you would have cracked your head open. That tile's pretty hard."

She suddenly thought about everything that had happened before she'd tripped. The awkward conversation when she'd rejected his *services*. Services he hadn't even been offering.

The way they'd drawn closer together, even while she'd been saying no, as if some unseen magnetic pull between their bodies was working them into close proximity.

Tripping over her own stupid feet. Falling. Him catching her.

The towel on the floor.

Gasping a little, she immediately looked down, not sure whether to sigh in relief or cry in disappointment that he wasn't naked. At some point, he'd grabbed a pair of jeans and yanked them on. They weren't even buttoned, as if he'd been in too much of a hurry to do more than zip. Maybe because he'd been busy lifting her onto the bed, fetching a cold cloth and water to revive her?

She swallowed hard, her mouth dry despite the water she'd been sipping. Because she had a mad impulse to grab the tab of that zipper and pull it down a little more, to see if he'd taken the time to put on anything else before the jeans. She suspected not.

"Well, you definitely seem to be feeling better."

That deep, husky voice suddenly sounded more amused than solicitous. Madison realized what she'd done—jerking her attention off his face and ogling him like a stripper at ladies night—and gulped. She took a deep breath, then worked up the courage to look up. It was a slow lift of the eyes. She just couldn't resist focusing on his body, so close, so big and warm and spicy smelling. She had to note the flat stomach rippled with muscle, the broad chest, wiry hair encircling his flat nipples. Those powerful shoulders, corded and thick, and on up the throat to the strong, lightly grizzled jaw.

And the face. Oh, lord, that face.

That smiling face.

"You done?"

She took a deep, even breath.

"I'm a little confused," she mumbled, lifting a shaking hand to her head.

"Yeah, right."

Well, damn, so much for her thinking he was a gentleman. He could at least have pretended not to notice she'd been struck dumb by his looks.

Then she remembered the way he'd swooped down to catch her, how he'd put her on the bed and tenderly taken care of her. She conceded he was definitely a gentleman. Just one with a sense of humor. Considering she'd accused him of being a male prostitute, that was a good thing.

"Am I *really* in your room?"

"I think so," he said. Then he frowned. "Although, to be honest, I could be in the wrong one. My key didn't work, so the bellhop let me in. He didn't speak English very well...maybe we got our wires crossed and he let me into the wrong one."

"Well, if that's the case, feel free to stay."

One brow shot up.

She flushed. "I mean, they can put me in another room. You've already settled in."

"I really don't mind being the one to move. You look like you need to stay right in this bed until tomorrow."

Yeah, and she couldn't deny she wouldn't mind if he stayed in it with her. Well, she couldn't deny it to herself, anyway. She'd deny it to her last breath if he accused her of feeling that way.

"Long trip?"

"You have no idea. I've been traveling for what seems like days."

"From where?"

"Hmm, kind of all over," she said, thinking about the crazy whirlwind her life had become in the past few weeks, ever since she'd become the woman who'd betrayed the beloved Tommy Shane. Whore, slut, bitch, user, taker, Jezebel—some preacher had lobbed that one from a pulpit—those were some of the names that had been launched at her.

So much for thinking she would escape the breakup unscathed. Could she possibly have been more naive? She'd never in a million years imagined that by becoming the bad girl who'd broken the heart of Hollywood's golden boy, she would be loathed, vilified and reviled all over the freaking country.

She'd had paparazzi follow her wherever she went. People who recognized her from her picture on the cover of every tabloid on the newsstand greeted her with catcalls and jeers. Her life had been ripped to shreds on blogs and Hollywood gossip shows. A woman had even spit on her while she was grocery shopping.

So she'd taken off to northern California. Unfortunately, everyone knew she had a twin sister who lived in Napa, and she hadn't been hard to find. Poor Candace and Oliver, who liked to live quietly, had come into the limelight, too.

Then it was off to Florida to visit her parents. Same

story. She hadn't stayed there long. It had been way too much to ask for them to play along when they saw how horribly she was being treated. They knew better than anyone that she and Tommy hadn't had a real engagement, and her father had been dying to defend her. Or at least to punch a few photographers. Heaven forbid she be the cause of his next heart attack!

So distraught over the whole thing that he'd decided to come out, Tommy had planned a press conference. Madison had told him to forget it. What he needed to do was buy her a ticket to somewhere warm. Before long, she was headed for the airport again.

Costa Rica. It should be far enough away for her to regain her sanity. Lord, did she hope so. If this scandal hadn't blown over by the time she went home, she didn't know what she would do.

"Hello?"

She realized her mind had drifted. She cleared her throat. "What?"

"Where'd you go?"

"Nowhere I want to return to," she insisted vehemently.

"You're on the run, huh?"

"You might say that." Something prompted her to add, "You, too?"

He nodded. "Yeah, I guess I am."

"Not a bank robber, are you?" she asked, her tone light and teasing, even though the possibility that he was an ax murderer had flashed across her mind. Of course, if he'd wanted to chop her into kindling, he could easily have done it while she was unconscious. Besides, nobody with eyes as warm and kind as this man's could ever be the violent sort. He looked and behaved like a real-life hero.

"No. I stick strictly to convenience and liquor stores for my life of crime."

"Penny ante," she said with an airy wave of her hand.

"What about you? Are you a secret double agent seducing your way into state secrets?"

She batted her lashes. "You think I could?"

"Honey, I *know* you could."

The vehemence in his tone made her smile fade a bit. They were no longer teasing and joking. The attraction between them had been thick from the moment he'd turned around and found her in his room, but they'd been successfully hiding from it. Except, she suddenly remembered, for that long, heated moment when he'd held her in his arms after he'd caught her. She wasn't a mind reader, but she'd had no difficulty seeing what was going through his head. Probably because the same wild, erotic thoughts had been going through hers.

Sex with a stranger. Nameless, guiltless, hedonistic. Wild and unforgettable and something never to be regretted.

Oh, yes. She'd definitely been thinking those thoughts.

The fact that he had, too, and that he hadn't taken advantage of the situation, reinforced her *hero* assessment. She couldn't think of him as merely a nice guy… that didn't do justice to this man. She barely knew him, yet she knew he was ever so much more than that.

As if he'd noticed the warm, approving way she was

looking at him, he cleared his throat and slid off the bed, standing beside it. "Think you can sit up?"

She nodded, knowing she could do it on her own but somehow unable to refuse his help when he bent and slid a powerful arm behind her shoulders. He helped her into a sitting position and it was all she could do not to turn her head and nip at the rigid muscle flexing near her cheek, or to breathe deeply to inhale his musky, masculine scent.

Tommy had obviously been right. She needed sex, badly. And for a moment, she found herself wishing her first impression had been correct and the man had been for hire. Because completely unencumbered, drop-your-pants-right-now-and-make-me-come sex sounded pretty damned awesome right now.

"By the way," he said as he stepped away from the bed, "I'm Leo. Leo Santori. What's your name?"

"My name?" Considering how desperately she'd been trying to evade the scandal her name created lately, she had to think for a second about how to respond.

"You have one, don't you? It's the thing they give you at the hospital before you get to go home."

"I thought that was a blanket."

"I don't think they give you the blankets anymore."

"Pacifier?"

"Judging by the number of kids my cousins have had, I'm thinking they pretty much ship you out the door with just a red-faced mutant and a big old bill."

She snickered, liking the good humor in his tone. Then she seized on the rest of his comment. "So you don't have any of your own?"

"Pacifiers?"

She smirked. "Kids."

"Nope." He hesitated the briefest moment before adding, "And there's no one waiting in the wings to supply any."

So, he was single? How interesting that he'd felt the need to point that out. How fascinating that the knowledge made her heart leap in her chest.

"What about you?"

"No pacifiers. No kids. Nobody trying to get me to have them."

"Well, that covers just about everything," he said. "Except one… Are you going to tell me your name?"

"It's Madison," she said.

She didn't add the last name. No need to tempt fate, right? He didn't look like the kind of guy who followed Hollywood gossip. Nor did he seem the type who would sell her out to the tabloids. But then, the host of that syndicated radio show hadn't seemed like the type who would release her private number on the air so she could be bombarded with hateful calls and texts, either.

If this Leo Santori was the curious type, he could get online—she supposed even this reclusive resort had internet access—and check her out on Google. If he had her first and last names, he'd come up with a ton of hits, none of which put her in a very good light. Any of them would probably tip somebody off that they could make a quick buck selling her out to the tabloids. That was one reason she'd chosen this resort—they apparently catered to wealthy clientele looking for privacy.

Which made her wonder just what Leo Santori did for a living, and what he'd come here to escape.

"Okay, Madison, how about you stay here? I'll go talk to the people at the front desk and try to get this straightened out. And I'll bring you something to eat when I come back."

"I couldn't…"

"Sure you could. Feel free to dive into the pool and cool off while I'm gone. You look like you could use it."

She glanced out the door, seeing the beautiful swimming pool, so secluded in a private, idyllic garden, and realized he was right. Gliding through that cool water sounded like heaven right now.

"You're sure you don't mind?" she asked, feeling badly but also really not wanting to make that long trudge back to the front desk again.

"I'm sure," he said, heading into the bathroom. The bed was angled so that she had a clear view of him standing in front of the large mirror, and she watched as he grabbed a shirt and pulled it on over his massive shoulders.

Gracious, the man's muscles had muscles. Her heart was being all spastic, thudding and skipping along, and she couldn't seem to even out her breaths to get the right amount of oxygen. She felt light-headed, no longer queasy but there were definitely butterflies fluttering around in her stomach. Her legs were quivering a little, and she was hot between them.

The stranger was totally turning her on, like she couldn't ever remember being turned on before. He was like a miracle worker, a sex god who got women all hot and bothered for a living…except he apparently didn't follow through.

Right. Not a gigolo. Check.

Which was too bad.

You're being ridiculous a little voice in her head said. One thing Madison had never been accused of was having a limited imagination. Considering she wrote stories for a living—one of which was an extremely erotic film that would surely earn an NC-17 rating if it ever got made, and that looked pretty iffy right now—she couldn't deny she'd been thinking about wild, wicked sex a lot lately. It seemed the longer it had been since she'd had it, the more it filled her thoughts.

So much for coming to a secret hideaway to get some peace and tranquillity. If this guy's room was anywhere near hers, she would probably turn into some female Peeping Tom before the week was out. Because her mind just wasn't going to stop thinking about that white towel until she knew what was under it.

"What do you do, anyway?" she asked when he returned, carrying his shoes. *Stripper? Male model?*

"I'm a firefighter."

Her jaw fell open, then she snapped it closed. Because, that totally made sense. She could easily picture him carrying ladders and big, thick hoses. He probably carried one around with him all the time.

Stop it. You're delirious.

"A real American hero?" she said, amused that her instant assessment of him was so dead-on. He really *was* a hero.

"I wouldn't say that," he insisted with a self-deprecating shrug.

"Have you ever saved anyone's life?"

Another shrug. He looked embarrassed. "I guess."

"That was a pretty vague answer to a yes-or-no question," she said, her voice wry. "'I guess' is the type of answer you'd give if someone asked you if you had a good time at a party or if you liked a movie. Saving someone's life seems to require a bit more specificity."

"Okay."

"Was that a yes?"

He grinned. "I guess."

She couldn't help chuckling. "Where do you live?"

"Chicago. You?"

Hmm. Good question. She'd been raised in Florida. Then she'd moved to New York after grad school, determined to be a world-class journalist. Only, she'd realized she kind of hated journalists. That was when she'd started writing screenplays. And when she'd gotten engaged to Tommy, she'd moved to Southern California. Now, she honestly didn't know where she was going to live.

"I'm sort of between housing right now."

That dimple reappeared. "That was a pretty vague answer."

"I suppose it was. I've been living in L.A. But I'm not sure what I'm going to do when I leave here. I might go back to New York."

"Chicago's got better pizza."

Her jaw dropped. "You must be kidding. That loaf of bread with cheese on it that they serve in Chicago has got nothing on a thin, crispy slice of pepperoni from Ray's."

He drew up, looking offended. "My uncle and cousin run a pizza place with food that would make your taste buds decide to commit suicide rather than eat pizza anywhere else ever again."

"With all due respect to your uncle and cousin, you're mental cheese has obviously slipped off its crust. Because you're crazy."

"I challenge you to a taste test."

"I don't think we're going to find very good examples of New York *or* Chicago style here in Central America."

"When we get back stateside then."

Implying they might see each other again after they left here? Oh, how tempting a thought. But she forced herself to concede, an impossible one.

"Maybe," she murmured, quickly looking away. A sharp stab of disappointment shot through her because she knew she was lying.

She couldn't see him again. Not at home. Not here. Once he got the room situation straightened out, she needed to avoid him altogether.

Maybe if he'd been the gigolo she'd thought him, she'd take a chance. Or if he'd been anything but the delightful, warm, friendly, protective man she'd already seen him to be. As it was, though, she couldn't get involved with anybody like Leo Santori. Her life was too freaking messed up right now to involve anyone else in it.

"Well, guess I'll head up to the lobby," he said, as if

noticing that she'd pulled away, if only mentally. "And I was serious, feel free to use the pool."

She nodded. "I might do that. Thanks. Maybe you should take my room key, just in case I'm outside and don't hear you knock."

He picked it up off the dresser where she'd tossed it and departed. After he'd gone, Madison thought about his offer to use the pool. She had been serious about how appealing it sounded, though she wouldn't swim the way she suspected he'd been about to. Judging by the towel he'd been oh-so-inconveniently holding, he'd been planning to skinny-dip. That sounded perfect, delightful, in fact. Letting her naked body soak up the breezes and the warmth was just about her idea of heaven.

Of course, she wasn't quite desperate enough to strip out of her clothes and pose in front of the door the way he had. Even if she did have a very nice ass, if she did say so herself. Still, she wasn't about to bare it for some stranger...a stranger she'd already decided she couldn't have, no matter how much she might want him.

Now that he was gone, now that the room wasn't full of his warm, masculine presence, she managed to pull the rest of her brain cells together. It wasn't just that she couldn't trust anyone she met to keep her secret; there was more to it than that. Coming here to Costa Rica had been about hiding out, licking her wounds, staying out of the limelight and being completely on her own. She needed to rediscover the Madison she'd been six months ago, before her crazy engagement, before she'd become chum for an ocean of avaricious sharks.

There was more, though. She just couldn't do that to *him*...or to any man. Because, even if she could keep him in the dark about who she really was—and the scandal she'd hopefully left behind in the states—she'd be exposing him to a lot of danger, too. The last thing she needed was to get involved with some guy, then get tracked down by the paparazzi. Any man she spent time with would be subject to the same vicious scrutiny she'd endured, maybe even accused of being the mystery lover she'd cheated on Tommy with. The one who didn't exist.

She just couldn't put anybody else through that, especially not someone as great as Leo seemed to be. So, no. There was no room in her life for a fling with a hot fireman. None whatsoever.

Even if she desperately wished there were.

As it turned out, they'd both been wrong...and right. They were both in the correct room. Apparently, the woman who'd been at the front desk when Leo checked in was the only one who knew how to operate the hotel's computerized system. She'd put Leo in the correct room, even though his key card hadn't been coded properly. Then she'd gone on break, leaving a less-than-capable replacement at the desk. That man had put Madison in Leo's room, too.

Leo couldn't deny that it might be interesting—or, hell, fantastic—to share a bed with the beautiful brunette, but it seemed a bit soon to ask her if she wanted to become roomies.

Maybe by the end of the week...

He'd told the clerk that Madison could keep the room and he'd been assigned to another one. The woman got a twinkle in her eye and offered him a slight brow wag when she noted that Madison was traveling alone, too. Maybe she'd also heard from the bellhop that Madison was young and gorgeous.

Yeesh. He wondered if the clerk had been born a matchmaker or if it merely came with the territory when women reached a certain age. Lord knew there were a lot of them in his family. Of course, even his youngest female cousins seemed to have the gene, so he supposed aging had nothing to do with it.

Heading back to fill Madison in, he couldn't stop himself from thinking about her with every step he took across the grounds.

Madison Reid. She hadn't supplied the last name, the front desk clerk had. He liked it. Liked the woman to whom it was attached, even though he had only just met her.

Leo wasn't a huge believer in fate, but he couldn't deny that this afternoon's incident—them both getting assigned the same room, her walking in on him, him being there to catch her when she fell—seemed pretty out of the ordinary. Like it was meant to happen or something.

He'd come here to enjoy himself, as well as to put the final touches on the coat of I'm-totally-over-Ashley paint he'd been wearing for six months. Truth was, ever since Madison Reid had walked in on him, he hadn't given his former fiancée a moment's thought. And now, as her name crossed his mind, there was only the vaguest sense of recollection, like when he ran into someone he'd gone to elementary school with and couldn't for the life of him come up with their name. He could barely remember what Ashley looked like, or why he'd ever thought he could be happy spending his life with her in the first place.

She'd been beautiful, yes. And pretty successful. But there had been a shallowness to her, not to mention a thin vein of hardness that he'd spotted from the start but had fooled himself into thinking was an indication of strength. Maybe he'd had it all wrong. Maybe the coldness had been a symptom of her weakness, her need to constantly make sure she was the most desired, the most loved woman in the room. Perhaps that was why she'd set out to prove it by getting involved in an affair with his friend. Hell, for all Leo knew, it hadn't been her first.

Funny how easy it was to see her—to understand her—now that the blinders had been so completely torn off his eyes.

Arriving back at his—no, *Madison's*—room, he thrust all those thoughts away. He didn't want to think about his ex now. Not when there were so many other good things to think about.

Lifting a hand, he rapped on the door. No answer. Hoping she'd gone ahead and taken a dip, he inserted her key card and pushed the door open a few inches, calling, "Madison?"

Again, nothing. So he went inside. She wasn't on the bed, and as he crossed the room, he heard a faint splash. Stepping over to the patio slider, which stood open, he glanced outdoors and spotted a dash of red in the clear blue waters of the pool.

A red bikini. God help him.

She was floating on her back, her eyes closed, her arms out to her sides. Her face was turned to the sun and a satisfied smile tugged at those lips. He thought he heard her humming a soft melody.

Madison had been incredibly hot in a skirt and blouse. Now that she'd donned a couple of triangles of scarlet fabric, leaving much of her body bare for his perusal, he could honestly say he'd never seen a sexier female.

Her legs were long—heavenly—and she gently kicked them to keep herself afloat. As he'd noted when she wore the skirt, she had some seriously lush hips, covered only by little sling ties that held her bathing suit together. Those feminine hips were made even more noticeable by the slim waist, flat belly and taut midriff. Her bathing suit top managed to cover only the most essential parts of her full breasts, pushing up those amazing curves, leaving a deep V of cleavage that glistened with droplets of pool water.

All of her glistened. Every inch of that smooth skin, from her pink-tipped toenails on up to her cheeks, on which those long lashes rested, gleamed invitingly. Her thick hair had spread out, floating around her face like a halo, and she looked totally lost to everything but physical sensation as she soaked up the sun and the water.

A sharp, almost painful wave of lust washed over him. His heart thudded, his mouth went dry with a need for moisture only she could provide. His hands fisted at his sides as he tried to push away the images of touching her, stroking her, gliding his fingers along every ridge and valley of her body.

"Oh, you're back!"

He flinched, not having even realized she'd opened her eyes. "Yes. Sorry."

She quickly dropped her legs, standing up in the pool, which was only five feet deep at the most, and smiled up at him. "You were right, this was exactly what I needed. I feel tons better."

"You look better," he admitted through a tight throat. God, he hoped the sun was glaring in her eyes and she couldn't see how taut his entire body was as he tried to keep himself from reacting to her. If she were a couple of feet higher, she'd be eye level with his crotch and would undoubtedly notice the ridge in his jeans. He was hard for the woman, wanting her desperately. Hell, he'd been half-hard for her from the minute he'd caught her in his arms.

"How did everything go with the front desk?"

"All settled. You get the house, I get the kids."

She giggled. The sound was light and sweet, and he liked the tiny laugh lines that appeared beside her eyes. "What kind of mother does that make me?"

"I guess I'm just more soft and nurturing."

Her laughter deepened. "Yeah, you look about as soft as a tree trunk."

Oh, if only she knew.

"What really happened?"

He filled her in on the situation. She didn't seem surprised to hear the guy who'd checked her in had messed things up. But she didn't get all ticked off about it, either. She was calm, chill. He doubted much fazed her... except naked guys catching her when she fell.

He needed to forget about holding her while he was

naked. That was not going to do his pants situation any good at all.

"I brought you back some fruit." The lobby had a large bowl of it available for their guests. It should be enough to settle Madison's stomach until she had a chance to sit down for a real meal.

"Thank you."

"I guess I'll grab my stuff and go. I'm in the Scarlet Room," he told her.

"Maybe the guy at the front desk is color-blind and that's how our wires got crossed. This is the Emerald one, isn't it?"

Grinning, he said, "Yeah, I'm sure that's it."

"Scarlet, huh?" She wagged her brows. "Sounds fit for a sinner."

"Huh, and a little while ago you thought I was a hero."

"I still think that," she said, the teasing note fading from her voice. "I really appreciate you, uh... Where do I start?"

"Flashing you?"

Her sultry laugh heated him more than the late-afternoon sun. "I was going to say catching me, putting me on the bed, putting water on my face, going down to the desk..."

"Not the flashing?"

"I think I fainted before I saw anything."

"You think?"

She gave him a mysterious, half-sideways look. "I'll never tell."

"Thanks for being a gentleman."

"An interesting description for a female."

"I don't know, it just seemed appropriate." Not that anybody would ever mistake her for anything but a pure, sexy woman. "I guess I'll see you later."

She hesitated, her mouth opening, then closing, and then slowly nodded. "Sure. Of course. I'll bet you're tired after your trip."

"Not as tired as you were after yours."

"I really am feeling better." She licked her lips, and furrowed her brow, as if considering something, then added, "I do owe you one for all you've done. How about I buy you a drink sometime this week?"

"I got the all-inclusive package," he said, wondering if she saw the twinkle of pleasure in his eyes.

"So you buy me a drink."

"I could," he said with a bark of laughter, "considering I paid for two packages."

She tilted her head in confusion. Mentally kicking himself for bringing up a subject he really didn't want to discuss, he edged back into her room. "Meet me by the main pool or the beach bar tomorrow and I'll buy you that drink."

"And then you'll tell me why you should be drinking for two?"

"Maybe I will."

"Sorry, that was pushy. You really don't have to."

"Well, then, maybe I won't."

"Touché," she said. "See you later, Leo Santori."

"Bye, Madison Reid."

Her smile faded a little. "How did you know my…"

"Your last name? They mentioned it at the desk."

Realizing she was truly upset about that, he couldn't help wondering why. Was she *really* in hiding? Incognito? He had thought from the moment he saw her that she looked familiar, but had been telling himself it was because she looked like the woman he would dream about if he wanted to have the best, most erotic dreams of his life. But maybe it was more than that.

"Are you famous?"

"Maybe infamous," she mumbled under her breath.

He quirked a curious brow. She didn't elaborate. A long silence stretched between them, and he realized she didn't intend to.

Hmm. Interesting.

But he wasn't here to dig into anybody else's secrets. He'd just wanted to get away from his own drama. No responsibilities, no angst, no worrying about a broken engagement or the fact that his family was apprehensive about him and his friends were insisting he get out there and get laid as some kind of get-back-at-his-ex game.

He wasn't into any of that. Coming here to Costa Rica was about leaving everything else behind and just indulging in some sun, some fun and some pleasure.

And now that he'd met Madison, he began to suspect things were going to be even more sunny, fun and pleasurable than he had anticipated.

BY THE TIME she awoke the next morning, having slept a solid, uninterrupted nine hours—largely because of the fresh air blowing in on her through the screen door all night long, not to mention the utter exhaustion—

Madison woke up the next day a little unsure of what to do with herself.

She'd never been on a vacation alone, though she'd been on plenty of family trips as a kid, of course. And she, Candace and Tommy had gone away together several times, usually on college road trips to dive-places on the beach. There'd also been one skiing trip with a boyfriend. But never had she been in a foreign land all by herself, with nowhere to go, no one to see, nothing to do and no schedule to keep.

All she had to do was stay hidden from the press.

She couldn't help wondering what was going on back in California. She hadn't spoken with Tommy or with Candace since she'd left Florida, although she imagined they'd both tried to reach her. She'd bet there were messages on her cell phone and texts and emails. They'd been so worried about her, for once both of them thinking they had to be the protectors, the caretakers. She suspected they were constantly on the phone with each other, trying to figure out what to do.

Though he'd lived with Madison for the past six months, in some ways, Tommy still seemed closer to Candace. Madison was never envious of that, however, knowing their friendship was very different. With creative, artistic, kindhearted Candace, Tommy could be carefree and a little more whimsical. With Madison— much more no-nonsense and blunt than her twin—he had to man up and take responsibility for what he did. And of course, with him, both the Reid twins could be more daring and adventurous.

As far as she was concerned, the three of them brought out the absolute best in each other.

Four. There are four of us now.

Right. Because Candace—her other half—had gotten herself a *new* other half in the form of a hunky lawyer who'd posed as a gardener and planted baskets of love in Candy's heart. Blech.

Madison liked Oliver. She really did. But she still wasn't sure she would ever get over the feeling that she'd lost something vital when she'd become the second most important person in her twin's life.

It's not four, it's five.

Pesky math. But the addition was right. Because Tommy had Simon, and Madison had the feeling he'd be in the picture for a very long time. Meaning she truly was, she realized, the odd man out. Literally the fifth wheel. It was the first time she'd acknowledged it, and a sudden hollowness opened up within her, swallowing some of her happiness and her certainty that nothing could ever really change the relationships she had with those she loved. Things had changed, and continued to change.

She was the only one who hadn't found that mystical connection called love. Honestly, she wasn't sure she ever would. She'd dated men, she'd slept with men, she'd even lived with one before Tommy. But never had she had stars in her eyes the way her sister did, and never had she tap-danced through her day because the right guy smiled at her the way Tommy did.

"Enough, no more feeling sorry for yourself," she muttered as she forced her mind toward other things.

Like what she could do with plenty of money and an exotic, tropical paradise to explore.

There were a lot of things she could do, and someone with whom she'd really like to do them. But having fallen asleep last night thinking of all the reasons that being with Leo Santori would be a really bad idea, she had pretty well decided not to do them. Or, to do them alone.

Zip lining, ecotouring, bodysurfing...they could all be done alone, or with a professional instructor. But the thing she most wanted to do wouldn't be nearly as fun without Leo.

Ah, well. It wouldn't be the first time she'd had sex alone, that was for sure. Lately it was all she'd had.

Of course, she hadn't exactly tucked any sex toys into her luggage. She wondered how often Customs asked travelers to turn on those odd-looking devices, and was glad she hadn't had to find out. But the point was, she was left totally on her own when it came to dealing with the intense, er, *interest* Leo had aroused in her from the moment she'd first seen him.

Oh, yeah, that picture had been burned in her brain.

Madison had always had an active imagination, and had never needed erotic stories or movies to rev her engines. Lately, just thinking about the hero of the screenplay she'd written was enough to get her going. The dark, angry, possibly murderous antihero liked his sex rough and dangerous, with floggers and leather ropes and lots of "Yes, sirs."

While she'd been writing it, that had been her fantasy: being tied up, forced to be submissive, learning how pain could be pleasurable. Well, maybe not her fantasy, but she'd certainly wondered about it, digging into a deep, previously untapped part of herself to create those scenes that disturbed more than titillated.

But now, with Leo's incredibly handsome face and warm, gentle eyes in her mind, she could only think of long, slow, sexy loving that went on for hours and needed no props, just two slick, aroused bodies bathed in sunshine and warm air. No touch off-limits, no sensation forbidden, every eroticism imbued with gentleness and intimacy. And trust. Lots of trust.

She moaned a little, and began to touch all the places on her body that would have far preferred his hands to hers. Running her fingers over her breast, she plumped it, knowing his big hands would overflow if he were to cup them. She reached for her nipple—hard and filled with sensation. Plucking it, teasing it, she acknowledged that she would never really have lived if that man never sucked her nipples.

She whimpered, one hand gliding even farther, over her hip, and then her belly. Farther. She brushed her index finger through the tiny thatch of hair—the landing strip look that was so popular in Southern California. Madison had gone for it once she'd moved out there, but hadn't had a lover since she'd first begun waxing her pubis, and had wondered, more than once, what it would feel like to have a man's mouth on that bare, sensitive skin. Her own fingers felt divine, made slick and smooth by her body's moisture. She moved them slowly, gently, stroking herself just right. Her clit was hard and ever so sensitive, and she made tiny circles around it, drawing out the pleasure, picturing his hands, his tongue.

Another stroke. She gasped, arching her back, curling her toes. Her climax washed over her, quick, hard and hot, and she sprawled out in the bed, trying to even her breaths and calm down.

It didn't happen. For the first time in her life, masturbating hadn't taken the edge off. Yes, she'd had an orgasm, but it hadn't satisfied her. She was still edgy, swollen and in need, as if she'd been cut off in the middle of intensely pleasurable foreplay.

It wasn't hard to figure out why. She wanted a man. One man. Leo. Her own hands just weren't going to cut it. She wanted him to be the one to make her come, wanted his cock inside her when he did it.

She'd told herself all last evening during her room service meal and the long minutes she'd thought about him before drifting off to sleep that she couldn't have him. Couldn't allow herself to take him. But never had she *really* acknowledged what that meant. Or how incredibly difficult it would be to stick by that decision. Because if she couldn't release this tension, she was going to lose her mind. And the only man who could release it for her was one she'd already decided was off-limits. He was too nice, too good, too heroic. Definitely not somebody who deserved to be tarnished with the scandal surrounding her.

"Damn it," she muttered. "Why did you have to go

and be so wonderful?" If he'd been a jerk or a player, it would have been much easier to let go of her concerns and *take* what she wanted.

There was, of course, no answer. Nothing could possibly explain why she'd met a man so sexy, so delicious, so freaking adorable, now, when she was in no position to have him.

Knowing she couldn't stay in bed and continue to be sexually frustrated, she got up and tried to decide between a shower and a morning swim. She intended to go down to the open-air restaurant for breakfast. From the hotel information sheet, she'd noticed that it adjoined the large resort pool. She planned to lie out beside it, so there wasn't much point in showering first, especially since she'd taken one last night before bed.

But she certainly wouldn't be able to swim naked in the public pool, and right now, swimming naked—letting cool water comfort and soothe her overly sensitized private parts—sounded like the perfect cure for what ailed her.

She'd gone skinny-dipping before; what adventurous, Florida-raised kid hadn't? But she'd certainly never done it in broad daylight. Considering the privacy of her pool, though, she figured she could risk it. Leo certainly had been about to yesterday. Good for the goose and all that.

Decision made, she got up and went into the bathroom to brush her teeth. She scooped her hair back into a ponytail, and grabbed the towel she'd used the afternoon before. The one that still carried the faintest scent of the man who'd been holding it when she'd entered her room.

Yeah, using Leo's towel had been pretty pathetic. It had also been pretty delightful, rubbing it against her cool body, smelling him, remembering him.

"Stop it," she ordered herself, determined to put the man out of her mind for the rest of the day. Hell, for the rest of her trip!

Going to the screen door, she pulled it open and stuck her head outside, peeking around. It felt so strange to step out into broad daylight—God, what a gorgeous, clear, sunny morning it was—not wearing a stitch. She caught her bottom lip between her teeth, glancing back and forth from one side of the walled-hedged area to the other. The tangle of green shrub was thick and practically impossible to see through. Plate-size pink flowers helped, too.

"Just do it. Just jump in!" she ordered herself.

So she did. She dropped the towel and wound her way around the lounge chairs that stood under the covered awning right outside the door. Free, excited and naked, she plowed forward, not thinking, just striding the five steps to the pool and taking a leap of faith.

It should have taken a few seconds for her to hit the water.

It didn't. It took forever, considering time had stopped.

She moved in slow motion, horror washing over her.

Because, after her feet had left the concrete deck—after she was committed to the pool and it was too late to change her mind—she saw a dark shape swimming toward her.

A dark, sinuous shape that hit on every one of her most elemental fears and sent hysteria coursing through her body.

There was nothing else to do. She screamed bloody murder.

5

THE ROOM SERVICE breakfast Leo had ordered lived up to the hotel's reputation for outstanding food. He'd enjoyed every bite of his meal, which he'd consumed outside on his patio, having moved his café table and chairs outdoors. It was midmorning, the sun was shining, the breeze was blowing, and he was on vacation. Life didn't get much better than this, especially when he thought about the chilly autumn and frigid winter that awaited him when he returned to Chicago.

He had made some plans for his first full day in Costa Rica, starting with dropping by his next-door neighbor's room.

He hadn't been able to put Madison out of his mind since he'd left her yesterday afternoon. Especially not once he'd realized the Scarlet Bungalow—his suite—was the very next one down the path from hers. Their private courtyards butted up against one another and he'd heard her humming again as she'd floated the previous afternoon. He'd stayed quiet, not wanting to disturb her, somehow knowing they could use a bit of a time before they saw each other again.

She needed some sleep, some food and some energy. He needed to think about what he was going to do about the incredible attraction he felt for the woman.

Today he'd knock on her door and see where things went.

He'd just finished off the last bite of his toast and reached for his coffee cup, sweetened with raw sugar and thick cream, when the morning silence was pierced by a dramatic, shrill scream.

He flinched, nearly dropping his cup, and was on his feet before he'd made up his mind to get out of his chair. His whole body went on instant alert, like it did whenever the alarm sounded at the station house, not knowing if he would be dousing a small oven fire or battling a monster blaze in an abandoned warehouse.

The scream had been cut off sharply—as if the screamer had run out of breath—and that made things even worse. Because he feared he knew where it had come from.

His stomach churned.

"Madison!" he said, knowing the woman's cry of terror had come from the other side of the hedged wall surrounding his pool.

Not giving it another thought, he ran over to the hedge, shoved his hands into the thick greenery and gripped the cool stone wall behind it. He clambered up, his bare feet and legs getting scratched, his arms covered with sticky green moisture, his face slapped with flowers. He lost his footing once, skidded down a few inches, then gripped the top even more tightly in his hand so he wouldn't go tumbling back down.

As he reached the top of the six-foot-tall wall, he heard splashes and another shriek. Was she being attacked? Drowning?

His heart raced. "I'm coming!" he called as he launched over the top of the wall, flinging himself into her private courtyard. He landed on his feet in the mulch, right beside her privacy hedge, and immediately looked for her. Having heard the splashes, his eyes turned right to the pool.

Madison was in it, her face twisted with fear, her mouth open as she exhaled shallow gasps. She didn't even appear to see him. All her attention was focused on the water before her. She was struggling to back up to the rear edge of the pool, reaching behind her, waving her arms, as if afraid to turn and look for it. Afraid to tear her attention off whatever had grabbed it.

"Madison, what is it?"

Her lips trembled. She cast the tiniest glance in his direction. But she didn't have to answer. He suddenly saw for himself.

"Stay still, don't move," he snapped, seeing the creature swimming in the shallow end of the pool.

A snake. Not huge, but big enough—thick, though not terribly long. Boa constrictor, if he had to guess, though he was no expert.

Jesus, no wonder she was screaming like somebody had come at her with an ax. He might have, too. He liked snakes about as much as Indiana Jones did.

But he needed to keep her calm. If she started flailing around, the thing might notice her and come closer to investigate. And while he would never let it get near her, his Tarzan-snake-wrestling skills were a wee bit rusty. Or nonexistent.

"It's okay," he told her, trying to keep her calm with his voice as he edged along the side of the pool. "He's not going to bother you."

"Snake. Oh, God, a snake. I hate snakes, Leo," she said, whimpering.

"I'm not a big fan either, darlin', but I don't think he's paying too much attention to you. He just wanted to take a swim."

"Aren't there j-jungles, rivers, entire oceans?" she said, panic rising in her voice. "Why my pool? Why now when I'm naked and jumped in without looking!"

His mind tried to make him think about that naked part but he was too focused on the way her voice was shaking and the danger the animal posed to her. If it *was* a boa, it wasn't poisonous, which was a good thing. But he doubted anything he said was going to make her feel better.

"Listen to me now," he said as he spied the pool supply closet tucked up against the corner of her bungalow. Hopefully it would contain a skimmer; he doubted the maintenance men would carry them room to room every day. "I'll take care of it, Madison. But I need you to very *calmly* get to the edge of the pool and climb out."

"I c-can't…"

"Of course you can. I'll watch it so you can turn around."

"No."

"Just move slowly."

"Have you forgotten the naked p-part?" she groaned, though he wasn't sure if her voice was shaking due to fear of the snake or embarrassment over her—*gulp*—nakedness.

"I won't look," he promised.

And he wouldn't. He was focused on the snake and the closet and would not allow himself to cast so much as a glimpse at her lithe form gleaming beneath the water. Not while he still had an unwelcome visitor to contend with.

It was just his luck to catch her skinny-dipping when she was in real physical danger.

He edged sideways, noting there was no lock on the closet and finding himself very thankful for that. Reaching it, he yanked the door open, tore his attention off the snake long enough to assess what was inside and gratefully spotted not only a skimmer on a long pole, but also a sizeable bucket that had once held chemicals but was now empty. A lid lay beside it on the concrete floor of the storage closet.

Looking back to assure her, he realized she had moved closer to the wall but still hadn't taken her eyes off the snake. "Okay, it's time to climb out now, Madison," he told her as he retrieved the items from the closet. "Once I try to grab him, he's going to panic and swim away."

She didn't argue anymore. From the corner of his eye, he saw her do as he'd said and put her hands on the pool's edge. Then his attention zoomed right back to her swimming companion.

He moved to the edge of the pool, placing the bucket

close by and trying to gauge just how quick he'd have to be if he wanted to swoop that sucker up and drop him inside it. Part of him thought about just leaving it, getting her inside and calling the hotel to deal with it. But he knew if he did, she would never have another moment's peace. It could easily slither away and if it did, she'd be envisioning it returning every time she closed her eyes. Hell, his bungalow was right next door…so would he!

"Ready?" he asked, not glancing toward her, though he saw her vague shape standing on the far side of the pool. He had a quick impression of hands crossed in the Eve-old woman's modesty pose, but that was all. "Madison?"

She only groaned.

He took a deep breath, then plunged the skimmer into the water, an inch below the animal, and jerked his arms to lift it out of the pool. It immediately squirmed and almost fell over the side, but luck was with him. He was able to flip it right into the waiting bucket.

The snake immediately began to slither up to escape, but he covered the opening with the skimmer, blocking its exit while he grabbed the lid. Then he switched them, catching the angry animal inside, grabbing a large, decorative rock to place on it so the lid wouldn't pop back off. It had taken no more than thirty seconds, but his heart was racing, and his breaths were choppy and forced, as if he'd just run a block wearing his protective gear and carrying a ladder.

"Oh, my God, thank you, thank you, thank you."

He turned just as Madison threw herself against him,

wrapping her arms around his neck, burying her face in the crook. She shuddered, her entire form quaking.

"It's okay, it's over."

"I hate snakes. I'm terrified of them. When I saw that thing in the pool a second *after* I'd leaped in, I thought I'd have a heart attack and die."

"Well, it's done. I'll call the front office and have them send somebody down to take care of it."

She shivered again. "I can't even look at one of them. I know it's irrational, it's stupid, but I just... I'm *offended* by them, somehow. Does that make any sense?" She pulled back a little and rubbed away some moisture that had appeared in her eyes. "My rational mind understands why snakes are needed for the environment, and I know the chances of ever being bitten by one, much less dying, are slim to none. But they just offend some deep, primal part of me."

He believed her. There was no way he couldn't. Her voice was hoarse, shaking, and her eyes were slightly wild. She looked almost on the verge of hysteria.

He slid his arms around her waist, holding her tightly against him, and stroked his fingertips in the hollow of her back. "It's okay. It's over. Shh."

Her head dropped onto his shoulder, and they stood there for few long moments. He could feel her gasping breaths, not to mention her racing heart thudding against his. He continued to whisper consoling words to her, brushing his lips against her damp hair, then against her temple where the pulse fluttered wildly. He would have thought she would have begun to calm down by now, but if anything her heart seemed to be pounding even harder against his chest.

His bare chest.

Which was pressed against her bare chest.

Which went along with her bare *everything*.

Holy shit. In the excitement, he'd momentarily forgotten what she wasn't wearing. She'd been—and was now—completely naked.

He should let her go, spin around, turn his back and toss her a towel. A nice guy would do that. The hero she'd called him would do that.

Leo didn't do that.

He just couldn't. Not yet. Not when she felt so good—so pliant and womanly. Now, when she was curled up against him like she needed his warmth to revive every cell in her body, how could he possibly step away from her?

He continued to stroke the small of her back, then let one hand glide down to brush against the top curve of her buttock. She sighed against his neck, pressing her lips against his raging pulse, telling him not to stop. Considering stopping hadn't even been on the top ten list of possibilities, that wouldn't be a problem.

Her body was all lush curves and softness, and he loved the texture of her skin beneath his fingers. He continued to stroke the curve of her bottom, tracing a line to her hip, which he cupped in his hand. She was so perfectly shaped, with the indentation of her waist designed to be wrapped in a man's arms, those hips intended to be clung to by someone buried to the hilt inside her.

"Leo," she groaned, kissing his neck again.

Her warm, soft tongue slipped out and tasted his earlobe, and he groaned low in his throat.

Her invitation wasn't voiced, but it was clear just the same. He didn't know whether they would have ended up like this if not for her fright. He had no idea whether she'd been tortured by the same kind of long, restless, sleepless night he had, filled with erotic dreams and even more erotic fantasies. He didn't even know if this was going to go anywhere else. All he knew was he had to kiss her.

So he did. Not saying another word, he lifted a hand to her hair, sliding his fingers into the tangled ponytail, and tugged her head back so she was looking up at him. Giving her face a searching glance, he dropped his mouth onto hers.

Soft at first. A tiny shared breath. Then they both fell into the kiss.

It was easy, so easy. And so good.

Her tongue met his with a languorous thrust, and he drank deeply of her, exploring every bit of her mouth. He found himself wanting to memorize the shape of her, the scent of her, the feel of her. They stroked and licked, tangled, gave and took. She tasted sweet and minty, delicious, and having his mouth pressed against hers felt as natural and right as coming home after a long time away.

His hand still cupped her hip, and he stroked her, held her tightly against him. With his other one, he traced a path up her midriff to the side of a full breast, pressed flat against his chest. He was dying to see her, to let his other senses be filled by her, but right now, memorizing her taste was enough. It had to be enough.

She was groaning, sighing, and her own hands explored, too. She tangled one in his hair, fingering it, twisting it, holding him close as if afraid he might end the kiss before they'd both had their fill.

Her other hand dug into his shoulder before sliding down his arm. Their fingers curled together, then she reached between them to stroke his stomach. Her hand drifted close, so damned close, to his rigid cock, which was so hard, it had pushed up beyond the top of his swim trunks.

"Oh, God," she groaned against his mouth, realizing what had happened as she caressed the swollen tip.

His body was helpless to resist the age-old urge to thrust toward her touch. Those soft, delicate fingers flicked lightly over his skin, the tip of her thumb smoothing out the moisture that seeped from him.

Before he could think or breathe or move, she'd tugged the trunks farther away from his groin, making room for her hand. She slipped it down, rubbing her palm all along the back of his cock, her long nails scraping ever so delicately on his tight balls.

He groaned, again rocking toward her, loving that she responded to his blatant need by wrapping her hand around him, at least as much as she could, and squeezing lightly. He heard her whimper. The sound seemed to convey both excitement and perhaps nervousness, as if she had just figured out, since her fingers couldn't close entirely around him, how much he had to offer her.

She didn't have to be nervous. He could make her

wet enough to take every inch of him. And he was *desperate* to do it. More than he wanted to live until sundown did he want to sink into her—her mouth, her sex, somewhere wet and hot and slippery. And tight. Oh, God, yeah, *tight*.

She stroked him, up and down, matching the movements with each warm thrust of her tongue. He edged away, just enough to slide his fingers over one full breast, until he could tweak the hard nipple between them. She hissed into his mouth as he played with her, stroking her into a series of slow shudders.

She made no sound of resistance at all when he moved his other hand from her hip, back around to her bottom, so he could toy with the seam separating those lush curves. A tiny stroke, another, then she relaxed enough to let him play a little more. She was pliant in his arms, arching a bit in invitation, and he dipped his fingers farther...enough to get wet, to sample the juices of her body, hot and slick and welcoming.

He had time to mentally process the fact that her plump, engorged lips were completely bare—*want, want, want*—when she whimpered. "You— We..."

He didn't know what she was about to say—to ask, to demand. Because before she had a chance to continue, they both heard a thumping sound coming from the ground near their feet.

She obviously realized what it was before he did, because she yanked back and leaped away so fast she almost fell into the pool. Leo got the tiniest glimpse at her utterly gorgeous, naked body—God, those breasts were a thing of art—before he focused his attention on what had made the sound.

Mr. Snake was trying to get out of his container. The lid on the bucket was jiggling up and down, and the whole bucket was a bit wobbly. He pulled his trunks up and retrieved another, heavier rock and replaced the one he'd put on there, being sure to leave uncovered a small hole in the old lid. He didn't like the intruder, but he also wanted to make sure the critter would get enough air during the few minutes it took to get somebody down here to get rid of him.

While he resecured the prisoner, Madison grabbed a towel off the ground and wrapped it around herself, sarong style. By the time he straightened and returned his full attention to her, she was covered from breast to upper thigh. He mourned that he had lost his chance to see that incredible, luscious body he'd felt pressing against him, and he knew there would be no diving back into the crazy-hot kiss they'd been sharing. Much less all the other crazy-hot things they'd been doing...and had planned to do.

"Wow," she whispered, lifting a hand to her mouth. That hand was shaking, those lips were trembling, her voice was quivery. Whether she was more freaked out by the snake or by the embrace, he didn't know, but he sure hoped he had a leg up on the slithery reptile.

"I guess I should apologize," he said, not really sure why. If she hadn't enjoyed that, he'd turn in his membership as a dude.

"For saving my life?"

He rolled his eyes. "I don't think it's poisonous."

"I meant, you saved me from a heart attack. I really don't think you understand how much snakes terrify me."

"I think I have a pretty good idea."

She was already shaking her head in disagreement before he'd finished his sentence. "I'm not just being a wimp. Believe me, I'm not scared of much." She thrust a hand in her hair, knocking the ponytail holder out altogether so that those honey curls bounced around her shoulders in a thick, sexy tangle. "I don't usually go around fainting, and I don't remember another time in my adult life that I have ever screamed with terror. Except, maybe, the first time I went skydiving."

Okay. So she was pretty brave.

"But snakes. Oh, God, snakes. They're my Achilles' heel. My sister, Candace, she can't stand spiders. Me? Hell, a guy I dated had a pet tarantula and I used to walk around with him sitting on my shoulder."

"The guy or the tarantula?"

She punched him lightly on the arm. Frankly, he preferred it when she used that hand to squeeze his cock.

But they'd moved past that moment. It was over... at least for now. Sanity and reality had intruded, and she was going to focus on the snake rather than on the near sex.

Letting her get away with it, knowing she probably needed to regroup and think about what had almost happened, he rubbed his upper arm, as if she'd hurt him, and grinned. "Sorry. I got the point, you're okay with bugs."

"Yeah, no big deal. I'd protect Candace from spiders,

she'd protect me from snakes, and Tommy would protect us both from guys who didn't take no for an answer."

"Tommy? Your brother?"

She opened her mouth, then snapped it shut. Some of the high color began to leave her cheeks, and he watched as she clenched her hands together in front of her.

"No, a friend. Boy next door. We grew up together."

"Okay."

He wondered if that was really all, considering how skittish she'd gotten when she'd mentioned the guy. But it wasn't his place to pry.

"Anyway, I know I have ophidiophobia. It's irrational and I've tried to get over it. I've studied, I even got myself hypnotized once."

One of his brows shot up. "Really?"

"Well, it was at one of those girls' naughty-panty party things, with a bunch of women drinking wine and buying fancy underwear. A friend of one of my college roommates was there and she swore she could hypnotize any of us into losing weight or quitting smoking. So I asked her to try to un-ophidiophobia me."

He was having a hard time paying attention, his mind still back on the whole panty party concept. Jeez, did chicks really do that? And how did one sign up to be a salesperson?

"It didn't work."

"No?"

"When she got me under and told me to visualize a snake curled up peacefully at my feet, I apparently threw up all over the saleslady's panty box."

Oh, did he need her to change this conversation. But

because he was a masochist, he replied, "Guess you bought a lot of underwear that night."

"Yeah, right. You hurl on it, you buy it." She wrapped her arms around herself, clinging to the towel, and continued, "So, you see, it's a big deal to me. I was on the verge of a full-on panic attack, and you saved me, and I appreciated it so much, and that's why I threw myself into your arms. It wasn't... I didn't..."

"I get it. You weren't trying to take advantage of me."

She nibbled her lip. "Right."

"Understood."

"And you're not, uh, mad?"

Oh, sure. Because every dude would be really angry about a beautiful, naked woman throwing her arms around him to express her gratitude. Or half jerking him off until he'd become nothing but nine inches of sensation.

"Not mad. I promise."

She looked relieved.

"Now, how about I go in and call the front desk and ask them to send somebody out here to get rid of our friend."

Her eyes rounded into circles. "I'm not staying out here by myself with that thing! He might tip the bucket over. He could..."

"Come with me then," he said, cutting her off and pulling her into her room. He shut the screen door behind them. "We'll make the call together."

She looked visibly relieved. "Okay. And then you can hand me the phone so I can call the airline. Because there's no way in hell I'm staying here and risking another run-in with the Creature from the Black Lagoon."

His heart skipped a beat and his stomach turned over. "You're leaving?"

She blinked, as if finally thinking about the words she'd said. She glanced at the closed door, shivered, then looked back at him. "That sounds ridiculous, doesn't it? I mean, there are snakes everywhere."

"Yes."

"I'm overreacting."

"Just a little."

"The thing is, I really don't know if I could ever be comfortable walking around the grounds again by myself."

"I'm sure you could."

"I've never vacationed alone."

"Me, either."

She tapped the tip of her finger on her bottom lip. "I'm wondering if we could, maybe, vacation alone… together."

His jaw fell open.

"I mean, it would be nice to know somebody had your back, wouldn't it?"

"Sure," he said with a nod. "I could totally use somebody to save me from any tarantulas that sneak into my room."

If he woke up with one of those suckers lying on top of him, the whole town would hear his screeches.

"And you've proved yourself to be a champion snake wrangler."

A slow smile tugged at his lips. It was answered by

one from her. Maybe her first real one since he'd heard her scream and ran forward to be her dragon, er, snake, slayer. Well, not slayer—he'd never kill an innocent animal that was just doing what animals did—snake *catcher* would be the better term.

"You asking me if I want to be your vacation buddy?" he finally said.

"Something like that. You know, like in kindergarten when you always had to have a partner to hold hands with in the lunch line."

He grimaced. "I'd never have held hands with a *girl*."

"I don't have cooties."

He grinned and walked closer, lifting a hand to push her hair back over her shoulder. "I can tell."

She stared at him, licked her lips, then edged away, as if confused, a little skittish and shy remembering that heated embrace they'd shared.

Again, he let her get away with it, knowing they'd get back there sooner or later. Right now, she was telling herself, and him, that she was just after a buddy to spend time with and cover her back during her vacation. But he knew deep down it was more than that. The encounter was driving her decisions, even if she hadn't yet realized it. Somewhere deep inside, she wanted more. This was a logical, acceptable way to tell him she wanted to spend time with him.

Of course, shoving her hand down his trunks and grabbing his cock had been a pretty good indication, too. In fact, he preferred it.

"I suppose I could check out your pool every day before you get in it."

She shuddered. "Definitely."

"And come running if you call?"

"How did you manage that, anyway?" she asked, as if finally remembering what had happened before he'd caught the snake. "Where'd you come from? I know my door was locked."

"Over the wall. We're next-door neighbors."

A laugh escaped her lips and for the first time that morning, he began to think she was really going to be all right. Her panic had eased its grip on her and she was regaining her equilibrium.

That was a good thing, even if her cute suggestion—that he be her vacation buddy—was driving him crazy. The idea that he could be buddies with a woman who had every one of his senses, and all of his male chromosomes, on high alert, was ludicrous.

But he knew she was only half-joking. The thought of leaving really had crossed her mind, all because of a run-in with a member of the local population. And he didn't want her to go. He *desperately* didn't want her to go.

So, not even giving it any more thought, he agreed to her suggestion.

"Okay, Madison Reid, you've got yourself a deal."

"I do?"

"Uh-huh. Let's be solo vacationers together."

And see just how long it took for them to progress beyond the holding-hands-in-the-lunch-line stage.

6

THE HOTEL STAFF was incredibly apologetic about the snake incident. After Leo had called the front desk and explained the situation, no fewer than four maintenance men had shown up at her door. They'd deftly taken care of her unwanted visitor, and had then, at Leo's suggestion, looked over every inch of her private courtyard, cutting back some of the lower tangles of hedge to make sure there were no holes, nests or sleeping family members. She had remained inside, unwilling to even look out the door for fear they'd stumble across Mrs. Snake and a passel of little snakelings.

They hadn't. They'd found an indentation under one corner of the wall, where they assumed the wild creature had made its entry, and had backfilled it in with packed dirt and stone. The foreman had gone on to assure her that nothing like this had ever happened before and it most certainly wouldn't happen again.

Right. Just her luck to get the pool with the big honking reptile in it.

Of course, it had also been just her luck to have a big, powerful hunk right next door to save her ass.

Lucky me.

Good Lord, was he big and powerful. Even now, a couple of hours later, she couldn't stop thinking about how his body had felt pressed against hers, so strong and masculine. Not to mention how he'd tasted. How he'd smelled.

How that massive ridge of heat had swelled between them during their passionate kiss, making her legs grow weak and her mouth as dry as straw.

She'd thrown her naked self into his arms, not even pausing to think of how he might react. And he'd reacted. Oh, had he ever. She knew for a fact she'd never been with a man who'd *reacted* more. Or had more to react *with*. Wrapping her hand around him the way she had had taken a lot of gall, and she knew it. But she hadn't cared. She still didn't. She'd wanted to touch him and had been desperate for him to touch her.

No, she wouldn't regret this morning. Not ever.

Unless, of course, it was never repeated.

Then she might regret it, because she would be left wondering just how amazing all the *other* things they could have done together would be.

She lifted her hand and fanned it in front of her face, needing it more for her heated imagination than the warm weather. As they lay on a pair of huge, padded lounge chairs beside the stunning tropical pool that dominated the center of the resort grounds, she found herself continuing to cast glances toward his swim trunks, wondering if the lumps in the fabric were caused by the looseness of the material, or by the fact that he was still half-aroused. As she was, even hours later.

She gulped and forced herself to focus on the book she'd brought along, not wanting to distract herself all over again by remembering how wonderful it had felt to be in his arms. And how wonderful it would be to be in his bed.

That was where they were heading. She could no longer deny it to herself. The attraction was too strong, irresistible, and now that they'd kissed, touched each other, she knew there was only one place this kind of want could take them.

He had to have figured that out, too. But for now, he seemed content to be her "buddy." He'd insisted on escorting her down to the pool, making a big production of showing her how carefully he was inspecting the path in front of them. She'd finally begun to laugh and admitted she might have overreacted just a bit, and had found that laughing with Leo was almost as delightful as kissing him.

"What do you suppose is this surprise the hotel is planning for us?" Leo asked, startling her. She'd thought he was sleeping—his eyes were concealed by dark sunglasses, and he'd been lying quietly for several minutes, which had enabled her to, she thought, sneakily glance at him and wonder how on earth his skin could stretch enough to accommodate all those muscles.

"I'm not sure." Madison reached for her drink—a tall, fruity concoction laced with rum that the bartender kept sending over. Apparently, word had gotten out about her close encounter with nature, and the hotel was bending over backward to make it up to them. "I've been wondering about it, too. Whatever it is, it sounds like it's going to be pretty special."

Not only had she been upgraded to a completely all-inclusive vacation, meaning she wouldn't have to pay for any more meals or drinks, she and Leo had also been invited to a private surprise dinner that evening. The hotel was making all the arrangements and kept insisting it was the very least they could do for the inconvenience.

Personally, she preferred they give her a pair of snakeskin boots, but she supposed that was being a little vindictive and bloodthirsty. She wasn't a subscriber to the adage "the only good snake is a dead snake." She simply didn't ever want to have to see, hear or interact with one again as long as she lived.

"I guess they take their snake incursions seriously," she said.

"I suppose it wouldn't do their hotel any good if word got out that their pools came complete with their own boa constrictors."

She shuddered, hating to even think about it. That thing had been a boa, one of the maintenance men had confirmed it. He'd also said it was extremely rare for them to come out of the jungle, but that they did sometimes enjoy taking a freshwater dip. Again, just her luck. Maybe she had a sign on her back that she couldn't see, saying Fuck with me.

"I'm surprised they didn't just offer you a spa day or something," Leo said. "No need to include me."

"Hey, you were the snake catcher. I just stood there naked and screamed."

He smiled broadly. "Yeah. I remember."

She leaned over and flicked his arm sharply. He just laughed.

"Of course, I have a feeling that the woman at the front desk is doing a little matchmaking," he said.

She gaped. "Seriously?"

"Uh-huh. I wouldn't be at all surprised if this turns out to be some romantic setup."

Hmm. That didn't sound so bad.

"Though, they didn't make it sound like we had to dress up or anything," he said, "which is a good thing since I didn't bring much more than jeans and trunks."

"Me, either."

"So you weren't planning on doing any clubbing or hobnobbing while you were here, huh?"

She snorted. "Definitely not. I planned to do exactly what I'm doing right now."

She just hadn't planned to do it with a hunky firefighter from Chicago.

"So why did you decide to take a solo vacation?" he asked, sounding a little puzzled, as if he'd been thinking about it since she'd mentioned this morning that they were both vacationing alone.

She tensed, but didn't overreact. It was a natural question. Everywhere around them were groups and couples. The airport had been full of them, as had the taxi line. And even here, at such a small hotel, one only saw pairs walking about. Right now, on the other side of the lagoon-shaped, flower-bedecked pool, she saw two cooing couples, one middle-aged, another young and honeymoonish. This wasn't the type of place one vacationed alone.

"I was going through some stuff and just needed to get out of town alone for a while." She shrugged. "As it turns out, it might be a great thing."

He smiled lazily.

"Because now I can finish up a project I'm working on," she said a little teasingly, knowing he'd thought she was referring to him. She had been. But that had sounded a little too fawning.

Besides, now that she'd voiced it, she had to admit, the project idea wasn't a bad one. She might be persona non grata around Hollywood right now, but once the press forgot about her, the studios might remember her screenplay. She needed to do some rewriting, tinkering.

Tommy was still insistent that he wanted to play the lead, and maybe an announcement that the two of them were going to be working together might throw some water on the fiery gossip. Since she hadn't ever conceived of him in the role, she wanted to go back over the script and tweak it, make it more suitable for him.

The more she'd thought about it, the more she'd realized he really would be right for the part. She just needed to change her dark, brooding, angry hero into a golden-haired angel whose good looks hid a dangerous, edgy soul. Plus, at least with Tommy, there shouldn't be any diva actor fits over the homoerotic threesome scene!

"What do you do, anyway?" he asked.

"I'm a writer."

He turned his head to look at her from behind the dark glasses. "Novels?"

"Not yet. I was a journalist when I lived in New York. I worked for one of the big papers and hated it. So earlier this year, I moved out to L.A. to market an original screenplay."

"Wow. Any luck?"

"Yes." *And no.* "There's some interest but nothing concrete yet."

"That's pretty amazing. Have you met any stars? Done the whole elite-Hollywood-decadence thing?"

Chuckling, she admitted, "A few. And maybe a little decadence." Then, remembering what he'd said yesterday about having two all-inclusive packages, she asked the question that had been flitting around in her mind.

"So, what about you? Why the solo vacation—and the two-person package?"

He sighed audibly, turning his head to look at the pool again. She lifted her drink, sucking some of the delicious sweetness through the straw, giving him time. She wondered for a moment if he was going to ignore the question, but finally, he cleared his throat.

"This was supposed to be my honeymoon."

She coughed out a mouthful of her drink, spewing it onto her own bare shoulder. Sitting up straighter in the chair, she coughed a few more times.

"Are you okay?" he asked.

He'd sat right up and swung around to face her, patting her back as if helping a kid spit out too big a mouthful of food. Well, she had to concede, that had been a lot to digest. Even in the crazy moment, when her mind had begun to spin over the whole idea that Leo was supposed to be here with another woman—his *wife*—she had time to think how nice his strong fingers had felt on her back.

"I'm fine," she insisted, nodding and scrunching her eyes closed. Some of her drink had flown out of her mouth, some she'd gulped down, and now she had a damned brain freeze. "I was just surprised."

"Sorry."

Finally, when she felt in full control of herself, she turned to face him. Their bare legs brushed against each other, their feet inches apart on the stone pool deck. The coarse black hairs on his legs tickled her smooth ones, just another vivid example of his maleness compared to her femininity. The soft sensation made her stomach flip and her bathing suit feel a tiny bit tighter against her groin.

She forced those sensations away to focus on their conversation. "You were supposed to be here with your *wife?*"

"I'm not married!" he assured her.

"Good thing. I mean, considering you came on your honeymoon alone. What happened?"

"Same old story. Long engagement, nonrefundable trip paid for, wedding got canceled."

"So, what, she kept the dress and you kept the trip?"

"Something like that. We returned what we could but both of us ate some of the costs."

"That must have been painful."

"Not too terrible, considering we broke up six months before the wedding date."

Six months. So he wasn't exactly on the rebound. That was good to know.

"But you still couldn't get a refund on this?" She gestured around the grounds.

"Nope. I'd prepaid for a whole honeymoon package. Nonrefundable."

Wow, that had been pretty optimistic, considering how frequently people broke up these days.

He must have read her expression. "I know, I know. I can't imagine what I was thinking. I wasn't just being a cheapskate, I swear. I think, deep down, doing it that way was an affirmation that I believed we really would get married, even though, somewhere deep inside, I'd already begun to have doubts."

"So it was a friendly, mutual breakup?"

He barked a laugh. "Oh, hell, no."

She didn't reply, not asking the natural questions. She'd already been incredibly nosy. If he wanted to share more, he would.

"She cheated."

Oh, no. Stupid, foolish woman.

"I'm so sorry."

Those broad shoulders lifted in a careless shrug. "I'm over it. What hurt the most was that she did it with my best man…can you possibly get more cliché?"

"Or more trashy?" she snapped. "What a bitch."

"It takes two…he's a bitch, too."

His tone held no heat; he didn't seem to be bearing any grudges or holding on to any residual anger. So maybe he really was over all that. He'd certainly seemed to be so far. She would never have guessed he'd been recently betrayed and hurt by someone he'd cared enough about to propose to.

It truly boggled her mind. She had no use for cheaters, anyway, something she'd never been more thoroughly reminded of than when she'd become the country's most infamous one. But to cheat on someone like Leo? She didn't get it. He was impossibly handsome. He was thoughtful, funny and heroic. He was built like a god, kissed like a dream and had hands that should be patented. She couldn't even begin to imagine how amazing he would be in bed…. He certainly had plenty to offer a woman there.

So why on earth would anyone risk that for a fling with someone else? Even more—how could anyone who proclaimed to care about him do something so hateful, so hurtful, to a man who was so wonderful?

"She's insane."

He waved a hand. "It worked out for the best. Maybe she sensed I wasn't as emotionally attached as I should have been. I think part of her wanted me to find out, wanted to see how I'd react and make sure she really was the center of my world. If I'd played the part of enraged, jealous fiancé, she might have felt more certain that I really loved her."

"Oh, genius plan," she said with a big eye roll. As if he'd have ever taken her back after she'd played such a game? What man would? "You didn't, I presume?"

He shook his head slowly. "I was embarrassed, and I punched the guy. I think I was more mad at him!"

"Bros before hos?"

He grinned, not appearing to mind that she'd just called his ex a ho. Then again, the ex was a ho.

"I didn't yell at her, didn't fight, just…left. I told her what I wanted out of the apartment and that I never wanted to see her again. The end."

"Wow," she murmured, suddenly imagining how that must have felt. Whatever punishment his ex had gotten, including the embarrassment and the ending of her engagement, must surely have paled next to the realization that Leo didn't give a damn that she'd cheated on him. Madison honestly didn't know if she could have survived that.

Not, of course, that she would ever cheat on someone to whom she'd committed herself. Except, of course, according to every damned tabloid in the United States.

"Well, all I can say is, she's an idiot."

He chuckled. "Thanks."

"And you're better off."

"Oh, no doubt about that. But I can't help wishing I'd figured it out sooner. Ah, well, lesson learned. If nothing else, it reaffirmed how incredibly lucky I am to be surrounded by people who really *do* love each other."

"Who?"

"My family." His laughter deepened. "My big, huge, obnoxious, pushy, bossy, demanding family."

"You have a lot of siblings?"

"Two brothers, one older, one younger. But also a ton of cousins, aunts, uncles, second cousins, grandparents. My family might inspire a sequel to *My Big Fat Greek Wedding,* only with Italians."

Good grief, there were more Leos in the world? It boggled the mind.

"And they're all happily married?"

"There's been one divorce in the Santori clan in the past ten years, and that was a great-aunt and uncle who got tired of waiting for each other to die."

She snorted.

"Otherwise, everybody's faithful, everybody's happy. They're pretty damned amazing and incredibly lucky." He shrugged. "It's set a standard for me. I almost took a step that wasn't living up to that standard, and I got slapped down for it. I won't make that mistake again."

No, she didn't imagine he would. He would never sell himself short again, that was for sure. Even she knew he'd never commit to a woman he wasn't completely sure about.

Her heart almost wept over that. To be the woman a man this steady, this sure, this *wonderful* really loved would be such a gift. What a miracle.

And, for her, what an impossibility.

Because all Madison could bring to Leo was embarrassment and scandal, and it sounded like he'd had enough of those to last his whole life. She might as well be walking around with a big scarlet *A* sewn to the front of her bathing suit. His association with her could only drag him through the mud.

He didn't deserve that. And she didn't deserve him.

She knew that. But that didn't change one damn thing.

She still wanted him desperately. They didn't have much time, only six more days, but the more time she spent here, the more confident she was of the privacy and security of this place. Maybe it was risky, maybe she was being selfish, but she couldn't deny that the thought of spending six solid days on the grounds of this resort, having a wild, passionate affair with the man sitting next to her, excited her beyond reason.

Should she, though? She'd made so many bad calls lately, had misjudged one situation after another, the most recent being just how interested the world might be in her love life. Could she really entice Leo Santori into a wild, passionate, short-term affair that they could both walk away from, unscathed, next week?

She honestly didn't know. Nor did she know whether she should.

She just knew she *wanted* to.

HAVING BEEN TOLD by the staff to come to the lobby at around six, dressed comfortably, Leo knocked on her door at five minutes before the hour.

"Right on time," she said as she answered.

"Promptness is my specialty."

"I thought snake wrangling was your specialty."

"That's another one," he said with a laugh as she came outside, pulling the door to her bungalow shut behind her.

She stepped out onto the path, into the sunlight, and he took a sharp breath, looking her over, from head to toe.

Madison was wearing a silky, wispy sundress, all color and light. It was strapless, clinging to her full breasts, tight down to her hips, then flaring out, falling to her knees. The bright, tropical colors made her newly tanned skin glow. Her brilliant green eyes were made even more dramatic with heavier makeup than she usually wore, and she'd swept her hair up onto her head in a loose bun, leaving several long curling strands to fall over her bare shoulders.

She wore simple sandals with a small, delicate ankle bracelet. Something about it, that tiny strip of gold, made his heart race. He wanted to take it off, wanted to kiss her ankle and lick her instep and taste his way all the way up the inside of those beautiful thighs.

"Do you think I look okay?" she asked, noticing his silence.

"No. Not just okay. I think you're beautiful," he said.

She smiled, pleased at the compliment, then looked him over. "I think you are too."

He hadn't been lying about the limits of his wardrobe, but he had remembered to pack a pair of khakis and one dress shirt. It wasn't exactly Chicago dress casual, considering he had brown leather thongs on his feet, but he figured it would do for whatever the hotel staff had cooked up.

They needed to go—it was at least a five-minute walk to the lobby. But something made him stop. This wasn't a date; they were simply getting comped a meal for what had happened this morning. But he couldn't go another minute without doing what he'd wanted to do ever since she'd left his arms earlier today.

Without saying a word, he slid his hands into her hair, knowing he was probably going to knock down more of those sexy curls and not caring. He pulled her to him, saw her eyes flare the tiniest bit in surprise, then he covered her mouth with his.

She didn't hesitate but slid her arms up to encircle his neck, holding him close. Madison tilted her head, parting her lips, gently sliding her tongue out to welcome his. They tasted and explored, slowly, lazily, and he realized he hadn't imagined how good things had been with them this morning. They had chemistry; it was instant, undeniable, almost heady. The more they kissed, the more they wanted to. She pressed her body against his, the pebbled tips of her breasts and the musky, female scent rising off her telling him she was every bit as ready to turn back around and go into her room, skipping dinner in favor of the most delicious physical dessert.

But he wasn't in a rush. No rush at all.

Leo liked taking things slow. There would be no mad, crazy, gotta-get-in-you-right-now coupling. Not with this woman. Oh, maybe that would happen someday, but for their first time, he intended to savor every inch of her. For hours.

Finally, knowing they were probably already late, he ended the kiss and drew away from her. He patted her hair back into place, fixed one dangling curl, and said, "I guess we should go."

"You still want to?"

He saw the question in her eyes, knew she was ready to say to hell with dinner, let's order room service. But like a kid who looked forward to the raw anticipation of Christmas Eve far more than the present-orgy of the next morning, he held firm.

"Yeah, I do. Let's go see what they've got cooked up for us."

She frowned a little. To make sure she understood this wasn't in any way a rejection, he brushed his lips across her mouth one more time. "I can't wait to take that dress off you."

Her eyes flew open and she gasped. "Do you think you can just…"

"Yeah, I can. You want me, Madison. It's dripping off you."

She opened her mouth, then snapped it shut. How could she possibly deny something so utterly obvious to them both?

"And that's good," he added. "Because I want you, too. All I can think about when I see the way your nipples are pressing against those red flowers on the fabric is that they'll taste like ripe berries against my tongue."

He couldn't resist reaching up and flicking his fingers against those taut tips, feeling her sway in reaction as he plucked and teased. He wanted to cup and stroke and suck her but there was no time. Not nearly enough time.

"Leo!"

"Yeah. You're going to taste better than anything they put in front of us for dinner."

She gulped, closed her eyes, obviously trying to steady her breaths. He noticed the way she clenched a lightweight shawl in her hands and wondered if she was picturing his neck in her grip. She appeared ready to strangle him for teasing her now, when there was no way he could follow through.

Hell, the woman obviously didn't appreciate the fine art of anticipation.

"I'll make it up to you," he told her. "I'll make it so worth the wait, Madison."

She opened her eyes, looking up at him, her frown softening, her lips curving into a trusting smile. Then, just to show he wasn't the only one who could play the game, she whispered, "If you think my nipples will taste sweet, just wait until you taste the rest of me."

It was his turn to pause for a deep breath.

"I haven't been with anyone in six months, Leo, and I'm dying to be explored, tasted, *taken*."

"Six months? Funny, same with me. Maybe six months is our lucky number."

It was as if they'd both taken a time-out from everyone else just so they could build toward this night, this joining.

"Mmm-hmm. And if I don't have you in me in the next few hours, I think I'll just die."

"A few hours, huh?" He glanced at his watch. "That doesn't leave much time for foreplay."

She hissed and grabbed at his arm, as if her legs had weakened.

"But I suppose I can make do."

She swallowed visibly. "Please, let's just skip dinner."

"Not a chance, beautiful."

Smiling, Leo took her arm and physically turned her toward the pathway, leading her to the lobby. She didn't say anything, and her steps were the tiniest bit wobbly, as if she was still affected by the sultry promise in his words.

Because he *had* been making a promise.

Hours of foreplay? Not a problem. As long as he could lose himself inside of her at the end of it.

The realization that they'd both turned the corner and admitted that this night would end up with them in bed was enough to slake his appetite for now. It would build, hour by hour, until they were back here. And by then, he looked forward to adoring every inch of her body the way it was meant to have been adored every day for the past six cold, lonely months.

7

As it turned out, the staff's "surprise" dinner wasn't in the upscale restaurant attached to the hotel. Nor was there a limo waiting to whisk them off to some fancy place up in Santa Cruz. Nor was there a bevy of staff carrying trays of room service for a poolside rendezvous.

Instead, they were told when they arrived at the lobby a few minutes after six that they would be going on a beach picnic.

They were instructed to head down to a small, secluded beach tucked into a private cove below the hotel, reserved only for guests. Leo had read about it in the brochures, and he and Madison had talked about heading down there tomorrow. Today they'd just soaked up some sun by the pool, talking, laughing, drinking. She'd filled him in a little on the Hollywood scene—ugh. He'd told her about life in the Windy City. More interesting were all the things they'd both been thinking about but hadn't discussed. Things like how she tasted, how her body molded so perfectly against his, fitting him like she'd been made to be his other half.

As they followed the directions, walking down the steps carved into the hillside below the resort, he realized the term *beach picnic* was far too simple and mundane for the reality. This was more like a picnic a sheikh might indulge in somewhere along the Mediterranean.

"Wow, this is stunning," she said as they reached the bottom of the planked steps.

"No kidding."

The water was a little rough, white-capped waves lapping ashore, not as gentle and soft as a typical Caribbean resort. He liked this better; the Pacific seemed wild and powerful, as timeless as the earth. There was nothing placid about it. It was full of passion and energy.

The shoreline was a broad swath of pale sand, not sugar fine, but still clean and beautiful where it met the blue-green edge of the water.

Not only did they have the cove entirely to themselves—it was near sunset, and, he supposed, the few other guests were eating in the restaurant or were already out on the town. But they also would be dining in splendor. He could only wonder at all the trouble the staff had gone to, and couldn't decide whether it was more a result of the snake or the matchmaking front desk clerk.

A flowing canopy, white and lacy, stood in a sheltered area of the beach, nestled near the curving hillside. Fabric twined around each of the four legs, and it billowed in the evening breeze. Beneath it were a small café table and two chairs.

A chef stood at a tabletop grill, beside which were platters stacked with skewered meat, marinating fish and fresh vegetables. The man smiled as they reached the canopy tent and immediately began to grill the food as the uniformed waiter led them to their seats.

A pristine white cloth covered the table. The center was taken up with a beautiful vase full of colorful, tropical blooms, and a bottle of champagne was laid on ice, two glasses at the ready.

"Good lord, this is like the deluxe wedding night meal in the brochure," Madison whispered as the waiter pulled out her chair and she sat down.

He took his own seat and nodded. This was feeling more and more like a setup, and he decided he needed to leave a large tip for the desk clerk when he checked out.

When he saw the bed-size double lounger, draped with soft, white fabric, he decided to make it an extra-large one.

"Glad we came?" he asked.

She cast a quick look at the lounger. "I think I'm going to be."

"I have no doubt you're going to be."

She shivered a little, though the evening was still warm, and a lovely pink color appeared on her tanned throat, as if her body was growing flushed. He looked forward to exploring that soft swath of pink skin later.

Before she could say anything else, they were startled by the strumming of a guitar. They hadn't even noticed the musician sitting a few yards away. He smiled and nodded as he began to play softly, the notes riding on the air, mingling with the call of seabirds and the never-ending churning of the ocean.

"Champagne?" the waiter asked.

They nodded, and he popped the bottle of an expensive vintage, then poured them each a glass.

"I suppose we should offer a toast to something," Madison said once the waiter had discreetly returned to the chef's table, leaving them in privacy.

"I don't imagine we should drink to the sn…"

She threw a hand up, palm out. "Don't say that word! No more mentioning him tonight."

"All right. How about we drink to…new friendships?"

"As in, vacation buddies?"

He shook his head. "That's not the term I'd use."

Their stares met, and the table suddenly seemed even smaller, more intimate. Because Madison's green eyes were glowing with something that went far beyond friendship. This was so much more than that. Whatever was happening between them, however long it might last and wherever it might go, it was about a lot more than either of them were probably ready to admit. Every minute they'd spent together had suggested that. The kiss they'd shared outside her room had reinforced it. Their conversation had cemented it.

"Let's drink to new beginnings," he finally said.

That felt right, at least for him. For the past six months, he'd been living in limbo. It was almost as if a part of him had been waiting for the original wedding date to pass so the reality that it would never happen would finalize itself in his mind. Now that it had happened, now that the day had come and gone, he felt no sadness, no wistfulness. There was only freedom. Relief. And, now that he'd met Madison, pure anticipation.

"I like that," she said, as if she, too, had something she wanted to move beyond.

Although they'd talked for hours today, while they'd enjoyed the pool—swimming, sunbathing, eating a light lunch—she hadn't opened up much about her past. But he sensed she had come here to escape from her troubles, much as he had. As well as seeking something new and different.

Well, they'd found it. Because they'd found each other.

Maybe just for the next few days. It was too soon to tell. But starting tonight, he and Madison Reid were going to become lovers. Of that he had absolutely no doubt.

It had nothing to do with the conversation they'd had before leaving her room, or with the romantic setup although the bed definitely didn't hurt. Rather, it had everything to do with the tension and awareness that had been building between them from the moment they'd met. Hell, even if he'd been fully dressed when she'd walked into his room yesterday, and she hadn't fainted in his arms and there had been no naked embrace this morning, this thing between them would still be happening.

It was overwhelming his senses, answering all the questions he'd been asking himself for the past several months. And it was making him more certain than he'd been about anything that he'd finally met the kind of woman he'd been waiting for. One who he couldn't stop thinking about, who filled his thoughts and fueled his every desire, until his hand nearly shook with the need to reach out and touch her. Take her.

"Leo?" she asked, her voice soft.

He shook his head, realizing she was watching him expectantly, her glass in her raised hand. He lifted his, too.

"New beginnings," she said.

He echoed her words. They clinked glasses, and both drank.

The champagne went down smoothly, and the conversation was just as smooth. They had fallen into an easy rhythm with one another sometime after they'd met, and as they waited for their meal to be prepared, answering the chef's questions about their preferences, they talked about a lot of nothing. But good nothing. Fine nothing.

Over fresh fruit, they compared family stories. He marveled that she was an identical twin—that there was another woman as beautiful and perfect as this one somewhere in the world.

She teased him about being the middle of three boys, correctly assessing that he'd been the easygoing one who was always smiling. Unlike his older brother, who was an Army Ranger, or his younger one who was a cop, Leo had always been the comedian of the family, the peacemaker.

When they moved on to a salad filled with exotic greens, they'd talked politics. Only a bit—enough to confirm they were both the same shade of light purple, i.e. a little of this, a little of that. Neither of them were militant on any point, though it seemed important to her that he agree with her on civil rights and gay marriage, which he did.

They didn't talk much when the grilled mahi, marinated beef skewers and crisp vegetables arrived, too focused on the perfection of the meal. And afterward, when the waiter delivered enormous strawberries freshly dipped in chocolate, he couldn't find anything to say. He was too busy watching the way those full lips of hers looked drenched in chocolate, wondering if she cooed like that and closed her eyes with pure, visceral pleasure when she had sex.

He was going to find out tonight.

Their eyes kept meeting. Their hands touched when they both reached for the butter or the water. Their legs brushed. And minute after minute, the pleasurable tension rose. He felt it. She felt it, too. She broadcast it with every flick of her tongue across her lips, every intentional tilt of her head, sweep of her lashes and the tiny sighs she couldn't contain when he leaned close to taste something off her plate or when she reached over to brush a crumb off his shirt.

Tension. Oh, such delightful tension.

"Would you like coffee?" the waiter asked after he'd cleared away the last of the dishes. The chef had already departed, after they'd extended their sincere thanks, and the musician was packing up his guitar.

"That would be nice, thanks," Madison said. She pulled her wrap around her shoulders. The sun had begun to set, the evening air gaining more of a chill.

After serving the coffee, the waiter walked out from under the canopy to light some tiki torches that had been planted in the sand. When he returned, he said, "Please enjoy the sunset. Staff will be down to clean up later tonight. It's been a pleasure serving you, and again, the management extends its sincere apologies for today's inconvenience."

"Thank you," Madison replied, and Leo echoed the sentiment.

Then the man departed, the guitarist following him. Leo and Madison were left alone on the tiny beach.

Without a word, he rose from his seat and extended a hand. When she took it, he helped her stand and led her to the plush lounger. Pulling her with him, he sat down on it, spread out, and helped her tuck herself in beside him. She was on her side, her head on his shoulder, one thigh lifted and curled between his, her hand traipsing lazy circles on his chest.

The sun slipped farther, ever farther, and they remained quiet, washed in the glory of it. There was no need for conversation. They both simply knew, somehow, that the moment deserved utter silence, the only sounds those of their beating hearts and the churning waves.

Red and orange beams chased each other over the surf as the massive golden orb descended toward the horizon. They began to dance across the water, sent forth from some far-off, mystical place, thousands of lines of light riding the waves and landing close to their feet. The entire world seemed to be made of glistening light, every droplet of water in the spray turned into a jeweled rainbow.

Against his chest, he felt Madison stop breathing, and understood the reason. He found himself holding his breath, too, as that globe dropped what seemed like inches into the vast blue. Farther. Farther. Until at last, with a final wink and a flash, it fell off the edge of the world.

She exhaled in a rush. "Beautiful."

It had been. "A once in a lifetime sundown."

Which seemed appropriate for the once in a lifetime night they were about to begin.

After the sun had descended beyond the horizon, Madison remained curled up against Leo, content to relive the beauty of the moment in her mind. She'd never seen a more glorious sunset.

Leo remained quiet, too, content to watch, and to stroke lazy circles on her back with his fingers. Her shawl had slipped down and there was nothing separating his fingertips from her sensitive skin, which grew more sensitive with each gentle stroke.

But despite being gentle, there was nothing simple or innocent about it. The same rapt attention she'd paid to the sunset now shifted and turned, zoning in on the feelings he was arousing in her with that deliberate touch. Every time his hand moved a tiny bit lower, pushing closer to the back of her sundress, she shimmied up a little, wanting those fingers to push the material away, to bare her to the cool evening air and the heat of his touch.

Though the sun was gone, darkness certainly hadn't descended. The sky was still awash with purple, orange and gold. Once it did grow dark, the torches would still provide enough illumination for them, though not for anyone standing high on the cliffs above them to actually look down and see them. Especially not beneath the graceful canopy.

The scene was designed for private seduction. For intimacy. And while she couldn't totally agree that the woman at the front desk was doing some matchmaking, she couldn't rule it out, either. Because this setting was simply too perfect for sensual interludes to be accidental.

"You warm enough?" he asked.

"I'm perfect."

He shifted, rolling onto his side to face her, looking intently into her eyes. "Yes, you are."

Placing the tip of his index finger on her chin he tilted her head up, then bent down to brush his lips against hers.

Madison had been in a state of high alert all evening. Hell, all day—ever since that wild, erotic encounter on the patio. She had been thinking of nothing else but being possessed by him—taken wildly, roughly, desperately.

But now, she realized, she wanted it slow. Wanted a lingering, deep kiss that lasted at least a hundred heartbeats, and wanted it to end only because there was so very much more to explore.

He seemed to read her mind. He kept the kiss slow, lazy and sensual, his warm tongue exploring her mouth thoroughly. He tasted every bit of her, breathing into her and taking her breath.

A hundred heartbeats passed. At least. Or perhaps a thousand. Time began to lose its meaning as darkness fell and the night became lit by only those torches and the glow of moonlight they could glimpse through the fabric of the canopy.

He finally moved his lips away, kissing the corner of her mouth. He moved to her cheek, tasting her jawline, and then her neck, until he was breathing into her ear, his tongue flicking out to sample the lobe.

"I've wanted you from the minute you fell into my arms and fainted," he whispered.

"I've wanted you since I walked into the room and saw you standing there."

"Finest male ass you've ever seen," he said with a laugh.

"I can't deny it."

She stretched a little, arching against him, sliding her bare leg up and down against him. Leo moved a hand down her arm, blazing a trail of heat against her cool skin, awakening every nerve ending. He was still focused on her neck, and he kissed his way down it, until he could bury his face in her neck. There he paused to inhale, breathing her in, as if intoxicated by her essence.

She twined her fingers in his hair, needing something to hold on to when he resumed his slow study of her body. Without a word, he reached up to the elastic top of her dress and tugged it down, following the material, kissing every inch of skin as it was revealed. She arched toward his mouth, her breasts heavy, aching and desperate. When the top hem finally scraped across her nipples and popped over them, she moaned. Every stroke was intense, every sensation built upon the last.

He leaned up on an elbow, staring down at her as he pulled the bodice all the way down, revealing her breasts. Even in the semidarkness she could see the hunger in his eyes, the way he had to part his lips to take a shaky breath.

"Taste me," she ordered, knowing he was dying to. He'd been dying to since they'd left her room.

He reached for one breast, cupping it in his hand, plumping it and lightly squeezing her nipple. Heat sluiced through her, as if there were a wire between her breast and her groin, and she jerked reflexively.

Leo didn't notice, he was far too focused on looking at her, studying her, as if he'd never seen anything more beautiful. The tension stretched and built, and she thought she'd die if he didn't suckle her. When she'd almost reached the point of begging, he bent to flick his tongue over her sensitive nipple.

"Oh, God, yes," she cried, waves of heat washing ever downward.

He needed no more urging, moving to cover her entire nipple with his mouth. His hot breath seared her, then he was closing tight, his lips capturing her, his tongue flicking out to taste. He sucked hard, making all her nerve endings roar.

She reached for his shirt, desperate to feel him, and ripped at the front. A few buttons flew, enough for her to reach in and stroke his powerful chest, feel the sheen of sweat on his body that spoke of hunger and desire and need far more than the temperature of the air.

He continued to suckle her, reaching for her other breast, stroking and squeezing it, playing with her nipple until she shook.

"Berries," he murmured. "Sweet and so pretty."

As if remembering she'd invited him to taste far more than her nipples, he finally moved down and kissed a slow path over her midriff. He sampled each rib, licking each indentation, scraping his teeth across her skin as he pulled the dress out of his way.

When it got down to her hips, she lifted up a little so he could pull it all the way off. Beneath it, she wore only a tiny, skimpy pair of panties, lacy and white, the kind made to be torn off by a hungry man. They might as well have been advertised that way on the package.

"Pretty," he said as he studied them. Closely. His mouth was beneath her belly button, his jaw rubbing against the elastic of her panties. She felt his warm breaths through the nylon, and arched up in welcome.

He moved farther, placing his open mouth on her mound and inhaling deeply, breathing her in through the material.

"Oh, God, Leo," she cried, dying—just dying—for him to lick every inch of her.

As if knowing she'd taken about as much as she could, he began to uncover her fully. But he didn't tear the panties off, he merely tugged them, slowly, inch by inch, watching closely as he revealed her secrets.

"Oh, man," he whispered, his voice shaking as he looked at her.

She smiled. He liked what he saw.

He proved it, pushing the panties the rest of the way off, and then reaching for one of her legs. He stroked her thigh gently before pushing it, parting her legs, opening them so he could enjoy her in all her wantonness.

There was no thought of shyness, no modesty, nothing but heat and desire, natural and earthy. He looked at her as if he'd never seen anything more beautiful and moved immediately to taste her.

His mouth moved to her sex, his lips gliding against her in an erotic kiss that defied description. He licked her thoroughly, scraping his warm, wet tongue all over her outer lips, then slipping into the folds for more.

A helpless, desperate cry escaped her mouth. It was carried off by the night breeze, and she wondered just how many more times the man would make her cry out tonight.

"Beautiful," he said, touching her, stroking her, gently plucking at each secret place so he could study her more intimately.

He flicked the tip of his index finger over her clit, which throbbed with sensation, then moved his mouth to it and sucked it gently. As if he knew her body already, he circled his finger around the base while he flicked her with his tongue. Everything—all sensation, all desire, all need—centered there. It built and throbbed until it finally exploded in a climax that left her shaking so hard her teeth chattered.

He noticed. Kissing his way back up her body, until he reached her face, he murmured, "Are you cold?"

"Oh, God, no," she replied, wrapping her arms around him.

He kissed her deeply, his mouth tasting like sex and desire, and she reached again for his shirt, determined not to be stopped by a few buttons this time.

Leo broke away long enough to take over the task, yanking the thing up and over his head and tossing it to the sand. She bit her lip, watching as he quickly undid his khakis, waiting to see that amazing erection she'd held in her hand just this morning.

He rose onto his knees, pushing his pants down. He hadn't been wearing anything underneath, and all her breath left her body in a deep, hungry groan.

"I didn't imagine it," she managed to whisper.

He didn't say anything, but focused on pushing his pants all the way off. Then he returned his full attention to her.

Madison parted her legs even farther in an age old invitation to claim her. Fill her.

"I'm on the pill," she told him when he paused, opening his mouth as if about to ask her something. "And there's nothing else for you to worry about."

"Or for you," he said.

Then there was no more talking. Nothing else to say. The only communicating they needed to do was with their bodies.

He moved between her parted thighs, bracing himself above her and staring down at her face. Just to melt her heart a tiny bit more, to reinforce the goodness she'd sensed in the man from the beginning, he asked, "You're sure? No second thoughts, no regrets?"

She reached up and encircled his shoulders, drawing him down to her. "I've never been more sure about anything."

"Neither have I," he admitted as he settled between her legs, nudging her sex with that massive erection that both thrilled and intimidated her.

She shouldn't have worried. He was careful, gentle, and he'd aroused her to the point of insanity. She was dripping wet, soft, welcoming and so ready to be filled by him.

He knew. And he began to fill her.

He slid into her warm opening, the passage easy and smooth. All the feminine parts of her reacted and responded the way they were supposed to, with utter surrender to pleasure. She clenched him, tugging him deeper, both with her arms and with her sex. Leo groaned, letting himself be taken in, still careful, but obviously starting to lose himself to sensation.

"Yes. Take me," she pleaded, tightening her arms around his neck, nipping at his throat. "Take me *now*."

That drove him onward. Without another word, he arched his hips and plunged, driving into her more deeply than she'd ever thought it possible to go. She let out another cry of pure, utter satisfaction, and focused on savoring the sensation of heat and power and such wonderful, delightful fullness.

"Are you…"

"I'm fine," she said, moving her mouth to his and licking his lips for entry.

They kissed hungrily, tongues entwining, and he slowly pulled out of her, only to sink again. She arched up to meet the slow thrust, curving her hips upward, wrapping her legs around those lean flanks.

"Madison," he whispered, still cautious.

"More," she demanded, knowing why he was being so careful, knowing he was afraid to hurt her. "Don't take it easy on me, Leo, I *want* it. Give it to me."

She tightened her hands in his hair, gripping him, almost at the point of begging him to pound and thrust.

And then he began to pound and thrust.

He pulled out and drove back in, going deeper and deeper. The walls of her sex wrapped around him, taking everything, greedy for more. Her heart pounded wildly and she found it hard to catch her breath. She couldn't think, couldn't focus, could only *be*.

Leo had obviously thrown off the last of his restraints, because he suddenly rolled over onto his back, pulling her with him. He sat her up, impaling her on his cock, holding tightly to her hips.

"Yeah, baby, please," she groaned, digging her fingers into the crisp hair on his chest.

He encircled her waist with his hands and thrust up, just as he tugged her down. The intensity was wild, and he bored a path even deeper into her. She let out a little scream, but when he paused, she glared down at him. "Don't you stop. Don't you dare stop."

"Not planning on it, sweetheart," he said between harsh breaths.

The muscles in his chest and arms clenched and flexed and his jaw was like granite. His eyes closed and he dropped his head back as he thrust up into her again. And again. And again.

Although she was on top, he controlled their every move, handling her as easily as if she'd been a doll. But she didn't care. Every movement he made was for her pleasure. As if to reinforce that, he moved one hand between them and rubbed her clit, just to make sure she'd climax again when he was ready to.

The heat began to rise again, the sensations spiraled. She was battered by the cool evening air, completely filled with his rock-hard cock, gripped and held and completely lost to pure sexual bliss.

And when he finally gave a hoarse shout, indicating he'd gained his own, she followed him to an explosive orgasm, and then collapsed onto his body, boneless, weak and exhausted.

8

As it turned out, Leo hadn't merely paid for an "all-inclusive" meal plan he didn't need, he'd apparently paid for an unneeded room, too. After he and Madison had become lovers on the beach, they had, by unspoken agreement, gone back to her room and slept together in her bed.

The sex was phenomenal.

Sleeping together afterward just made it better.

He liked drifting off with her head resting against his shoulder, her arm curled over his middle, their legs entwined. He liked it even better every time he woke up to find her warm beside him, ready for more.

They'd spent the deepest, darkest hours of the night exploring each other in a slow, sultry orgy of lust that seemed to go on forever. Or, at least, as long as he could hold out. Madison had once again proved to be impatient, as greedy in bed as she was generous out of it. At one point, he'd been able to do nothing but laugh—and comply—when she'd demanded that he stop with all the oral sex and just fuck her into the headboard.

Hoping to start the day off the same way, he reached for her as soon as he woke up the next morning. Her half of the bed was empty. It was warm, though, as if she'd just left it a few moments ago. Sitting up, he glanced toward the bathroom. The door was open, but she wasn't inside.

A muffled voice was talking nearby, and he finally glanced out the patio door and saw her sitting in the sunshine, talking on her phone.

She was stark naked.

Damn, he liked this place.

Beams of sunlight illuminated every delicious bit of her, catching all the gold highlights in that honey-brown hair. He'd touched and kissed almost every inch of her last night, but he hadn't seen her in all her glory until this moment, and the sight of her nearly stopped his heart. She was all softness and curves and smooth, silky skin.

And he'd left his mark on her.

Even from here he could see the slightly reddened spots on her throat and breasts, left there by his hungry mouth. There was a small bruise on one hip, and he suspected he'd held her a little too tightly when she'd been riding him.

He didn't feel too badly, though, suspecting that if he looked at his back in the mirror he'd see plenty of war wounds, too. He certainly felt them. But he didn't regret one damn thing. The memory that he could get her out of her mind, raking at him, begging him, and utterly helpless to do anything but take what he gave her turned him on almost as much as looking at her sitting naked in the sunshine.

Smiling, he got up and stretched, not surprised to see he had some major morning wood. Hell, just thinking of her was enough to make him want to go outside and push her legs apart. He couldn't think of a better way to scrape up his knees than kneeling in front of her. Draping her legs over the arms of her chair would put all those beautiful, slick secrets right in front of his face; he wanted to see, explore and taste her all over again.

But she seemed pretty involved in her conversation. So he instead headed to the bathroom to wash up. When he came out, she was still outside, still talking, and he went over and pulled the patio door open.

"No, I swear, I'm fine," she was saying into her cell phone. "You don't need to do anything right now, just let it go. It'll die down, these things always do."

Not sure whether her conversation was a private one or not, he was about to close the door again when she glanced up, saw him standing there and offered him a bright good-morning smile.

"Hi," he murmured, bending down to kiss the top of her head.

"Hi back," she replied before returning to her telephone conversation. "What? Uh, yeah. Someone I met here in Costa Rica."

Ah, she was explaining him to someone.

"Oh, be quiet, you know-it-all," she said good-naturedly. "Of course he's hot."

He snickered.

"Leo. Like the lion."

Rowr.

She sighed heavily, obviously getting the third degree. "No, not DiCaprio for God's sake!"

He laughed.

"Yeah, yeah, you're a genius. It was great advice. Blah, blah, blah."

So this someone had been after her to have a wild, sexy fling during her vacation? Interesting, considering that was also what his friends had told him to do, which made him wonder again what it was that haunted Madison. They hadn't discussed it, beyond her admission that she'd come here to get away from her troubles for a while. What were those troubles, though? Had her friends told her to go off and have an affair to get over a broken heart? And if so, who'd broken it?

The idea of someone hurting her made his whole body stiffen in anger. He walked over to the pool's edge, not wanting her to interpret his reaction as jealousy.

Even if, he had to concede, that might be part of it.

Yeah, he hated the idea that anyone might have hurt her.

But it was more than that. The very thought of any other man having his hands on her, making her cry out in pleasure the way she had for him last night, made him want to punch the bungalow wall. How crazy was that? He was jealous over somebody she might have been with even before she'd met him? He'd only known her a couple of days, but the very idea of it made him more ready to do violence than the reality of his former best man sleeping with his ex-fiancée.

"You are losing it, man," he muttered.

"Did you say something?"

He hadn't even realized she'd ended her call and walked up behind him until she spoke. Before he could turn around, she'd slipped her arms around his waist and stepped in close, hugging him from behind. Every bare inch of her body delighted him, but, to be honest, he'd rather be the one coming at her from behind.

Hmm. Nice mental images filled his head.

"I just checked," he told her. "The pool is reptile-free and ready to go."

She shivered against his back, her pert nipples scraping his skin, driving him a little nuts. "Yikes, thanks for reminding me. I'd managed to forget all about that this morning."

He turned around, lining the hug up better. Full frontal under the full sun...it was kind of spectacular.

"Sorry I slept so late. You didn't have to go outside to take your call," he said.

"No problem. It was just a friend from California." She smiled broadly, her eyes twinkling with humor in the sunlight. "Before I came here, he had suggested I find a beach bum to hook up with on my vacation. He was very happy to hear your voice and realize I'd taken his advice."

Thrusting off the quick flash of jealousy that her friend was male, Leo pretended to be offended. "Beach bum?"

"Well, no, I guess I have *slightly* higher standards."

"I'm going to have to punish you for that."

"Promises, promises." Her saucy tone and pursed lips said she was thinking of naughty punishments.

Which sounded just fine to him. God, how he enjoyed this woman's blunt approach to everything, from life to sex. He'd never been with anyone who was so open about what she wanted and what she didn't. And when she did or didn't want them.

"Are you, by any chance, a little wicked?"

"Haven't you figured that out by now?"

He stared into her eyes. "I'm getting the picture."

"Are you liking what you see?"

"Yeah." He raked a slow, thorough stare down her body, from the long hair draping her shoulders and playing peekaboo with those pebbled nipples, to the slim middle, to those eminently grippable hips and drool-inspiring long legs. All naked. All completely his, for now at least. "Oh, *hell,* yeah."

"Good. As for the punishment, despite some curiosity, I'm fairly certain I'm not into pain," she explained. "If you ever spanked me, I would probably cut your hand off."

Chuckling, he replied, "No interest in spanking, sweetheart."

She continued. "Nor am I into rape fantasies. Any man who tries to force me won't lose a hand, he'll lose what he uses that hand to play with."

He didn't play along by grimacing, cringing or feigning horror at the idea of losing every man's most prized possession. Instead, he grew serious, reaching out to touch her hair. It was warm beneath his fingertips, baked in the sun. "Every Santori man was raised by a Santori mother who taught him how to treat women.

Lesson number one—men who hurt women are cowards," he said. "I'd never do anything to hurt you."

She turned her face to kiss his palm. "I know that, Leo. I know you'd never really hurt me." Her impish smile returned. "But if you wanted to, say, get a little creative with some…"

Positions? Toys?

"…handcuffs…I might not object."

He coughed into his fist. Jesus, the woman was killing him here.

"Problem?"

"Nope. No problem. Kind of hard to get handcuffs down here, I imagine." He could hear the heat in his tone as he speculated, "We might have to make do with silk scarves or something."

It was her turn to look affected by the conversation. She was breathing across open lips and her eyelids had dropped to half-mast. She might have been teasing, trying to arouse him with some suggestive ideas, but those ideas were obviously exploding into full-fledged X-rated movies in her mind.

"That could be arranged."

"And maybe then you'd have to shut up and wait and take what I want to give you."

"Maybe," she said, completely unrepentant for being so demanding.

Oh, hell, who was he kidding? He loved that she was so demanding. Loved that he got her so worked up she couldn't do anything but scream and beg and threaten him if he didn't proceed. She'd gone so far as to call him a clit tease last night. He couldn't say he'd ever heard the expression, but had to admit, he'd found it pretty funny. And he'd been determined to live up to it.

"Maybe I'll punish you by making you wait all day for your punishment."

"That'd be punishment for you, too," she said, her voice almost a purr.

He knew she was taunting him, and decided to pay her back. Not warning her, he swung her up into his arms, bracing her under the shoulder, crossing-the-threshold style. As she squealed, he stepped to the very edge of the pool, dangling her over the crystal clear water. "Ready to get wet?"

"Don't you dare!" She twined her arms tightly around his neck. "It's too early, the water's too cold."

"Not for a beach bum."

"Superhot fireman, that's what I meant to say. Strong, professional, determined, hardworking hero." Loosening her grip, she traced the tip of her finger across his lips. "Please don't throw me into that cold water, Leo. Pretty please?"

"What are you going to give me if I don't?"

She thought about it, tapping the tip of her finger on her mouth. Then, smiling as if the proverbial lightbulb had just gone off in her head, she replied, "A blow job?"

He was torn between laughing and groaning with pure want. He'd already been aroused and another ten gallons of blood rushed to his cock just at her suggestion.

"You always say what you're thinking, don't you?"

"Pretty much," she admitted. "That's why my closest

friends always called me Mad. It wasn't just a shortening of my name."

"Hmm. Mad. You don't seem like the angry type."

"Not angry. It's short for Mad, Bad and Dangerous to Know."

"That I can see." He glanced at the glistening water, as if he really had to think about it, and said, "Okay, Mad. I guess I won't toss you in this time."

"You really are my hero."

She leaned up and brushed her lips against his. He immediately opened his mouth and deepened the kiss, invading her, taking the sassiness right off her tongue. Madison needed to be kissed, well and often, if only as a reminder that she wasn't always in charge.

When they finally ended the kiss, they were both panting. But he wouldn't put her down yet. He liked holding her, liked being in control for now. She might demand what she wanted, but he was making it pretty damned clear that, physically, he had her right where he wanted her.

She twined her fingers in his hair and looked up at him, her expression purely happy. "That's a very nice way to start the day."

"I had another one in mind when I woke up."

"Sorry I wasn't there."

"It's okay. Like I said, I slept too late anyway. I never sleep so late in the morning unless I'm on nights and have just gone to bed."

"I figured you could use your rest. You got quite a workout last night."

He scrunched his brow, as if giving it careful consideration. "Really?" Lifting her up and down a couple of times in his arms like a barbell, he added, "Funny, I feel great."

She squealed a little and hung on to his shoulders, saying, "That's good. Because I think you're going to get another one today."

"One?"

"Four."

He barked a laugh, then thought about it. Four. Hmm. Not very impressive. "Come on, challenge me, babe."

"Am I going to need to do any walking for the rest of this vacation?" she asked.

He tilted his head, as if considering it. "Not that I can think of."

"Okay, then. I *guess* you can go for a world record."

"What's the record?"

"Twenty-seven."

He snorted. "Yeah, uh, by that point you wouldn't be able to put your legs together, much less walk. And I wouldn't have a dick, much less one capable of getting hard."

She licked her lips, her expression evil. "Back to that blow job idea, are we?"

He didn't tease her back. She'd mentioned that one too many times for him to pretend he wasn't dying for her to use her beautiful mouth on every inch of him.

"I think we could fit that in today, if you really want to."

"I already know it's not going to fit," she said with a smirk. "But I do really want to and I'm always ready to give it the old college try."

"Rah-rah. So, where does that leave us? Somewhere between four and twenty-seven, with a blow job and a serious licking in between?"

She swallowed visibly. "*Serious* licking?"

"Oh, very serious."

"I noticed you kind of like that."

"No, honey, I kind of love it. You taste better to me than anything I've ever eaten in my life."

"Mmm." She wriggled in his arms, obviously reacting to this verbal foreplay.

So was he. In fact, he couldn't lower her to her feet right now because, if he did, she would hit a major obstacle on her way down.

"Okay, then. We're agreed," she said, as if firming up terms for a business proposition.

"We are? What's the final number again?"

"Six." She quickly added, "Plus the licking and the blowing."

Six. She was challenging him to make love to her six times today. Plus the…extras.

No sweat.

He was twenty-eight. His job kept him in peak physical condition. Until last night, he'd been celibate for six long months.

And he was hotter for her than any man had ever been hot for a woman.

Six would be absolutely no hardship.

"And if it'll *really* kill you not to suck my nipples until I scream, I guess you can do that, too," she said, doing him a very great favor by offering up her beautiful breasts for his devouring.

He lifted her higher, bent his head and flicked his tongue over one pretty tip.

"Thank you, that's so selfless of you," he murmured as she sighed with pleasure.

"That's just how I roll."

They both started to laugh, softly at first, then growing louder. There wasn't another woman he could *ever* remember talking to like this, especially one he'd been holding naked in his arms, whose nipple he'd just licked. She was so damned open and quick, witty and confident. Most women he'd dated hadn't been able to take a joke that *wasn't* about sex, much less any that were.

Before Madison, sex had always been twice as serious but only half as good. Adding warm humor to intimacy—at least before the brain cells evaporated and lust took over completely—enhanced the experience in ways he'd never thought possible. Hell, just having a woman smile up at him tenderly, twining her fingers in his hair, was incredible all on its own. As demanding as she could be in bed, Madison still surprised him with moments like those. Every woman he'd ever been with before had been entirely serious, and, he suspected, focused on gaining advantage in the relationship outside of the bedroom.

He and Madison didn't have a relationship—not yet, anyway, not in the real world. This was a vacation fling, although something inside him rebelled at calling it that. Still, it was a freeing proposition; neither of them were playing games, keeping score or exchanging in any kind of tit for tat.

It was easy with Madison. Hot, incredibly hot, but just so easy.

"Okay, then, I think we have a deal," he finally said.

"This is going to be quite a day, isn't it?" Her eyes were wide, gleaming with excitement, and she was practically panting each breath. He could feel the thudding of her heart in her chest and drew her a little more tightly against his body, knowing now where he intended to put her down.

On the bed.

"I think it would be quite a day even if we had to stop after one," he replied, wondering if she heard the tenderness in his voice and correctly interpreted it.

He wanted to spend the day with her. Yes, that day would include a lot of mind blowing sex. But even if it didn't, he would still be looking forward to it. Just being with her, getting to know her, hearing that laugh, watching those green-gold eyes sparkle in the sun…sounded like the perfect vacation day to him.

She nodded slowly, silently agreeing with him. "Maybe we could just go on and on for hours and call it one."

"Sounds good to me."

Slowly loosening her arms from around his neck, she said, "Don't you want to put me down?"

"In a minute."

He walked across the patio and went inside through the open door. Carrying her to the huge bed, he didn't so much lower her as toss her onto it. Madison stared up at him, those eyes flashing in challenge, and reached for him.

He shook his head slowly.

"What?"

"Move up," he ordered her, nodding toward the pillows.

She did, edging closer to the headboard. When she was close enough, he said, "Get all the way up on your knees. Turn around facing the wall and hold on to the headboard."

She caught her lip between her teeth. He knew this was driving her crazy, both with lust, and because his tone of voice brooked no disobedience. He was calling the shots for now. It was about time she figured that out.

She didn't move. Neither did he.

He could outwait her, of that he had no doubt. Knowing how to prove he could take care of his needs a little more easily than she could right now, he reached down and grabbed his cock. Encircling it in his hand, he stroked. It wasn't nearly as good as she would be, but it got the job done. She hissed, her gaze dropping so she could stare, and he saw her lick her lips.

She made as if to move toward him. He put a hand up to stop her. "Me first. Then your turn."

That was when she finally figured out what he wanted. A sultry smile broke over her face. She stopped stalling, rose to her knees and crawled toward the head of the bed.

Just because she was a witch and she knew how badly he wanted her, she put some serious wag in that ass, parting her legs a little more than was necessary. A flash of glimmering pink—oh, how that smooth skin felt against his lips, he could have died of sensory overload last night—greeted him. She was practically daring him to resist. She wanted him to climb onto the bed behind her on his knees and ram into her.

"Later," he promised.

"Everything's later," she grumbled.

"So stop stalling so we can get on to the now," he said with a lazy grin.

She grinned back, admitting she liked this push and pull between them, the sparring over who called the shots.

She finally reached the top of the bed, shoving the pillows out of her way and kneeling. He walked closer, took her hands and rested them on the top of the tall wooden headboard, making sure she remained on her knees but completely upright.

Kissing her on the mouth, hot and hard, he dropped onto his back on the bed and slid up toward her. "Show me, Mad. Show me everything."

She looked down at him, over her shoulder, and slowly eased her legs apart, opening for him.

"Beautiful," he growled, unable to tear his eyes off her glistening, sensitive folds. She was swollen and plump, pink and perfect.

When her knees were far enough apart to accommodate him, he slid all the way up so his head was between her thighs.

"Hold on tight," he said.

"Is it going to be a bumpy ride?"

"Uh-huh."

"Oh, good. That's my favorite kind."

He didn't give her any more time to prepare or talk.

He just couldn't wait to taste her fully. Wrapping his arms around her thighs, he tilted her sex toward his mouth and slaked his thirst for her.

She cried out when he flattened his tongue and licked her from stem to stern. Knowing he had her attention, he slid his tongue deeper, between those luscious folds. He lapped into her, sliding his tongue deep enough to make her sing, then moving out again. She tasted as amazing as she looked, as she smelled, as she felt, and he had to tell her so.

"I could do this every day for the rest of my life and die a happy man," he muttered.

"You're killing me, Leo," she groaned, sounding hopeless and desperate.

Almost laughing, he moved his mouth to her pebbled clit and sucked it between his lips. Her hips jerked, but he held her tight, nowhere near ready to let her do what he knew she wanted to do: slide down his body and impale herself on him. Although part of him would love that, considering his need was almost painful, he wasn't going there until she'd completely lost herself to everything but sensation.

Continuing the relentless assault, he brought her higher and higher. She quivered and moaned, but didn't release her death grip on the headboard. He explored her completely, pleasured her until his tongue ached, until, finally, a cry of utter satisfaction signaled her orgasm.

"Yes, oh, lord, yes," she said, her voice weak.

He moved out from under her, his face wet, his every sense filled with her. Madison sagged against the headboard, sucking in deep, needy breaths, completely wrung out. She made as if to turn around, and he knew she still wanted to use her mouth on him, but he was barely holding it together. He had to be inside her, right now.

Rising to his knees, he moved in behind her. Madison smiled at him over her shoulder, suddenly looking a lot more energetic, and scooted back to meet him, her legs parted invitingly.

"Yes," she told him. "I want you to be buried so deep inside me I'll remember you there for a week."

He smirked. "A week? Oh, please."

She licked her lips and curved that gorgeous ass a little higher in welcome. He didn't need any further invite. Taking her hips in his hands, he held her tight and nudged into her. Pleasure washed over him the moment hot, hard cock met warm, slick channel, and he groaned as he sank deeper and deeper, every inch feeling like a step closer to heaven.

She cried out when he finally sank all the way, making a place for himself deep inside her willing body.

"You okay?"

She literally purred. "So okay."

Not wanting to hurt her, and knowing the angle had to be pretty intense for her, he moved slowly at first. He made easy love to her, caressing her hips, her thighs and the small of her back between each deep stroke. But as the intensity built, as her cries increased and she pushed back ever harder, he knew she was long past any need or desire for gentleness.

Which was good. Because he'd reached the point where he needed to pound into her in a mindless frenzy.

But he also wanted to see her beautiful face, wanted to kiss her and share the gasps as they both hit that cliff and flew off it.

Pulling out of her, he flipped her onto her back. Her eyes were sparkling with excitement and wanton pleasure. Her face was flushed, her every breath a gasp, and her whole body sheened with sweat. They were slick and hot and so well matched he wondered how he'd ever done this with anyone else.

"That was…"

"The halfway point," he muttered, making sure she knew they weren't done. "At most."

A sultry smile widened those lips. "One-twelfth of our day, then, huh? You'd better slow down."

He laughed out loud, but grew serious when she reached for him, wrapping her arms tightly around his neck and pulling him down for a deep, hungry kiss. Her thighs parted again and he settled between them, getting back into her with one hot, hard plunge. He reached for one of her slim legs, lifting it over his shoulder, lightly biting the thigh as he drove a little deeper. The angle was incredible. He felt so completely taken in by her, welcomed and pleasured.

She thrust her hips to meet his every downward stroke. Soon she was rolling her head back and forth on the pillow, biting her lip to try to hold back her cries.

"Nobody can hear you, sweetheart," he told her as he felt waves of heat radiating through his body, preparing him for a mind-numbing explosion.

As if she'd just been waiting for permission, she let out a tiny scream of pleasure with the next thrust. An even louder one followed, and he knew by the way her head fell back and her fingers tightened, digging into his shoulders, that she had come again. Seeing her losing herself to glorious pleasure was enough to send him tipping over the edge, too, and with one more deep thrust, he flew apart as well, coming into her in wave after wave of ecstasy.

He didn't roll off her right away, wanting to watch sanity return to her face and feel the raging heartbeat begin to slow to a normal rhythm. He lowered her leg, keeping himself propped on his elbows so he didn't crush her, sharing heaving breaths and then, when she opened her eyes again, satisfied smiles

"That," he told her, "was…"

"Number one."

9

ALTHOUGH THEY HADN'T hit the world record—whatever that might be, and she doubted it was anywhere near twenty-seven—Madison still found it deliciously difficult to walk the next day. For thirty-six hours, she and Leo hadn't left her room, except to go out into the private pool. They'd ordered room service when hungry, had slept when exhausted, had soaked in the pool when overheated, and had made love so many times, she'd lost count of the positions, sensations and orgasms.

And throughout all of that, she hadn't given more than a passing thought to all the nonsense going on back home. It was like they were living in a completely different world. Things like tabloids and paparazzi and movie stars didn't exist.

Being with Leo had made her troubles disappear.

He was funny and smart, could be bossy, which she liked, and could also be incredibly tender, which she also liked. He was, without a doubt, the most amazing lover she'd ever had. Patient to the extreme, powerful and exciting. But the sex was also playful and fun.

Honestly, she didn't even want to think about what it would be like to give him up at the end of this vacation.

Not that they'd talked about that. Neither of them had mentioned the real world or going back to it. She knew she might be riding a cloud of sexual euphoria, but she was happy to be airborne and didn't want to come back down to earth.

Of course, *this* wasn't exactly what she had in mind.

"I'm sorry, I changed my mind, I don't think I can do it." She heard the nervousness in her own voice and while she hated herself for it, she couldn't prevent it.

"Come on, I know you're not scared of heights. You've been skydiving," Leo said, looking surprised.

"Over North America. Not over the freaking jungle."

It was probably a bad time to get cold feet, considering they had already ridden the party bus several hours to get here. They'd also already paid the exorbitant fee for the double experience—a treetop tour on some swinging wooden walkways, plus zip lining out to a beautiful waterfall in the middle of nowhere. Not to mention they were already standing on a small platform hundreds of feet in the air, getting strapped into harnesses for their zip-line adventure!

She'd been very excited about it, right up until the moment she'd seen a vine dangling from a nearby tree and had a sudden image of a long, slithery animal.

"It's the snake factor," Leo said, understanding immediately.

Yeah. That. Madison had seen that vine, recalled what kinds of creatures made their home in the jungle, and her feet had turned into icicles.

She gulped and nodded. "I want to do this, I really do. It's gorgeous." She spread her arms wide and looked around them at the incredible green canopy blocking out the blue sky above their heads. She truly had never seen such a remarkable palette of different shades of green—her favorite color. Part of her wanted to soar through the sky, to explore the wonders of nature that made this place so different from anywhere back home.

Part of her wanted to carjack the nearest tour bus and hightail it back to the resort.

Because of those pesky snakes.

The guide—young, cute and English speaking— had obviously overheard. "Oh, no, no snakes to worry about, *señorita*."

Madison just lifted a skeptical brow.

The young man shrugged. "Maybe a few."

She reached for the clasp of her harness, ready to strip out of the contraption.

"But you'll do nothing more than wave to them from the air as you fly over," Leo insisted with a chuckle.

"What if the harness breaks and I fall a hundred feet into a nest of fer-de-lances?"

"That won't happen," the guide assured her.

"Plus, I think if you fell a hundred feet, you'd have more to worry about than some snakes," Leo pointed out. "Broken limbs, crushed skull, that sort of thing."

"Ha-ha."

The guide didn't laugh at that part, either. They'd gone over the rules for this adventure many times; the company prided themselves on their safety record.

"Impossible," the man said, looking offended.

"I know, we wouldn't do it if we didn't think it was safe. It's just, she had a snake encounter at the hotel the other day," Leo explained.

"Oh, then all is well!" he exclaimed. "It is like lightning. You've been struck once, you never will be again."

"Huh." She wasn't buying it.

"He's right, you know. What are the odds?" Leo prodded.

Probably not as good as getting engaged to the tabloid-proclaimed sexiest man alive, yet she'd managed to do that, if only for a very unusual reason.

"Come on, are you really going to let a phobia about something that probably won't happen stop you from doing something you really want to do?" Leo asked.

When he put it like that, it did seem crazy.

"I'll go first if you want, clearing the way."

"My hero."

A grin lifted a corner of his mouth and one of those sweetly sexy dimples appeared. Leaning closer, so the guide wouldn't overhear, he whispered in her ear, "The faster we get back down to earth, the sooner we'll be back at the hotel with those pretty new scarves you bought at the bazaar."

Her heart sped up. The bus had made a couple of stops during the trip here, including one at an open-air market. She'd found a stall selling long, beautiful silk scarves and had bought a few of them, knowing when Leo's brow shot up that he knew why.

"All right, all right. I guess I'll do it."

"Are you sure?" Leo asked, searching her face carefully, all kidding aside. "If you really don't want to, I'll understand."

She gazed at the canopy—all that green—at the zip line extending as far as she could see toward that waterfall, which sounded absolutely beautiful, and nodded. "I'm not going to let a phobia deprive me of something I've wanted to do for a long time."

"Good girl."

Pressing a quick kiss on her mouth, he stepped to the edge of the platform. Within a moment, he was gone, flying like a bird, whooping as he went, his laughter floating back to her on the air.

"Ready *señorita?*" the guide asked.

"Ready as I'll ever be."

She stepped to the edge, took a deep breath and did what she'd been doing ever since she met Leo Santori.

She leaped feetfirst into adventure.

LATE IN THE DAY, after their jungle excursion—which Madison had loved in spite of herself—they boarded the tour bus for the trip back up to their resort. The bus was crowded with other tourists. They'd met some very nice people from various parts of the world. Now, though, after a day with them, she really just wanted some alone time with Leo.

She kept thinking about that beautiful waterfall, and how much she would have liked it if they'd had it all to themselves. Making love in the water, she had recently discovered thanks to her private pool, was one of her favorite things. She could only imagine how it would have felt to stand beneath those cascading sheets of cool liquid and lose herself in his strong arms.

She suspected every other couple there had had the same thought. Unfortunately, nobody'd had the nerve to say, "Hey, how about we take turns, you guys go explore the jungle and give us a half hour." It wasn't like college when they would know by the sock hanging on the doorknob that it wasn't safe to come back yet.

Tucked together on the bus, she and Leo kept their voices low, not talking a lot to the people around them, who were well on their way to being drunk. It was a long drive and the rum punch was complimentary. There was also a guy playing a guitar up front, tourists shouting out windows and being a little stupid. But here in the back, cocooned as they were in their own private little nook, she was able to forget any of them were even there.

"That was pretty spectacular today, wasn't it?" Leo said.

"Definitely."

"Glad you went for it?"

"I am. Thank you for doing it first and scaring the wits out of all the snakes so they got out of the way before I arrived."

"Just call me Saint Patrick."

She sipped her drink, which was heavy on the rum and light on everything else. Half of one was knocking her on her butt, and she couldn't imagine how the people closer to the front, who'd downed three or four, were feeling.

Or, actually, considering they'd had to pull over once for some guy to get sick, maybe she could.

"So, tell me about these Santori men raised by Santori women."

"Huh?"

"You said something about it the other day. About how men in your family learn to treat women right."

"Well, they do," he said with a shrug. "I've told you there aren't many breakups in the family."

"Except for Great-Uncle Rocco and Great-Aunt Gertrude," she said with a laugh, "who got tired of waiting for each other to die."

"Actually, their names are Vinnie and Sarah. But like I said, they're the exception, not the rule. My parents have been married thirty-five years, my dad's brothers even longer. Uncle Anthony and Aunt Rosa just celebrated their fiftieth. All six of their kids, who are happily married, celebrated by giving them a trip to the old country."

"Old country?"

"Italy." The dimple flashed. "I'm Italian, if you didn't notice."

She giggled. Big, brawny, dark-haired, dark-eyed, sexy as hell. Oh, yeah, she'd noticed.

"Are they all Italian? I mean, the wives and everyone?" she asked, hoping he wasn't hearing a question that was dancing around in her brain. That question being—*is one-eighth Italian, by virtue of having maybe an Italian great-grandparent somewhere in the family tree, good enough to get the welcome mat put out by the family?*

She wasn't exactly hinting that they might end up married, but she also wouldn't mind if this vacation fling turned into something more when they got back stateside. She was pretty much homeless right now, and not tied down anyplace, who was to say she couldn't check out the Windy City and decide to stay?

"Definitely not," he said. "Tony's and Nick's wives are—they're also sisters. But most of my other cousins didn't go looking for 'traditional' wives."

She thought, *Good.*

She said, "Interesting."

Although he'd mentioned it, they hadn't talked a lot about his broken engagement. He didn't seem to be dwelling on it, that was for sure, and she hoped it wasn't a sensitive subject. She wanted to know more.

"What did they think of the *former*-future Mrs. Leo Santori?"

It took him a second to process the question and figure out what she was asking. Once he had, he grinned. "My brothers hated her."

"That's not a good sign."

"I know, right? Rafe, my older brother…"

"Army Ranger?"

"Right. He only met her once and told me that she reminded him of a crocodile—big, bright teeth, always ready to bite."

She chuckled.

"And Mike…"

"Cop?"

"Right. He said anybody who took six years to get through college for a degree in decorating was an idiot."

She had to agree with that one.

"So what on earth were you doing with her?"

"I don't know, to be honest." Sounding sheepish, he admitted, "This'll seem stupid, but the truth is, I think she just kind of decided she wanted to get married, I was the one she was dating, and I didn't have much say in the matter."

"Oh, poor wittle you."

"Not saying I was blameless, believe me, I wasn't. I floated into it, having seen all my cousins getting married and pushing out the babies. My mother kept hinting that it was my responsibility to get married first since Rafe was in the military."

Oy. Old fashioned, indeed.

"Looking back, her cheating on me—and me finding out—was the best thing that could have happened. Otherwise, I have no doubt I'd be breaking the Santori family record by being the only one of my generation to get a divorce."

That made sense. Heaven knew, Madison had done her fair share of drifting into things because she had nothing better to do at the time. Look at her engagement to Tommy! Sure, she'd been helping her sister, and helping her friend. But hadn't one small part of her decided to do it because she was bored with her life, unhappy with her job, wanting a change?

"On the plus side, I think my near miss has cooled my mom's jets for a while. She's not going to be pushing any of us anytime soon. Right after the breakup, she called my brother Mike and said, 'Michelangelo, you bring home a girl who spends more money a month on makeup than on food and I'll smack you in the head.'"

Laughing, she said, "Your brother's name is really Michelangelo?"

He shrugged. "Yep."

"And Rafe?"

"Raphael," he admitted.

"Leo…short for Leonardo?"

"Uh-huh." He sighed heavily. "You can say it."

Bursting into laughter, she said, "Your parents named you after Teenage Mutant Ninja Turtles?"

"That's certainly what all my friends thought, growing up."

"They must also have thought you had the coolest parents in the world."

"Well, with that, and my uncle Anthony's famous pizzeria, I didn't lack for friends."

His self-deprecation was cute. The fact that he was a hell of a guy, nice, smart and funny, didn't seem to enter into the equation.

"Truth is, my grandparents emigrated and were very traditional, and my parents wanted to please them. So they went with really traditional names."

"Would there have been a Donatello?"

He shook his head. "Don't think so, though Donato was on the short list when they named Mike."

She twined her fingers with his. "So, Leonardo, huh? That makes you the lead turtle—smart, always has a plan and fights with two Japanese katana swords… cool!"

Lifting a brow in surprise, he said, "You do know your turtles."

"What can I say?" She wagged her brows up and down. "I was into dangerous males from a very young age."

"But not reptiles."

She thrust her bottom lip out. "Turtles aren't reptiles…are they?"

"Amphibians, I think."

"Whew!"

"For what it's worth, I bet those dangerous males were into you, too." His brown eyes gleamed with approval as he stared at her, and she saw his lids drop a little. She had no doubt he was thinking wicked, sultry things, and she wished this bus would hurry the hell up.

He lifted her hand and brought it to his mouth, brushing his lips across her knuckles. His tongue flicked out to taste her—just a tiny flash of moisture—and she quivered in her seat.

"Did I mention that Leonardo was always my favorite?"

He squeezed her hand once more as he lowered it. "Glad to know it. I'd hate to have to katana my brothers' asses if you decided you preferred a hotheaded fighter type like Rafe or a wise guy like Mike."

"Not a chance."

She preferred him. Just him. Over any other man she had ever known.

"We'll be there soon," he said, reading her mind.

As if realizing they both needed to focus on anything other than the cloud of sexual awareness building between them, he went back to what he'd been saying. "So, was your sister a Turtles fan, too? I thought girls preferred Powerpuff Girls."

She laughed out loud. "That's so funny, I was just thinking about those characters!"

"I suppose only people our age would have any idea what we were talking about."

"Nickelodeon generation."

"Exactly. Are there any other ways in which you and Candace were different?"

"She was always very sweet."

A slow, sexy smile. "You're sweet."

He didn't say it, but she knew that somewhere in his mind, he'd reworded that sentence and added the word *taste*.

"I meant well behaved. She was the good girl."

"Making you the bad one?"

"Let's just say I was the one who found all the squeaky floorboards in our house and knew how to avoid them when sneaking out. And was almost always the one who instigated a twin-swap whenever there was a test I wanted to get out of that I knew Candace could do better on."

"Lucky!" he said. "I look a lot like my brothers, but not close enough that either of them could ever bail my ass out when it came time for the next English exam."

Before she could reply, they noticed the bus was stopping. Madison glanced out the window, surprised to see they were still on the road. A long line of cars and trucks were lined up ahead of them.

"What's going on, man? What's the holdup?" one of the passengers asked.

One of the tour company reps, who'd been checking his phone for information, replied, "Angelina and Brad are in town at a charity event! Miles of traffic."

She assumed he meant Jolie and Pitt. Funny how superstars needed no last name, even when in a different country.

"So, you want to stop by and say hi to Brad and Angie?" Leo asked. "You run in their circles, right?"

She snickered. "Not exactly." She'd spied the couple from a distance once at a premiere Tommy had taken her to, but hadn't gotten anywhere close to them.

"But you will be someday."

"You don't know that," she said, wishing the whole topic of Hollywood hadn't come up. That brought back issues she'd been trying very hard to run from this week.

"You never have told me what your screenplay's about," he said. He leaned against the window of the bus in their double seat, turning slightly to face her. His hair was windblown, his face tanned and flushed, his eyes sparkling after their exciting day.

"You don't really want to hear about that," she said.

"Yeah, I really do."

Well, she might not want to discuss why she'd fled Hollywood, but she did like talking about her work. She was proud of her project, protective of every word she'd written, and found herself wanting to share some of that with him. "It's a dark thriller about sexual obsession and murder."

His eyes popped.

"Sorry you asked?"

"Uh, no." He grinned broadly. "As long as you're not here doing research on the murder part of the story."

"No. Just the sex part. Thanks, by the way. I'll be sure you get an acknowledgment in the credits."

"My mom'll be so proud."

"Oh, I'm sure all your friends will line up to see it."

"What will my title be? Maybe gripper. Or best boy." His dimple appeared as he loaded the movie tech terms with innuendo. "I've always wondered what that person did on a movie set."

"It's key grip, not gripper, and *you* don't grip, you caress."

His voice low, he said, "And? What else do *I* do?"

She dropped hers too. "You stroke."

"And?"

"And squeeze."

"And?"

"And pound, and thrust, and kiss, and lick, and hold and…"

He lifted his rum punch to his mouth and took a sip. "I shouldn't have started that."

"No, you probably shouldn't have."

He dropped an arm across her shoulders, tugging her closer so she rested against him. Gently squeezing her, he said, "We haven't talked about this, but…"

"Yes?"

"Well, to be honest, I don't know how I'm going to leave here without you on Monday."

Hearing a note in his voice that said he wasn't finished—and that he might have been thinking about something they could do to remedy the this-was-a-vacation-fling-and-we'll-never-see-each-other-again thing, she said, "I know." Then, thinking a little more, she blinked. "Wait, Monday? You mean, tomorrow?" The idea horrified her.

He appeared puzzled. "No, I mean Monday…four days from now. Today's Thursday."

"No, it's not."

"Uh, yeah, babe, it is."

Not totally believing it, she grabbed the backpack in which she'd carried her wallet and some other stuff from her purse. She found the small calendar that went with her checkbook and looked at it, counting back the days since she'd left California.

He was right. It was Thursday. Good lord, she'd been traveling so much in recent weeks—from L.A. to Napa to Florida to Central America—that she'd totally lost track of not only where she was, but *when* she was. How bizarre!

"See?"

She nodded slowly. "That's so weird, I completely messed up the days. I have no idea why I was so sure today was Sunday."

Of course, it could have been more than the travel and the jet-lag. There'd also been the matter of the stress, the tears, the long, sleepless nights, the races with the paparazzi. All of which had been the driving forces in her life until she'd come here and met *him*.

So yeah, it must have been all those confusing things that had led to the screwup in her internal clock.

But something was niggling at the back of her mind. Some small detail or memory that told her there was more to it. She just couldn't grab the thought, and it was irritating her. She swiped a hand through her hair, loosening the ponytail that had begun to give her a bit of a headache, and tried to focus, but nothing came to mind.

"So, now that you know what day it is, can you tell me how long you're staying?"

"I guess until Monday also. I booked for a week."

Or, well, Tommy's travel agent had booked her for a week. She thought.

It was late in the evening, which meant they had only three more full days. That didn't sound like very much time at all.

Part of her wanted to ask him if he could stay a little longer —if they gave up one of their rooms, perhaps they could put it toward extending their stay.

Another part wanted him to make the suggestion.

You can't hide here forever. You've got to go home and straighten your life out before you can take this thing much further.

"You're sure?" he asked her. "You might want to double-check your reservation."

He was teasing, but only just. And she realized he was right. "I know. At least, I *think* it was a week. This trip was planned on the fly and I've been pretty out of it, obviously."

"Remind me to never let you be in charge of the scheduling calendar."

Scheduling calendar.

That thought whizzed by again. Suddenly, she wrestled it into coherence and when it formed in her brain, she gasped.

"What?"

She didn't answer, bending over to grab her backpack again, worry overwhelming her. *No, you couldn't have been that stupid, right?*

"Madison, what is it?"

She kept digging, looking for a small, hard plastic case. Casting quick glances up at him, hating to admit what was going through her mind, she said, "I had a thought about why I might have had my days mixed up. If I'm right, the bus is going to have to pull over for *me* to throw up this time because I feel just sick about it!"

His worried expression told her he was concerned only for her, not for himself, not for any repercussions. He didn't get what she was worried about.

Hell. If her suspicions were correct, there could definitely be some repercussions for them both.

"What can I do?"

"Pray."

He gaped, obviously seeing how frightened she really was.

Finally, she found the object she'd been looking for and pulled it out of her backpack.

Her birth control pills.

"Are those…"

"Yeah."

She gulped, flipped the lid with her thumb and studied the dial of pills. She was very careful, every month, to set the starting day correctly, because she'd had problems with the pill in the beginning. And there had been that one pregnancy scare in her high school years that she had never wanted to repeat.

According to this package, those pills, and the little days of the week imprinted above them, tomorrow she should be taking Monday's pill. That was why she'd thought today was Sunday.

Only, today was Thursday.

For a second, she prayed she'd taken them ahead of time, too many instead of too few. Crazy hopes blossomed within her and she sought frantically for an explanation. *You took extra protection for all the extra sex, right?*

But she knew she hadn't done that, not consciously, anyway.

Leo had obviously been studying the case, too. His brow was furrowed, his expression serious. "What's the verdict? Are there too few or too many?" he asked, jumping to the same conclusion.

She thought about it. Last week she'd been in Florida, the week before in Napa. She'd started this package of pills while she was still in L.A.

The days rolled out in her mind, and by the time she'd finished calculating them, she realized she was in trouble.

"There are too many pills left," she whispered. "Three more should be missing. So I have apparently missed three doses at some point over the past few weeks."

He was silent. She was silent.

Dropping the plastic case into her backpack, she

threw herself back in the seat and closed her eyes, her mind swimming with confusion.

Three pills. Three little pills. That couldn't be a catastrophe, could it? She'd been on the pill for ten years. After all that faithful service, surely one minor mistake like this wouldn't result in…couldn't mean she was…

"So you could be pregnant."

He'd put it right out there, voicing the words she'd been unable to even think. She flinched, slowly lowering her glass of rum punch and putting it into the drink holder in her armrest. She told herself it was instinct— that she felt queasy. But she couldn't deny that something, some tiny spark of oh-my-God-what-if-it's-true, had thought *this isn't good for the baby.*

"No. Of course not," she insisted. "It's crazy."

He wasn't in a panic and he wasn't angry. Not happy, certainly, but not reacting the way she'd expect most twentysomething single men to react to the news that they might have knocked up a woman they'd met a few days ago.

"It's possible, though."

She gulped and slowly nodded. "I'm so sorry, Leo. It's been… I'm *never* so careless. I've just had an awful few weeks, my mind's been spinning. I screwed up. I totally screwed up."

She finally worked up the nerve to open her eyes again, knowing there were tears in them. Blinking rapidly to hold them back, she looked at him, dreading his reaction. Maybe his was a calm before the storm.

But oh, that warmth, that understanding in his expression. If she'd been standing, she would have lost her legs and fallen to the ground, so overwhelmed was she by the tenderness in his handsome face.

"Shh, it's okay," he insisted. "Stop beating yourself up about it. I'm sure it won't happen. The odds are crazy."

"Right."

"Worse odds than encountering two snakes in Costa Rica."

She forced a chuckle that came out a little like a sob. "Yeah. Of course they are."

He lifted her across the seat onto his lap, wrapping his arms around her and pulling her head onto his shoulder. His hand gently stroking her hair, he said, "It's okay, Madison. It'll be fine."

"I can't believe you're not freaking out."

"Over a mistake that anybody could make that *might* lead to a bigger problem? Why would I freak out over that?"

Amazing. She didn't know any other guy who wouldn't have already started losing it, or stated his stance on abortion, or accused her of dumping pills into the toilet to trap him, or at least calling her careless.

This man was unique and so wonderful. Aside from that, he also calmed her, steadied her. She'd always been told she was too volatile, that she had a temper, that she could be thoughtless at times.

Leo was everything she wasn't. He was like a port in a storm, soothing and so damned strong. She wondered if there was any crisis he couldn't weather, and acknowledged that, God forbid this slipup of hers resulted in pregnancy, she couldn't imagine anyone better to go through it with.

"If there's something to worry about, let's deal with it when it happens," he said, brushing a kiss across her temple. "In the meantime, let's just make sure we stop in my room when we get back to the hotel so I can grab some condoms."

She tried for a real smile. "That's a deal." She promptly ruined that with a big, sad-sounding sniffle.

"And maybe a blue necktie. I can tie holes in it and tie it around my face, and maybe get some fake katanas and *really* be your hero."

The smile was a little more genuine this time. "You already are."

They were silent for another moment.

Finally, he said, "It's really okay. It'll be fine, Madison. Let's not worry about it until next month."

Next month. They hadn't even exchanged phone numbers, yet Leo was assuming they would still be… something. She really believed he thought they were going to have some kind of future after this Monday.

Oh, she hoped so. She most certainly hoped so. Because, no matter what day of the week it was, or how many weeks it had been, she was falling for Leo Santori. Falling head over heels, out-of-her-mind, crazy-in-love with him.

She might have come here to escape and to hide.

Now, she suspected she'd been found…and didn't want to be lost ever again.

10

THEIR THREE DAYS left together flew by way too fast for Leo's liking.

Once Madison had stopped beating herself up about what might happen due to her mix-up with her pills, she'd let him coax her back into a good mood. He'd done it with lots of laughter, long walks on the beach, midnight swims in their private pool, surfing lessons, a wind-sailing expedition, dancing at the club of a big touristy resort nearby. And lots and lots of sex.

Damn, he didn't think he would ever have another week like this in his entire life. And he knew he'd never had one before.

They didn't talk about the birth control pill issue, instead using condoms as a matter of course. He wasn't thrilled about it—having been inside her warm, wet body, skin to skin, he really disliked there being any kind of barrier between them. But there was no sense in taking risks.

Although, to be honest, part of him wasn't sure he minded so much.

Yeah, it was crazy to be thinking about having a kid with a woman he'd met a week ago.

But yeah, he was thinking about it.

Whatever he'd thought about his life, his future, his relationships or his prospects before coming here to Costa Rica didn't matter a damn. Because, since he'd met her—since he'd begun to fall in love with her—he was seeing whole new worlds of possibility. Worlds that included him and Madison, committed, together, bringing more little Santoris into the world. No, he wouldn't have chosen to do it so soon, but he wasn't going to deny that, if it happened, he wouldn't be absolutely devastated.

He just wanted to make sure that Madison wanted him as much as he wanted her…and that, whatever happened between them, *didn't* happen only because of a possible pregnancy. That was why he hadn't pushed her for any confirmations on where things would go after they both left this wonderful place. But now it was Sunday night. And in the morning, they were both going to leave this wonderful place.

It was their last night in paradise, but rather than going out somewhere, they'd decided to have a room service dinner. The hotel might be small, but the chef was outstanding, and, once again, they were served an amazing meal.

They shared it outside on her patio at a small table draped with a snowy-white cloth and lit by a few tapered candles. Again, the staff had gone overboard. He had no doubt word had spread that his bed wasn't being slept

in—while hers usually looked like a troupe of monkeys
had been doing acrobatics on it all night long.

"What are you thinking about?" she asked.

"Monkeys."

She tilted her head, visibly curious, but he only
laughed.

"What about you? What are you thinking about?"

"I'm thinking I want one more naked swim in that
pool."

He shifted in his seat.

"And wondering how long we'll have to wait until
room service comes to take all this stuff away."

He dropped his napkin onto his plate, reached for
his water and finished it, as well. Although they had
never even discussed it, neither of them admitting any
reason for it, he'd noticed that neither he nor Madison
had been drinking any alcohol during the past couple
of days. It was as if she were already protective of the
life that might be growing inside her. And he. Well,
he wasn't sure whether it was solidarity or a desire not
to jinx anything, but he was laying off, too.

"There's a Do Not Disturb sign on the door. The
waiter offered to put it there and said we can just call
when we want them to come back," he said with a suggestive wink.

"Do we need to wait a half an hour after eating before we can swim?" she asked.

"I don't think so, considering the water's not even
over our heads."

"Perfect," she said, already rising to her feet and
pushing at the straps of her sundress. They fell, re-

vealing those soft shoulders, and then the whole dress dropped with a whoosh.

She hadn't been wearing anything underneath.

He swallowed hard, staring at her, awed, as always, by that perfect body, so curvy and feminine. She was lightly tanned all over, no lines to mark the infrequent presence of her skimpy bathing suits.

"Come and get me wet," she said, throwing him a sassy look.

He played along. "The pool's not too cold this time?"

"Not talking about the pool," she promised.

"Good."

He pushed back from the table and stripped off his clothes, grabbing a condom from his pocket before letting his shorts hit the patio. Madison watched him, her eyes zoning in on all the places on his body that she seemed to like a lot.

He was already as hard as a rock.

"Okay, never mind, I don't think I need your help. I'm already there," she exclaimed with a visible quiver of excitement. She clenched her thighs tight, as if to catch the moisture building between them, and his mouth went wet with hunger.

"I think I should check and make sure."

He walked to her, dropping the condom on the pavement right beside the pool, knowing there would be a lot to do before he would want to put it on. He slid his hands around her waist, stroking her hips, pulling her to him. She tilted her face up and their mouths met in a warm, lazy kiss. Their tongues twisted and mated, each stroke languorous and hungry, each breath shared, their heartbeats falling into the same rhythm.

When they finally broke apart, she whispered, "Thought you were going to check it out."

He nodded. Hiding a grin of mischief, he wrapped his arms more tightly around her and jumped into the pool, bringing her with him.

She came up sputtering, splashing his face with water and swimming away. "That was a dirty trick."

"What? Now I'm positive you're nice and wet."

"Maybe not everywhere."

"Everywhere," he said, totally confident.

"Wouldn't you like to know."

He stepped toward her, enjoying the coolness of the water against his naked skin. "Yeah. I would like to know."

She stopped moving away, her teasing words dying on her lips, as if she knew, as he did, that their time together was too short to delay. They wanted—needed—each other, tonight more than ever, and all the playfulness evaporated. There was just intense heat, and, he suspected, a hint of desperation. They both knew they had to leave in mere hours.

Madison watched Leo approach, and saw the same note of, not sadness, but maybe wistfulness on his face that she sensed was on hers. Saying goodbye to this man would be next to impossible, and frankly, she didn't want to think about it. Not when she still had him for a little while longer.

They came together, their bodies meeting beneath the surface. She loved this sensation, had loved it from the first time they'd swum naked together. Water caressed her, cooled her, even as his slick skin warmed and aroused her. There was no weight, no gravity to combat, and they could float and thrust and twist and love to their hearts' content, wrapped in their own wet world.

"I'm going to miss this," she admitted.

"Me, too."

"Not many opportunities for skinny-dipping in Chicago?"

He didn't smile. "Nobody I'd want to do it with if there were."

Madison sighed a little, loving that admission.

"This has been the best week of my life, Leo," she said, reaching up and wrapping her arms around his neck.

He encircled her waist and held her tightly against him. Bending to kiss her, he replied, "Mine, too."

The kiss was sweeter, soft and tender, and in it Madison read a lot of emotions neither of them had expressed. Although she wanted to express them now, to let him know she longed for so much more than this, she knew she couldn't. There was too much to deal with, too much to fix in her life, before she asked him to be a more permanent part of it.

Not that she was about to let him go completely. God, no. She just wanted to be able to come to him with a clean slate. She longed to admit to him exactly what she'd been running from and why. Until that time, telling him she cared about him—hell, that she *loved* him—seemed unfair.

After the kiss, he said, "Are you cold?"

"No."

He lifted her higher as he dropped lower in the water so he was eye level with her breasts. "You look cold."

She laughed softly. "*So* not cold."

"Maybe I should warm you up, just in case."

"You do that."

He did, lapping up some of the water off the curve of one breast, kissing his way toward its tip. He breathed a stream of warm air over the puckered nipple, and then covered it with his mouth and suckled her.

She threw her head back, groaning with pleasure. Lifting her legs, she wrapped them around him and floated there, rubbing herself against his heat, indulging in all the sensations battering her body. His mouth on her breast, his hand on her hip, another twined in her hair, his big, thick cock between her legs, brushing against her core.

There was nothing better than this on earth. Nothing.

He moved to her other breast, pleasuring her just as thoroughly, and then began to draw her back toward the steps at the end of the pool. She saw the condom lying on the pool deck where he'd dropped it but wasn't ready to lose all that hot male skin just yet.

When they got to the steps and he reached for the packet, she said, "Wait."

He eyed her quizzically.

Giving him her sultriest look and licking her lips, she said, "Sit on the top step."

One brow rose. He did as she asked.

Kneeling below him, most of her body still in the

water, she kissed her way up his powerful leg. The wiry black hairs teased her lips as she nibbled and tasted her way ever higher.

He dropped a hand onto her shoulder and tangled the other in her wet hair, obviously knowing where she was headed. When her cheek brushed the side of his erection, he jerked a little. And when she ran the tip of her tongue all the way from its base to its tip, he groaned out loud.

"Madison…"

"I love how you taste," she admitted, licking the moisture that seeped from the tip of his cock.

"Jesus," he groaned.

He liked it, she knew that much. She'd loved doing this to him at various times this week, but they'd never done it in the pool. And the position was so easy and so perfect, the steps lining up exactly the way she needed them to be.

Opening her mouth as wide as she could, she sucked the thick head of his cock.

His guttural groan told her he liked what she was doing, as did the gentle squeeze of his hand on her shoulder. She slid her mouth down, taking more of him, filling her mouth with him, licking the salt and the chlorine and the *male* right off him.

When she could go no farther, she began to pull away, sliding up, knowing her pace was both a torment and a delight. Another flick of her tongue as she lapped up more of his body's delicious juices, and she went down again. Up and down, slow, then faster, soft, then harder, until her jaw hurt and Leo was thrusting a little with every stroke.

"Enough," he said with a gasp. "Get up here."

She wanted to finish, wanted to swallow him down, but she was also dying to have him inside her. So with one last powerful suck, she released him and kissed her way up his stomach, tracing his abs, licking his nipples, biting his neck.

"You definitely should hold the world record for *that*," he said before sinking both hands in her hair and dragging her mouth to his.

He kissed her deeply, thanking her with every thrust of his tongue, releasing her only so he could grab the condom. Tearing it open, he sheathed himself and then pulled her onto his lap. She straddled him, her knees beside his hips on the step.

Another kiss, deep and hungry, but also incredibly tender, and he began to ease his way into her. She took him, every inch of him, every breath of him, every ounce of him, grabbing and holding and loving and savoring. Wanting all of him. Wanting this memory to imprint itself on her very soul so she would always be able to return to it and relive such glory.

When they were fully joined, as close as they could be, she looked into his eyes—those beautiful brown eyes—and said all the things she couldn't yet say aloud.

She'd swear he said them back.

REALITY RETURNED WITH a vengeance the next morning. As if to punctuate the regret both of them were feeling, Leo awoke to the sound of rain. It was the first time they'd seen anything but a blue sky, and the weather suited his mood.

They were both ass-dragging, having stayed up way too late last night indulging in a long, lethargic lovefest that had left him weak but utterly satisfied. Because of that, they'd overslept a little.

Not wanting to suffer the long drive all the way back to the airport in San José, Madison had been able to get a ticket on a puddle jumper that would take her from Liberia, the same airport from which he was flying, to the capital. That meant they had a little more time together. During that time, he intended to ask her when they were going to see each other again.

He'd prefer tonight in Chicago. But it seemed pushy to ask. So he would have to settle for the weekend.

She'd admitted she wasn't working on anything right now except her screenplay, and he knew she was between permanent homes, though he'd never found out exactly why. She'd said she was heading back to her parents' place in Florida while she regrouped.

Chicago was a very good place for regrouping, if he did say so himself. Plus, flights between there and Florida were pretty cheap. Hell, if she couldn't come to him, he'd go to her.

When they reached the airport and checked in, they hesitated before going through security. Their gates were far apart and they had some time before their flights would start boarding, though his was earlier than hers.

Sitting together in a bar in the main terminal, each of them drinking a Virgin Mary, he said, "So. Madison."

A tiny smile tugged at the corners of her mouth. "So. Leo."

Their eyes met. He knew she knew what he was about to say.

"Facebook?" she asked.

He barked a laugh. "I'm not on it."

"You're joking!"

"Sorry, I prefer regular media to the social kind. I like actually knowing people I call friends."

She nodded in commiseration. "I guess I understand that. And I was just kidding since I don't have a profile anymore, either."

"Really?"

"I got rid of it once I started getting too much attention."

"Because of your screenplay?"

She nibbled her bottom lip and hesitated, staring at him searchingly. It looked as if she wanted to say more, and he wondered if she was finally going to reveal just what she was running from.

The fact that she was running, and that she'd gotten rid of her Facebook profile because of too much attention, suddenly made a sharp fear stab into him. *Had she been stalked? Was she on the run from an abusive ex?*

His hands fisted on the table, but he covered by reaching for his drink.

"Something like that," she finally whispered.

He knew it wasn't the whole story. But he also knew she wasn't ready to tell him the whole story.

"Just tell me one thing. Are you in any kind of danger?"

Her jaw fell open. "Oh, God, no, of course not."

"Okay then."

"It's…it's complicated," she admitted.

"I hear ya. It's all right. I can wait, though not forever."

"You won't have to, I promise."

Good. Her secret would give them plenty to talk about when they saw each other back home. Tonight or next weekend or next month. Hopefully no longer than that.

"So I guess we'll have to do this the old-fashioned way," he said, trying to lighten the mood. "You're hot. Can I have your phone number?"

Her green eyes twinkled and she replied, "Well, I don't usually give my number out to strange guys…"

"Hey, I'm not strange. Just Italian."

A broad smile. Thank God. "Okay, I *guess* it's okay if you call me." She reached into her carry-on and pulled out her cell phone. "Tell me yours so I can punch them into my address book."

He rattled off his numbers—home, cell and the station, and threw in his uncle's restaurant just to be on the safe side. She was laughing and complaining about sore fingers by the time she'd finished entering. After she was done, she raised an inquiring brow.

"I hate to admit it, but we're gonna have to do this the *really* old-fashioned way. I didn't get an international SIM card, and knew my phone wouldn't work here so I never even took it out of my suitcase."

"Which you already checked."

"Right."

"I'll text them to you."

"No way. I don't trust technology when it comes to something this important. Write them down."

"Okay, but I don't want to hear any excuses about you losing my number," she said. "Remember, I have yours and I can stalk you and be all vengeful if you give me the brush-off."

He reached across the table and took her hand. "Not gonna happen, Madison Reid. That is *never* gonna happen."

Their gazes met and held and he knew that, once again, they were saying a *lot* more things that didn't really need to be verbalized. In utter silence, they were thanking each other for the amazing week they'd shared, and promising each other it would be continued. They were admitting there were feelings and promising they would be explored. All without a word being spoken. Just like when they'd made love in the pool the night before.

Without ever even opening his mouth, he'd told her he loved her. He even suspected she'd heard it. And that she felt the same way.

Someday soon they'd say it out loud.

"Here you go," she said, pushing a small sheet of paper across to him. It contained a number marked "cell," and another marked "parents in Florida."

He carefully folded the paper and tucked it into his wallet, right next to his license and certification cards. No way would he lose it. Hell, he'd probably be digging it out to call her within an hour of landing at O'Hare.

They finished their drinks, not saying much, both

stealing glances at the clock. Until, finally, knowing he couldn't delay any longer, Leo got up and held out a hand to her. She rose, too, sliding up against his body. He felt her, even though an inch of air separated them, vibrating with life and passion. He felt her magnetism even when they weren't touching.

"Soon," he demanded, a wave of want washing over him, the way it always did when she was near.

She nodded. "Soon."

Before he could say more, they were startled by raised voices. A large crowd of people had gathered at this end of the terminal. They stood right outside the bar, which was open-air, separated from the main section of the airport by only a half wall. That might explain why it was so damned loud.

He hadn't been paying attention, but now all those people—most carrying cameras—came to life and began shouting questions and snapping pictures. "What the hell?"

"Angelina and Brad are flying out this morning!" someone at the next table whispered, peering around and out into the main terminal.

He rolled his eyes, not interested in the celebrity stuff and only hoping the rolling out of the red carpet didn't delay his flight.

Hell, what was he thinking? This could go ahead and delay it indefinitely, as long as Madison's was delayed, too. Of course, with their luck, they'd each be on their respective planes when the delay happened.

"Think they're following us?" he asked her, laughter on his lips.

It died when he saw her expression. Her eyes were wide and glassy, her mouth rounded in shock. She was staring at the crowd gathering a couple of yards away and he could actually hear her harsh exhalations as she struggled for breath.

"Mad, what is it? What's wrong?"

"Oh, my God," she whispered. She spun around, burying her face in his neck, hugging him tightly and mumbling, "We should go."

"You going to walk backward?" he asked, placing a gentle hand on the small of her back.

She looked up at him and now he didn't just see shock, he saw something that resembled panic. "I mean, you should go. They'll be boarding your flight any minute," she said, suddenly jerking away from him and giving him a push. "I have a little more time."

He couldn't understand her sudden change in mood, but she was right. They would be calling for his flight soon and he still had to get through security.

"If I didn't know any better, I'd say you were trying to get rid of me."

"I shouldn't have come here with you," she said, casting quick glances over her shoulder. "I should have taken a cab to the other airport." She looked at him, her eyes wide and wet. "I never dreamed they'd find... Oh, Leo, please forgive me. I was being selfish, I just wasn't ready to say goodbye. Now I've exposed you to..."

"Madison, whatever it is, it's okay," he told her. Dropping his hands to her hips, he pulled her close, so their bodies touched from thigh to chest, and dropped his mouth onto hers. He kissed her deeply but gently, saying goodbye and reminding her of all the things they'd be missing until they saw each other again.

He usually didn't make out in public, but kissing Madison always made him a little crazy. He deepened things, liking how she clung to him, kissing him back, wildly, hungrily.

They didn't break apart until they heard someone calling her name.

"Madison!"

Then another voice.

"Over here, Miss Reid!"

And another.

"Is he the guy, Madison? Is this where you've been all this time?"

"Any chance you and Shane will reconcile?"

"What's going to happen to the house you two were sharing in California?"

Looking down at her and seeing the utter misery in her face as she grabbed a sun hat and glasses and pulled them on, he could only stare.

"What's your name, buddy? Where are you from?"

"Are you the one she cheated with?"

"Come on, Madison, lay another kiss on him! The world wants to know who you prefer to Tommy Shane!"

Tommy Shane? The movie star?

His heart stopped and his stomach flipped. The room suddenly seemed to spin and it had nothing to do with the heat. He found it hard to think, hard to see, hard to process much of anything except those voices and those snapping cameras.

And the guilt on her face.

"Madison…?"

"I'm sorry. I'm so sorry you got dragged into this, Leo," she whispered, tears falling from her eyes. "I didn't want this to happen to you, I'd never wish it on my own worst enemy, much less…"

Those awful, intrusive voices continued, digging into his brain like sharp, spiky instruments. "Madison, how did you two meet? When did the affair start? How'd Tommy find out?"

Affair. Tommy.

God.

The pieces started to come together in his mind. Tommy Shane—everyone on the planet knew his name. And while he didn't pay attention to Hollywood gossip or junk like that, he now remembered having heard something about a breakup. He'd been visiting his cousin Lottie. She'd just had her second child and he'd glanced through some gossip rags someone else had brought her to look at while nursing.

She'd gone on an indignant rant about poor sweet sexy Tommy Shane, wondering how any woman could cheat on him. A woman who'd been *engaged* to him.

This woman. The woman he suddenly wasn't even sure he knew.

She'd been engaged to one of the most famous men in America. *She cheated.* She'd been hounded by paparazzi. *She cheated.* She'd fled to Costa Rica. *She cheated.* And put another notch on her bedpost?

She cheated.

Every instinct he had rebelled against the idea, but he could think of no other explanation. She wasn't screaming at these people that they were liars. She looked utterly ashamed. Guilty as sin.

His sweet and sexy Madison had betrayed the man she'd promised to marry and had used Leo to lick her wounds while the scandal died down. It was the only thing that made sense.

What he couldn't figure out, though, was what had happened to her lover. Considering she'd lost Shane over the man, he had to be pretty damned important. Which made Leo wonder what the hell she'd been doing slumming around with *him* for the past seven days. She'd cheated on a man who women threw themselves in front of.

So why had she just spent a week here with him, a regular guy?

"Leo, please, let me explain," she insisted, raising her voice to be heard over the paparazzi.

"How about starting with the basics. Were you engaged to Tommy Shane, the movie star?"

She nodded slowly.

He thought he'd been prepared for the answer, but considering he thought he was going to puke, he guessed he hadn't been.

"You lived with him. That's why you're between addresses now."

"Yes."

It got better and better.

"And you came here to get away from all the bad publicity you were getting because of your breakup."

"Yes, but you don't understand," she said.

His whole body rigid, he stepped away from her.

"Speak up, I'm sure everyone would love to hear the story."

She closed her eyes, shaking her head in sorrow and regret.

He wanted to shake her, wanted to yell at her for lying to him.

Only she hadn't, not really, except by omission. She'd never said anything about a broken engagement or an affair. She'd kept her secrets well. He'd just been stupid enough not to see the truth.

Again.

Christ, what was it with him picking women who couldn't be faithful? Was it some character flaw he had?

Part of him screamed at the very idea of putting Madison in the same category as his ex. But in the end, they weren't much different, were they? In fact, Madison's affair had been a whole lot more public.

"I've gotta go," he said, trying to be heard as the photographers and reporters who'd struck out getting the good stuff on Brad and Angelina pressed inside the bar and swarmed them like flies on meat.

"Yes, you should, get out of here before this gets worse."

"It can get worse?"

"You have no idea," she said, her tone bleak.

He was angry. Furious, in fact. He wanted to walk out and leave her here to deal with her own mess.

But he just couldn't do it. He couldn't walk away and leave her in the middle of this feeding frenzy to be chewed up by these animals, even if a part of him thought she probably deserved it.

"Come on," he ordered, grabbing both their carry-ons. He dropped a possessive arm over her shoulders and pulled her along with him, elbowing people out of the way with every step.

The barrage continued.

"Just tell us your name!"

"Do you have anything you want to say to Tommy? Do you feel bad about stealing his woman?"

"Are you two living together somewhere?"

He ignored them. So did she. Together, fighting for every step, they pushed through the crowd. Leo threw a few elbows at those who wouldn't move voluntarily. Finally, they reached the security area, through which nobody without a boarding pass could come. He waved theirs and jerked a thumb toward their pursuers. "I don't think they're passengers, and they're harassing us."

The guards immediately stepped in, ushering them into a secured line, leaving the crowd behind. Still the shouts continued, and Leo could practically feel the cameras taking pictures of the back of his head.

That finally struck him. It wasn't just the shock and betrayal of her not being who he thought she'd been. He'd now been dragged into this. His picture was going to be plastered on their tabloids, his name, his home, his job, his family…everything was going to be thrown out there for public consumption if they found out who he was.

Fuck.

"Thank you," she said as they finally turned a corner and got out of sight of the crowd.

He immediately dropped his arm and stepped away from her.

"If you can, please keep my name out of it, would you?" he bit out from a granite-hard jaw. "I don't imagine it would go over very well with my lieutenant or with my family."

"I'm so sorry," she whispered, watching him, tears falling freely down her face. "I never imagined that would happen, not in my worst nightmares."

He'd heard enough. He just couldn't listen to any more. So when they reached the end of the first line and he saw that there were several checkpoints, each with its own separate queue, he watched her go into the closest one...and headed for one as far away from hers as he could get.

He told himself it was because it was shorter and his flight would board soon.

He knew the truth, though. He needed to think and to breathe. Needed to absorb everything that had happened in the past ten minutes and figure out what it meant and what he was going to do about it.

He needed to get away from her.

"Leo," she said as he turned his back and began to walk away.

He didn't turn around, not trusting himself to look at her face. Instead, he called, "I can't, Madison. Not now. I just can't."

And he didn't. He didn't look back. He didn't wait for her. He didn't try to find her at her gate.

He simply got on his plane and went home.

11

MADISON MADE THE trip home like a zombie, barely cognizant of her surroundings. She'd been able to focus only on the look on Leo's face when he realized he'd been thrown into the deep end of the ocean by a woman he'd thought he could trust.

Her father picked her up at the airport in Florida. As soon as he saw her by the baggage claim, he pulled her into his arms, hugging her tightly. "I'm so sorry, baby girl. So sorry, honey."

She clung to him, feeling tears well up further.

"It didn't help, huh?"

Had her trip helped? Well, the majority of her week hadn't just helped, it had been downright magical. But the ending had been like something out of her worst nightmare.

"I'm okay, just tired," she said, knowing he would see right through it. Her emotions were spinning wildly, and if anybody would recognize that, it was her wise, attentive father.

"Listen, why don't I get your bag? You duck behind

the escalators, I'll grab the suitcase and go get the car.
Once I've pulled up to the front, you can dash right out."

Distressed that he had to go to these lengths, especially considering his recent heart attack, she said, "I
shouldn't have come here. I should have just gone back
to California."

"Forgedaboutit," he said. "Come on now, get on over
there. I've always wanted to play James Bond."

"Did you bring weapons?" she asked, heavy on the
sarcasm.

"No, but I brought a new secret-agent-mobile that
none of those cockroaches will recognize."

She gaped. "You got a new car?"

"I wanted to be less noticeable when you came back.
Traded in the old jalopy." His smile said that hadn't
been a hardship.

"You got the SUV you've been bugging Mom about."

"Yup." He hugged her again. "Thanks for the crisis, honey."

Knowing he was trying to cheer her up, she forced
a laugh.

"Oh, and if it's okay with you, we're going to head
over to the condo instead of the house."

Her parents lived inland, but had bought a place on
the beach as an investment years ago. She supposed
it was possible they'd planned a beach trip, but she
doubted it.

"The reporters drove you out of your house?"

"Are you kidding? You know your mother. She's
gotta have those ocean breezes. Can't keep her away."

Probably an exaggeration, but she didn't call him on

it. Her parents were doing what parents did, taking care of their kid in her moment of need. Even if the kid had screwed up royally by getting in a situation she hadn't been prepared for and making a decision she'd pay for until the end of her days.

She wasn't just the woman who would go down in infamy as the cheater who'd broken Tommy Shane's heart. She'd also lost the one man who'd ever made her feel as though she was capable of loving someone with every fiber in her being.

"I'm glad you're here," her dad said. "You can pay me back for the ride by making me one of your chocolate cakes…your mother tries to sneak zucchini and wheat germ into hers."

"Ick," she said with a soft laugh, then murmured, "Thanks, Dad."

Their plan worked. He picked her up outside and she didn't hear anyone demanding answers that were nobody's business. They arrived at the condo, which was gated, making it difficult for them to be harassed if anyone tracked her down.

Nobody did. And for the next several days, Madison began to heal.

There was never a sign of a photographer, and while she saw the photos of herself and Leo on the cover of a tabloid at the grocery store, she didn't see his name. She prayed they hadn't discovered who he was, and so far it appeared their luck was holding.

She couldn't imagine how he was explaining it to his colleagues, or anyone in his family, but hoped they were trustworthy enough not to sell him out to the *Tattler*.

Her mother had seen the pictures, too. They'd been standing in line at Publix, and her mother's gasp had cued her in. But being just as supportive and protective as Madison's dad, she didn't say a word. She instead reached up and *accidentally* spilled her cup of iced coffee on the cover of the tabloid.

She hadn't even asked Madison to explain who it was she'd been kissing in Costa Rica, as if realizing the hurt she was feeling might have more to do with that than with what had happened out in L.A. Not for the first time, Madison acknowledged she had the best parents in the world.

She was loved. She knew that. She'd never doubted it. And out of the spotlight, at the small beach town, she began to find peace, to think about her future and figure out what to do.

Calling Leo had been on her mind a lot. A whole lot.

She couldn't begin to count the number of times she had picked up her phone, looked at his numbers in the address book and thought about dialing.

Would he answer? Would he listen? Would he hang up on her?

Did it matter?

Because, even if he would listen, how could she explain? She couldn't tell him the truth without revealing the nature of her engagement to Tommy. Couldn't drag Tommy out of the closet to someone he didn't know when he'd tried so hard to stay in there for the rest of the world. She had seen her sister go through the exact same dilemma when Candace had fallen in love. She'd just never thought it would happen to her, too. Who could ever have imagined a Leo coming into her life?

Besides, he obviously didn't want to talk to her. She kept her phone nearby but he never called. She checked for messages even though it didn't ring. But nothing. He hadn't tried to reach her.

She didn't blame him. He was too decent a guy to be dragged into her garbage. She should never have let herself forget that.

Sitting on the balcony of the condo, watching the waves churn one evening after she and her parents had shared dinner, she began to drift off to sleep, lulled by the ocean and the call of the seabirds. In that lazy place between asleep and awake, she replayed all the lovely moments the two of them had shared.

Their first meeting. The room mix-up. The lovemaking on the beach. The stupid snake in the pool. The zip-lining tour. The long bus ride back when they'd talked about a lot of nothing.

A lot of...*nothing.*

Her eyes flew open. "Oh, my God," she muttered.

"What, honey?" asked her mother, who'd been sitting nearby doing a Sudoku puzzle.

"What's today?" she snapped.

"Thursday, why?"

Thursday. Of course it would be Thursday. Wasn't it always freaking Thursday? "Do you know the date?"

Her mother told her, and Madison started calculating.

She'd been in Florida for seventeen days. She could hardly believe it. Apparently, she'd been so numb, she hadn't noticed the passage of time. Each lazy day had rolled into the next, none bringing a solution to her problems or offering a glimpse of happiness with the man she missed so terribly.

Seventeen days.

That day on the bus with Leo, she had figured out when she'd started her last pack of pills. The date was emblazoned in her mind and it wasn't hard to count backward to see just how long it had been: six weeks ago.

She was late. Two weeks late.

Calm down. It might not be that. Could be stress, anything.

But Madison was never late—she hadn't been in years. Besides, something deep inside her already knew the truth.

She was pregnant.

Pregnant by a man who obviously never wanted to see or hear from her again for the rest of his life.

"What's the matter, Madison?" her mom repeated.

She couldn't tell her folks—not because they were old-fashioned or wouldn't be supportive, but because she just couldn't drag them into even more of her drama. None of this was their fault; how could she add to the worry that was already making her mother so sad? Put more stress on her father's recovering heart?

"Sorry, Mom, I just remembered some stuff I need to take care of." The next words left her lips without her giving them much thought. "In California."

Her mother didn't look surprised, as if she had already come to that conclusion herself and had just been waiting for Madison to figure it out. "All right, honey."

Yes, it was time to go back to California and deal with this once and for all. With a baby to consider—and she truly believed there was one—she could no longer be the story-of-the-week for the cheap news mags. She would be in no position to run around evading the paparazzi.

Besides, she was a fighter, not a quitter. She was good-and-damned tired of having her life ruled by strangers dying to find out sordid details that were not their concern.

She had to see Tommy—and Candace, who she needed now so much her heart ached—and figure out what to do. It was time to reclaim her life. Maybe by doing so, she could go to Leo and tell him the truth.

She hoped he would not only listen…but that he could deal with the fact that he was going to be a father.

"HEY, BRO, HOW'S it going?"

Leo heard his brother Mike's voice, but didn't slide out from under his truck. He continued with his oil change, wishing his brother would go away but knowing he wouldn't.

"You gonna come out or are you hiding?"

"Bite me," he muttered.

"I did when we were four and six. You gave me a fat lip."

"And mom spanked me," Leo said, smiling reluctantly.

"So are you coming out?"

"If you're here to pump me for information, forget about it. I don't want to discuss it."

"Can't a guy just stop by on his lunch hour to say hello to his brother?" Mike squatted down beside the truck, peering at him. "Seriously, I'm not here to bust your balls. I was in the neighborhood and just wanted to see how you're doing."

He sighed heavily. "Give me a minute." At least Mike hadn't come over here to rag on him about the pictures in the tabloids like the guys at the station did.

It had been a crazy couple of weeks.

He'd been *in a mood,* as his mother would describe it, since the minute he'd left Madison at that airport in Costa Rica. The flight stateside had been miserable. He'd vacillated between anger, regret and humiliation the entire way.

Things hadn't improved much once he got home. His family and friends had noticed, but he hadn't told them anything. He was still too raw, too unsure what to believe, to talk about it.

Once the heat of anger had died down and he'd really begun to think, he'd realized there was no way he knew the whole story. First, he didn't think anybody was a good enough actress to pretend the happiness Madison had seemed to feel when they were together. She hadn't behaved at all like a woman pining for another man— her ex-fiancé *or* her mystery lover.

Second, everything inside him rebelled at the idea that she was the type who would cheat. She didn't come across as anything less than an honest person. The moment he'd met Ashley, he'd seen that tiny hint of selfishness that had made it less of a surprise that she couldn't be faithful. He'd never seen that in Madison. Never.

Besides those factors, he also couldn't stop thinking about one of their first conversations, the one when she'd said she hadn't had sex in six months. That hadn't felt like a lie. Besides, why would she make it up? There would be no need for her to invent a detail like that.

But if it were true…what did *that* mean?

That she was innocent and hadn't cheated?

That she hadn't slept with her fiancé—the sexiest man alive, per magazines—since long before they'd broken up?

Confusion didn't begin to describe the state he'd been in. Finally, knowing he had to get the answers or go crazy, he'd pulled out the slip of paper with her phone numbers on it. It had been late, and he'd been leaving the station after a long twenty-four-hour shift. But he hadn't wanted to wait until morning, knowing that in the light of day, when he was less fatigued, he might rethink the decision.

No answer. He hadn't left a message, instead deciding to try the other number for her parents' house in Florida.

It had been disconnected.

Well, if she really had gone back to their home after the nightmare in Costa Rica, he could understand why the phone was no longer connected. Hell, if the paparazzi figured out who he was and where he lived, he'd not only want to change his address and phone number, he'd want to change his damn face!

The very next day, when he'd been about to try to call her again, the story had broken. Those leeches had published the pictures from the airport. He was officially being called "the unidentified man who stole Tommy Shane's fiancée."

And his life totally went to hell. Everybody saw it, everybody commented on it. He was able to laugh off what he called a "resemblance" to people he didn't know. Those he did know, who were aware he had, indeed, gone to Costa Rica, weren't buying it.

"You need a hand?" Mike asked.

"No, I'm done," he said as he finished tightening the filter. Double-checking the seal, he slid out from under the truck and sat up. "Bring any beer?" he asked his brother.

"I'm working."

"I'm not," he said, enjoying the first morning of his long, three-day stretch off. Rising to his feet and wiping his hands with a rag, he added, "Come on in."

Before they turned to walk through the garage into Leo's small house, Mike dropped a hand on his shoulder. "You holding up?"

"I've been better."

Mike followed him inside, and Leo went to the fridge to grab himself a beer and his brother a bottle of water. Going into the living room, they sat down and eyed each other in silence for a minute.

"So, heard from Rafe lately?" he asked, wondering how their older brother was doing. An Army Ranger stationed in Afghanistan, their other sibling didn't communicate much. The whole family was anxious for him to finish up his tour of duty and get the hell out of there.

"No, not a word. Mom's hoping he'll make it home for Christmas."

"Think that'll happen?"

"I doubt it."

They fell silent again, and Leo knew his brother had something else on his mind. This wasn't just a stop-by-to-say-hey visit.

Finally, Mike spoke. "Have you heard from her?"

Leo merely stared, surprised by the question. It was the first time anybody had asked him that. Most of his friends just ragged on him, trying to get information out of him, asking what it had been like to bang a movie star's ex. His family pretended it hadn't happened, changing the subject, not wanting any details.

Nobody had even asked how they'd met, what they'd done, or how he felt about her. *Really* felt.

"No."

"Have you tried calling?"

"I did before the pictures hit the press."

"And she hasn't called you?"

"I didn't leave a message. The last time we spoke at the airport, I made it pretty clear I didn't want to talk."

"Harsh, dude."

His jaw stiff, he admitted, "It wasn't my finest moment."

"I guess you had provocation."

Maybe. Or maybe he'd just been a jerk, acting like the injured party when he really didn't know what was going on. He should have at least given her the chance to say something—anything. He'd been on autopilot, in shock, operating on instinct and emotion. And he regretted it.

"Was it pretty serious?"

He nodded slowly. "I thought so." Swallowing, he admitted, "To be honest, Mike, I was picturing marriage and babies and all that crap, right up until the minute the press showed up."

His brother leaned forward in his seat, dropping his clenched hands between his splayed legs and hunching over.

"What is it?"

"There's something you should know."

His heart skipped a beat. "About Madison?"

Mike nodded. "And maybe about you." He reached into the pocket of his jacket and pulled out a folded piece of newsprint. "Mom saw this article this morning and asked me to come talk to you. She wanted you to hear it from one of us."

Leo reached for the paper, unsure why his mouth had gone so dry and his heart was beating so fast. Unfolding the square, seeing it was a torn-out page of a tabloid, he felt a little sick, but forced himself to look at the "news" article anyway.

At first, the words didn't make sense. As they began to sink in, though, the world seemed to stop spinning, then to suddenly lurch wildly. He spun with it, unable to do anything but stare at the words on the page.

Who's the Daddy, Madison?

He scanned the article, crumpled the paper in his hand, looked up at his brother and said, "Get me to the airport."

"ARE YOU OKAY?"

Madison awakened from a light nap as her sister

stuck her head into the bedroom, offering her a gentle smile. Candace had flown down the day before yesterday, a few days after Madison had returned to California. They were both staying with Tommy in Laguna Beach.

"I guess," Madison mumbled. "I'm just tired all the time now."

"I suppose that's to be expected," her twin said, entering the room and sitting down on the corner of the bed. Although Candace was concerned, there was also a gleam of excitement in her eyes. Ever since she'd found out that Madison was pregnant, she'd been torn between being upset for her and being utterly thrilled that she would be an aunt in about eight months.

That was now official. The three pregnancy tests she'd taken since she'd arrived in California confirmed it.

She was pregnant with Leo Santori's baby.

"You aren't feeling nauseated or anything, are you?"

She sat up, leaning back against the pillows. "No, not really. A tiny bit queasy in the evenings, but mostly I'm just tired." She rubbed at her eyes and asked, "Where's Tommy?"

"He and Simon are downstairs making dinner."

"Are the shades drawn?" she asked, sounding bitter.

They really didn't need to worry too much about that behind the gates of this secluded mansion. Tommy had bought it for privacy, after all. The front lawn was large and gated, the house set well back from the road. The backyard comprised a steep, rocky hillside that led down to the beach and nobody but a goat could climb it. So, yeah, her comment had just been sarcastic. The paparazzi might be cruising the street in front of the house, but they weren't snapping embarrassing pictures, the way they had when she'd first arrived at Tommy's place a week ago and run the gauntlet to get to the gate.

She hadn't had the stomach to read any of the articles or watch the Hollywood "news" shows since her return. She knew full well everybody was speculating that Tommy, being the great guy he was, had taken back his cheating ex-fiancée.

"I need to talk to you. It's about the press."

"Screw them all," Madison muttered, unable to help it.

Candace reached out and took her hand, which Madison had noticed was actually a bit pale, despite her tan. She suspected she'd lost a little weight and knew she wasn't getting enough exercise. She'd been practically hibernating, consoling herself in the company of her sister and her best friend as they all brainstormed on how best to deal with this.

Tommy had offered to marry her. Same old knight in shining armor. Simon, his partner, hadn't seemed too thrilled about it, but hadn't objected. He knew full well how Madison's life had been shredded because of all of this.

Madison had of course declined. It wasn't the 1950s—she didn't need a father's name on the birth certificate. If there was a name to put on there, she wanted it to be the real one. She only hoped that by the time she'd gotten things straightened out here, Leo would listen to her when she showed up in Chicago to break the news.

This wasn't the kind of thing she could say on the phone, so she'd already bought her ticket. She was leaving in two days. Tommy had told her to tell Leo anything she had to in order to make him understand the truth of the situation. He'd offered to go with her. Hell, he'd offered to hold a press conference to stage a big coming-out party.

All she'd really needed was that permission to share his secret. She didn't want him throwing himself on his sword for nothing. Her real hope was that by staying here with him for a few days, maybe the press and the public would see she and Tommy were still friends. Maybe they'd begin to believe she hadn't broken his heart, that their engagement had just been a mistake.

Maybe they'd let her get her life back.

Get Leo back.

"Mad, something's happened. Mom called this afternoon."

Hearing the note of anxiety in her sister's voice, she gripped her hand tighter. "Is Dad all right? His heart…"

"He's fine. It's just… I don't know how to tell you this."

So it had something to do with *her*. "Just say it."

Candace swallowed. "The *Tattler* has a big story about you."

Oh, great. "What else is new?"

"*This* is new. It seems somebody—probably one of their slimy reporters—dug through Tommy's trash the day after you arrived."

Slimy indeed. She hoped he'd gotten a handful of fish guts.

"Mad, he found the test kits." Candace's hand tightened. "Your pregnancy's all over the tabloids."

She froze, unable to process it, hoping her sister was joking. But Candace was dead serious—the tears and sympathy in her eyes proved it.

"You mean they printed…"

"Yeah. Big headline, nasty article, lots of speculation over who the father is." Candace drew her into her arms and held her tightly, as if fearing Madison was about to break apart.

Funny, though, as the immediate reaction died down, she realized she wasn't devastated, wasn't furious. Mostly, she was just terrified. *What if Leo saw it?*

"I've got to go!" She launched out of the bed. "I have to change my flight to Chicago."

Candace nodded. "I'll call while you pack."

But before they could do either, the intercom in the room buzzed on. Tommy loved the stupid thing and played with it all the time. "You awake?"

"I'm busy."

"Mad, you have a visitor."

"No time," she snapped, wondering who on earth would be coming to see her, and, more importantly, why Tommy would let them in.

"He's coming up the driveway right now. Get your ass down here!"

"He who? What are you talking about?" she asked, finally paying attention.

"A gorgeous Italian guy who demanded to be let in,

and then flipped off a dozen photographers in the street as he drove through the gate."

She gasped. *Leo?*

"Do you think it's him?" Candace asked.

She considered, thought about the articles, remembered the conversation they'd had. He would know the baby was his.

"It's him," she whispered, her hand rising to her mouth as she dashed over to the dresser to check her face in the mirror. "Of course, I haven't bathed in two days and I look like a red-eyed raccoon with these bags under my eyes."

Candace leaped to the rescue. She quickly grabbed Madison's makeup bag and touched up the dark circles. There wasn't much she could do about her hair, so she slung it into a ponytail. It took only a minute or two, but even that was too long.

She hurried downstairs, her heart racing, arriving at the bottom of the steps just in time to see Leo Santori throw a punch at her former fiancé. Fortunately, Tommy ducked to the side and evaded the shot.

"Stop, Leo, don't!" she shouted.

He jerked his attention toward her. His dark eyes studied her, his gaze sweeping over her, from messy hair down to bare feet. She saw the tiny furrowing of his brow and knew he didn't like what he saw. She hoped it was because he was worried about her and not because she looked like total shit. Or because he hated her guts.

"This isn't Tommy's fault," she said immediately, trying to diffuse the tension. "And the papers have everything all wrong."

"Are you pregnant?" he snapped, cutting right to the issue at hand.

She nodded slowly.

"Is it mine?"

Another nod.

His bunched shoulders relaxed a little and the dark frown eased. He didn't exactly look overjoyed about the news or ready to pass out cigars, but at least he no longer appeared about to beat the crap out of Tommy.

"So you're not going to deny it, try to claim it's his?" he asked, jerking a thumb toward Tommy.

"Why would I do that?" she asked, genuinely puzzled.

Candace had followed her downstairs, and Simon had come in from the kitchen. He ignored them both.

"I don't know, Madison, I don't have any idea what you might be thinking. But I do know one of those fucking articles is saying lover boy here can't have kids so you went out and had an affair only so you could give him the baby he wants."

Her legs went weak as dismay washed over her. How could people invent such horrible, vicious lies? She lifted a hand to her forehead, suddenly feeling light-headed.

"Mad?" Tommy said.

Leo didn't speak. When he saw that her weakening limbs were about to betray her, he launched himself forward and caught her in his arms. She fell into them gratefully, inhaling his unique scent, feeling the heat of his body and finally allowing herself to believe he was really here.

And then, for the second time in her life, she fainted.

12

LEO DIDN'T KNOW his way around this gaudy California mansion, so when he realized Madison had passed out from shock, weariness or the pregnancy, he simply strode through the nearest doorway, hoping there was a soft surface on which he could place her.

It turned out to be a dining room. The rich wood table was as big as his own kitchen. Jesus, had Madison really been living like this?

"In here," Shane said, gesturing toward another doorway.

Glaring at the man, not wanting his help with anything, Leo nonetheless carried her into the other room. Spying a large plush sofa, he gently lowered her onto it. "Get her some water and a cold cloth."

"Here." Someone thrust a wet facecloth toward him, obviously having gone for it the moment she'd fallen. He glanced up long enough to realize it had been Madison's twin sister, Candace. He nodded his thanks, thinking she might be identical in features, but she certainly didn't make his heart dance around in his chest the way it did when he looked at Madison.

He placed the cloth on Madison's brow, not liking the paleness in her face and the circles under her eyes. She looked like she hadn't slept at all in the weeks since he'd seen her. There were hollows in her cheeks that hadn't been there before, and her hands and arms looked so much smaller and more fragile than he remembered them being.

"Madison, sweetheart, wake up," he whispered.

Her eyelids fluttered. A pause. Then they flew open.

"It's really you. You're really here."

"Yeah. Did you think it was a dream?"

She nodded. "It wouldn't be the first time."

So she'd been dreaming about him? Well, that was only fair, wasn't it, considering she'd inhabited his dreams and his fantasies every day since he'd walked away from her at that airport?

"You haven't been taking care of yourself," he scolded.

"You're not looking so great yourself." She lifted a slender hand and brushed her fingers across his lips. "You've lost weight."

"So have you. And you should be gaining it, shouldn't you?"

Her hand immediately dropped to her waist. She again displayed that protective instinct he'd already seen when there was just the possibility of a baby.

How could she be a cheat and a liar? How was something like that even possible?

He no longer believed it was. Which was why he'd

gotten on that plane this morning, right after Mike had shown him the article, and flown out here to get to the truth.

"I was coming to tell you," she said, as if reading his mind. "I have my tickets booked."

"Really?"

"Really," she assured him. "The confirmation is in my purse. I was coming in two days. I never wanted you to find out about the baby like you did."

"Okay," he said, believing, because, as always, he could sense no deceit in the woman.

"I'm so sorry you had to read about it in the damned tabloids. That's so wrong."

"It's all right. They're like piranhas, aren't they?"

"Wish you'd run a few of them over when you flew through the gate," said the world's sexiest man.

Leo stared up at him, his expression hard and unyielding. Although the rest of the world was boo-hooing about poor Tommy Shane and his broken heart, Leo knew—*knew*—there was more to this whole thing. Madison was the one who'd been hurt. She was the one who'd been nearly crushed by the weight of all this, and he believed she deserved it about as much as he believed in the Easter Bunny.

"Ooh, fierce," Tommy said. He held his hands up, palms out, in a conciliatory gesture. "Take a breath, big guy."

"What the hell is going on?" Leo asked, looking away from Tommy and down at the woman trying to sit up on the couch. He put a hand under her arm and helped her. "Explain this to me because I've read all the stories and the gossip and the innuendo, and I don't believe a word of it. So somebody needs to start talking."

Madison glanced first at Tommy, and then at the other man, who was dark haired, well dressed and standing close to the famous actor. Then at her sister. "Would you excuse us, please?"

They all immediately mumbled apologies and scurried out of the room, leaving them alone.

Leo ached to reach out and pull her into his arms, to hold her again, this time while she was conscious. He held back, though. They had to clear the air and he didn't want to make this any harder than it was already going to be.

"I've missed you so much, Leo," she said. "I've thought about you every minute of every day."

He dropped onto a nearby chair, surprised those had been her opening words, though he certainly echoed the sentiment.

"Wow. I hadn't planned to start off like that," she said, swiping a hand over her brow. "I'm not trying to manipulate things, gain your sympathy or anything."

He didn't reply, still savoring that admission, still wondering what was yet to come.

"Tommy Shane and I were engaged, but we were never planning to get married. He's been one of my dearest friends all my life, and that's all we have ever been to each other, and all we ever will be."

About twenty pounds of weight lifted off his shoulders. But a lot more remained.

"So why the engagement?"

She gestured toward the window. "You think they're

ruthless now? Imagine what they'd say if word got out that the hottest action star in the country…is in love with a man."

The lightbulb clicked. The presence of the dark-haired guy made sense.

Leo closed his eyes and dropped his head back onto the chair, letting out a heavy sigh. It was as if some-body had set a domino in motion and all the other pieces began to fall down, one after another, everything slid-ing into place.

When he thought his voice wouldn't shake, he said, "You were his beard."

"Exactly. It wasn't supposed to last forever. And when he got serious with his partner, we decided the time had come to break up. Only, we needed a reason. A really *good* one."

"Why?"

"Because what woman in her right mind would break up with the sexiest man alive? Unless he did something horrible. Which would really take a chink out of that superhero-of-Hollywood image."

Right. Nice guys didn't cheat. Not when they had relatively new careers *and* a big secret to hide.

"So you pretended you'd had an affair."

She nodded.

"*You* took the fall, carried the burden for weeks while he…while he…"

"While he offered to come out in the open, to throw away his career and his life and his privacy," she said gently. "Tommy's heart is breaking for me. *I'm* the one

who won't let him make this more of a spectacle than
it is."

Spectacle. Yeah, that pretty much described the life
she'd been living lately.

"To be honest, I also didn't want to let those bastards
win. Why should they get their way?" She punched the
seat cushion. "Why should they be free to hound people
to death, prying in their closets, and under their beds
and…and in their trash cans!"

He'd read the articles about her pregnancy and knew
where that information had come from. How low did
somebody have to be to dig stuff out of the garbage? He
supposed only someone who wallowed in it for a living

"I never thought it would be such a big deal…slow
news month, I guess."

"It's not news," he snapped. "It's gossip and slander
and they're all sick, miserable people with black souls,
no lives, and…small penises."

She smiled weakly, nodding in agreement.

"You went to Costa Rica to hide, didn't you?"

"Yes."

"Never planned on meeting anyone, I'll bet."

She peered at him and her voice throbbed with intensity as she replied, "I never expected to meet *you*. Not
in Costa Rica. Not anywhere. Not in my whole life."

She was baring herself, laying out her every emotion, exposing herself to more heartache—on top of the
mounds of it she'd already been dealing with. All for
someone who'd never once told her how he felt about her.

"And I never thought I'd find you, either," he said
softly.

Unable to stay away from her any longer, he rose from his chair and sat beside her on the couch. He put his arms around her and gently—oh, so gently—pulled her onto his lap. She wrapped her arms around his neck and tucked her face next to his.

"I missed you, too, Madison."

He couldn't see her smile. But he could feel it.

Maybe they were being cautious, telling the truth, but not telling all of it. What he felt for her was a lot more than absence making the heart grow fonder. He'd missed her, yeah. Because he loved her like crazy.

Unfortunately, they were in someone else's house, with three strangers right outside the door. They hadn't seen each other in weeks. She was exhausted, pregnant, emotionally wrung out.

And she hadn't said she loved him, either.

She does. He knew she did.

But maybe it wasn't quite time to say it yet.

"I'm sorry I didn't come find you sooner."

"And I'm sorry I didn't come tell you the truth sooner. I was going to, I just had to make sure Tommy knew and understood, since it's his secret that's at risk of getting out."

He thought about her friend, considered the life he led. Tommy Shane was an international sensation. He'd risen out of relative obscurity just three or four years ago and had become a superstar. He made millions, lived in a mansion, had women hanging on his every word, turned down movie offers that other actors drooled for…and could never *really* be who he was.

He never would have imagined it, but he truly felt sorry for Shane. It was one hell of a choice to have to make.

"How are we going to get out of this mess, Madison?" he whispered, tenderly kissing her temple. "Because I want it over. I want you in my life and I want our baby."

"I don't know," she admitted. "I honestly don't know."

ALTHOUGH LEO HAD hit it off with Tommy after Madison told him the truth, and also got along great with Candace and Simon, they decided to leave for Chicago that very night. For one thing, he needed to get back to work, having used almost all his vacation time in Costa Rica. And Madison needed to get out of this atmosphere. It was toxic and she knew it was bad for her health, and for the baby's.

More than that, though, she just wanted privacy so she and Leo could spend some time together in the real world. Time to accept all that had happened, to explore the feelings they had for each other and see if they were really as strong as she suspected they were.

They could also use some time to get used to the idea that they were going to have a child together.

They couldn't do that here, certainly. Nor did Leo intend to leave her here, living like a bug under a microscope, while he went home alone.

They'd thought about how to slip away, and it had been Candace who'd come up with an idea—which was why, late in the day, a limousine with blacked-out windows pulled up in front of the house, parking at an angle to help block the view from the road. Each of them wearing a jacket, hat and dark glasses, Madison and Leo said their goodbyes and dashed to the car. The driver let them in, closing the door behind them.

Some of the photographers ran to their cars as if to follow. But before they'd even left the driveway, Candace had come outside, waving enthusiastically at the limo as it departed.

The press stayed. Madison could see the confusion on their faces as they peered at the limo, trying to see who was inside.

Somehow, they'd missed her sister's arrival the other day and had no idea her twin was on the premises. When she'd shown up, they'd probably just assumed it was Madison—that she'd gotten out of the mansion under their noses and was returning.

Whatever the case, the press mistook the sisters for each other again now. Ignoring the mysterious vehicle, they focused instead on the fresh meat standing in the driveway, waving happily, acting as though she didn't have a care in the world.

Madison glanced back, her heart twisting as she saw her brave sister standing there, sticking up for her. Their lives had gone in very different directions, and she doubted they'd ever live in the same state again. But some things never changed—like the instant connection they shared, the way they would drop everything on a dime to be there for each other.

They had each found love with great men. But they would always be twins.

She continued to stare, sending warm, loving thoughts out to her sibling. Suddenly, Tommy walked out of the house. So did Simon. That hadn't been part of the plan. Both of them walked up to Candace, stood on either side of her, and slid an arm around her waist. They laughed together and all three waved, looking like one happy family.

She giggled. "I have no idea what the vultures are going to make of that!"

"Hopefully it'll give them all aneurysms just thinking about it," Leo said, sharing her laughter as he pulled her close on the leather seat, draping an arm across her shoulders.

"I hope my father doesn't have one," she said, shaking her head.

She'd called Florida right before they'd left. Her parents hadn't been thrilled that she'd run away the moment she'd found out she was pregnant. Nor were they happy to have found out about it from friends who read the tabloids. But she'd heard the excitement in their voices and, at the end of the conversation, they'd admitted they were *thrilled* to be having their first grandchild.

"Let me kiss you, woman," he growled. "It's been way too long."

She didn't hesitate. The privacy screen was up. Needing desperately to feel him, touch him and know he was real, she moved over onto his lap, twined her arms around his neck and pulled him close for a long slow kiss. He cupped her face in his hands in the way she so loved—so tender, yet sexy. Sultry but sweet. They kissed and kissed, laughing and whispering between each brush of their mouths.

"I could get used to traveling like this," he said. "Think he'd drive us all the way to Chicago?"

"Sure. We'll send the bill to Tommy."

Chuckling, he kissed her again. "Don't I wish. I do have to go back to work, though."

"Too bad. We could get him to drive us all the way to Florida. My parents are dying to meet you."

"I'm looking forward to meeting them, too," Leo said, sounding sincere.

"They're wonderful. They'll love you." She sighed heavily. "They've known Tommy forever and are in on his secret, so they won't hate you on sight like your folks will me."

She was more than a little terrified about meeting his family, having them think of her as some tramp loathed by the entire world.

"Stop it," he ordered. "They'll love you as much as I do."

She froze. Still, so still. Surprised, happy. Wondering whether he'd meant those words or they were an expression.

Love. He'd said the word *love*. She hadn't misheard it, had she?

As if reading her mind, he lifted her chin so their eyes met.

"I love you, Madison Reid."

Her heart thudded, practically escaping from her chest. That was fine. She didn't own it anymore, anyway. This man did. "You're sure?"

"I've never been more sure of anything."

Slowly nodding, she allowed the truth of it to fill

her up, let it sink in to all those empty places that had been hollowed out by the days and weeks of being without him.

He loved her.

He'd come for her.

He wanted her and he wanted their baby.

She could face anything.

When she was able to speak, she said, "I love you, too, Leo. I am totally and completely yours."

"I know."

She couldn't help poking him in the ribs. "You cocky Italian."

He grinned up at her, that gorgeous dimple appearing, his face glowing with utter happiness. "Come on, what's not to love? I mean, you'll never do better than me, babe. You must've hated life in that huge mansion with the beach and the pool and the art and the movie stars dropping by all the time."

Giggling, she replied, "Oh, definitely. The horrors!"

"I ask ya, what could be better than a little two bedroom house right around the corner from a noisy fire station?"

"Two bedrooms are enough for me."

In fact, it sounded like heaven to her.

She realized they'd both just assumed she would live with him. This didn't feel like a vacation. It was crazy. She'd left most of her things behind in California or in Florida, but it felt like she was on her way home. At last.

As long as she had a computer on which to write and a phone with which to make and receive calls, she could continue pursuing her screenwriting career. If that didn't pan out, well, there was always the *Chicago Tribune,* or another big city paper. Most of them would probably be chomping at the bit to scoop up a journalist with a masters from Columbia.

"Southern California? Who needs it?" Leo asked as they cruised up the coast. "Limos and Porsches and beaches? Screw that. Nothing beats the Windy City. Lake-effect snow, crime, cold that cuts right through your bones."

"Can't wait," she said with a laugh. "I'll be able to take you up on that pizza challenge."

"You'll love my cousin Tony's food. In fact, you'll love the whole family. And they *will* love you. I swear it."

"You really think so?"

"I know so."

"Even if this whole nightmare doesn't die down? We can't just tell everyone the whole story, you know. I'm sorry, that has to be Tommy's decision."

"I understand. But I'm telling you, sweetheart, there's only one thing my mom'll need to hear—that she's going to be a grandmother."

Remembering her own mother's reaction, she believed that one.

"As for the rest, we tell them it's a bunch of sensationalistic lies. That you and Tommy were childhood friends who decided you just worked better as friends, and the tabloids made a bunch of nonsense out of it. Who doesn't know that, anyway? I mean, really, how many martian spacemen have you seen flinging a Frisbee in Central Park?"

Laughing out loud as she pictured some of the more outrageous tabloid headlines she'd seen, she nodded helplessly. "Okay."

Their laughter faded. Growing serious, as if knowing she needed the reassurance, he said, "They're good judges of character, Madison."

"If they're anything like you, I know I'll love them all." She nibbled her lip. "But Leo, sooner or later, the press is going to figure out who you are. Somebody will out us and the maniacs will descend on us, no matter where we are."

He smirked. "Oh, honey, there's no place in Chicago that the Santoris can't block the press in and stop them from getting anywhere near us."

"There are that many of you?"

"I've got more relatives than a new lottery winner—cops, bodyguards, lawyers, construction workers, business owners, strippers, politicians…"

"Strippers?" she said, gawking.

"My cousin's wife. You'll love her. She also bakes—oh, *madone,* you haven't lived until you've tried her cannoli."

"I'll add it to my list."

"The point is, there's a Santori on every corner, and every one of them will serve as a barricade to anybody who tries to mess with one of their own."

Swallowing, she asked, "And I'll be one of their own?"

He brushed his fingers against her cheek, reached for her left hand and laced their fingers together. He lifted it to his mouth, placing a tender kiss on her ring finger.

She knew what he meant. Knew exactly what he meant.

"You already are, Madison. You're mine."

"Forever?"

"Forever. Rings, vows, whatever you want." He bent to brush his lips across hers, sealing the promise with a gentle kiss. "I'm never letting you get away again."

Epilogue

LEO WAS AS GOOD as his word. The family loved her. And she loved them.

Going from a small family with one sibling and only a few other relations into a clan like the Santoris was a bit of a culture shock. Madison was thrown into a whirlwind of aunts, uncles, cousins and in-laws.

It was crazy. It was wonderful. And Leo was by her side through every bit of it.

Although none of them ever made her feel at all unwelcome, or questioned the story she and Leo had told them, she had to admit she felt a lot better after Tommy's press conference.

The one where he'd shocked Hollywood.

No, he hadn't spilled everything, but he'd come pretty damned close. Telling the world that it was wrong for *anyone* to have to feign an engagement with one of his oldest friends, and then see that friend ripped to shreds in public over it, he asked the media to take a good, hard look at themselves.

Of course, the tabloids wouldn't...they thrived on

gossip. But there had been plenty of supposedly "legitimate" news outlets that had ripped them apart, too. So maybe his words would do a little good there.

Lots of people speculated that their fake engagement, and his demand for privacy, for the right to live the way he wanted to, meant he was gay. But so what? More fans stepped out in support of him than criticized, and a lot of other celebrities had backed him up with similar comments.

His last film had opened at number one and stayed there for weeks. His career was thriving. He was happy—if discreet—with Simon.

And she and Leo were, blessedly, being left in peace.

"How are you feeling?" Leo asked, coming up behind her as she typed the last few words of her screenplay. She'd been doing revisions for a studio that had optioned it, wanting to get all the work behind her before their upcoming trip to California.

"I'm fine," she insisted, hearing the worried tone in his voice. He wouldn't stop worrying until their daughter was safely in their arms and Madison had fully recovered from childbirth.

If there had ever been a more overprotective father-to-be, she had yet to meet him. Absolutely the only time she could persuade him she wasn't about to break, and was perfectly healthy, was when she seduced him into some seriously naughty sex. Seriously. Naughty.

Yum.

It turned out that being pregnant pumped up her libido to astronomical levels. She found herself ripping Leo's clothes off every chance she got.

He didn't seem to mind.

"You're sure you're going to be okay to fly? I'm sure Candace would understand…"

"I'm six months pregnant, not on my deathbed," she said, rolling her eyes as they went over this again.

"Six months. Our lucky number, remember?" he said with a suggestive wag of his eyebrows.

"I can't wait to see what happens six months from now next October." Then she got back to the subject at hand. "But as for now, I am *not* missing my sister's wedding. We're going to Napa. End of discussion."

"Bossy chick."

"Hey, what can I say?" She adopted a fake accent and made a hand gesture she'd seen her new father-in-law make many times. "I'm Italian, ya know?"

He broke up over her awful imitation. "Brilliant," he said.

"Hey, I learned from the best. I guess that's why your bossiness has rubbed off on me."

"Baby, you were trying to run the show from the day we met."

Oh, that wonderful day they'd met. How she loved to think about it, and most of the days that had followed, right up to and including their own special, intimate wedding ceremony here in Chicago a few weeks ago.

Well, it had been private, but it certainly hadn't been small. Her family had come, of course, along with Tommy.

And then there had been the Santoris. All the Santoris.

They'd filled the church without inviting a single outside guest. A few *un*invited ones had tried to sneak in—they followed Tommy everywhere he went and were still looking for dish about Madison. But one of Leo's cousins, Nick, was a former bouncer and ran a popular club. He'd *bounced* one photographer out on his ass and the others had scurried for cover.

"So, you're really feeling all right?"

"Indeed I am."

"Then finish that sentence and come to bed."

She glanced out the window at the bright blue sky and raised a brow. She was only teasing him, of course. She and Leo had never felt the need to restrict themselves to the dark of night. Their baby had probably been conceived in broad daylight in a swimming pool for heaven's sake.

"What's that look?" he asked as he took her hand and helped her out of her chair.

"Thinking of our last vacation."

He closed his eyes, obviously picturing it, too. "Guess we won't be able do that again until the kid's twenty."

Hmm. Maybe not.

They should certainly be able to afford it, anyway. Her screenplay had not only made a splash, it had made a tidal wave. Once Tommy had held his press conference, and she'd been the object of sympathy worldwide, the studios had swooped in and fought like dogs over her work.

She supposed she could have felt a little offended, could have thought about it as a pity bidding war.

But screw that. She cashed the check.

"Maybe we can take her with us and go when she's three or four," she said. "I think she should learn how to swim naked."

He nodded, liking the idea. "As long as she's potty trained."

"Good point."

They were laughing together as he bent down to pick her up. He often did that, sweeping her into their bedroom. She thought she might cry on the day she became too heavy for it and told him so.

"Never gonna happen."

"I'll be big as a house in three months."

"I'll eat my Wheaties." He pressed a kiss on her cheek, on her nose, then a long, lazy one on her lips. "Because I learned a long time ago when I'm holding you in my arms, I can do absolutely anything."

* * * * *

"Now is the time to sell this relationship…"

Angie gave Cole a wary look. "What do you have in mind?"

"Something like this." He lowered his head and claimed her mouth with his.

Cole knew he was playing with fire. He was only going to graze her lips. But he found that he couldn't pull away. He needed another kiss and then another. He traced her full, soft lips with the tip of his tongue.

Angie opened her mouth and drew him in. Triumph swept through him. He cupped her jaw with both hands and tilted her head. She kissed him as if she couldn't get enough of him. Excitement pulsed through Cole as she grabbed his shirt and pulled him closer.

Cole wrenched away from Angie. Damn it, he thought, as he gulped in air. He forgot. He forgot where they were and why they were kissing.

Most of all, he forgot that kissing Angie was like sharing a piece of his soul…

THE BRIDESMAID'S
BEST MAN

BY
SUSANNA CARR

First published in Great Britain 2013
by Mills & Boon, an imprint of Harlequin (UK) Limited,
Eton House, 18-24 Paradise Road, Richmond, Surrey TW9 1SR

© Jasmine Communications, LLC 2013

ISBN: 978 0 263 90327 0
ebook ISBN: 978 1 408 99705 5

14-1013

Harlequin (UK) policy is to use papers that are natural, renewable and recyclable products and made from wood grown in sustainable forests. The logging and manufacturing processes conform to the legal environmental regulations of the country of origin.

Printed and bound in Spain
by Blackprint CPI, Barcelona

Susanna Carr lives in the Pacific Northwest with her family. When she isn't writing, Susanna enjoys reading romance and connecting with readers online. Visit her website, susannacarr.com.

To Kathryn Lye, with thanks

1

THE DANCE MUSIC pulsed through the floor and the lights flashed across the shadowy room. As the bare-chested men danced for the screaming women, Angie Lawson glanced at her cell phone to check the time. How much longer was she required to be at this bachelorette party?

She jumped when she felt someone tap her on the shoulder. Angie whirled around and saw the bride-to-be behind her. Brittany was dressed to attract attention from her fire-engine-red bandage dress to the rhinestone tiara and veil perched on top of her long, coppery hair.

"Angie, you are supposed to be having fun." Brittany's whine seemed to pierce through the music. Her hands were on her hips and she tapped her foot impatiently. "You're my bridesmaid. It's practically required!"

Angie stared at her and then looked at the women standing on the table and chairs as they screamed for the well-endowed Tiger to take it all off. She returned her attention to Brittany. "This is what you notice?"

"And what *are* you wearing?" She gestured to Angie and gave a look of disgust. "It's a bachelorette party."

"There are half-naked men everywhere," she reminded the bride-to-be. "I didn't realize there would be a dress code."

"Absolutely, it is *my* party." Brittany flattened her manicured hand to her chest. "I am a personal shopper for an exclusive clientele and they're here."

Exclusive? Angie wanted to snort at the word. She had worked with some of the most accomplished and talented women in the Seattle area. The women here at Brittany's invitation were sloppy drunk and out of control. She was pretty sure one of them had tried to bite a stripper.

"Not only do I have to look good," Brittany said, "but so do my bridesmaids."

Angie glanced down at her clothes. She wore a glittery black tank, dark skinny jeans and—with great reluctance but her mother had insisted—strappy heels. There was nothing strange or offensive about her outfit.

She scanned the room, taking note of the other women in the upscale strip club that had been reserved for Brittany's bachelorette party. The guests were not like the flannel-shirt, thick-framed-eyeglasses and designer-boots crowd she knew. They weren't even the yoga-pants and organic-coffee group from the suburbs. The women wore flirty dresses and skintight miniskirts. The outfits were wild and sexy.

Oh. Those were two words that wouldn't describe her. Ever. Angie sighed and fought the urge to hunch her shoulders. Once again, she had dressed all wrong. She thought what she had worn was sophisticated and trendy enough that she would blend in. Instead she looked like a dark giant among the sugarplum fairies.

"I mean, really, Angie." She tossed her hands up with frustration. "What's wrong with showing a little cleavage?"

Now Brittany was really beginning to sound just like her mother. "Nothing." Angie shrugged. And it was a good thing she felt that way, since she was going to flash the whole world when she wore her bridesmaid dress. It was tight, shiny and barely covered the essentials.

"I give up. Just try to look like you're enjoying yourself," Brittany said as she marched off.

Angie froze at those parting words. She had made a valiant effort to get into a party mood but she was bored. And that was cause for worry. Actually, she hadn't been interested in any man since Cole walked out of her life. That was months ago and yet, watching these gorgeous men had left her cold. Why couldn't she enjoy watching a man dance? It didn't make sense. She was young and healthy. What was wrong with her?

"Don't listen to Britt."

Angie peered down and saw Brittany's assistant at her side. Cheryl, a petite and curvy blonde who usually wore jeans and animal-print tops, was dressed in a leopard-print tube dress and skyscraper heels.

"She gives unsolicited fashion advice all the time," Cheryl said with a weary smile. "She doesn't mean anything by it."

"It's okay. It doesn't bother me," Angie assured Cheryl, but the woman was already trailing her boss.

And it didn't bother her that much. She heard the complaint so many times that it had become white noise. Boyfriends had always wanted her to wear revealing clothes and well-intentioned friends kept trying to give her a makeover. No matter how much they insisted, she wouldn't give in. She knew she would never meet their expectations. What would be the point of trying?

She had learned to resist this type of help from a young age. Her mother used to make her go on shopping expeditions that felt more like death marches. Despite her mother's perseverance to create a girly look for Angie, it never stuck. Angie preferred the hand-me-downs from her brothers rather than the ruffled dresses and makeup.

But maybe she had gone too far. Her mother thought Cole had lost interest because Angie didn't work hard enough on her appearance. Her friends weren't quick to shoot down the idea, either.

She didn't want to believe it. When they had first met at a gym, Angie hadn't been dressed to impress. She had been sweaty and in desperate need of a shower after an intense workout. And yet Cole couldn't stop flirting with her.

Even after that Cole never asked her to dress up and he didn't make any complaints about her customary ponytail or lack of pretty lingerie. He didn't suggest that she needed to wear tight clothes to reveal the hard work she put in exercising. He thought she was strong and sexy.

But maybe she hadn't been sexy enough.…

"Angie!"

Angie cringed when she recognized the maid of honor's voice. She looked for an escape route but she was stuck unless she wanted to get on stage with the strippers. That wasn't going to happen. Angie sighed with defeat and watched Heidi approach.

Heidi was tall, rail-thin and her short dark hair made the most of her dramatic features. Her blue one-shoulder dress and stiletto heels would have gotten Brittany's stamp of approval. Just being near Heidi made Angie feel drab and frumpy. The only thing they had in common was the gold bracelet they had received as a bridesmaid gift.

"You need to keep me away from Robin," Heidi declared.

Angie wondered where it was written in the bridesmaid handbook that she had to be the referee? Heidi and Robin might be Brittany's sorority sisters but they hated each other. It was as if they were in competition over who was Brittany's favorite. Why anyone would spend energy on that was beyond Angie's imagination. And from what Angie could tell, Brittany seemed to genuinely enjoy pitting the two against each other.

Unfortunately, she wasn't surprised by this side of Brittany and wished for the millionth time that she had found a good excuse to get out of being a bridesmaid. But Patrick was the groom and her best friend since kindergarten. It was important to him that she was part of his wedding.

"I couldn't stand her in college," Heidi continued. "And she's even worse now."

"I admire your restraint," Angie deadpanned. "You're really doing everything you can to keep the drama out of Brittany's bachelorette party. That's a true friend."

"I know, right? I couldn't believe that Robin said the bridesmaid dresses are tacky. How could she say that? I love Britt's sense of style. I think the dresses are sexy and colorful."

Colorful? Angie bit down on her lip. Bile-green was a color, so Heidi was technically correct.

"And you can wear them again," Heidi informed her.

Angie nodded slowly. "Sure." But why would she want to go somewhere that required her to wear a bustier dress?

"Of course, Robin can't let anything other than designer touch her skin." Heidi crossed her arms and looked over her shoulder. "I think she's just bitter because the dress didn't come in vanity sizes. Her dress size is in double digits."

Angie gritted her teeth. This was exactly why she preferred hanging out with the guys. She was tempted to put Heidi in a headlock and tell her to grow up. It always worked on Patrick but she had a feeling it would cause a meltdown for Heidi.

The strip club plunged into darkness and the spotlight zeroed in on Brittany. "Oh," Heidi squealed as the DJ asked the bride-to-be to go on stage, "the strippers are going to give a special dance for Brittany. Go find a seat."

Angie watched Heidi run to the edge of the stage, teetering dangerously on her silver stilettos. She took a deep breath. So what if she wore the wrong clothes? Who cared if she was too shy to grope a man? It didn't mean she was sexually repressed, right? She could smile, clap and make sure everyone was having a good time. She was going to have fun tonight even if it killed her.

"What did she say about me?"

Angie jumped as Robin stood beside her. The woman's orange beaded halter dress was so short that at first Angie thought it was meant to be a shirt. "Heidi? She said the strippers were going to dance for Brittany."

"She was talking about me, wasn't she?" Her sleek black ponytail bobbed as she nodded her head.

"No," Angie lied.

Robin arched a perfectly groomed eyebrow. "She's just mad because Britt loved the bridal party spa and that was my idea. We all needed it, don't you think?"

Going to the spa had been a new experience for Angie. She had felt awkward in the hushed and ultra-feminine surroundings. The moment she had walked through the ornate doors, she had felt like a clumsy duck next to elegant swans. "You know, that was the first time I've been to a spa."

"No need to tell me that. I've seen your cuticles," Robin said. "But still, that event was designed to help the bride relax. And Britt has been incredibly stressed out."

Angie wholeheartedly agreed with that. Brittany had a strong vision for the wedding and reception, but there were too many details to keep track of. Even with her highly efficient assistant and three bridesmaids at her beck and call, there had been a series of problems to solve. "Maybe if she started eating."

"Don't even say that!" Robin shook her head vigorously. "Not until after the wedding. She has to fit into that dress."

No solid foods for a week? It sounded like torture to Angie. "The dress fits perfectly. She doesn't have anything to worry about. But she should stop the liquid diet. It can make a person tired and irritable."

Robin's eyes widened. "You think Britt is irritating?"

She really needed to be more careful with her words. Didn't she know by now that the bridal party was a walking, talking minefield? All the competition, insecurities and petty jealousies. Angie already had a sneaky suspicion that being Brittany's brides-maid wasn't going to strengthen their relationship. She needed to work harder if she wanted to stay friends with Patrick. "No, I said—"

The hot pink stage curtains were ripped back and five strippers stood silently on the dark stage. They wore black neckties and low-slung leather pants. Angie jumped, startled, as the women around her went wild.

Robin raised her arms and whooped with delight as the first few notes of "It's Raining Men" played. Angie dutifully smiled and clapped as she watched the men start their routine around Brittany. The audacious choreography and frenetic lighting hid the fact that only a few were good dancers.

Angie's mouth dropped when she saw Brittany eagerly lay on the stage as one of the strippers straddled her. No one could accuse the bride-to-be of being shy. Brittany enjoyed the special attention.

The men had lean, athletic builds. Angie admired the hard abs and strong arms. She knew the work they had to put into getting sculpted bodies. They were attractive. Sexy. But she didn't feel the need to go crazy at the sight of them.

Perhaps it was because she worked as a personal trainer and was surrounded by muscular men every day. Or it could be that she felt self-conscious having a man gyrate in her face until she stuffed money in his sequined thong.

Or it could be none of those reasons. It could be that she wasn't acting as assertive and enthusiastic as the other women because she couldn't let go of her inhibitions. She tried that before. She had felt safe when she was with Cole. She knew she could be as outrageous and as daring as she wanted. She'd played out her deepest, darkest fantasies with him.

And then he dumped her. She was hurt and humiliated. Was she more mild than wild? Was she unable to compete with other women? She was afraid of the answer and had kept the sensual side of herself under wraps ever since.

Angie looked away from the stage as the knot in her stomach tightened and a flush of embarrassment crept up her neck. Not only had she felt safe with Cole, but at the same time, she'd also felt wild. She found it weird. No other man made her feel that way.

But she didn't want to think about that. She couldn't. It was better to accept that she didn't have a sensual side and move on. One day she'd regain her confidence. However, she wasn't going to lower her guard here, and definitely not with a stranger. It would be with someone she loved and trusted.

"Aren't these guys hot?" Robin yelled over the music.

"They are." Angie continued to clap to the beat as Brittany got to her feet and danced with the strippers. Some of her moves were downright dirty.

Robin elbowed her. "The bridesmaids get the next lap dances."

Angie lurched forward and her stomach twisted violently. "Up there on stage?"

"No, that honor is reserved for the bride. But you better pick one before Heidi grabs them all. Which one do you want?"

"Oh…it doesn't matter." She knew what would happen. The more audacious the dancer, the more uptight she would be. She was going to be laughed at for her discomfort. She wanted to refuse the dance but she had to act like a team player. She studied the men on stage, hoping to find one who understood personal space and boundaries.

"I can't decide between the guy groping Brittany or the one in the back."

Angie looked at where Robin pointed. The guy reminded her of Cole, from his short black hair to his solid, muscular build. She felt a surprising flutter of interest as her gaze traveled down his smooth chest, defined abs and lean hips. He had power and grace. He looked a lot like Cole. In fact—

She gasped and dragged her gaze to the man's face. She recognized the square jaw and full lips. The high cheekbones and strong nose. The short dark hair that felt soft to the touch. "No…way."

"What?" Robin asked. "Are you okay? What's wrong?"

Angie slumped into the nearest chair. She felt hot and cold from the shock but she continued to stare at Cole Foster from across the room. Her ex-boyfriend was on his hands and knees as he sinuously rolled his hips.

"Where the hell did he learn how to move like that?" She realized she had said it aloud and pressed her lips together.

"Who?" Robin asked. "The stripper? Do you know him?"

"No. I don't know him at all." She had shared intimate moments with this man. Loved him with her body and soul. Once she had bared it all to him, but it had been a mistake. It turned out she wasn't enough for Cole. And now she saw the truth with her own eyes as he stood on stage, performing for a group of panting women. "I thought he looked like someone I used to date."

Robin gave a bark of laughter. "Yeah, right. You dating a stripper."

"Stranger things have been known to happen," Angie murmured. Like Cole *becoming* a stripper. It didn't make sense. When she dated him, Cole had been a detective on the police force. And a good one at that.

Angie watched, stunned and openmouthed, as Cole ripped off his necktie and wrapped it around Brittany's waist, pulling the bride-to-be closer as the group of women screamed louder and reached for him.

Angie crossed her arms and sat stiffly in her chair. She wanted to disappear into the shadows. Leave before Cole saw her. She felt confused. Stupid. Territorial.

She felt betrayed and that didn't make any sense. At one time, this guy had made her feel special. Now it looked as if he knew how to make every woman feel that way. She wasn't dating Cole anymore and it didn't matter what he did. So why did she feel angry?

Cole turned his head and his gaze snagged hers. Angie's breath hitched in her throat as she stared into his blue eyes. He didn't look surprised to see her. It was as if he had known she was here all along.

She saw the determination flash across his face. *Uh-oh.* She knew that look. Angie wanted to leap from her seat but instead she braced herself. Her eyes widened with horror when she watched Cole jump from the stage. The women grabbed at him but he didn't pay them any attention as he strode straight for her.

THESE WOMEN WERE animals. Cole Foster tugged his leg away from a woman's fierce grip and ignored the fistful of dollars that another waved in his face. He'd never felt like a piece of meat until tonight. The crowd was rabid and ready to rip off his clothes.

He was having a difficult time focusing on his case and that wasn't like him. He was committed to this job—his real job—and prided himself on his professionalism. Yet all he could think about was Angie sitting in the back row.

She hasn't changed a bit, Cole realized. Angie Lawson was strong, athletic and a natural beauty. Her wavy black hair was pulled back in a casual ponytail and she wore no makeup. She didn't need to. She had a healthy glow and vibrant energy that a person couldn't get in a bottle.

He noticed she wore a black tank top and jeans. He saw the strappy heels and knew that had to be her mother's interference. Angie dressed to hide or blend into the crowd. But she couldn't hide from him. He was always aware of her and nothing would ever change that.

It wasn't his plan to blatantly approach her. It could risk his assignment but he saw her rigid stance and crossed arms. Her eyes were wide and her mouth was tight with anger. Cole knew she was trying to hold it all in but she was about to blow his cover.

Maybe he should have given her an early warning. He knew she would be here, he had been tracking the bridal party for the past week. But he hadn't been able to determine how close Angie was with the other bridesmaids.

He stood before her, his heart beating fast, his skin slick with sweat. The leather pants clung to his legs and rode low on his waist. Angie was doing her best to keep her gaze somewhere around his ear.

She didn't say anything. There were a lot of things he wanted to say to her. Things like "Sorry," or "You're better off without me." Instead he said, "You're next."

Her eyes glittered with anger and she held out her hand to stop him. "No, thanks."

"Angie, what are you saying?" The woman he knew as Robin tapped her on the shoulder. "You just told me he looked like your ex. Go for it."

He got here in the nick of time. What else did she say about him? "I insist," he said with a hint of warning. "Bridesmaids are next in line."

She jutted out her chin. "How did you know that I'm a bridesmaid?"

"I was told ahead of time," he replied. He loved the sound of her voice. It was low, rough and sexy. He remembered it at the most inconvenient times.

Angie glared at him with suspicion. She crossed her legs and held her arms tighter around her. "Sorry, I don't have any dollar bills."

"Didn't you know you were coming to a strip club?"

"Don't mind her," Robin said. "She's new at this."

He leaned forward and rested his hands on the top of her chair. He caged her in and she pressed her spine against the back. Cole inhaled her scent and the memories bombarded him. "No money at all?" he asked.

"Not unless you want coins."

Cole's smile grew wide. He looked at Robin. "Tiger told the rest of us that he wants to be the one to give you the lap dance."

"See ya!" Robin blurted and raced to the stage, leaving them alone.

"There was no reason to send her away," Angie said and her words vanished as he straddled her legs. She immediately tensed up. "What are you doing?"

"This is the only way I can talk to you here," he said, but his mind was elsewhere. He was painfully aroused being this close to Angie. How was he going to put two words together while he was touching her? "Don't worry, I'll be gentle."

For some reason his assurance was met with a frosty stare. He watched with fascination as Angie's skin flushed red. "Don't worry about me," she said in a clipped tone. "Give me all that you've got."

"Angie, I know you're uncomfortable with all this." He saw the flash of injured pride in her eyes and he fell silent. Everything he said was being taken the wrong way.

"No, no, Cole. I'm curious. I've already seen some of your new moves. I didn't realize that you had been holding back with me."

"Holding back?" He never held anything back with Angie. Well, not physically.

"Go ahead, Cole." Angie leaned back in her chair. "Drive me wild."

2

COLE DIPPED HIS head and Angie closed her eyes. It was a defensive move but it didn't help. She could still feel the heat from his body. She licked her lips, remembering how his skin tasted. Warm and masculine.

"I need to talk to you," he said against her ear.

She felt his breath against her skin and shivered. "Apparently so. You've gone through a few life changes since I've seen you." Cole's bare chest grazed against her breasts and she jumped. She opened her eyes wide. "Or have you?"

Cole paused. "What do you mean?"

He was so close that she found it difficult to think. It was as if her body had been asleep and now energy sparked inside her. Her heart pounded against her chest and her blood pumped hard through her veins. Her skin stung with awareness. Why? Why did she only feel like this around Cole? It wasn't fair.

A sickening thought occurred to her. "How long have you been a stripper?" she asked. "You're very good at it."

"Should I be flattered by your surprise or insulted?" he asked as he rolled his hips.

Angie curled her fingers tight into fists. She wasn't going to touch him. Hold him. Guide his hips. No, she wasn't, no matter how much her hands tingled with need. "I notice you're not really answering the question," she said, all too aware of how her voice cracked. "Were you stripping when we were together?"

Cole jerked back as if he'd been struck. His smile disappeared and his mouth tightened. "Do you really think that?"

"I don't know what to think." She really hoped he didn't have a secret life, but the man had always been private. He kept things to himself and now she wondered if she knew him at all.

"This is not what it looks like," he said as he kneeled down before her.

She tensed up as her heart pounded faster. "It never is."

"I'm not a stripper." He placed his hands on her knees and pulled them apart.

"Really?" Her voice was high and every muscle in her body locked. How could he touch her so intimately and yet so casually? "Because you're faking it very well."

She looked down at him and tried to fight off the memories. How many times had they been like this? How many times had their position been reversed? Cole knew how to touch her, please her with his hands and mouth. She never found that kind of satisfaction anywhere else.

Cole lifted her leg and placed it over his bare shoulder. Angie saw his expression. She recognized the desire and something else. Something bittersweet. She didn't know why he felt that way. He was the one who walked away.

She couldn't fight the pang of misery. Angie yanked her leg away. She held up her hands in defeat. She couldn't do this. Not with Cole. When they were together, the sex they had was romantic. Intimate. It had meant something. She didn't want to respond to the same routine he did for any woman who had a dollar. "This lap dance is over."

"Not yet." Still kneeling between her legs, Cole slowly slid his body up against hers.

Angie inhaled sharply as she remembered every plane and angle of his body. How it felt to curl up against his hard chest, cling to his broad shoulders and wrap her legs against his waist.

She felt the sweat beading on her skin and tried to remain calm. She saw the knowing twinkle in Cole's eyes. Did he remember, too? Or did he know the effect he had on her? Angie looked away. "I'm not sure what you're trying to accomplish here…."

"Then this must be your first time at a strip club."

She turned back and frowned at him. "But you're wasting your time with me."

Cole gave a crooked smile. "It's never a waste of time being with you."

She stilled as the words washed over her. How could he say that when he'd dumped her and never stayed in touch? "We're done."

"No, wait." He quickly straddled her legs and grabbed the back of her chair again. She was trapped and considered pushing him away. But that meant touching him. Pressing her hands against his naked skin… "I have something to tell you."

"Yeah, I got it." She searched for a safe spot to focus

on, trying not to notice the way his broad chest rose and fell, or how his rock-hard abs gleamed with sweat from dancing. "I heard what you said. You're not really a stripper. Let me guess. You're in between jobs. You're doing a favor for a friend?"

He thrust his hips to the music. "I'm undercover."

Angie slowly shifted her gaze to meet his. That was one excuse she didn't expect. A chuckle erupted from her throat. "That's a good one."

Cole stopped moving and frowned. "You're not supposed to laugh while getting a lap dance."

"I'm sorry. I can't help it." She shook her head as she continued to laugh. "It's not like I'm pointing."

He sighed and moved forward until his mouth was against her ear. "Angie, this is serious."

The bubble of laughter died in her throat as she felt his lips against her skin. "Then stop joking." She squirmed away. "I know you're not undercover. You quit the police force after you broke up with me a year ago."

"Hey, Angie, it's my turn," Heidi called out as she approached them.

Angie was unprepared for the fierce territorial streak that sliced through her. She knew Cole was no longer hers, but she couldn't share him. It was bad enough seeing him dance with Brittany. She didn't want him anywhere near Heidi.

"Stall her," Cole demanded.

Angie felt a flash of relief at his reluctance to leave, but she knew it wasn't because he favored her over the others. He needed something from her and it wasn't to relive the memories or have one night together.

"Come on. No playing favorites," Heidi said as she waved a fistful of cash. "I have money to burn."

"Why should I do what you ask?" Angie asked Cole between her teeth. "I should throw you to the wolves."

He looked into her eyes. "I really need to talk to you."

His voice was harsh, but she saw the pleading in his gaze. What was so important? Curiosity got the better of her. She sighed and looked at the maid of honor. "Sorry, Heidi. I'm still waiting for him to rock my world. I'll send him over to you once that happens."

Heidi rolled her eyes. "I'll be back." She stormed off into the crowd of women, who were encouraging the other strippers to take it all off.

"Really?" Cole said. "Like you couldn't come up with something more flattering?"

She shrugged. "I didn't want to set her expectations too high."

Cole did a sinuous roll of his hips that made Angie squeeze her legs together. "Get some money out so you can hold me here longer," he suggested.

Angie shook her head. "I told you that I don't have any cash."

"You always have money in case of emergencies."

She was surprised that he would remember that. For some reason she assumed he'd forgotten all about her when he'd moved on. "This is not an emergency."

"Angie," he warned.

She pressed her lips together as she considered her options. She decided to do as he asked if it meant she didn't have to share him with the others. "Fine." She reached inside the front pocket of her skinny jeans and pulled out a twenty. "What will this get me?"

He shook his head and clucked his tongue with regret. "You're not ready for that."

"Don't be too sure," she said with an angry smile.

She wasn't going to let him see how his assumption hurt. "Now what do you need to tell me?"

COLE HESITATED. SHOULD he tell Angie? He hadn't planned on it. Was he considering it just to prove he wasn't a stripper? No, he decided. He needed her help and her insight. In the past he had no problems confiding to her about his job when he worked in Missing Persons. He trusted her and valued her advice.

And his instincts told him that he could still trust her. She wouldn't do anything to hurt him or sabotage his assignment. He didn't have a lot of faith in people, but Angie was different. She would help him even though they were no longer a couple.

Angie moved to get up. "It was good seeing you, Cole, but I was about to call a cab and leave."

"You can't leave," he said, refusing to move out of the way. His hands clenched the back of her chair. He didn't want her to go. It had been too long since he'd seen her and it was difficult to keep up the pretense while he was conducting surveillance. There were a few times when he wanted to forget about his professional distance and approach Angie. Now she was right next to him and he wanted the moment to last.

"Why?" she asked as she crossed her arms. "No one will notice."

He would, but she wouldn't care about that. "The bride will. She'll never forgive you."

"How would you—" Her voice faded when he abruptly turned around. He grabbed her hands and rubbed them against his chest and he swayed to the music. "What are you doing?"

"Keeping my cover," he said. He dragged her hand down his chest until her fingers brushed against his waistband. His stomach clenched as she lowered her hand even more before she snatched it away.

"Will you stop that?" She pushed against his back. "It's kind of hard to listen when you're distracting me with those moves."

He paused and turned to face her. "I'm a private investigator."

She nodded. "You went over to the dark side?"

"Yeah, I did." He liked being a cop, but this was something he needed to do. His goal was to find missing relatives and reunite families. He always wanted to do that ever since he was a teenager.

Angie narrowed her eyes as she watched his face carefully. "Let me see your P.I. license."

He clenched his jaw. This was a side of Angie he hadn't experienced before. He didn't like how she questioned his word. "It's not like I have it on me."

"You don't have to make up a story for me. So you're a stripper and you take your clothes off for a living. I'm not going to judge." She tilted her head and pursed her lips. "Much."

"Why don't you believe me?" he asked irritably.

"I don't know." She shrugged. "But I'm very curious what you would do for a twenty. Is it something I've seen before?"

Cole stopped moving and slowly stood to his full height as the cold anger seeped through him. "Are you comparing what we had together with this?"

"Don't worry." Angie held up a hand as if it would erase his hurt and frustration. "I get the feeling that there is no comparison. You needed to find excitement elsewhere and this is where you wound up. How could I possibly have competed with this?" She splayed her hands out and gestured at the club.

"I didn't leave you for this," he said through clenched teeth. The anger gripped his chest and he took a deep breath. "I really am a private investigator."

"Mmm-hmm. And you needed to infiltrate a strip club? Why? Are the guys jewel thieves by day?" She made a show of looking around her before she leaned forward and stage-whispered, "Is Tiger really an assassin?"

"I'm investigating the maid of honor."

"Say what?" Her voice went high. "Heidi?"

Cole clapped his hand over her mouth before she said any more. "Yes. And don't look for her. We can't let Heidi know we're talking about her."

"Heidi," she repeated against his hand. She pulled his hand away. "Why are you investigating her?"

"I can't tell you. I've already said too much." He had to keep some things confidential but he wanted Angie to know what he was doing with his life. Despite the fact they were no longer together, he wanted her to be proud of his accomplishments.

She pressed her fingers against her forehead as if she were trying to wrap her mind around the news. "Heidi is not interesting enough to have a secret life."

"Don't blow this for me." He looked over his shoulder. Everyone was still cheering as Tiger and Robin played up to their audience. He didn't see Heidi in the crowd.

"You already blew your best bet for the night. Heidi wanted a lap dance from you. Why are you wasting your time with me?"

He refused to give a lap dance to Heidi or any other woman in this club. It was different with Angie. "I can't interrogate her while I'm thrusting in her face."

"That would require special coordination," Angie admitted. "But listen, I won't say anything to Heidi."

"Thank you." He stood between Angie's legs but was reluctant to leave. "One more thing."

"Oh, my God, what?" She looked upward and groaned with frustration. "I swear this is the longest lap dance in history."

"What can you tell me about Heidi?" he asked. "What do your instincts tell you?"

Angie's eyes widened as if she were shocked. "Is this why you came over?" she asked indignantly. "To pump me for information?"

"It's not the *only* reason." He also had to stop her from telling anyone about his work history. But he wasn't about to mention that to Angie.

"I don't know much about her," Angie said through clenched teeth, "But I can tell you that she's no criminal mastermind."

"What's your impression?" He could rely on her opinion. Angie had to figure people out very quickly as a personal trainer.

"She's shallow. Fake," Angie stated. "Doesn't play well with others."

From the surveillance he'd done, that could describe the bride and the other bridesmaid. "What else?"

"She's very loyal to Britt— Hey—" she flattened her hand against her chest "—I'm not your informant. If you want to know anything, go give a lap dance to Brittany's assistant. Cheryl knows everyone and everything about this wedding."

Cole sighed. There were occasions when he really questioned what he had to do for his job. *Think of the end result. You are bringing a family back together.*

You are giving someone else the happy ending you didn't get.

"Here." She thrust her twenty-dollar bill in front of him. "Don't let me keep you."

Cole looked at the money and waited. He had called in a lot of favors to masquerade as a stripper for his surveillance, but it had been made very clear that he had to act like the other dancers. No exceptions. "I can't take it like that. House rules."

She made a face. "Like there's a policy?"

"Actually, there is." He smiled, knowing Angie wasn't going to like what he had to say. "If you don't want to put it in my pants, I can take it with my teeth. But first you would have to put it between your—"

"All right! I'll just give it to you."

Cole braced his legs and laced his hands behind his head. He leaned back and tilted his hips forward. He watched Angie silently, wondering what her next move would be. He assumed she would be quick, but instead Angie curled her fingers around the waistband of his leather pants.

His muscles clenched as her knuckles rubbed against his hipbone. Cole hissed in a breath as he felt his penis get hard. He wasn't going to be able to hide his reaction. It would take the last of his self-control not to take her hand and press it against his erection.

Cole closed his eyes, praying for restraint, when a frightened scream ripped through the air. He whirled around and instinctively held Angie back when she jumped from her chair.

"Over there." Angie motioned at Brittany, who stood by an empty table. The bride-to-be pointed at the floor.

Cole ran forward. He felt Angie right behind him.

There was something about that scream that had sent a chill down his spine.

He saw a woman lying on the floor, partially under a table. She was facedown and a tablecloth hid her from the waist up. All he saw were two legs and silver stilettos.

"It's Heidi," Angie said.

3

"Back up," Angie ordered the women surrounding Heidi. She followed Cole, pushing her way through the crowd. "Give her some space."

Angie crouched down next to Heidi and watched Cole carefully roll her onto her back. She knew first aid and CPR for her job, but she was glad he was with her. He was calm and in control during times of crisis. She knew she could depend on him.

"Someone call an ambulance," she called out to the crowd as Cole checked the maid of honor's airway.

"I'm on it," Cheryl said as she got her phone out of her tiny purse.

"What do we have here?" she asked Cole. She slid Heidi's golden bracelet aside so she could check the woman's pulse. She noticed Heidi's skin was warm to the touch.

"Airways are clear and she's breathing." The relief in his voice was unmistakable.

"Pulse is strong." Angie addressed the other guests. "What happened? Did anyone see her fall? Did she faint?"

She saw the women shrug and shake their heads. From the murmurs and snatches of conversation, it was clear that no one had seen Heidi after her lap dance. She had her spotlight and then melted back into the crowd.

"Is she on anything?" Cole asked in a low, confidential tone.

"I have no idea." She had spent a lot of time with Heidi in the past week, but she wasn't that knowledgeable about the maid of honor.

"I didn't catch that." Brittany was at Cole's side. Her movements were choppy and frantic. "What did you ask?"

"Is she on any medication?" Angie quickly rephrased the question and Cole gave her a look of gratitude.

"How should I know?" Brittany tossed up her hands as her voice rose to a shriek. "Check her purse."

Angie looked around. The floor was sticky and pink from a spilled drink and a martini glass was next to Heidi's hand. She found the handbag under the table and opened it. "Cell phone. Credit card. Dollar bills. Lipstick."

Cole glanced up. "That's it?"

Angie had thought the same thing. For someone who was as high-maintenance as Heidi, she expected more. At least a bag of beauty products. "I don't think anything is missing. This purse is too small."

"Keys? Driver's license?"

"I don't think she brought them along," Angie said. "She took the party bus like the rest of us."

"We should roll her onto her side."

Angie knew why Cole suggested that. Heidi could vomit if she was intoxicated or under the influence.

They eased her sideways and put her in the recovery position.

To her, it was very obvious how she and Cole still worked in sync. In the past they could share a mere look and understand. Or she could say a word—not a sentence, not even a phrase—and Cole would know what she was talking about. She thought the year apart would diminish their shorthand communication, but it was all still there.

"Does anyone have a jacket I can use?" Angie asked the other women. "Something to keep her warm while we wait for the ambulance?"

"I'll go find something," Cheryl said before she hurried away.

Cole gently tipped Heidi's head back to keep the airways open. He went still when he cupped her head. Angie was immediately aware of his wariness. That was one thing she wished had disappeared since they broke up. She was too aware of him. She knew the instant when his mood shifted. He would show no change in expression but somehow she knew.

She leaned over Heidi and blocked Cole's face from the crowd. "What is it?" she asked.

He pulled his hand away. She saw the dark stain on his fingers. "Blood."

"What did she fall on?" She examined the table next to Heidi. There was no blood on the white tablecloth.

Cole's expression was grim. He leaned forward to whisper in her ear. "I think she got hit."

"With what?" She glanced around. All the tables and chairs were in place. The metallic vases were upright and not a flower was out of place. The drinking glasses were plastic. She had no idea what could be used as a weapon.

"This isn't happening," Brittany wailed as she stomped off. "I should have known Heidi would do this to me."

Robin ran over to her and wrapped her arms around Brittany's shoulders. "It's going to be okay."

"How can you say that?" Brittany started to cry. "My party is ruined."

Angie rolled her eyes and moved closer to recheck Heidi's pulse. "Remind me never to be around Brittany when there's an emergency."

"I recommend staying clear when she finds out one of her friends did this."

COLE SQUINTED AS he checked out the strip club. The building was a lot different when all the lights were on and the music stopped. The paramedics had left with Heidi on a stretcher and now the place felt barren and deserted. The white tablecloths and colorful flower arrangements couldn't hide the utilitarian setting.

"Anything else?" he asked Linda, the first officer on the scene. He remembered her from the force. Sometimes he missed the camaraderie at the police station. He missed having a partner. Having backup.

"Yeah, I really like the outfit, Foster," Linda said as she tapped her pen against her notebook. "It's so you."

He crossed his arms and glared at her. He couldn't wait to get out of these leather pants and put a shirt on. "Yeah, yeah, yeah. I've already heard it from the other guys. I'm sure all the customers are curious about how I know everyone."

"They can think you're friends with a few guys in law enforcement. Get over it. We have more important concerns. Now let me go over this statement again."

Cole took a deep breath. Linda was right. It didn't

matter if they found out he was an ex-cop or a private investigator. He needed to know what happened to Heidi. It bothered him that he got distracted and she was injured on his watch.

"So," Linda began as she perused her notes, "you were giving a lap dance."

He pressed his lips together. "I was undercover."

She raised her eyebrows. "To your ex-girlfriend."

"She's a bridesmaid." He glanced over to Angie. She was sitting alone, her arms and legs crossed, her face tilted away from the rest of the guests. She was quiet and thoughtful while the others chatted or used their cell phones.

"And the lap dance was how long?"

"I wasn't keeping track." Cole spotted Linda holding back a smile. He winced. He was never going to hear the end of this. "What hospital is the victim going to? I should notify her family."

The woman's smile disappeared and she gave a nod, sliding back into her professional demeanor. "I'll find out and get back to you."

"Thanks." He gestured back to where they had found Heidi on the floor. "What do you think happened?"

Linda shrugged. "I think drinking and high heels don't mix."

He shook his head. "I don't think that's it. Something is not right."

"You suspect foul play? Because I don't see that. I see it as bad luck. Is there something about your case that you're not sharing?"

"It's about the angle that she fell. We found her face-first but her injury was on the back of her head. And why didn't she break her fall with her hands?"

"That doesn't necessarily mean someone hurt her." Linda pocketed her notepad and stepped away. "We'll find out more when she regains consciousness."

Cole rubbed his hands over his face. He had found Heidi two weeks ago and had been investigating her life. He wished he had more answers.

He turned and walked over to Angie. He paused in midstep. Was that wise? She was distracting him. It would be best to talk to the other women and to ignore her presence.

No, he couldn't do that. He quietly sat down next to Angie. He wasn't sure what to say but he wanted to be there for her. He knew what she was like after a scare or an emergency. She did what needed to be done and then her adrenaline kicked in. He wanted to keep watch over her.

"Why are you sitting all the way over here?" he asked. Angie was always friendly and could talk to anyone about anything. He always liked that about her and wished he could be the same. It was a skill he had to develop for his job but it didn't come easy.

"I'm about ready to tackle Brittany if she doesn't shut up," she answered. "I'd rather not do it in front of the police."

Yes, he'd made the right decision. He would have to watch her closely or she would let her emotions get the best of her.

"Don't you find it weird that Brittany hasn't shown any concern for Heidi?" Cole asked as he watched the bride-to-be pace the floor. "All she's worried about is whether this affects her wedding ceremony."

"You never know how someone will react in a stressful situation," Angie said. She paused and glanced at him. "But, honestly, I expected this from Brittany."

"Why?" Brittany wailed as she sat down with a thump. Several women rushed over to pull her back up. "Why did she have to have an accident right before the wedding?"

"Does she expect you to go over there?" Cole asked. "You are a bridesmaid. Isn't taking care of her one of your duties?"

"Not going to happen," Angie said. "What did the police say about Heidi? Was it an accident?"

"The police are treating it as one. I can't say that it wasn't." He hoped it was an accident. If someone harmed her, he had no evidence of motive or means.

"I warned her not to wear those heels!" Brittany's voice rang through the club.

"Great, now she's revising history." Angie slid down in her chair. "You may have to hold me back."

He knew it was all talk. Angie could take down a man twice her size but the only time he'd seen her use those skills was in the bedroom. Cole smiled as he remembered those lighthearted moments and the hot sex that came after. He shifted restlessly in his seat and tried to focus on something else. "How do you know she's not telling the truth?"

"Brittany told Heidi to buy those shoes," Angie said. "We were at the mall picking up last-minute stuff for the party."

Cole watched the police leave the scene. "Seems like everyone can go home now. I can finally get out of these leather pants."

"And this bachelorette party from hell has officially ended." She tensed beside him. "Brittany is coming over here. I will not be held accountable for my actions."

"Think of Patrick," he advised. "The guy has been your best friend for years."

"That should count for something. He's only known Brittany for a year."

"Doesn't matter," he said, feeling suddenly weary. He knew from experience that Angie needed to take a step back and keep her mouth shut or she would regret it. "Patrick will choose Brittany's side over yours every time. Take my word for it."

Angie gave him a sharp look as if his advice revealed something she hadn't seen in him. He was almost grateful that Brittany was suddenly standing in front of Angie.

"We'll need an emergency meeting," Brittany told Angie as she tried to wipe the mascara streaks with a tissue. "Meet up at the usual Starbucks tomorrow afternoon at four."

"Why?" Angie asked. "Are we going to visit Heidi?"

"We don't have time for that," Brittany said, dismissing the suggestion with the wave of her hand. "We have to decide what happens if Heidi can't be maid of honor. A groomsman will need to be let go. Then we have to rework the processional and recessional. I really don't need this extra work."

"Your maid of honor was seriously injured at the bachelorette party," Angie reminded her.

"Careful," Cole muttered.

"Shouldn't you postpone the wedding? Maybe downsize it?" she said hopefully.

Brittany took a step closer. "I'm already down one bridesmaid."

Angie frowned and her mouth was set in a straight line. "But…"

"Angie—" Brittany's voice dropped "—I have

planned my wedding for years. I have waited for this day. Nothing and no one is going to get in my way."

Cole didn't like the threat he heard in Brittany's voice. He grasped Angie's forearm, reminding her that he was there as backup. He was tempted to pull her behind him and wedge himself between Angie and Brittany.

Angie went rigid. He sensed her struggle, but after a tense moment, Angie nodded and smiled. "Got it."

"Good." Brittany glared at Angie before she swiveled on her impractical heels and stalked off. "Be at Starbucks by four."

Cole watched the bride-to-be leave. Every step pulsed with hostility. "What would happen if you didn't show?" he asked Angie. "Would you get kicked out of the bridal party?"

"Oh, if only," she said as she pulled from his grasp.

Cole studied Angie. "You're really not enjoying this wedding."

"I have to deal with that," she said, gesturing at Brittany, "and I have spent way too much money on the dress. Brittany also expects us to attend all these events. I've been to six wedding showers. Six! I don't think I can take much more."

"You can't miss anything?" An idea started to form.

"Not one! Which is why I had to take off work for the next week." She stopped and took a long, deep breath then released it. "I shouldn't complain. This is Patrick's wedding and I'm glad he wants me to be part of it."

"But?" he asked as they walked to the exit.

"This wedding is a train wreck and nothing is going to stop it."

"Do you want it to stop?" Was she worried about her

friend? Did she feel the need to take matters into her own hands? No, he discarded that idea immediately. That was not Angie's idea of friendship.

"I would never sabotage a wedding— Wait." She whirled around and looked at him. Her eyes narrowed as she considered the meaning behind his question. "Do you think I tried?"

"No." He'd always admired Angie's loyalty to her friends and family. She tried to be supportive even if she didn't understand their choices.

"Because there has been one setback after the next now that I think about it. So many...but I've been helping to fix the problems. Patrick wants Brittany to have the perfect wedding and I'm doing everything I can."

Cole raised his hands in surrender. "I believe you."

She pointed her finger at him. "And if you think I had something to do with Heidi's accident—"

"Whoa! It never crossed my mind. I'm your alibi, remember?"

Angie poked at his chest. "I want to get this wedding over and done with. That's all."

"That's not surprising since you have to go to every event." He needed that kind of access if he was going to find out more about Heidi and her accident.

"Weddings used to be so simple," Angie said as she continued walking. "When I get married, it's going to be on a beach with a few friends and a minister. Shoes optional."

Cole felt the weight of regret settle in his chest when he heard those words. *When* she got married. Did she have someone in mind or was this in theory? All he knew was that he wasn't part of those plans.

Angie dipped her head as if she were embarrassed for mentioning her ideal wedding to an ex. "I should get going," she said, awkwardly motioning at the door. "I hope your undercover work goes well."

"Thanks," he said gruffly. "You need a ride?"

"No, I'm on the party bus," she said as she moved backward. Her steps were slow, as if she wanted to say something more.

"Angie?" Cole hesitated. He wasn't sure if he should do this. If he should say anything. If he had any other option, he wouldn't pursue this.

She kept walking backward. "Yeah?"

He shifted from one foot to the other. This was probably a bad idea. "I know we didn't end well and I'm really sorry about that, but…"

She stopped walking. "Yeah?"

"I need to get into the wedding." He said the words in a rush. "Are you going with anyone?"

4

"THE NERVE OF that man," Angie muttered to herself. "Did he think I would jump at the chance to take him?" He most likely did. She had never denied him anything in the past.

Angie blew out a puff of air as she ran around the empty high school track. It was a cold and damp morning. The evergreen trees, spindly and clustered together, did nothing to stop the breeze as the sun weakly shone through the haze of clouds. She splashed through the puddles from last night's rain and kept moving.

Most people would be reluctant to get out of bed on this kind of day. She had wanted to toss the covers over her head and act like last night didn't happen. Push away the memory of Heidi injured and unconscious. Forget about Brittany and her demands. Erase Cole completely out of her mind.

Seeing Cole Foster last night had left her unsettled. Every time she tried to sleep, her fragmented dreams were about him, bare-chested and wearing leather pants. Only this time, she boldly touched his muscular body. In her dreams, she encouraged him for more. She wasn't afraid to take charge.

Angie clenched her teeth and pumped her arms and legs harder. What was it about that man? When she had been with him, she'd felt like she could ask for anything. Try everything. But she had gone too far. Deep down, she must have known. She had held back from exploring her fantasies until she felt secure in the relationship. But it didn't matter how long she waited. He still ran.

She thought he was different from the other guys. She heard enough boasting to know the men in her world liked their women clingy and submissive. She couldn't be like that. She was forthright and a little impatient, but she was never aggressive in bed until she was with Cole. She didn't ask for anything she wouldn't give to him.

But apparently he didn't like a strong and powerful woman in bed. A woman who made it very clear how much she wanted him and what she wanted from him. She had felt safe but excited. She trusted he wouldn't judge her, wouldn't think less of her. When she had looked into his eyes, she felt like a goddess. But she had been wrong. She had mistaken adoration with intimidation. She had scared him off.

She had learned her lesson. Next time, she would allow the man to take the lead. From now on she would keep her fantasies to herself.

If she wanted to feel strong and powerful, she'd focus on other parts of her life. Like her job and on the track. There she would be encouraged to push herself to the limits. There she could shine.

Angie rounded the bend and saw someone standing at the gate that led to the parking lot. Her steps faltered when she recognized the car parked next to hers. Her heart kicked against her ribs when she saw that it was Cole waiting for her.

Why was this happening? Angie's chest tightened at the sight of him. She hadn't seen him for a year and thought he had moved out of Seattle. They had never crossed paths since he returned. Now she'd seen him twice in two days. She wasn't sure if she was ready to deal with him again. How often would she look at him and think of the broken dreams and the ruined promise of a future together?

And it wasn't fair, she decided as she maintained her pace. Cole still had the ability to make her pulse skip hard. While she was expected to put effort in her appearance, Cole could throw on some clothes and still manage to look sexy.

Her gaze traveled down the length of his body. The blue buttoned-down shirt skimmed his lean, muscular chest and strong arms. He had incredible strength but he could still gently embrace her. Her gaze lowered and she noticed his faded jeans that emphasized his powerful legs. She always admired how he moved with lethal grace, yet she could outrun him.

She had always been attracted to his mix of force and restraint. He liked to dress casually but had a commanding presence. He spoke with authority in his low, husky voice. Her heart would do a slow flip whenever she saw a twinkle in his dark blue eyes or a curve of a smile on his stern mouth.

As she got closer, she saw his serious expression. The lines on his tired face were deep. It looked as if he hadn't slept.

No, she wasn't going to feel sorry. It wasn't her job to worry or look after him. She wasn't his girlfriend anymore. She didn't want to see him. Feel anything for him. She felt too raw, too unprepared.

But she couldn't avoid him. She had a few more laps to go, but she knew she wouldn't be able to concentrate with him watching her. If she ignored him here, he would keep at it until she listened. She used to like his persistence. Now, it was just annoying. She knew it was better to get this over and done with.

Angie slowed down and walked to the gate. Her legs were burning and shaking. Sweat glistened on her skin and dampened her gray tank top. Her hair was coming out of the ponytail and she brushed off a few tendrils from her flushed face.

She felt his gaze on her. Her top and shorts felt too small. Her skin tingled and she suddenly didn't know what to do with her hands. She wanted to cross her arms and hide her small breasts. She felt exposed.

She wasn't sure why she felt this way. Cole no longer cared. Heck, at one time she thought he found her sexy. That only showed how delusional she truly was.

Resisting the urge to pull on a jacket or sweatpants, Angie grabbed onto the chain-link fence and started her cooling-down routine. "You're up early."

"I haven't gone to bed," he said quietly as he watched her stretch her legs. "I've been at the hospital."

"I see." She bent down and hesitated when she felt Cole's gaze linger on her legs. "How is Heidi?"

"I'm told she's awake," he said gruffly. "I can't get much information because I'm not a friend or next of kin."

Angie grabbed her foot with one hand and slowly raised her leg behind her. She immediately realized her mistake. She wanted to stretch her quadriceps, but it required her to thrust her chest out. Her nipples tightened and her breasts felt full and heavy. She glanced at Cole just as he dragged his gaze from her breasts to her face. She abruptly looked away.

"Why are you here?" she asked as she dropped her leg. She could skip her cooling-down routine for today. "You're not dressed for a run."

"I need your help." He reached out and offered her the water bottle she had placed next to the gate. "Heidi's family in California hired me to track her down. I've done that and I informed my clients about what happened."

"What does that have to do with me?" she asked. She grabbed the water bottle, careful not to graze her fingers against his.

"I have to find out what caused the accident. She had a wild lifestyle a while back. Her family wants to know if she's still into that. If they need to get her some help."

"I don't know anything about Heidi," she reminded him as she took a sip. Her throat didn't seem to want to cooperate as Cole watched her drink. She wiped the water away from her mouth with the back of her hand. "I don't think I can help."

"You have access," he pointed out.

She glared at him. "Is this about you going to the wedding? I already said no." She didn't even have to think about it. The word had fallen from her lips. She had been stunned by his request. How could he ask her on a date—even a fake one—when he had broken her heart? Didn't he have any feelings?

"I need more than a wedding invite," he explained. "I need total access. The rehearsal dinner. Behind the scenes."

"It's not necessary." Angie shook her head and

started for her car. "Heidi may be out of the wedding, period. She has a head injury."

"But the people at the bachelorette party would be there," he said softly.

She stopped and turned. "You don't think it was an accident."

"It could be an accident. The police think so, and I haven't seen any information about her blood alcohol level," he admitted. "I think someone may have tried to hurt Heidi. It probably had something to do with her private life. I just don't know how they did it."

"Private life?" She thought that was an odd choice of words and she thought about the other comments he'd made about Heidi. She lifted her chin when she realized what he was trying not to say. "You mean drugs. That's why you asked if she was on something."

His eyes widened with admiration. "Good catch. I don't know if she's still using."

She pursed her lips as she tried to remember how Heidi had acted over the past few days. "I haven't seen any signs of it."

"You weren't looking for signs, but maybe if I hung around while you were preparing for the wedding…" he said hopefully as he let his words trail off.

Angie sighed and crossed her arms. "Why do you have to drag me into this?"

"Why won't you let me be your date?" he countered.

"I think it's obvious." It didn't matter if it was a pretend date. Spending a day with Cole would remind her of what she once had with him. What she had lost.

Cole's jaw tightened. "Are you taking someone else?"

She went still. Angie would love to lie and avoid any

discussion on her nonexistent love life. But it wouldn't take much for him to find out the truth. "No."

His blue eyes darkened. "Will someone get jealous if you take me?" he asked stiffly.

She wanted to scoff at the suggestion. "No."

He spread his arms out. "Then what's the problem?"

He didn't get it. How was that possible? For a private detective, Cole Foster was oblivious. "I don't have to give you a reason." She turned and marched to her car.

"Come on, Angie," he said right behind her.

"After all," she said, "you didn't give me a reason why you broke up with me."

"Is that what this is all about?" His voice rose with incredulity. "I told you why I needed to break up with you."

"You weren't ready for a relationship." She yanked her car door open. "It's you, not me." She threw the water bottle into the backseat with more force than necessary. "Something about how I deserved better."

"You do," he said quietly.

She wasn't going to fall for the sincerity in his voice. No, what Cole really meant was that *he* deserved better. "Are you dating anyone?" she asked huskily as the emotions clawed her throat. "Wouldn't she be upset if you started hanging around your ex? Or would she understand that it was just for an assignment?"

"There hasn't been anyone since you."

Angie didn't realize how much she needed to hear those words until he had spoken them. If he'd been in a relationship with someone else, it would have destroyed her. "I find that hard to believe," she said hoarsely.

"It's true." He took a step closer. She took a step back and bumped up against her car. "I've spent all my time and energy building up my agency."

"And what's up with that?" she asked, her voice rising. "Not once did you talk to me about having your own business. You were passionate about what you did. About working with Missing Persons."

"It's still what I do," he said, his eyes sparking with annoyance. It was clear he didn't want to discuss it. "My agency specializes in tracing people. Reuniting families."

"I thought everything was fine and then it was like you changed overnight." And it wasn't easy to ignore when his abrupt change occurred. It was right after she lowered her guard. Once she started taking charge in the bedroom.

Her face burned as she remembered that. She had felt sexy and desirable. Strong and assertive. She thought Cole loved it. That he wanted her to reveal this side she didn't share with anyone else. Those moments had been special. Intimate.

She had only been fooling herself. Seeing what she wanted to see. She thought they were solid as a couple, but she was blindsided when he dumped her two weeks later. He had walked away, saying he couldn't give her what she needed.

But what he really meant was that she was undesirable. Unwanted. Her fantasies were not his. She couldn't give him what he needed. She had given him everything but she hadn't been good enough.

"I didn't mean to hurt you." His whisper was heavy with regret.

She straightened up and offered a tight smile. "I'm over it," she lied. "I just thought you were different from the other guys."

Cole frowned. "What do you mean by that?"

"That you weren't in it for the challenge." What a

few men had tried to do in the past. To take on Angie Lawson. Soften her up and tame the tomboy.

COLE TOOK A step back and stared at Angie. "You think I dated you because I like a challenge?"

Angie was a challenge, all right. She was stubborn and impatient. Independent almost to a fault. She was brazen but he also saw the insecurities she tried to hide.

"I don't know why and I don't care," she declared. "All I know is that I'm not going to put myself through that again."

"Angie, our time together meant a lot to me. I can't tell you how difficult it was to leave you." It had been the hardest thing for him to do, but it had been necessary. He had started to think he could be with Angie forever. That she could fall in love with him. But that was a fantasy. Even if he tried harder and tried to be better, he wasn't worthy of love. His family had proven that to him years ago.

Cole stepped away from Angie and looked down. He didn't want her to see the struggle in his eyes. "Angie, it's very hard for me to ask, but I need your help."

He felt her hesitation. She was the kind of woman who automatically offered her help, but it was different now. He knew how awkward it was to offer help to someone who had once discarded you.

"You were always there when I needed you." He hated how his voice cracked. Hated how much her loyalty had meant to him. "And I was there for you."

"We were a couple then," she said softly.

"You are still very important to me." She was the most important person in his life, but he couldn't tell her that. Angie wouldn't believe him, anyway.

"So important that you couldn't stay in touch?" she asked bitterly.

He dragged his gaze to meet hers. Staying in touch would have been a constant reminder of what he couldn't have. "I thought a clean break would be best. It hasn't been easy for me, either. It still isn't."

"And you think that being my date for the wedding will make it better?"

"No, but I think we're at a point where we can be friendly with each other. Do you really want to deal with that bride on your own? Think of me as backup."

"She is unbearable," she said as she considered his suggestion. "It would be nice to show up with a stripper boyfriend."

He jerked back. "Say what?"

"Most of the wedding guests will think that you're a stripper." Angie bit her lip as she tried to contain her smile. "Patrick and some of the other guys will know the truth but I could tell them that our breakup sent you into a tailspin."

He had crashed and burned once he left Angie. It had taken him nearly a year to get back on his feet. "You want me to continue the role as a stripper?"

"Why not? You're the one who started it. And no one would question my sudden wedding date. After all, you showed me special attention last night. Thanks for that."

He ignored her sarcasm. "You're really considering this?"

"Brittany is going to have a fit that I'm bringing a date at such late notice." She grimaced as if she were imagining the bride's reaction. "I'll talk to Cheryl, her assistant. She's in charge of the details."

"Think you can get me into Heidi's room today?"

He knew he was already pushing her, but he was running against the clock. If he didn't get answers in the next few days, chances were he never would.

"I was going to visit her today after Brittany's meeting," she revealed reluctantly. "I'll meet you at the hospital and we'll go in together."

"Thank you," he said. He wasn't sure if the relief he felt was because he could move forward with his assignment or because Angie was on his side once more.

Angie gave a sharp nod and got into her car. "By the way, my stripper boyfriend is totally into me," she said. "He can't believe his luck that he landed me."

"I can do that." He wouldn't even have to pretend. He had felt that way since she had accepted his invitation for a first date. He had no idea what he did to convince her and often felt he was living on borrowed time. He knew someday she would wake up and see she could do much better than him.

"But I'm not really into him," Angie warned Cole. "Everyone would get suspicious if I was all clingy and affectionate."

Especially since she didn't act that way in public, Cole thought. But when they had been alone, she was very demonstrative and explicit in her requests. "So it's only physical attraction?" he teased.

She grinned. "Yeah, something like that."

"Then that will be our cover. By the end of today, everyone will think we're having a red-hot but brief reunion," he promised. It had to be short-term for his sanity. One touch from her and he'd want another. One kiss and he wouldn't stop. Unless this had a predetermined end date, he'd start to believe he had another chance. He'd forget that she never loved him—couldn't love him—in the first place.

"A wild fling?" Her smile disappeared. "No one will believe that."

"They will." Because he was going to make the most of this temporary affair. "I guarantee it."

5

"THIS WAS A bad idea." Angie felt her ponytail swing against her shoulders as she strode down the hospital corridor. She was nervous and it showed. She took a deep breath and gripped the flower arrangement tighter.

"Don't back out on me now." Cole draped his arm around her shoulder.

A sense of longing crashed through her unexpectedly and she tried not to react. It had been common for Cole to touch or hold her whenever they were together. She shouldn't be so surprised.

"Oh, are we pretending to be a couple already?" she asked lightly as she struggled with the opposing needs to shake off his touch and to curl into his body. "Heidi can't see us from here."

"You don't start pretending the minute you walk into the room," he explained. "You assume the role as soon as possible. And you never know whom you're going to bump into on the way. What if we see someone from the bridal party?"

Angie pressed her lips together. Cole always had an

answer for everything, but she didn't think this was going to work. "No one will believe this."

"That we're together?" He stopped and looked down at her, his arm cradling her closer. "No one questioned it when we were dating."

Was he kidding? His friends probably didn't ask or care. She wished she had been so lucky. Her relatives teased her about how opposites attract. Her female clients asked if she used any sexual expertise in grabbing Cole's attention. One acquaintance had asked why Cole was dating her when he could have any woman.

She guessed no one dared to ask Cole those questions. Lucky him. "I mean that no one would think I would hook up with a stripper."

It didn't help that she had done nothing different with her appearance. Angie knew she should have worn something suggestive or pretty. She winced at the thought. Instead she wore her favorite standbys. The white long-sleeve T-shirt and black track pants were comfortable and her running shoes were top-of-the-line.

She should have given her appearance more thought. After all, she was going to stand next to Cole Foster, whose masculine beauty was emphasized in a blue henley shirt and jeans. Most guys in Seattle wore that combination, but for some reason, Cole stood out in the crowd. It wasn't just her opinion. She had seen more than one person in the hall give him a flirtatious glance.

"But it's not unreasonable that you would backslide," he argued. "Ex sex happens more than you think. Why do you think they give it a name?"

Ex sex. She didn't like that label. It made something that was so emotional into something very casual. She imagined most people had sex with their ex because it would offer some familiarity and comfort. She never had that with Cole. When they were together it had been an exciting roller-coaster ride.

Sometimes the intimacy they had shared felt risky. There were moments that had changed her and made her see Cole differently. Those were the times when she felt they had formed a stronger bond. Backsliding wouldn't let her recapture those life-transforming experiences.

She stumbled to a stop and pretended that she was reading the room numbers. Why was she thinking about that? They weren't backsliding. Cole had no interest in having sex with her. If she responded to any of his gestures or touches, then she would be in trouble. She felt jittery and alive next to him. She was very aware of his clean, masculine scent, how warm and large his hand felt against her shoulder.

"Okay, Heidi's room is over there." She pointed at the door across the hall. "Ready?"

"Yes." He squeezed her arm and drew her closer. "Just follow my lead."

"Wait a second. Let me do the talking," she suggested. "It would look weird if you started asking questions."

Cole showed no expression but she felt the tension in his body. Did he think she would mess up? Or was it hard for him to give up any control in his case? He obviously didn't like it if she took charge in or out of bed.

He nodded. "Fine."

"Really?" She wasn't expecting him to yield. But then, he had surrendered quickly in bed and then she paid for it weeks later. "Are you sure?"

"Yes, absolutely. She'll talk to you because she knows you."

"Okay, let's do this." Angie thrust out her chin and walked out of Cole's embrace. She knew he wanted to enter as a loving couple, but that would distract her. It was bad enough that she already felt the loss of his touch. That bothered her. A year without Cole and she was craving for him more than ever.

Angie knocked on the door and peered inside the room. "Heidi? Do you feel up for visitors?"

Heidi's hands flew to her face. "Oh, I look horrible."

"No, not at all," Angie insisted. It was the truth. The woman's short hair was ruffled and her face was pale, but she was still stunning. The hospital gown did nothing to detract from her fragile beauty.

"Who's that?" Heidi asked as Angie set the bouquet of flowers on the bedside table. "Wait a second, you look familiar."

"This is Cole." She only paused for a second before she hooked her arm around his waist and leaned into his body. It felt as good as she remembered. "He was one of the strippers last night."

"You two got together last night?" Heidi stared at Angie, her mouth hanging open with shock. "You landed a stripper? *You* did?"

Angie cast an I-told-you so look at Cole. He seemed more confused by Heidi's reaction than anything. "Well, last night was crazy," she said as she returned her attention to Heidi. "Don't you remember?"

Heidi pressed her hand against her head. "No. A lot of it is fuzzy."

"I don't remember you drinking that much," she said. She felt awkward and didn't know how Heidi would respond. But if there was one thing Angie knew about being a personal trainer, she always broached difficult topics head-on.

Cole reached up and wrapped his finger around the end of her ponytail. She bit her lip, remembering the bite of pressure when he tugged her hair. He did it to get her attention, either to tease or to warn. She'd almost forgotten how they had silently communicated.

"I don't drink. All those calories, you know?" she said in a rush. "It's either juice or water."

"I suggest that to my clients all the time," Angie murmured. Heidi hadn't been drinking? That threw out the theory that she was too drunk to stand. Or was the maid of honor lying? She couldn't remember what Heidi had been drinking. She hadn't paid any attention.

Angie wasn't sure if she could trust Heidi's answer. Avoiding calories was something she expected from Heidi, but it didn't ring true. Angie also remembered the spilled drink next to Heidi when they had placed her in the recovery position.

Angie jumped a little when she felt Cole's fingertips trail down her spine. "Do you know when you'll get out of here?" she asked in a rush.

"I'm under observation. I'm told it's something they have to do for head injuries." Heidi bit her lip as if she were reluctant to say something. "But the strangest thing happened."

"Oh? What?" Angie's breath caught in her throat as Cole dragged his fingers up and down her back. Did he think it was comforting? She was breathing fast as her entire world centered on the gentle caress of his fingertips.

"My parents called to see if I was okay," Heidi said, her eyes wide as she revealed the news. "I haven't talked to them in years. Not since they kicked me out of the family after I...well, there was a time during college when I was out of control. I thought they didn't want to have anything to do with me. I didn't contact them even after I got my life back on track because I thought they gave up on me. I have no idea how they found out where I was or what happened to me."

"I guess they've always been looking out for you," Cole said quietly. "They just needed a reason to reach out."

As Heidi leaned back on her pillow to consider what he said, Angie looked up at Cole and gave him a warning glare. "Well, Heidi, we should go so you can get some rest. I hope you'll still be at the wedding."

Heidi's mouth trembled. "The doctors don't think that will be possible." Tears welled up in her eyes. "I feel terrible about letting Brittany down. She's never going to forgive me."

"Don't worry about her. She—" Angie forgot what she was about to say as she felt Cole's hand glide against the curve of her hip. She had to get out of here before she bucked against his touch. "This wasn't your fault."

"Thanks," Heidi said as she watched Angie move away from Cole and take a few steps for the door. "And thanks for the flowers."

"You're welcome. Get better soon!" Angie hurried out of the room but she couldn't escape. She didn't have to look back to know that Cole was right behind her.

COLE SAID A quick goodbye to Heidi and then followed Angie. She was moving fast, almost breaking into a run. He was tempted to reach out and grab her ponytail. Wrap it around his hand and hold her still.

He caught up with her several rooms down and blocked her path. "What's the rush?"

She looked over her shoulder as if she were focused on a destination. "I had to get out of there before you blew your cover."

She thought he was blowing their cover? He wasn't the one who had bolted. He would have liked to have asked a few more questions but the opportunity was gone. He had to admit, though, that Angie's questions were helpful. She did well for her first interrogation. "We were very convincing."

Angie rolled her eyes and leaned against the wall. "First you talked about the parents as if you had intimate knowledge of the situation," she whispered fiercely. "And then you went a little overboard with the public displays of affection."

Was that why she abruptly ended the interview? Was his touch unbearable to her now? He wanted to stroke her skin and curl her against his side. He wished she would respond by boldly touching him, publicly acknowledging his claim with a simple gesture or touch. Yet she had to get away from him.

Or was it the opposite? Did she still like it when he held her? Was she holding back because this was supposed to be all pretend? It didn't feel pretend to him. Did she also think it felt too much like the real thing? He tried to tamp down the hope billowing inside him.

"You were never this touchy-feely when we were together," she complained.

"Then you are remembering it wrong." Still, she may have a point. In the past, one touch or one look held the promise of something more. Now that wasn't the case and who knew how many chances he would get to hold her like this? This could be his only opportunity to relive these moments.

Angie smoothed her hand over her hair and tilted her head back. "It's too bad Heidi didn't have a lot of information."

"But she did. She said she wasn't drinking."

"Of course she's going to say that," Angie argued. "She doesn't want Brittany mad at her. The fact is there was a spilled martini next to her."

"It doesn't mean she had any of that in her system." He rested his arm against the wall and looked down at Angie. "I really wish I could get my hands on her blood test."

"Good luck with that." Angie said. "I don't know much about investigations but I know the medical staff will protect Heidi's privacy. No one is going to give it to you."

Cole saw a movement from the corner of his eye. "Here comes the other bridesmaid. Let's sell this relationship once and for all."

She gave him a wary look. "What do you have in mind?"

"Just this." He lowered his head and claimed her mouth with his.

Cole knew he was playing with fire. He only intended to skim her lips. But he found that he couldn't pull away. He needed another kiss and then another. He traced her full, soft lips with the tip of his tongue.

Angie opened her mouth and drew him in. Triumph swept through him. He cupped her jaw with both hands and leaned in. She kissed him as if she couldn't get enough of him. Excitement pulsed through Cole as Angie grabbed his shirt and pulled him closer.

"Hey, you two," Robin said loudly. "Get a room."

Cole wrenched away from Angie. Damn it, he thought as he gulped for air. He forgot. He forgot where they were and why they were kissing. Most of all, he forgot that kissing Angie was like sharing a piece of his soul.

"Oh, it's you from last night." Robin gave a sly smile to Angie and tapped her arm with the box of chocolates she held in her hand. "Good for you. I thought the two of you would hit it off."

"What are you doing here, Robin?" Angie asked as she pushed away from the wall. "I thought you didn't like Heidi."

Cole was suddenly taken aback. He knew from surveillance that Robin and Heidi didn't get along, but he didn't think Angie would say it so bluntly. Yet Robin didn't seem to mind.

"Eh," she said and gave a shrug. "The best way to describe it is that we're frenemies."

This was a person he needed to speak to. Robin knew Heidi from the past and could give him some insight. "The doctor just went in to check on Heidi," Cole lied. "It may be a while. Let's get some coffee while we wait. My treat."

"Lead the way," Robin said.

By the time Cole brought the drinks to their table in the café, he noticed that Robin was relaxed and talkative. He was glad Angie didn't start asking questions right away. It surprised him that Angie knew how to approach Robin. The two women were very different. Robin wore impractical heels, skintight jeans and a fussy pink blouse that looked like an explosion of ruffles on her chest. He preferred Angie's casual look and natural beauty.

When Cole gave Angie her drink, Robin noticed

the complicated order written on the disposable coffee cup. "You guys met last night and he already knows your coffee order?"

Angie's mouth opened and closed. She wasn't sure what to say. Cole knew that they had to stick close to the truth if they wanted this ruse to work. "I dated Angie in the past."

"So he is your ex-boyfriend! That explains why you're hanging around during an obligatory hospital visit." She gave Cole a thorough look. "Most one-night stands would find an excuse to get out of it."

"I wasn't ready for the day to end," Cole said as he rested his arm along the back of Angie's chair. "I had to convince her to bring me along."

"Interesting." She studied Angie with narrowed eyes. "I never thought Angie had that kind of pull."

Cole frowned. Why did these women think he wouldn't be interested in Angie? Were they blind? Angie was the most sensual woman he knew. He could see it in every move, every smile.

"Want something to eat?" Angie suddenly asked, obviously determined to change the subject. "Danish?"

"No thanks." She held her hand up. "Food allergies."

Angie rested her arms on the table and leaned forward. "So what's this about you and Heidi being frenemies? Was it because of her drug use?"

Cole reached up and grabbed the tip of her ponytail. He gave it a sharp tug and hoped she understood his message. There were times when Angie's straightforward attitude was a disadvantage. She couldn't bulldoze her way into delicate discussions.

Cole could see Robin look at Angie with caution. "How do you know about that?"

Angie shrugged. "I've heard the rumors."

Robin sighed and made a face. "Brittany could never keep a secret." She looked around the café before she bent forward and spoke softly. "Yeah, Heidi made my life miserable in college. The lying, the stealing. I thought she had cleaned up, but then she winds up in the hospital after a drunken night. I guess I was wrong."

"Sounds like a lot of drama," Angie said sympathetically. "I can't imagine Brittany putting up with that."

"She wouldn't normally, but Heidi was more a groupie than a friend. Brittany is always on the lookout to add to her entourage."

Angie pursed her lips. "She wanted a minion."

Cole gave another tug on Angie's ponytail. Angie silently responded by pulling her hair over her shoulder so he couldn't reach it. He flexed his fingers and held back.

He wished he could interrupt the conversation. Angie was getting Robin to talk but she was skating on thin ice. It was like watching someone on a tightrope. One wrong word and Robin would stop talking. Or worse, she would notice their interest in Heidi.

When he first took on this case, Heidi's family only wanted to locate her. He had been able to track her down so easily that he wondered if the family had even tried. Once he gave the information to his clients, he soon realized that finding her was only the beginning. What they really wanted from him was to do surveillance. He was supposed to follow Heidi and see if she was still having trouble with drugs and alcohol.

He didn't have a definitive answer and he needed to be sure before he gave his report. What if the family didn't welcome Heidi back because they didn't like the answer? Would they only repair the relationship if Heidi met certain conditions?

He needed to know the truth. A lot was at stake. Unfortunately, the investigation wasn't going as planned. The people who knew Heidi best only seemed to remember how she used to be. They gave no insight into her life today.

"Brittany knew that Heidi would put up with a lot of crap to be friends," Robin explained as she took a sip of her coffee. "I think Heidi wanted to be part of everything."

"That's why she agreed to be maid of honor even though she knew it was going to be an ordeal." Angie tapped her hand on the table. "I wondered why anyone would willingly take on that role. Especially after getting that very demanding email that listed all of Brittany's expectations."

"Oh, I bet Heidi jumped at the offer," Robin said with feeling. "If anyone should be maid of honor, it should have been me. I'm the closest sorority sister to Brittany."

Angie clucked her tongue. "You should have gotten the honor."

Cole winced when he heard Angie's sarcastic emphasis on the word *honor,* but Robin didn't seem to clue in. He was beginning to wonder what had happened in the past year that made Angie bitter about weddings.

"I should have," Robin agreed, "but I don't take orders very well. Heidi will do anything for Brittany and she knows it."

Angie nodded slowly. "I'm sure that's it."

"I should go see Heidi before visiting hours are up. Thanks for the coffee," Robin told Cole before she gave him a speculative look. "Will you be at the wedding?"

"Yes, I insisted."

"Interesting." Robin seemed confused as she cast a look at Angie before returning her attention to him. "Save a dance for me," Robin said before she strode away.

Cole waited until she left the café before he spoke to Angie. "That was a close call," he said, his gaze still on the doorway.

"You mean about Heidi's past?" Angie asked. "It could have gone badly, but Robin assumes Brittany said something. She won't track it back to you."

He hoped that was the case, but he wasn't sure how much Robin gossiped. She could relay everything to whomever would listen, or she might be the kind of person who held back pertinent information until she found the right—and most damaging—moment. "Don't you find it strange that Robin isn't maid of honor?"

"No," Angie said as she sipped her coffee. "Robin may feel she's closest to Brittany, but that doesn't mean Brittany feels the same."

"True." But something didn't quite add up. He felt like he was missing something.

"Is everything okay?" Angie set her cup down and watched him carefully. "What are you thinking about? It doesn't look good."

He shoved his hand through his hair and sighed with frustration. "There's something about last night but I can't remember."

Angie reached out and patted his arm. "You'll get it."

He wanted to cover her hand with his. Keep her there and soak in her encouragement. Angie always made him feel like he could accomplish almost anything if he worked hard for it. "Thanks for meeting me here. I appreciate it."

She awkwardly drew her hand away. "You're welcome," she mumbled as she took a hasty sip of her drink.

"You were very good at getting information out of the bridesmaids," he said and watched Angie blush from his praise.

"I'd like to take all the credit, but Heidi and Robin love to talk about themselves and each other."

"It's more than that," he insisted. "It's like you understand the feminine psyche."

Angie pressed her lips together and her mood shifted subtly. "I should hope so," she said slowly. "I *am* a woman."

He was fully and painfully aware of that. "You know what I mean."

"Yes." She nodded, then rolled her shoulders back and thrust out her chin. "You're amazed that someone like me can understand how a woman thinks."

"That's not what I said at all. It's just that you're nothing like those women." When she was around, he was oblivious to anyone else.

"That's true." Angie suddenly stood up. Her face was pale and expressionless, as if she wore a mask. "I need to get going."

Did he say something wrong? He was trying to compliment her but he made a mess out of it. "What's the rush?"

"Personal stuff," she said, avoiding eye contact. "I'll see you around. Thanks for the kiss, er...coffee."

"It was my pleasure," he said. "Always."

6

"I'M OPEN!" ANGIE waved her hands in the air as she tried to get her basketball partner's attention. Tim, her opponent, bumped into her. Angie pushed back. The game was aggressive and close. She'd already gotten an elbow in the face during a jump ball. She gave as good as she got.

Angie was glad she didn't skip her weekly game. She needed the familiar sight of the dark green trees, the long stretches of thick grassy lawns and the faded basketball courts. She found comfort in watching the seniors on their benches, the kids running free and even the dog walkers, who tried to balance leashes, cell phones and coffee cups with only two hands. But most of all, she enjoyed being with her real friends. This was where she belonged.

She needed this, Angie decided as she wiped her sweaty hands against her long basketball shorts. It was good to take a break from dress fittings and bridesmaid meetings. And Cole. She definitely needed a break from him.

Angie frowned. She hadn't heard from him since the

day before, at the hospital. That was good. That was what she wanted. It took her a year to get over that guy and she didn't want to go through another Cole detox.

But how was she going to forget that kiss? Angie bit her lip as she fought back the memory of Cole's mouth against hers. The kiss started out soft and teasing. She tried to hold back but then his kiss grew demanding. Or maybe she had demanded more. There was a moment when she wasn't sure who was in charge. She had tried to resist, but his kisses were better than she remembered. His touch still excited her. She never responded as wildly with another man.

Tim blocked her and Angie shook her head, trying to get her head back into the game. She dodged and Tim tried to grab her oversize shirt but failed. She wasn't as tall as her basketball buddies, but she made up for it with speed. "C'mon, Steve!" she yelled as she ran next to the basket. "Give it to me."

"I'd throw it to you," Steve said as he tried to set up a difficult shot from the three-point line, "but I'm afraid you'll break a nail."

Angie smiled as the other guys laughed. "Why don't you come a little closer and I'll show you how strong my nails are."

"Yeah, right— Hey!" Steven complained as Patrick stole the basketball. "Foul!"

Angie watched as her best friend sank the ball in the basket. She groaned and dropped her shoulders in disappointment. "Steve, next time throw me the ball."

"It's much more fun teasing you," he said.

"Be careful," Angie warned. "You and I are walking together at the end of the wedding. I just may trip you."

Steve's eyes widened with horror. "You wouldn't dare."

She pushed her finger against his chest. "Don't tempt me."

"You don't have anything to worry about," Tim told Steve. "Angie has to wear high heels. She'll be too busy clinging onto you, never mind trying to trip you."

"Clinging? Not going to happen," Angie insisted as she made a face. "I've worn heels before."

Tim and Steve gave each other a look of disbelief. "She's going to take the whole procession down," Steve predicted to Tim. "It'll be one big pileup."

"A stack of dominos," Tim decided.

"I'm not listening." She pressed her hands over her ears. "La-la-la-la." She wouldn't tell them that the heels were a concern. She actually followed her mother's advice and had been practicing walking in her bridesmaid shoes. They were taller than anything she'd worn and she wasn't as graceful as she wished.

"Hey," Patrick said as he bounced the ball to Angie and jerked his head to the park entrance. "Is that Cole Foster?"

Oh, damn. She winced as she slowly turned to where Patrick indicated. Cole was walking through the city park and heading to the basketball courts. Her heart gave a jolt. He was dressed in a hoodie and jeans, warding off the cool Seattle breeze, but she remembered how strong and lean his body felt against hers.

"Yeah, that's him." she answered weakly as pleasure, dark and heavy, settled low in her pelvis. How did he find her? It wasn't as if he would remember her schedule.

Patrick placed his hands on his hips. "What is he doing here?"

"You want us to get rid of him?" Tim offered.

"Uh…no." Angie pressed her palms against the basketball. She dreaded having to tell her friends about Cole. They knew how much she had suffered when Cole left. She didn't talk about it but they had tried to keep life normal for her. They probably wouldn't believe she was back with him, but she couldn't tell them the whole truth. That this was merely pretend. Or at least, it was supposed to be. That kiss sure felt real.

"Really?" Steve asked. "We can do it. It's three of us against one of him."

"No!" she said sharply and gripped the basketball tighter. She knew Cole could handle any situation but she still felt very protective of him. She had worried about him when he had been on the force. Cole's colleagues had told her stories about his heroism. The idea of him hurt or in trouble had plagued her, but she had learned to trust that Cole wouldn't take any unnecessary risks. She had known that his top priority was being with her, safe and sound at the end of the day.

"What's going on?" Tim asked. "You're acting weird."

"I've been meaning to tell you guys." She cleared her throat and spoke quickly. "Cole is my wedding date."

"What?" Steve said in a squawk. "Is this a joke?"

"It's the funniest thing." She gave a nervous laugh and bent her head, concentrating on her dribbling technique. "I bumped into Cole and one thing led to another. And, I, uh…invited him."

"Have you lost your mind?" Patrick asked, his deep voice booming.

"One too many basketballs to the head," Tim muttered.

"You guys, it's fine." She held up a placating hand

as she watched Cole getting closer. "There are no hard feelings."

Patrick shook his head. "Well, *you* may not have them, but we do."

She tossed the basketball to the side and let it bounce away. "Patrick, I swear, do not—"

"Hey." Cole gave a nod as he stepped on the basketball court. She saw the caution flicker in his eyes as he saw her friends form a protective wall in front of her. "Haven't seen you guys for a while."

"Yeah," Tim said as he puffed out his chest. "Not since you dumped Angie and broke her heart."

"Tim!" She tried to step in front of Tim and Steve but they weren't budging.

"Now you're sniffing around her again?" Steve asked. "I don't like the sound of that."

"You have no say in the matter," Angie pointed out.

"I disagree," Steve said. "I don't stand by quietly when someone hurts my friend."

"I'm fine, you guys," Angie repeated. She jumped but couldn't see over their shoulders. "No harm done."

"Are you kidding?" Patrick looked back at her. "Cole played with your head. You don't date. You haven't looked at another guy since."

"Okay! That's enough." She jogged around her friends and held up her hands for them to stop. "I can take over now."

"We got your back," Tim told her. "If he's causing trouble, just let us know."

"Thank you." Angie pulled Cole's sleeve, silently encouraging him to walk away with her. "Ignore them," she said quietly. "They get a little aggressive but it's all show."

"Don't believe that for a second." He looked over his

shoulder and smiled at Tim's posturing. "Those guys would take a punch for you."

"And they know I would take one for them." Angie grimaced when she realized how unfeminine that sounded. If she wanted to remind Cole that she was a woman, then that was not the way to go.

Cole stopped when they were off the basketball court. "Is it true? That you don't date?"

Patrick and his big mouth! Angie felt the heat of embarrassment in her face. "He has a tendency to exaggerate when he's trying to make a point."

Cole looked in her eyes and then abruptly looked away. "I didn't mean to hurt you," he said solemnly.

"Yeah, I know." Angie began to fidget. She didn't want to discuss how he broke her heart or how she'd never be the same. She believed she had found someone who adored her for who she was. She wasn't sure why that wasn't true.

"I had some personal stuff to get through," Cole continued to explain. "I was hurting and the last thing I wanted to do was cause you pain. That's why I broke up with you but it turns out I hurt you, anyway."

"Personal stuff?" Angie asked, crossing her arms. "Too personal that you couldn't share with your girl-friend? I knew you were holding back."

Cole sighed and raked his hand through his hair. "I thought it was best to let you go than to drag you into it."

Angie stepped around him so her friends couldn't see her anger. "You know, you may think that sounds all noble, but it's not. It's an insult. Do you think I'm fragile? That I couldn't have understood or helped you?"

"It wasn't something I could share."

"And something you still don't feel like sharing. I get it." He clearly didn't want to tell her even though it had come between them. Was still between them. Cole was always private but this was too much. "Why are you here?" she asked abruptly. "I'm in the middle of something."

Cole hesitated. "I need a favor," he mumbled.

Angie clenched her jaw and slowly shook her head. She wanted to refuse. Or tell him she would do him the favor only when he confided about his personal problem. Although if she tried that, there was no guarantee that he would tell her the truth.

Maybe her friends were right to form a wall between her and Cole. All he had to do was show up and she got sucked back into his world. She was reluctant to tell him to leave yet she knew that was the smarter move.

But the sooner she helped him, the quicker he would get out of her life. She could stop thinking about him and be able to concentrate on the things that were important to her. "You are going to owe me so big after this wedding. What's the favor?"

Cole squeezed his eyes shut as if he knew he was pushing his luck with her. "I need the invitation list for the bachelorette party."

That wasn't the request she was expecting. "I don't think I can help you with that. I've never seen it and I didn't know many people at the party. Cheryl was in charge of all that."

"Do you think you can get it from her?" Cole asked. "I want to see if anyone else from Heidi's past was at the party. There may have been other sorority sisters who had a grudge against her."

She considered the best way to approach Brittany's assistant with a request. The woman looked sweet and

friendly but Angie had seen during the wedding preparations that Cheryl could be stubborn. "I can call her
or drop by Brittany's office, but I don't even have a
reason to ask for the guest list."

"You'll come up with something." He reached out
and wrapped his fingers around her wrist. "I know it."

She was reluctant to pull away but she was sure he
could feel her racing pulse under his touch. "Your faith
in my abilities is misplaced."

"No way." He gradually brought her close until they
almost touched. "I've seen you finish a marathon when
you had nothing left. I've seen you build your business
from nothing to a success. I've even seen you win an
argument with your mother. You will come up with a
brilliant excuse."

"Fine," she reluctantly agreed. She hated how much
pleasure she felt when she saw his appreciative smile.
"But you're coming with me. If I talk myself into a
corner, you'll have to get me out."

"I'm with you all the way."

Yeah, right. Angie broke from his hold. *We'll see
about that.*

COLE STOOD AT Angie's side as they visited Brittany's
office. The suite was probably as big as his agency but
he still felt claustrophobic. The dark green walls in the
front room made the place feel smaller. The floor was
painted in black-and-white stripes and the bookshelves
were crammed with magazines and catalogs.

He felt like a giant standing next to the delicate furniture. Cole wrinkled his nose and glanced at Angie.
How could she chat effortlessly with the assistant and
not keel over from the headache-inducing scented
candles?

"I'm sorry?" Cheryl asked as she set down a pile of pastel—and probably scented—files. "You want to do what?"

"I want to get a hold of everyone from the bachelorette party and see if they'd like to chip in for a special gift for Brittany," Angie replied with a bright smile. "It would make her feel better, like the bridal spa did. And what with Heidi in the hospital and all. Cole, don't you think Brittany needs a little pampering?"

"Absolutely." But what the heck was a bridal spa? He felt as if he were in a different land, where they spoke a foreign language.

Cheryl gave him a cursory look. It was clear she didn't understand why he was accompanying Angie. It was time to sell the adoring-lover routine but Cole was slightly worried. He had gotten carried away when he kissed Angie the last time and she'd been pushing back ever since. Would she automatically reject his touch?

He had never taken Angie's affection for granted. He always knew that if he reached out his hand she would take it in hers. She knew how to arouse and how to comfort him with a simple touch. She could tease him during the day and at night she held him in her sleep. He'd never felt alone when she was in his life.

Cole hesitated before curling his arm around Angie's waist. He didn't realize he was holding his breath until she instantly leaned into his embrace.

"What's the special gift?" Cheryl asked Angie. She said it with nonchalance, but there was something about her tone. As if she expected Angie to want her approval.

"Uh…it's, uh…" Angie looked up at him.

He saw the flicker of uncertainty in Angie's brown eyes. "For the honeymoon," he stated.

She flashed him a grateful smile. "Yes, a thoughtful gift for their wedding night."

"Something that both the bride and groom will enjoy," he added.

Cheryl chose to ignore him. "That's really sweet of you, Angie, but I can't give out the guest list. A lot of her clients are on there."

"I understand, but—"

He pressed his fingers against Angie's waist. He had done a lot of legwork in his past career to know when someone was going to be helpful or not. No one could persuade Cheryl to hand over that list.

"And I can't let someone they don't know have access to it," Cheryl explained cheerfully, but he heard the firmness in her voice.

"What if I—"

"And, to be honest," Cheryl interrupted with a smile, "I don't think they would appreciate being hit up for more money. It's a great idea, but it could create a negative feeling."

He felt Angie's shoulders slump in defeat. "You're right."

"But if you want to give Brittany a gift for her wedding night, I'll make sure it's in the honeymoon suite." Cheryl rose from behind her desk. Cole knew it was a move to end this meeting.

"Thank you. I'll let you know." She turned to him. "Let's go."

"See you later." He saluted Cheryl with a wave but the woman continued to ignore him.

He opened the door for Angie and she stopped at the threshold. "Cheryl, have there been any updates on Heidi?"

Cheryl pressed her lips. "She's out of the hospital

but she can't be part of the bridal party. Doctor's orders. It's a disaster."

Angie clucked her tongue. "Poor Heidi. She was so looking forward to it."

"I couldn't tell by the way she kept complaining about the work," Cheryl said. "Robin will be maid of honor. Honestly, I don't think she's up for the job."

"Fortunately, Robin and Brittany have you to help," Angie said sincerely.

Cole saw the anger and irritation flash in Cheryl's eyes. "It's overwhelming but I want Brittany to have a perfect wedding."

"Will Heidi be at the ceremony at least?" he asked. He muffled a grunt when Angie dug her elbow in his side.

"She doesn't know yet." Cheryl looked at him with open suspicion. "Why?"

"Just wondering," Angie answered for him. She grabbed his hand and led him out the door.

"Well, that didn't work at all," Angie whispered the minute he closed the door behind them. She let go of his hand once they passed the window to Brittany's office and walked ahead of him to the parking lot.

"It was a long shot. We're working under the assumption that someone tried to hurt Heidi because of the past. As far as we know, the only people who knew her were Brittany, Robin and the sorority sisters who attended the party.

"But why wait and do it in such a public place? And why now?" Angie asked.

"I don't know but I have to find out. This may have something to do with her past, but what if it's about something that's going on in her life now? What if she hasn't changed and her family can't accept that?"

"You're putting too much responsibility on your-self," Angie said. "There is only so much you can do."

"If Heidi gets back together with her family only to get kicked out again, it'll be devastating." He knew what it was like to hope for a reconciliation only to have everything fall apart. To discover that your worst-case scenario was nothing compared to what actually happened. "I want to prevent it. I can if I have enough information."

"You will," Angie promised. "You found Heidi, you did the surveillance and now you're looking into the accident when no one else is. If there is any kind of evidence, you will find it."

"I wonder why Cheryl wouldn't give us the list," he said. "You think she's hiding something?"

"No, that list represents Brittany's business. She has to protect it. I think I would do the same. It took me years to build up my list of clients and I would want to maintain their privacy. Cheryl's just doing her job."

"I wish I had a Cheryl working for me," Cole said. There were times when he could use any help he could get. But the only person he wanted in his corner was Angie. "Except I would want someone that didn't give me the evil eye."

"Ah, you noticed that, too? Maybe she doesn't ap-prove of strippers." She paused as they stepped out onto the parking lot. There was a light drizzle of rain that they ignored as the drops danced on the cars and rippled puddles on the pavement. "I'm sorry I didn't get that list. I should have come up with a better story."

"Hey, it was a good one." Cole wanted to comfort her. He gathered her in his arms and held her close. "We'll come up with something else."

Angie's shoulders stiffened and she stepped out of

his embrace. "Cole, you don't have to act love-struck. No one is watching."

"That's—" He bit back the words as the hurt cut through him. She was right. He had stepped out of line and blurred pretend with reality. "Sorry, Angie. It won't happen again. I promise."

7

COLE LEANED BACK in his chair and stared at the computer screen. He had been trying to write his report on Heidi but he wasn't getting far. All he could think about was Angie.

They were once a good team. It didn't matter if they had been enjoying a night out or had suffered through the worst weekend getaway—they had faced each moment as partners. In the beginning it had made him uncomfortable. He did better alone.

The last people he had relied on were his mom and stepdad. Only their love had been conditional. No matter how much he tried to do better, *be* better, it wasn't good enough. They had deserted him when he needed them the most.

When he was with Angie, he had tried his best. He wanted it so much for them to work. He tried to hide the darkness but she seemed to know and understand. She didn't push, but most importantly, she never pulled away. Even when she saw him at his worst, she was there at his side.

Which was why it stung when Angie pulled out of his arms in the parking lot.

He didn't touch her because he thought someone was watching. He wasn't thinking about his surroundings at all. He had simply longed for the connection they once shared.

It was his fault and he deserved to have her shut him down. He had gotten carried away in the role and slipped back into a time when he could hold her. Show his claim with a possessive touch. But Angie wasn't his anymore.

Cole heard the outer door to his office open. He sat up straight and listened to the door close quietly. That was strange. He didn't get many walk-ins.

"Hello?" The deep male voice echoed in the waiting area.

Cole dragged his hands over his face and sighed before he stood and left his tiny office. He should have known Patrick would not let this matter rest but he didn't feel like dealing with it right now.

"Patrick," he greeted the other man, noticing his wet hair and soaked coat. There were dark patches on Patrick's shoes and jeans that indicated he'd stepped into a deep puddle. What they said was true, Cole decided. No one in Seattle owned an umbrella. "What brings you here?"

He glared at Cole and shook his head as the water sprayed from his drenched hair. "I want some answers."

Cole should have known he wasn't going to get out of this. "Sure. Sit down."

"No, thanks. It won't be necessary." Patrick braced his legs and crossed his arms. "This will be very short."

Cole waited. In the past, he and Patrick tolerated each other. They were both territorial about Angie. It took a while before Cole realized Patrick had no romantic interest in Angie. He never understood that. Angie was the most fascinating and sensual woman he'd ever met but her friends saw her as one of the guys.

At first he thought it was unusual that Angie's closest friends were men. He didn't like it. But he never complained or asked that she didn't hang around those guys. He didn't want to make it a competition, especially since he had a feeling he would lose. It took him a few months before he realized he was being ridiculous.

Unlike the women he had dated in the past, Angie wasn't flirty or suggestive with other men. She didn't want to make him jealous. Instead, she went out of her way to make him feel like he was the most important man in her life.

"Don't mess with Angie and don't mess with this wedding," Patrick warned.

"I don't plan to do either." But his original plan was unraveling quickly. All he wanted to do was find Heidi and determine if she still had a substance abuse problem. Now he was tangled again in Angie's life, resurrecting feelings and struggling between make-believe and reality.

"Brittany really needs this wedding to be perfect," Patrick insisted. He suddenly looked weary. "She is so stressed out that she's breaking out in hives. The last thing I need is for you to bring more drama to the situation."

"Okay." Unlike the rest of the bridal party, the wedding was the least of his concerns. All he wanted was to find out what happened to the maid of honor.

"I don't know why you're back in Angie's life, but I don't like it," he said. "It can only mean trouble."

Cole stood very still. Patrick didn't know the truth.

After what happened on the basketball court, he was sure Angie would tell her best friend the real reason they were together. Did she keep his secret to protect him or to keep Patrick from worrying?

"I'm sure you've discussed this with Angie," Cole said. Was that why Angie pulled away from him? Did Patrick express the many reasons he thought they shouldn't be together? Cole didn't doubt that the list was a long one.

"I did, but she's not listening." He made a face that Cole understood. Angie could be very stubborn. "She always had a soft spot where you were concerned. But I don't. And I'm not going to let you hurt her a second time."

"I don't want to hurt her." Why did everyone think he didn't have her best interest at heart? "I care about her more than anybody."

"And look at where that got her. She was ready to move in with you." Patrick shook his head with disbelief. "She was afraid you'd say no, but she went for it, anyway."

Angie had been nervous? He would never have known. She seemed almost casual when she suggested they move in together. But it had been a big deal for him. He had wanted to jump at the offer but experience taught him to hold back. He made a decision to revisit his past instead and was still reeling from that trip down memory lane.

"And you couldn't get away fast enough." Patrick looked at him with disgust. "I told her it was a bad idea."

"I loved Angie but I couldn't live with her." He realized how that sounded. Angie wasn't the problem; he was. Cole was tempted to explain, but that would require revealing too much. "It would never have worked."

"You loved her?" Patrick gave a harsh bark of laughter. "You have a funny way of showing it."

"It doesn't matter now," Cole said, forcing back the anger. He learned long ago not to show how much someone meant to him. That knowledge would be used against him. "I messed up and she's won't give me another chance. She'll drop me once this wedding is over."

"Good." Patrick's tone was low and emphatic. "She needs to move on and stop listening to the gossip."

Gossip? He couldn't imagine anyone judging Angie. That could only mean he was the subject. "What gossip? Was it about Angie and me?"

"I'm not getting into it." Patrick turned and headed for the door.

"You came here and started this," Cole reminded him. He needed to know what was said to Angie. "What were they saying?"

Patrick faced him and scoffed. "There was some talk about why you broke up with Angie."

His gut twisted. That was impossible. No one knew about his family life around here. They didn't know about his history, but maybe that didn't matter. People made assumptions when they didn't know the truth.

Patrick's gaze slid away. "Rumor was you wanted someone hotter."

Cole slowly blinked. "Excuse me?"

"You wanted a hotter girlfriend. Someone—" he motioned at his chest "—you know. Sexier. Girlier." He dropped his hands. "A lot of people told Angie that she lost you because she wasn't doing enough to keep you interested."

"I... *What?*" How could anyone think that? Angie was fun, sexy and had a wild streak that left him breathless. She was uninhibited in bed and demonstrated a woman could be strong and feminine.

Patrick shrugged and took a few steps to the door. He was clearly uncomfortable with this discussion. "I'm only repeating what I heard. I didn't say I believed it."

"Good, because that is the furthest thing from the truth. Angie is more than beautiful. She's amazing and—"

He held up his hand. "Dude, I really don't want to hear it."

"Why would she think that?" Was it something he said or did? But what? He didn't feel that way about her at all.

"She's been told that crap for years," Patrick said. "Angie's different from the women around here. Always has been. She got teased a lot about that at school until she started kicking ass in sports."

Was that why she was shutting him out? Was it because she believed he was faking his attraction? He thought she complained because it reminded her of their past. Could it be because she felt insecure about her sex appeal?

"And remember," Patrick said, "you didn't hear it from me."

Cole nodded absently, trying to think of a time when Angie had felt shy with him. "And I promise, I'm not going to cause any problems with Angie and the wedding."

"We'll see about that," Patrick muttered as he left the office. "I won't hesitate to kick you out of the church."

"I've been warned." And he deserved to get banned from the ceremony if he tried to sabotage the wedding.

But right now he had more pressing matters. He had to clear up these lies with Angie. Right now. He didn't want her to think for another moment that she wasn't good enough for him.

Didn't she realize that it was the other way around?

COLE STOOD BY Angie's apartment door and flexed his hands. He looked around and counted all of the security features that were lacking in her hallway. He hated that she chose to live in a renovated factory in one of the most run-down neighborhoods. But he had to admit that the old brick building suited her. The large arched windows would welcome the rare sunshine and the oddly shaped studio apartment was the perfect backdrop for her flea-market finds and mismatched furniture.

The only thing that didn't fit in her home, her life, was him. He took a step back, prepared to abandon this idea. Dipping his head, he drew all the courage he had and knocked on the door.

He really didn't think this through, Cole decided as he stared at the heavy, plain brown door. He wasn't sure what he was going to say. How was he supposed to erase a year of hurt with a few words? He couldn't.

He heard the scratch of the lock. His heart thudded against his ribs as the door swung open. Cole's eyes widened as he watched a sleepy Angie stumble into the lit hallway.

Her thick black hair was tousled and cascaded past her shoulders. His fingers itched to sink into the soft waves and draw her close to him.

Angie glared. Her face was soft from sleep. She really was a natural beauty. She didn't need anything to highlight her big brown eyes or her full pink lips.

His mouth dropped open as he stared at her clothes. Her small breasts were pressed against her thin camisole. The top was almost sheer and he could see her nipples through the thin white fabric. The black boyshorts accentuated her sleek lines and incredible legs.

"Do you always answer the door like that?" he asked gruffly.

"Did you come all the way to my home to comment on my sleepwear?" she asked as she rubbed her bleary eyes.

"No." His voice sounded strangled to his ears. He liked what she wore a little too much. She didn't need frilly nighties or barely there lingerie to capture his attention. The camisole and shorts were more her style and showed off her sexy and athletic body.

"What do you want, Cole?" Angie flipped her long black hair away from her face. "Another favor?"

Yeah, and it was huge. He wanted her to forgive him. Forget that he left her. Welcome him back into her bed and in her life.

"What could possibly be so important at this time at night?" she asked.

He checked his watch. "It's ten-thirty."

She groaned. "That's the middle of the night for me."

That was true, Cole thought as he bit back a smile. As a personal trainer, Angie had to get up before dawn to meet with her clients. She had always apologized for her early hours, but he didn't mind. He wasn't looking for nights in dance clubs and bars when he could be alone with her.

"Is this about your case?" she asked. "The wedding

is in three days and then everybody goes home. I don't think there's much more you can do."

He could lie and say he was here for the case. But he had used his assignment as an excuse to get closer. He wasn't going to hide behind his job. He had been too private and guarded in the past. It protected him but not Angie. She believed in what other people said. He won't let that happen again.

"I made a mistake."

Angie frowned. "About Heidi's accident?"

"No, I meant about us." He took a deep breath. "I made a mistake breaking up with you. It's my biggest regret."

She looked down at her bare feet. "What brought this on?"

"You think I'm overplaying the role as your on-again boyfriend. You're right." His words were choppy. He wished he could be a smooth talker but it was difficult getting his feelings across. "Being together reminds me what I've lost. I miss being with you."

Angie's eyes narrowed and her mouth tightened. "You knew what you were giving up when you walked away."

He should have known he wouldn't get any sympathy from her. "You suggested we move in together and I panicked." It wasn't the whole truth. There was so much more to it but he didn't feel safe in revealing it all.

"That's why? Seriously?" She stood straight and grasped the door handle, ready to slam it in his face. "I mentioned it once. It's not like I tried to give you a hard sell."

"I felt that if we lived together, you would see the sides of me that aren't so—" he gritted his teeth and pushed the word out "—loveable. You wouldn't like what you saw."

"I never thought you were perfect."

"You would have grown to hate me." Like his family did. He had gotten in the way of what they always wanted. "I thought it was best to end things so you had a chance to find someone better. Someone you could really love."

Angie slowly shook her head. "You shouldn't have done that."

Cole nervously rubbed the back of his neck. "I know that now. I wish I'd never made that mistake and been the boyfriend you needed."

"You were the boyfriend I wanted but your attitude changed in that last month." Her voice carried a hint of the confusion and hurt from that time. "I had loved you, Cole. Didn't you see that?"

He was stunned. His heart stopped and his ears started to buzz. The room kind of slanted as his whole world went off balance. *"You loved me?"*

Angie blushed but she held his gaze. "Why are you so surprised? I wouldn't have talked about moving in otherwise."

She loved him. She had never said those words before. All he wanted was Angie's love but he didn't think he had it. He had left because he didn't think he could earn her love. Now he realized he had thrown it away.

The regret and loss weighed heavily on him. He felt like he needed to hold on to something before he slid down to the ground. He wanted to lean against Angie and hold on to her until his world righted itself.

She had loved him. Once. How did she feel about

him now? No, he didn't want to ask that question. What if she couldn't love him again? What if he couldn't get her back?

He'd take whatever she was willing to give as long as she didn't shut him out. Cole took a step closer. "Invite me in," he said in a husky voice.

Angie swallowed roughly. "That's not a good idea."

"It's a very good idea. I've been thinking about it and so have you." When she didn't deny it, he boldly took a step closer. "I can't stop thinking about you. How good we were together."

"It's best if we don't try to recapture what we once had," she whispered.

He wanted what they once had. Angie was the only one who had cracked the protective wall around him. She was the only person he could trust and the only woman who could turn him into knots. The power she had over him was at times troubling. There was so much he kept to himself because he knew from experience that knowledge was power. But as their relationship grew stronger, he noticed that he was sharing more about himself and his life with her. It was scary and at the same time deeply gratifying. He'd never had anything like it and he never would again.

He knew they couldn't get what they had. Too much time had passed. Too much distance. But he wanted her back. He was willing to work toward something different. Something better. He wanted a fresh start.

Cole's body grazed hers. He wanted to demonstrate how much he missed her. How much he loved her. "Let me in."

She stared at him with wide eyes. "This is insane."

Cole lowered his head and brushed his mouth

against hers. Angie's lips clung to his. Hope squeezed his chest when she didn't pull away. He gathered her close, stepped into her apartment and kicked the door behind him.

8

ANGIE PRESSED COLE against the door. Her apartment was dark and quiet but her mind was a whirlwind. She'd wanted this since she had seen him on stage. His lap dance had invaded her dreams. It had been so long since she had felt aroused. Felt anything for a man. It was sharp and instant, making her movements clumsy as the lust poured through her veins.

A sense of urgency pulsed through her but Cole was in no rush. He savored her mouth with thorough kisses. He teased her with his tongue, darting the tip along her reddened lips before plunging into her mouth, only to withdraw.

She shivered when she felt his large, rough hands slide down her back. She leaned into Cole, arching her spine as he trailed his hands down to her bottom. He squeezed hard and she growled in the back of her throat.

Angie froze. She shouldn't do that. The last thing she needed to remind Cole was how unladylike she was in the bedroom.

She rubbed her body restlessly against him. She

wanted to tear off his clothes and climb onto his naked body. She flattened her hands against his chest and felt the heavy and uneven beat of his heart. She didn't want to follow his lead and go slow. She needed this to be hard and fast. Next time they could have a leisurely exploration.

Next time. The words swirled in her head and she stopped rocking her hips against Cole. There would be no next time. Nothing had really changed. He said he missed her. He missed this.

This was sex.

Angie hesitated as the realization hit. Should she grab this opportunity or kick him out? Sex with Cole was once about love and connecting two souls. She had shared everything with him when they were in bed. Now he was offering this one night. There was no promise of a future yet she wanted more. It wasn't enough.

But it was more than she had yesterday

She should end this. One more kiss and she would break away. Cole gently cupped the back of her head and suckled her lips. She felt the pull to her core. One more kiss, she decided. And it would be the last one. The last time she shared a kiss—shared anything— with Cole Foster.

Cole broke the kiss and pressed his mouth against her ear. "You have no idea what you're doing to me."

She knew. His skin was hot and his raspy breath couldn't hide his excitement. She felt his erection pressing against her. His penis was hard and thick. Angie moaned with anticipation.

A thought wafted through her mind like smoke. They should stop now. Pull away before they reached the point of no return.

Cole placed his hands on her hips and turned her around. The move was so sudden that she fell back against him. He burrowed his face in her hair as he dipped his hand lower.

Angie's breath staggered from her throat as Cole boldly cupped her sex. She instinctively flattened her hand against his.

"Angie." He dragged her name out in a rough whisper. "Let me touch you." His fingers flexed. "Please you."

She bit her lip as the erotic memories crashed over her. Cole not only knew how to satisfy her, but he also gave her maximum pleasure. He was generous and imaginative. Strong and loving. With one intimate touch, he could make her believe that they were made for each other.

But would she feel the same tonight? He didn't love her. He didn't want to share a future or even a home. All he wanted was to share a bed. Would this one time taint those special memories? Was she willing to risk feeling empty and alone for a shadow of what they used to share?

Cole delved his other hand beneath her camisole and covered her breast. He lightly pinched her stiff nipple as he stroked the folds of her sex with his other hand.

Yes, she was willing. Angie rested her head against his broad shoulder as her knees threatened to buckle. *Yes,* she mouthed in the darkness as she pressed the heel of her palm against his hand. She bucked against him. *Yes.*

"Take off my clothes," Angie ordered softly.

"Patience," he said.

She frowned. This was not a time to be patient. She hadn't been able to see Cole, touch him, or hear his groans of satisfaction for a year. She needed to feel his skin on hers with no barriers. No restrictions. Angie grabbed the hem of her camisole.

"No." Cole gave a warning nip to her earlobe. "I'm in charge."

Angie's fingers dug into the cotton as she considered her next move. She should have known. Last time she had been demanding and insatiable. She hadn't held anything back, confident that Cole wanted her just as much. That he was turned on by her assertiveness.

"Let me take care of you." Cole's voice was low and mesmerizing. "I know what you like." He pressed his fingertip against her throbbing clit.

"But…" Pleasure rippled lightly through her.

"I'll give you anything you want." His voice was urgent with need.

He would give her anything…as long as he was in charge. As long as she surrendered. She shouldn't care, Angie decided as she closed her eyes. She hadn't always been brazen in bed. Not until she had felt secure with Cole.

And that had been a mistake. She wouldn't repeat it again. If she held back, if she didn't follow every animal instinct or reckless impulse, she could have her ex-boyfriend for one more night.

Angie gradually let go of her shirt and was rewarded with Cole's sigh. She looped her hands over his shoulders. Now she was open to his touch, giving him total control. It shouldn't make her so nervous.

Cole grasped her jaw and tilted her head toward him. She felt the kick of power at how his fingers trembled against her chin. But his kiss was confident and demanding as he claimed her mouth.

Her skin tingled as the shameless need built inside

her. She swallowed back a keening cry as she writhed against his hand. The pleasure promised to be intense. Her heart raced as her stomach twisted with wild expectation.

Angie wished Cole would stop teasing her. She wanted to turn around, strip him bare and take over. But that would put a stop to everything. There was only one thing she could do.

"Please," she said in a jagged breath.

She bucked when Cole squeezed her nipple while also pressing against her swollen bud. The pleasure exploded inside her. Her mind shut down and she cried out. Angie slumped forward, her legs going limp. Cole caught her and gathered her close.

She was dimly aware of him carrying her. His shirt pressed against her cheek and she heard his heartbeat close to her ear. Her chest rose and fell as her muscles shook slightly. Her skin felt hot and her clothes were too confining.

Cole lowered her onto her warm, welcoming bed. She reached out for him and he wrapped his hands around hers. "First I need to find the light."

Something close to panic gripped her chest. "No," she said. "No lights."

She felt Cole's pause. "Why not?"

Angie didn't know how to explain it. They had been lovers but this time it was different. This time she knew she wasn't feminine enough for him. She lacked big breasts and generous hips. She didn't have anything sexy to wear that could heighten his pleasure before he unwrapped her like a present.

She was the same person he left a year ago. A little wiser and more cautious this time around. She wasn't going to be free and uninhibited with him. Men wanted a little mystery. A fantasy.

"Angie?"

She drew his head down and kissed him. It was meant to distract him from the light but it only managed to lower her guard. She instinctively tangled her legs with his. His jeans were scratchy against her bare skin. She was tempted to roll over, straddle Cole and shuck off his clothes.

Her body must have signaled her intent. Cole wrapped his fingers around her wrists and held her hands over her head. Her first instinct was to wrestle for control. Roll him under her and tease him with her mouth and hands. Drive him wild until he was begging for release.

Cole had loved that. Or so she thought.

He kissed a trail down her throat and circled the tip of his tongue against her trembling pulse point. She rolled her hips in response and bumped against his rock-hard penis. Her flesh clenched with desperate need. "Take off your clothes," she insisted. She didn't care how bossy she sounded—she wanted him naked now.

"You first," he said with his mouth pressed against her shoulder. She gasped with appreciation as he dragged the camisole strap down with his teeth. Angie couldn't stop herself from thrusting her breast to his mouth.

Her nipples stung and she couldn't remain still. She wiggled her hips against Cole and her legs locked behind his. She fought for self-control until he took her breast in his mouth. Angie surrendered to his touch.

She allowed her legs to drop as she sinuously arched her back. Her short, choppy breaths mingled with his.

He drew sharply on her nipple and let go of her hands so he could fondle her breasts. His touch grew increasingly impatient as his restraint started to crumble.

Angie grabbed the back of his head, her fingertips tangled in his thick hair. Sweat bathed her skin as the heat billowed inside her.

Cole slid her boyshorts down her legs. She kicked them off as he settled between her thighs.

"Wait," he said hoarsely. She heard the metallic sound of his zipper and the rustle of his clothes. His shoes hit the floor. She lowered her hands onto the bed, clutching the sheets, as she held back from shoving his jeans off him.

She licked her swollen lips, excitement squeezing her lungs, as he placed his firm hands on her thighs. Angie took a deep breath when she felt the tip of his penis pressing against her. Her sharp intake echoed in her ears as Cole surged forward.

Angie went still for a brief moment as her body yielded to his. Blood roared in her ears as her skin flushed. Immediately, she tilted her hips and drew him in more.

Cole's thrusts were strong and steady. His hands were everywhere. Her stomach fluttered from his gentle, clumsy caress and her nipples tightened as he massaged her breasts.

Her heart skipped a beat when he stroked her hair before drawing his fingertips along her cheek. He placed his thumb against her chin, guiding her mouth open before he kissed her hard.

His kiss was possessive. Elemental. He was reminding her of his claim. And it triggered something primal inside her. Angie wrapped her arms and legs tightly against him and rolled them over.

Now she straddled Cole. He didn't seem to mind. She couldn't see his face but she heard snatches of his encouraging words. His fingers pressed into her hips, clearly approving of her frenetic pace.

She tore off her camisole and tossed it away. Angie flattened her hands on his chest, twisting his shirt in between her fingers as she followed an ancient rhythm. Her hair fell in her face, her skin felt like it was going to burst open and the desire coiling deep in her pelvis sprang wildly.

Her muscles locked and her body stilled as she climaxed. It stole her breath and she felt as if she were falling. She held on to Cole, grinding her hips against his hurried thrusts. She tumbled against him just as she heard his hoarse cry of release.

She lay next to him, her face pressed against his, as she struggled for her next breath. As she closed her eyes, Angie realized that nostalgia had played with her memory.

Sex with Cole was better than she had remembered.

COLE DIDN'T WANT to move. Angie was curled around him, soft and naked. She was his for the night and he wanted to hold on to this moment. He waited until Angie had fallen asleep before he changed positions. She didn't make a sound of complaint when he turned over and laid her tenderly on her pillow.

He wanted to stay with her. In the past he would toss the blanket over them to keep the world at bay and hold her all night. Those quiet minutes always meant a lot to him. Too much. Angie had made him feel special and wanted. She had made him feel as if he had found home.

He felt that tonight. He had been hesitant to embrace the feeling because he knew he couldn't hold on to it. He knew it wasn't real. They weren't a couple anymore and he needed to remember that. If he fell for the illusion, it would break him and he wouldn't be able to recover.

He reluctantly got out of bed and tucked the blanket over Angie. He tripped over his shoe and winced. Cole was about to turn on the bedside lamp but stopped as his fingertips brushed against the switch.

Why didn't Angie want the light on? That was unusual. She was not shy when it came to sex. In fact, she was the opposite. He loved that about her, but tonight he wanted to make it all about her pleasure. Why did she want it dark? Was she ashamed that she had fallen back in bed with him? Or did she still believe in the gossip that he didn't find her sexy enough?

He was going to fix that, Cole decided as he grabbed his jeans and yanked them on. He wasn't sure how he could prove his desire. Wasn't it already obvious? He was always aware of Angie and constantly dragging his gaze away only to find he was still staring at her.

And these days he couldn't stop touching her. Cole sighed as he picked up his shoes. He had found every excuse to hold her hand or touch her hair. And if he wasn't doing either of those things, he was likely touching her back to guide her as they walked. She didn't say anything when he placed his hand on her shoulder or waist. Did she know it was his way of showing the world that Angie was still his?

Now if only Angie felt the same, Cole thought as he made his way to the door in the dark. If only she wanted him back. She had loved him once. Could she fall in love with him again?

Cole flattened his hand on the door and looked over

at Angie. Would she welcome him back into her life or would she think this was all for appearances' sake? That he was doing all this for his case.

He shouldn't consider whether or not he could get Angie back. History had proven that it would not work in his favor. A year ago he had searched for his mother and stepfather and contacted them. The people who should automatically love and care about him rejected him again.

Still, Angie was different. She had accepted him even though he held back. If he wanted to have a fresh start with Angie, it had to begin now. Cole relocked the door and turned around. He slowly padded back to bed—back to Angie—as he shed his clothes. From now on, he was going to give everything he had to her. And pray that it was enough.

9

COLE FROWNED WHEN he heard an insistent buzzing sound. He rolled over and opened his eyes. He blinked when he saw the glass chandelier above him. Slowly sitting up, he noticed the sunlight streaming through the windows. He smiled contentedly when he saw the exposed brick walls and eclectic furniture. Everything in Angie's studio apartment reflected her personality.

Looking beside him, Cole found Angie still asleep. Her long black hair fanned against her colorful pillow and partially hid her face. The patchwork blanket had slid down to her waist, revealing her athletic body and firm breasts. He was tempted to lie back down and cradle her against his bare chest.

He heard the buzzing noise again. Cole glanced over at the bedside table and saw Angie's cell phone vibrate. He knew it would be her mother calling even before he could see the image of the older woman on the tiny, lit-up screen.

He smiled when he saw the casual snapshot of Angie's mother, glamorous as usual. She wasn't the kind of mother Cole had wished for growing up when he watched TV sitcoms. Angie's mother didn't bake or sew, although she certainly made sure her two sons and daughter had been fed and clothed, and were safe. Her first priority would always be her husband but she was also a constant presence in her children's lives. Sometimes a little too involved, according to her children. Angie had no idea how lucky she was that her parents even cared.

"Angie," Cole said as he shook her arm. "You need to wake up."

"Five more minutes," she mumbled. He was about to try again when he felt Angie's arm tighten. Cole knew she was suddenly and fully awake. She was now realizing that what happened last night was real and not a fantasy.

"Your mom is calling," he told her.

Angie reached for the blanket and dragged it up to her chin. "Ignore it."

"She's been calling. You know how worried she gets when you don't answer." He knew how this would play out and he liked how it never varied, even when her mother was angry with Angie. "If you don't answer, she'll make your dad call. And then your brothers."

"I'll call her back later," Angie said as she curled deeper into her pillow.

"If you don't answer it, I will." And he knew the havoc that would cause.

Angie bolted up and grabbed the phone. She glared at him while she carefully wound the blanket around her body. "Hey, Mom," she said, her voice rough from sleep. "Can I call you back?"

He knew that wasn't going to happen. Cole smiled when he heard Angie's sigh as she tucked the phone more comfortably next to her ear. He hadn't been around the Lawson household for a year, but he still understood the natural rhythms and the rules they lived by. The close ties and predictability drove Angie crazy, but he had secretly yearned for it.

He didn't idealize Angie's family. The Lawsons were loud and they didn't always get along, but the family offered solid support for each other. That was something he didn't have when he was growing up but he got it from the Lawsons. They had included him in their family with such speed that it had embarrassed Angie and it had made him nervous. He saw it as a privilege and a gift, but unlike Angie and her brothers, it was not given to him unconditionally.

Cole lay back down and got an unobstructed view of her strong and naked back. He was about to reach out and stroke his fingers down her spine when he noticed how she stiffened. It was as if Angie were on guard and sensing danger.

"Yes," she said tightly. "Cole is my date for the wedding. How did you know?"

Cole's chuckle was rewarded with the sharp swipe of her hand gesturing him to remain quiet. He didn't think it was necessary. When was Angie going to learn that she could not hide anything from her mother?

"No," she said firmly to her mother, "it doesn't mean anything.... No, it doesn't. I needed a date to the wedding and Cole was available."

He found it interesting that she wasn't telling her mother the real reason. But he also refused to think that this meant something. Did she worry that they had taken the pretense too far? He would prove to her that this was very real.

"No, there is nothing to discuss.... He's just returning a favor. No, you are not inviting him over for the family dinner. Mom…Mom?" She huffed and waved her hand in the air in surrender. "I give up. Do what you want. I have to go. 'Bye."

"I don't remember you being this grumpy in the morning," Cole said as he watched her end the call and toss the cell phone back onto the bedside table.

Angie tucked her knees to her chest. "If she calls you over for the Sunday dinner, don't accept."

"But I love those dinners," he teased. It had taken a while for him to get used to the chaotic meals and lively arguments with Angie's dad and brothers. They were casual, fun, and he felt like he was part of the family.

Angie reached over the bed and yanked her discarded camisole from the floor. "Do you really want to be interrogated by my mother?"

"I survived the first time." He laced his hands beneath his head and smiled with pride. "In fact, I passed with flying colors. She said I was a keeper." That casual comment had meant a lot to him.

"She is so embarrassing," Angie muttered as she put on her top. "I know you think she's adorable, but that's probably because you miss having your mother around."

Cole wasn't paying attention anymore. Angie's voice faded as she pulled on her clothes while listing the reasons why her mother drove her crazy. His heart began to thump and dread twisted his stomach. Cole battled back the nauseating fear. If he were going to stop holding back and start sharing, he had to do it now.

He looked down at the bedsheet. "I have a mother."

Angie stopped moving and stared at him. "I'm sorry, what?"

Cole forced himself to look at Angie. She seemed

stunned. "My mother is still alive," he said. "So is my stepdad."

Anger flashed in her eyes. Her mouth opened and closed. "You told me they were dead. You said you didn't have parents."

He rubbed the back of his neck as the shame clawed at him. "They stopped being my parents years ago, but they are still alive." Still married. Still a family without him. "I just thought you should know."

"You just…" She pressed her lips together into a stern line. "Of all the…"

Cole closed his eyes. He should have kept his mouth shut.

COLE LIED TO HER. His parents were alive. The words kept repeating in her mind. The hurt and surprise had reverberated inside her and she'd followed her first instinct to sprint for the bathroom. She felt betrayed and she didn't think she could control her wild emotions.

She had taken her time in the shower and changing her clothes, hoping Cole would have gotten the idea and slither out of her apartment and far, far away from her. Instead, he stayed. She'd seen the determined, almost defiant look in his eyes and she knew she was in for a battle. Angie had immediately scooped up her keys and walked out of the apartment, only to have Cole follow her.

Cole lied to her. His parents were alive. Angie glanced up at the gray sky and noticed the dark, ominous clouds. She took an unsteady breath and inhaled the scent of rain.

"I can't believe you didn't tell me," Angie said to Cole as they walked to the Starbucks at the corner of her street. She huddled in her jacket to ward off the cool morning breeze but she also wanted to distance herself from Cole. "I never thought you'd lie to me."

"I didn't lie," Cole said calmly. "My parents haven't been part of my life since I was fifteen. They may as well not exist."

"You acted like they were dead. Actually, you let me think they were dead." Angie frowned and shook her head. "Who does that?"

"Angie," he said with a deep sigh. "Don't you think you're overreacting?"

"No," she said as she marched down the crowded sidewalk. She didn't pay attention to the people striding past her or the sound of the bus whooshing by. The world was cold and colorless. Silent and still. She needed to move to get this billowing hurt out of her, but she wasn't getting far.

"It has nothing to do with us," Cole insisted.

Angie stopped and stared at him. "Are you serious?" From the look on his face, he was. How could Cole be so smart and yet so clueless? "It has *everything* to do with us. I always thought you were private. You were reluctant to share anything about yourself, but once you did, I assumed it was the truth. What else have you hidden from me? Is there a Mrs. Cole Foster? Is Cole your real name?"

Cole's eyes narrowed with anger. "Do you really think I would keep something like that from you? What kind of man do you think I am?"

"Are you really thirty years old?" She thought about the other things he had said in the past. Those anecdotes that she had treasured because he had shared them freely. "Did that scar on your arm come from falling out of the tree when you were ten? Are you an only child or do you have a bunch of brothers and sisters I don't know about?"

Cole clenched his jaw and a ruddy streak entered his cheeks. "That's enough," he said in a low growl. "It wasn't easy for me to tell the truth. I knew it wouldn't make me look good but I did it because I *have* been holding back. I was trying to share something and now it just blew up in my face. This is why I don't talk about myself."

"How did you expect I would react?" she asked as she followed him to the Starbucks. "Did you think I would say, 'Oh, thanks for clearing it up, sweetheart. I'm sure that was the only thing you lied about. My trust in you is still absolute.'"

"Wouldn't that have been great?" he muttered as he opened the bright green door and motioned for her to step ahead.

"And why are you telling me now?" She lowered her voice as they entered the long line.

"Like I said, I was trying to share," he bit out the words. "Communicate. Shouldn't I get bonus points for that?"

She rolled her eyes. He just didn't get it. "Don't you think it's too little, too late? We had a booty call and—" The woman standing in front of her turned around and gave a curious look over her thick-rimmed glasses.

Cole lowered his head and whispered, "What we had was more than sex. More than great sex between two people who are still hot for each other."

Angie turned and faced Cole. She saw the desire in his eyes as he remembered.

"It was not a booty call," he whispered in her ear. "It was not a one-night stand. Do I make myself clear?"

"Yes," she answered hoarsely. Last night had meant

something to him, too. He wanted to hold on to their connection. Strengthen it. That was why he was compelled to share something about himself.

She was secretly thrilled but she was still rattled by his revelation. And how long was he willing to share? Until the weekend when the wedding was over? Or was he doing this so they could build something more permanent? Something told her that Cole wouldn't be able to give an answer.

"And I don't want to talk about my parents anymore," Cole said. "They are no longer in my life."

"Are they in jail?" she asked. "Witness protection?"

His expression hardened. "No. The subject is closed."

She took a step closer and touched his forearm. She could tell this was difficult for him, but she needed to know. "Just one more question, I promise."

Cole closed his eyes briefly. "Fine. What is it?"

She wanted to ask why they weren't in his life anymore. Was it his decision or theirs? She couldn't imagine Cole doing something unforgivable.

But he wasn't ready to discuss it. She could see it, sense it. She wanted to know what made him this guarded and cynical.

"Angie?" Angie tensed when she heard Brittany's voice from across the coffeehouse. She saw the redhead from the corner of her eye. "Hey, Angie."

She wasn't going to let Brittany interrupt her. Cole was already regretting telling her. She admitted she hadn't handled this well and she may not get another opportunity. "Were your parents the personal stuff you were dealing with a year ago?"

A muscle bunched in his jaw. "Yes," he said in a hiss. She saw the misery etched in his face. She wished she could soothe him, take the pain away and carry the burden for him. She wanted to protect him from the memories but she didn't know how.

"Angie…" Brittany approached them, her heels clacking loudly on the floor. "Did you get my email about the changes in the wedding ceremony? You haven't responded."

"Sorry. I've been a little busy." She slid her arm around Cole's and gave him an encouraging squeeze. *Lean on me,* she wanted to tell him. *I'll take care of this.* "But, yes, I saw all six emails this morning."

"You know you have to respond to all bridal party emails within an hour of receiving them," Brittany whined. "Those are the rules."

"Along with not getting pregnant, keeping my hair color and no body modifications like tattoos or piercings," Angie added. "Believe me, those rules are burned into my brain."

Brittany crossed her arms and gave Cole a dirty look. "Angie, if I had known you were going to be distracted by a man, I would have also included no dating."

"That's my fault," Cole said, pasting on a polite smile. "When we're together I demand her full attention."

"Well, you need to try and restrain yourself for the weekend. The countdown for my wedding has started and I've already lost one bridesmaid. I can't let anything happen to the rest." Brittany looked at her tiny diamond watch and then at the line. "What is taking so long? My drink is not that difficult to make."

"You couldn't find a replacement for Heidi?" Angie asked.

"Not at this late date," she said with a huff. "It's so

inconvenient. If she had her accident earlier I could have found a substitute."

"You could have Cheryl step in and do it." Cole tilted his head toward her assistant, who was waiting at the counter for their drinks.

"Cheryl?" She gave Cole an incredulous look. "No. She's tiny, blonde and curvy. The other bridesmaids are tall, lean and have black hair. Cheryl would have thrown off the entire color scheme. Anyway, she's my *assistant.*"

"Fine, look on the bright side," Angie said, wishing the line would move faster. "Heidi and Robin were not getting along. You would probably have had to deal with a cat fight on your wedding day."

"No kidding." Brittany pressed her hands against her head as if she were getting a headache just thinking about it. "They knew this day had to be perfect but all they cared about was who got to be maid of honor."

"Yeah, I noticed that. So self-involved." And she really didn't understand why they were fighting over what was genuinely becoming a miserable job.

"I should have known they would act this way." She held her hand up as if she were swearing in for office. "I forgot how they were when we were in college. They made my life miserable when I pledged to their sorority. Heidi thought I was on Robin's side and Robin thought I was teaming up with Heidi. Hazing was brutal."

"But you became friends," Cole said with a raised brow.

"Uh, yes. We *are* sorority sisters." She turned to Angie. "Although after my ceremony I'm not going to have them in the same room again."

Angie was recalling what Robin had said at the hospital the other day. The bridesmaid thought she deserved to be the maid of honor. Was it so important to her that she would hurt the competition?

"Nonfat triple-grande sugar-free extra-hot extra-foamy caramel macchiato," the barista called out.

"That's my drink. It's about time," she said as she started to walk away. "Cheryl and I have so much to do and I'm in desperate need of caffeine. Don't forget the mani-pedi at five."

How could she when Brittany sent hourly reminders? "Can't wait."

Cole waited until he saw Brittany and Cheryl exit out the door before he spoke to Angie. "I'm beginning to think Heidi's fall had nothing to do with substance abuse. But I still want to get her blood test results to rule it out."

"I agree." The bespectacled woman in front gave another curious look. Angie beamed a bright smile and tightened her hold on Cole's arm. "We should focus on Robin."

"Robin? No, Brittany."

"Are you kidding?" She looked up at him. "Brittany is trying to make this ceremony perfect. The last thing she wants to do is create problems."

"Didn't you hear what she said? Heidi and Robin were terrible to her when she rushed for a sorority."

"And what better way to get revenge than make them her bridesmaids?" She saw the woman in front of her nod in agreement. "There is a twisted sense of justice in that but Brittany isn't that complex."

"Why do you think it's Robin? She hasn't gotten along with Heidi for years. Why act now?"

"Because Heidi had something Robin wanted."

"And you think she caused an accident so she could

be promoted to maid of honor? No, my money is on Brittany."

"How would she have hurt Heidi?" Angie asked. "She was the center of attention at the bachelorette party."

"Not for the whole party," Cole said. "And who was it that found Heidi? Brittany."

He had a point. "Brittany wouldn't do it," she insisted. At least, she hoped Brittany didn't. The woman was marrying her best friend.

"Maybe we should go back to the strip club and see if it was possible."

Angie groaned. "Do we have to?"

"Don't worry, Angie." He gave a comforting pat on her hand. "I'll be with you every step of the way."

"Okay," she reluctantly agreed. "But first I want you to take me somewhere."

"Name it."

She paused and stared at him. "I want to see your agency."

Cole tilted his head back in surprise. "Why?"

She shrugged. "I'm curious." His apartment and his car never held any personal items. No trinkets, souvenirs or pictures. His office may show something different.

Cole gave a long and deep sigh. "I really am a private investigator."

"I know and I'm sorry I questioned that. I was angry," she said. "You don't have to show me your license. But I've never seen a detective agency and I'm curious."

"It's not that special."

But it may show what was special to him. "Cole, let me be the judge of that."

10

COLE MADE ANOTHER attempt to slide the key into the lock. He hoped Angie didn't see how his hand shook. Quickly glancing at her, he noticed she was brushing her fingers along the lettering on the window.

"Foster Investigations," she read softly. "Sounds very impressive."

He shouldn't be nervous. He was proud of his business. It was small and struggling, however, it was his. The agency was in a neighborhood mostly populated by college students who couldn't afford much and plenty of seniors who'd been there for years. It was humble in every sense of the word, yet he wanted Angie to see what he'd done on his own. He didn't realize how important her opinion was until he opened the door.

He stepped in the outer office and flipped on the lights before he let Angie inside. Glancing around the waiting room, he tried to see it from Angie's perspective. The room was small and beige. There were a few antique chairs, a coffee table and lamps. Nothing that would wow and amaze her.

"This is nice." She trailed her finger along the stained-glass lamp. "I like this. Where did you get it?"

"Antique store," he said gruffly and ignored her look of surprise. He didn't want to explain how he wound up looking at antiques or how he bought the lamp because it had been handed down from generation to generation.

He bought the furnishings more for the story that came along with them. Every piece of furniture he had in his office and in his home had once been important to a family. He didn't have heirlooms of his own, but he took care of the ones people discarded.

Angie stepped in front of a framed print of Norman Rockwell's *The Runaway*. She looked confused and yet charmed as she studied the police officer sitting on a stool at a restaurant while talking to a runaway boy.

When she left the picture and focused on him, he felt as if she were studying something else. She was trying to understand the connection between him and the print. "What kind of clients do you have?" she asked.

It was a simple question and he could give an easy answer, but the knot in his chest tightened. "Families, mostly."

"What do you do for them?"

"Contact missing relatives for one reason or another. I track down people who don't want to be found or think they've been forgotten. A have a few cases finding heirs named in a will and a few deadbeat dads."

Angie strolled around the room. "So the case with Heidi is different for you."

"It's the kind of work I want to do."

She looked at him sharply. "Why is that?"

"Years ago, Heidi and her parents had a falling-out because of her substance abuse. They lost contact with her and they were worried. Heidi didn't know that her family was looking for her. They didn't know if she was alive or in trouble. Now they have a second chance."

"I knew you were good at your job at Missing Persons, but you never explained why it was your passion."

He didn't discuss it because it would have brought up his family life. Working in this field was a constant reminder of what he didn't have. There were no worried parents looking for him. He didn't have a family who wanted him to come home. He had used his skills to find his parents, then waited years to contact them. Unfortunately, they didn't want him to find them.

"What's in here?" she asked as she stood by the doorway that opened into a darkened room.

"That's my office." He almost stopped her from going in. That room felt more personal but there was nothing private in there for her to see. He slowly followed her as she turned on the light. Cole watched her eyes widen when she saw the two mismatched sofas and a low coffee table. A laptop computer sat on a small wooden desk in the far side of the room.

"This isn't at all what I had expected," she said as she slowly entered the room. "I thought I would see a gun collection and a couple of fedoras. It looks like a place where people hang out and talk."

"Most of my work is done on the computer. I use this room when I'm interviewing the families." He spent countless hours listening to people tell their stories, their side. He saw and heard it all. The lies and the excuses. The good and the bad memories. He saw the tears and anger. The shame and the regret.

"I never thought you were a Norman Rockwell fan,"

she said as she pointed at the famous print of a big family having dinner. "You think you know a person…"

He wasn't about to explain the pictures. He didn't think he could. Whenever he looked at them, he felt conflicting emotions. They reminded him of too many broken promises. What he didn't have, but what he could get for others.

Angie sat down on the edge of a sofa. "Okay, I know you're not ready to discuss it, but I have to ask. Were you a runaway? Is that the personal stuff you were going through with your family?"

"Why would you think that?"

"Your interest in missing persons," she said as she began to tick off a list with her fingers. "The pictures in this office. The fact that your family isn't part of your life anymore."

Cole forced himself to remain where he stood. "And you think I chose that?" He couldn't keep the defensiveness out of his voice.

She leaned back on the sofa. "And there's the fact that you walked out on me."

He crossed his arms. "I told you why."

"Yeah, you didn't like the idea of living together. You weren't ready to make a commitment."

"That's not exactly how I would put it."

She glanced at the framed print and then returned her attention on him. "Did you run away from home?"

"No, I stayed." Until he was driven out. Until it was made very clear that his parents did not love him. That no one could love him. "That's when I learned to rely on no one. I had to stand on my own if I wanted to survive."

"That's a very bleak outlook on life."

"It is, but I managed to do that for a long time." He

had survived. Thrived. For a time he had convinced himself that he wasn't missing out. "And then I met you."

She winced and covered her face with her hands. "I scared you off. I knew it."

"Not in the way you think. You made me believe I could be someone different. Someone better. But I can't."

Angie leaned forward and rested her arms on her knees. "Cole, I don't want you to be different."

"You say that now. If we had lived together, you would have kicked me out within a month." Probably sooner, he decided. She would have been under no obligation to stick around.

"Ah."

Cole scowled at her. "I hate when you do that." It meant she had figured out something he rather would have had kept safely hidden.

"That's why you ended our relationship. It wasn't because I was unladylike and too aggressive in bed. It was because I was getting too close."

"Aggressive?" He didn't know if he would call it that.

"You weren't comfortable with me seeing the real you. All of you. Well, guess what, Cole. It wasn't easy for me to bare it all with you."

"Get back to that aggressive-in-bed part."

"Oh, please. What was I supposed to think? We had talked about moving in once and it was maybe a month before you ended things. But two weeks before you left, I had become a little…" She waved her hand as if she were trying to find the right word.

"Demanding?" he said, remembering one intense

night they had shared. "Passionate? Strong? Confident? Take your pick."

"Pushy," she said. "I know guys don't like that much of a challenge in bed and I thought I scared you off."

"Angie, I never had a problem with that. You know what you want and you're not afraid to go after it. That's kind of hot."

"Right," she said with a twist of her lips. "It's so hot that you had to be in charge last night."

"I wanted to show you how much I missed you. How much I still wanted you. I didn't want there to be any question about that." And he had made the wrong move. Instead of showing how he felt, he managed to raise more questions. "Next time you make the first move."

She scoffed at his suggestion but he saw the flare of interest in her eyes. "Like that's going to happen."

"Don't deny it," he said with a knowing smile. He thought of Angie's warmth and affection. "Last night you proved that you want me as much as I want you. You can't keep your hands off me and I don't see why I can't encourage it."

She raised an eyebrow. "What happened to my making the first move?"

He wasn't that patient. He had one night with Angie and he wanted more. He wanted it all. "I never said I was going to be a gentleman about it."

"I should have known," Angie said with a small smile as she rose from the sofa. "In that case, I should leave and remove the temptation."

"Leave?" How could he have gotten this all wrong? "I don't understand."

"I need to meet with Brittany," she said as she headed for the door.

"That's not it. You're making excuses." Cole tried to hide the frustration from his voice. "Why don't you want to make the first move?"

"Because no matter how good we are together, nothing has changed," she said. Angie averted her gaze as she walked away. "History will repeat itself and I can't go through that again."

ANGIE LOOKED AROUND the nail salon Brittany had reserved exclusively for her bridal party. Everything was sleek, modern and blindingly white, from the walls, chairs and tables to the nail technician's uniforms. This was a side of Seattle she didn't know. Located downtown between the famous designer stores and small expensive restaurants, Angie felt on edge.

She wished she were back in Cole's office. She had finally seen a side of him she hadn't expected. He wasn't hiding in that office. If anything, he was sharing with his clients. He was sharing his hopes and his disappointments.

And she couldn't get those framed prints out of her mind. They didn't reflect how she saw Cole—a cynical loner who hid in the shadows. Those pictures represented a positive, almost innocent, time. They obviously meant something to him.

Angie wished she knew more about his life. All this time she had assumed he had been orphaned as a teenager. She had made this conclusion by the few things he said about his childhood and his clear enjoyment of being surrounded by her relatives. She figured he missed having a mother. She assumed he longed for a family. Now she realized that she had been completely wrong about him.

It was a startling feeling. It felt like her world had

shifted. The man she loved was someone else entirely. Or was he? He didn't have contact with his family and the way he acted with her family was genuine. Maybe these clues would give her a better understanding about Cole.

"You look very serious," Robin complained, disrupting her thoughts. "Have another sip of champagne."

"No, thanks." Angie stared at the bright pink polish applied to her toenails. It almost hurt to look at and she was sure it would clash violently against the bile-green bridesmaid dress. "Where have I seen this color?" she asked.

"Definitely not in nature," Robin muttered and shared a smile with her.

Angie snapped her fingers. "Oh, now I remember. It was that drink at the bachelorette party. The psychedelic pink one."

"The Britini," Cheryl said without looking up from tapping the keypad on her phone. "It was made in honor for Brittany's special day."

"I didn't get a chance to try it," Angie said. It didn't sound like her kind of drink, anyway. She didn't drink anything that pink on principle. "What does it taste like?"

"It was a martini made with bubble-gum-infused vodka," Cheryl informed her. "It was a hit at the party."

Angie pursed her lips. "Seriously?"

"They'll have it available during the rehearsal dinner and wedding reception," Cheryl said as she stood up to speak privately on the phone. "You should give it a try."

"Does it really taste like bubble gum?" Angie asked Robin.

"Yes, it's very sweet," Robin confessed in a whisper and looked over to where Brittany was getting her nails done. "But it wasn't a popular drink. Cheryl kept trying to get people to order it because it's named after Brittany."

Heidi probably ordered the drink to please Brittany. She had noticed a bright pink stain when they put Heidi in the recovery position.

"So, how's it going with the stripper?" Robin asked, wagging her eyebrows.

"Stripper?" Oh, right. Cole was supposed to be a stripper. She almost forgot that was how the bridal party met him. She wanted to tell Patrick and her friends what Cole was really doing. That he had been investigating Heidi and needed to know if someone intentionally hurt her. He was determined to find out if it had something to do with her troubled past or if she were in trouble now.

Angie wanted everyone to know that he was using his skills to help others. That he was an honorable and dependable family guy. He was still the man she fell in love with. "His name is Cole. Cole Foster."

"It sounds like it's more than a one-night stand," Brittany called over from where she sat getting her nails done. "I saw them this morning at Starbucks."

"I knew him before the bachelorette party," Angie was quick to clarify. "He's an ex-boyfriend."

Robin leaned back and studied Angie, from her messy ponytail to her tank top and yoga pants. "Yeah, about that. What's his deal?"

Angie frowned. "His deal?"

Robin gestured at her. "Is he into muscular women?"

"Does he have a sports-bra fetish?" Brittany asked with a sly smile.

Angie clenched her jaw. This was why she couldn't

wait for her bridesmaid duties to be over. She could do without the sharp remarks. Just when she thought she was finding common ground with these women, they put her down with a zinger or two. "Is it so strange that he finds me attractive?"

Robin drew back as if she weren't prepared for a pointed question. "Well…no," she said, "but did you get a good look at him? He could have anyone."

"Mmm-hmm," Angie agreed, faking the confidence she wished she had. She leaned back comfortably in her chair. "And if he plays his cards right, he can have me."

"Seriously, Angie—" Brittany took a sip of champagne and gestured to the empty glass "—how did you catch him?"

Angie looked at Brittany and then at Robin. They didn't know anything about Cole. He said little and tried not to show what he was thinking, but the man felt things deeply. Intensely. He tried to keep it in because he felt vulnerable. Unworthy. Cole had been devoted to her but broke up with her because he didn't think he was good enough. What had he said? He was afraid she would have seen his unlovable side.

She knew that feeling. All this time she thought she wasn't good enough for him. That he would eventually dump her for someone glamorous and beautiful. Yet every time he had looked at her, she had felt sexy and brazen. She had seen the desire and adoration in his eyes. She'd seen how his features tightened with lust when she made the first move. She had felt his wonder and awe when they lay exhausted after making love.

But once he was gone, she had questioned everything—the smoldering looks, the secret touches and the anticipation that throbbed between them. They faded from her mind to the point where she thought she'd imagined it all. She'd allowed other people to question and revise what she had shared with Cole. They couldn't understand why he was attracted to her.

"Are you freakishly flexible or something?" Robin asked.

"He's attracted to me because I'm strong, beautiful and smoking hot." At least, that was how he felt when they were dating. She didn't really know if what he felt now was pretend or not.

The women exchanged looks. "Is that what he told you?" Brittany asked with apparent disbelief.

"Yes." Angie smiled and closed her eyes. "Every time he's with me." And during the weekend, she would make sure he found her irresistible.

11

ANGIE TRIPPED WHEN she reached the front door of Foster Investigations. She slapped her hand on the door frame and fought for her balance. Damn shoes. She checked and was grateful no one was around to see how clumsy she was.

How do women walk in these things? She looked down and glared at the black platform heels. Whoever designed them was just evil. Angie stood straight and paused until she stopped wobbling. She smoothed the black bandage dress down her hips and then flipped her long hair over her shoulders.

She was ready. This time she was going to be dressed like the other women at the strip club. Instead of boyish and out-of-place, she would look fun and flirty. Sexy.

She reached for the door and then dropped her hand. What was she trying to do? When Cole saw her, he was going to see this dress as a suggestion. An invitation. Would he see her choice of outfit as the first move?

Angie bit down on her lip and looked back in the direction of the parking lot. It wasn't too late to go home and change. She could always cancel. But deep down, she didn't want to. She wore this dress with Cole in mind. She wanted him to see her as a woman. A sensual and confident woman who didn't let a breakup sideline her.

Angie opened the door and stepped inside the office. "Okay, Cole," she called out from the waiting room. "Let's get this over with."

Cole stepped out of his office. He was rolling down his sleeves and stopped abruptly when he caught a glimpse of her. His eyes widened. "Angie?" he said hoarsely.

She saw the lust in his face. He wasn't even trying to hide it as his gaze traveled leisurely from her eyes to her heels. Her skin tingled with awareness. She felt powerful and exposed at the same time. She wanted to please Cole but she felt like this dress was making a promise she couldn't meet.

Angie suddenly longed for the comfort of her jeans and T-shirts. She wanted to cross her arms and hide the thrust of her breasts. Instead she kept her hands at her sides. "Are you ready?"

Cole slowly walked toward her. His jaw was clenched as his skin flushed. "I don't remember that dress."

"My mom bought it for me last Christmas." It was tradition for her mother to buy a dress and a makeup kit every year. Angie considered it a waste and always felt guilty for not using the gifts but her mother wouldn't let her return them. "I may have to take a picture but I'm worried it would encourage her."

His gaze snagged hers. Her breath caught as she stared into his dark, glittering blue eyes. "You look… wow."

Angie swallowed hard. "Thank you." She felt the tension whipping through him. He wanted her. He wanted to drag her against his body. She could tell he was restraining himself from touching her. Keeping a safe distance, as if he didn't trust himself. "So, what are we looking for? At the strip club?"

"I want to see where Heidi got hurt and decide if it was an accident or a crime. Maybe even come up with a possible weapon," he murmured, distracted by her high hem and bare, toned legs. "Put together a timeline."

"Okay." Angie resisted the urge to tug her dress down. "I still think Robin did it."

He nodded absently and then jerked to a stop as if he remembered something. "I also got Heidi's blood results."

"How did you do that?"

"My clients told me," he said as his gaze lingered on her scooped neckline. "They're taking her back home."

Her breasts felt full and heavy under his gaze. Angie couldn't decide if she wanted to preen or turn away. "That's good, right?"

"It is."

He didn't say anything else. "So what's the problem?" Angie prompted.

He shook his head, as if trying to clear his mind. "She hadn't been drinking," he said, not looking at her. "Apparently she's been sober and clean for years."

"I wonder if Robin or Brittany knew that. I don't think they'd seen her for a while."

"I bet they still view Heidi as a troubled sorority sister," Cole said as he opened the door and gestured for her to go first. "One of them could have tried to make it look like a drunken fall."

"Let's go test our theory." She turned and her heel

snagged on the carpet. Angie reached out and grabbed Cole's arm. His muscle went rigid under her touch. "Sorry."

"Are you going to be okay in those heels?"

"Probably not," she admitted. She held on to his arm. Cole was solid and strong. She felt safe next to him. "I'll just hold on to you, okay?"

"Sure." He reached for her hand and held it against his arm. "I don't mind. Hold on as long as you want."

COLE DIDN'T THINK he would last much longer. The music pulsed a primitive beat. Colorful lights streamed through the dark club. Well-endowed men wearing sequined thongs pranced on the stage and the crowd of women kept screaming for more.

But none of that mattered. All he noticed was Angie. She sat at the bar on a high stool. Her dress had inched up and revealed more of her thighs.

This was a test. He was sure of it.

"What were we thinking?" Cole asked Angie as he stood protectively behind her. He had given every stripper a warning look when they tried to approach. They backed off but he knew it wouldn't last much longer. "This is crazier than the bachelorette party."

Angie swiveled in the chair and her foot bumped against him. "Don't worry, Cole. I'll protect you."

"Very funny," he said as he watched her cross her legs. He was mesmerized by the sensual and fluid motion. His body hardened and his heart pumped harder. Cole gritted his teeth when her skirt drew higher on her thighs.

Angie tilted her head back and smiled. "We'll see how funny it is when these women take one look at you and expect a lap dance."

"They will be disappointed. I dance exclusively for you," he teased. Cole saw her smile dim. "What's wrong?"

"Nothing. Let's consider the timeline. I remember Heidi coming up to us because she wanted a lap dance. She must have gone to the bar after that."

"Why do you say that?"

"She had come over when you were giving me a lap dance." She blushed and looked away. "Heidi had money in her hand but no drink."

"But when we found her there was a drink on the ground next to her."

"It was a Britini. I'm told it's the drink of the wedding. Would Heidi have ordered one to please Brittany?"

"If so, she would want Brittany to see it." He looked around the room. "Brittany wasn't on stage the whole time. The attention was on the dancers. It would have been easy for Brittany to lose herself in the crowd."

"She wore a tiara and a bright red dress. Brittany would have been noticed," Angie said. "And why do you think it was Brittany? It doesn't make sense."

"They could have had a fight," Cole said. "Or Brittany could have seen an opportunity and jumped on it."

"Robin was the one who really hated Heidi. She didn't try to hide it."

"But it sounds like the wedding preparations brought forward a lot of hurtful memories. Remember, Heidi and Robin had been her tormentors when she first rushed the sorority." He looked around the club. "There was nothing here that could be used as a weapon. Unless Brittany brought it and left with it."

"No," Angie said as she reached for her drink. "Security checks the purses."

"Wait a second…" He looked at the tables near the stage. There was nothing on the tabletops except for purses and drink glasses. "The flowers."

"There are no flowers," she said against the rim of her glass.

"Exactly. There were flowers at the bachelorette party."

"Oh, yeah." Angie rolled her eyes. "Brittany wanted the same flowers that would be at the wedding. You would not believe how expensive that turned out to be. It took forever to find the vases that she wanted."

"Were they heavy?"

"They were metallic." She paused and then raised her eyebrows. "Oh, I see what you're saying. Yes, they were heavy enough to cause injury."

"Where are they now?"

Angie shrugged. "Cheryl will know. She has a checklist for everything."

"Whoever did this had nerves of steel. Somehow she hit Heidi and then had the presence of mind to put the flowers back, leaving the scene undisturbed."

"You still have to find the vase." Angie saluted him with her drink. "Good luck with that."

Cole saw a glimmer of sequins from the corner of his eye. He turned and saw Tiger, the most popular stripper in the club, walking toward them. Cole saw the appreciative look Tiger had for Angie. Cole grabbed her hand. "Let's get out of here."

"Wait." Angie clumsily set down her glass. "I wasn't finished."

"Hey, lady." Tiger stood in front of Angie and flexed his chest muscles. "How about a lap dance?"

Angie stared at him. "Who, me?"

"That's not going to happen." Cole had to fight back

the raw, ugly emotions that poured through him. He felt possessive. Territorial. He helped Angie out of her chair and dragged her away. "No one gives this woman a lap dance but me."

"Cole? What is your problem?" Angie asked as she hurried behind him as fast as her heels would allow. "I could have taken care of that myself."

"I declined for you. You're welcome." And yet he wondered if Angie would have accepted the dance out of curiosity or attraction. His gut twisted at the thought.

She tugged hard at his hand as they exited the building. The cold rain pelted them and they huddled together. "Cole, listen to me."

"Once we're in the car." He tried to shelter her as he guided her to the parking lot. Their shoes splashed in the puddles and Angie slipped. He put his arms around her, holding her securely against him until he got her safely in the car.

"You don't speak for me," she said the moment he slid into the driver's seat. "And you don't have any claim on me."

"Yes, I do." He wouldn't let her deny that.

"Because of last night?" she asked as she brushed her damp hair from her face. "That doesn't mean we're back on."

Cole rested his hands on the steering wheel. What would it take to get her back in his life? How many tests would he have to pass to make up for what he'd done? There were some things he knew he wouldn't accept.

"Did you want the guy to dance for you?" he asked accusingly. The idea sickened him. "Did you want me to watch? Give you dollar bills so you could have every stripper in there?"

Her mouth dropped open. "No! I don't want any of those guys. I—"

"Good." He reached for Angie and kissed her. Threading his fingers in her hair, he held the base of her head as he deepened the kiss. He needed to claim her. Brand her with his kiss. It was only fair—he was hers and always has been.

Cole felt the soar of triumph when she softened against him. But then she went stiff and pulled away. Angie drew back in her seat. Her chest rose and fell as she glared at him. "What was that for?"

"Come on, Angie." He didn't mean for his voice to sound harsh, but he was fighting a desperation he didn't understand. He wanted Angie, but he wanted Angie to accept him, as well. "You want this as much as I do. It's been a long time for both of us."

"And you think I would be an easy tumble in bed?" she asked, her voice rising with anger. "Because the guys told you I don't date? That I haven't looked at another guy since you left?"

"I wasn't thinking that at all." But it had given him hope. He wanted it to be a sign that he could fix the mess he'd made. That they shared a bond that couldn't be broken.

"What are you thinking?"

He shoved his hand in his hair. "That I want to drag you into the backseat, rip off that insanely sexy dress and—"

"So you want me."

"Yes."

Angie didn't look away. "Right now."

"Yeah." Immediately, if not sooner. He was rock-hard and had been the moment he saw her in that dress. There would be no foreplay and no lingering touches.

It would be a hard and fast ride the moment he sank into her.

"And then what?" she asked. "What about tomorrow or the next day? How long do you plan to hang around until you walk away again?"

Cole stared at her. Didn't she see that he was still crazy for her? That he wanted to try again. He wasn't planning to walk away again. It nearly broke him the last time. He didn't have the strength to do it again. "I'm here to stay."

Angie crossed her arms. "Why?"

"It's very simple." He pointed at her. "I want you." He pointed at himself. "You want me."

Her mouth formed in a disbelieving smile. "That wasn't enough before."

He scoffed at that statement. "I've always wanted you. From the moment I met you." He had seen her in the gym and had been immediately thunderstruck. He had tried to impress her with his strength and speed only to discover she was just as strong and fast as he was. If she thought that would scare him off, it had the opposite effect. He had been more intrigued than ever.

"But you went away and you stayed away," she pointed out. "You didn't contact me until you needed help on this case. Then you had to pretend to be hot for me. How do you think that makes me feel?"

"I have no idea what's going through your mind. You are driving me crazy. What do you want from me?"

"I want the truth," she said. "The whole truth."

He looked into her eyes. "You are everything I want in a woman."

She blinked, obviously not expecting to hear those words. "What do you want from me now?" she asked.

"Forgiveness? Sex? Do you want to be friends with benefits?"

He held her gaze as the fear pulsed through him. It was too soon to say anything but he had to take the risk. "I want another chance."

She lowered her gaze. "I don't think I can do that again," she whispered.

He held on to the steering wheel and squeezed as the pain rushed through him. "Because I made one mistake."

"No, because I can't be with a guy who won't share his life."

"I just did this morning," he blurted out in frustration. He shared something about his past and it did not go well. "Look at what happened."

"That was one time and you're still holding back," she accused. "You don't trust me. Not enough."

"That's not true," he insisted. "I trust you more than anyone I know."

"You don't trust me enough to talk about yourself. I don't know about your past, I didn't know about your dream of opening an agency and I don't know how you feel about me. And I was with you for over a year." She took a deep breath. "Cole, I'm done with this. This was a mistake."

Cole closed his eyes as her words ripped through him. He was not a mistake. "Angie..."

"Just take me back to your office. I parked my car there," Angie said. Her voice was dull and tired as she looked out the car window. "We got caught up in the pretense. Let's forget this ever happened."

12

As Cole parked in the front of his office building, he felt the weight of this moment. He knew he had to do something or Angie would never be his again. Angie, the only woman he loved and if he were honest, still loved.

Angie had been the most loyal person he knew. She didn't agree with everything he did, but she was there for him. She cheered him on when he needed encouragement and gave him advice when he asked. When he made a mistake, she called him on it. This was a woman he wanted at his side. Yet he never thought she would reach the point where she called it off. But he had found her limit.

That was his specialty. Driving people away.

"We need to talk," he said as he put the car in Park.

"Cole, I'm done talking."

"It won't take long," he said as he watched her unbuckle her seat belt. "Just come into my office. There are a couple of things I need to tell you."

"Like what? About your case?" She exhaled sharply. "Face it, Cole. The whole thing was probably an accident. I can see how it happened after wearing these stupid heels all night. Heidi likely spilled her drink and fell. She hit her head. I don't know why she was facedown. She could have tried to get up but failed."

"That makes sense." His instincts told him something different, but he had no proof. It was time to stop and move on to the next assignment.

"Your case is over," she continued. "Heidi's family reconnected with her. You don't have to investigate anymore. You don't have to go to the rehearsal dinner or the wedding. It's all good."

There was something about Angie's voice that bothered him. She sounded tired. Disappointed. She sounded like she was giving up on him. "That's not what I want to talk about," he said, his voice rough as the fear clawed his chest. "Come on, let's go inside."

Angie paused before she gave a sigh of defeat. "Fine. But you have five minutes."

He helped her out of the car. The rain was now a mist, clinging to their skin and clothes. Angie didn't touch him or hold on to his arm as she navigated the puddles. She didn't say a word as they walked into his office suite. She didn't look around but headed straight for the other room, slapping the light switch as she entered.

"Well?" Angie asked once he stepped into the room after her. "What is so important that we had to discuss it here?"

He took a deep breath but it didn't diminish the nervous energy coursing through his veins. "You're right," he said as he started to pace. "I didn't trust you enough. I didn't realize it until you said it just now."

Angie didn't say anything. She stood by the sofa, arms crossed, as she watched him walk around the small room. She glanced at her wristwatch and the fear gripped him harder. He needed to explain himself and reveal his darkest moments, but he didn't think he could do that under the clock.

"I didn't tell you some things about me because…" He floundered, trying to come up with the right words. He wasn't much of a talker and what he said now would have a great impact on his future. "Because it would open some old wounds."

"It was more than omitting a few important facts," she pointed out. "You lied to me. You led me to believe that you didn't have a family. Why would you lie about something like that?"

"I felt…" He stopped and gathered all the courage he had. "I felt that if you knew all about me, saw the real me, you would leave."

"Okay, that's kind of what you said before. I'm not really sure where this is heading." She sat down on the sofa. "Is there something you've done in your past that I should know about?"

"No." He crossed his arms tightly. "It's about the personal stuff I was going through when we were together. You suggested moving in and that "

"Scared you off, I know." She leaned back into the sofa and crossed her legs. "You didn't want to make that kind of commitment."

"No, you're wrong. I *wanted* to make a commitment." When she had made the suggestion, he wanted to instantly agree before she would have changed her mind. "But I didn't want to make the mistakes I'd made in the past."

He saw the hurt and surprise flash in her eyes. She pressed her lips together. "You lived with someone before me?"

"No, I didn't want to before. I'm not easy to live with. I never have been." He made a face. That was an understatement. He had chosen not to live with anyone, not even a roommate when he was younger, because he knew they would grow to resent and hate him. He hadn't been interested in living with a girlfriend until he met Angie.

She made him want things he told himself he couldn't have. She showed him a world that sounded almost too good to be true. He knew it wouldn't last. He would ruin it just like he always did.

"I wanted…" He paused and tried again. "I wanted to know where I went wrong before I moved in with you. In the past, I had pushed away the people I love. Like my parents."

Angie frowned. "So, what did you do?"

"I tracked them down." It had been incredibly easy. They weren't trying to hide. Not from the government or the rest of the world. Their goal was simple: they wanted to be rid of him.

"Your parents?" She glanced at the family dinner picture on his wall and then back at him. "How long had it been since you'd seen them?"

"Fifteen years." He looked at the floor as he remembered that horrible day. He usually tried not to think about it, or relive that sense of absolute rejection and fear. "One day I had returned home from school and they were gone."

She blinked and leaned forward. "I'm sorry, what?"

"My mom and my stepdad had left me." He rubbed the back of his neck as he felt the heat flood his skin. "There was no note or any contact information. They had taken all their stuff and took off while I was at school."

Her eyes narrowed. "I don't understand."

"I wasn't a runaway, Angie," he said gruffly as he felt the dark emotions welling up inside him. "I was a throwaway. They kicked me out of the family because they didn't want me. They left and started another life."

She stared at him. "What did you do? How did you survive?"

"My friends helped me a lot. But there were nights when I had to live on the streets. I kept going to school because it was warm and I could get a meal. It took a while before I got enough jobs and could support myself."

"Why would your parents leave?"

"My stepfather and I always fought. He was bigger than me and would hit me often. One day he hit me and I hit back hard." His mouth twisted as he remembered how powerful he had felt. He had believed that his stepfather couldn't hurt him anymore. How wrong he had been. "The next day my parents were gone."

"It's taken you this long to track your mom?"

"No." He went and sat next to Angie on the sofa. He felt weary and old. Thinking about that time in his life always dragged him down. "I found out her information a long time ago but I didn't go searching for them. And they definitely weren't interested in looking for me."

"They told you that?" she asked, clearly horrified.

"They didn't have to." He saw it in their faces when he found them. They asked no questions about him or his life. They just wanted him gone. "But when you talked about moving in, I knew I had to find them and answer some questions."

"Did they give you any answers?"

"No." He regretted looking for his mom and step-father.

Angie was quiet for a few minutes before asking, "Where do they live?"

"Across the country. Virginia." He shifted as the image of his mom's new home bloomed in his mind. It was tiny but well-loved. It was a house he would have been grateful to grow up in. "They're doing better than when I lived with them."

"I can't believe your parents didn't look after you." Angie curled in closer. She wrapped her arm around his chest. "They messed up. Not you. What mother would do that?"

"My mother never wanted me. I was an accident." She had ranted about it so many times. How his biological father abandoned them when she got pregnant. How no man wanted her because he was part of the package. How he had better not mess it up with his stepfather. "I was a mistake that changed the course of her life."

"You're not a mistake." Angie leaned her head against his shoulder. "When your parents left you to fend for yourself? That's a mistake. That's a crime."

"I survived." Barely. There were times when he wanted to give up, but pride kept him going. He had been determined to show his parents that he could take care of himself. He had carried the fantasy that his parents would eventually come crawling back to him begging for forgiveness.

"Why didn't you tell me when you found them?" Angie asked. "You didn't need to keep it a secret."

"All this time I thought they were incapable of loving anyone. But I was wrong. They were incapable of loving me. There was something wrong with me."

She pressed her hand against his chest. "That's not true. Don't ever think that."

"It is true. I know because when I tracked them down, my mother was still married to my stepfather. They were happy and doing well." The pain tightened his throat and it hurt to tell the rest of the story. "And they had more children."

She lifted her head. "No."

"Two girls, not yet teenagers." It had been a jarring discovery when he met his half sisters. He had been devastated. "My mom and stepfather take good care of them and are very involved parents."

And if their desertion had been the wound, seeing his parents transform into good parents had been the twist of the knife. It was as if they wanted to start from scratch instead of a do-over. They were able to give those girls a secure and stable home life. Why couldn't they have done it for him when he needed it the most?

"Oh, my God." Angie's eyes held of sheen of tears. "What did your mom say when you found her? Was she ashamed of what she did?"

"No." By the time he had realized that, he had been numb. "She had to make a decision between my stepfather and me. She picked him and she doesn't regret it. And she made it very clear that she doesn't want anything to do with me."

ANGIE DIDN'T KNOW how long she sat with Cole as they held each other. She wished she could do something to take the pain away. She wanted him to know that he was loved, but she knew he wouldn't believe her.

She gave him a light punch on his shoulder. "You should have told me."

He reached up and covered his hand over hers. "It's

difficult to talk about it. My friends' parents would let me stay for a while but they were suspicious. People looked at me differently when they learned the truth. They wanted to know what horrible thing I did to cause my parents to leave. I was a lot of trouble. I wasn't an easy child to love."

"Are you kidding me? You're still taking the blame for what they did?" What kind of mind games did they play on Cole? The anger boiled inside her. "You should have taken me with you. We had been partners. We were in this together."

He squeezed her hands. "I didn't know what I was going to face."

"So you went alone to protect me?" That shouldn't surprise her. He made decisions, dealt with problems and took actions by himself. "Don't do that again."

"Again?" he asked in a teasing tone. "I thought you were done with me."

"Stop throwing my words back at me," she said in a grumble. "I can't believe they left you alone to fend for yourself. That is not acceptable. It's a good thing I didn't meet them or I would have kicked their asses." She glared at Cole when he smiled. "What? This isn't a laughing matter."

"I love seeing this side of you. It's sweet."

"Sweet?" She didn't feel sweet. She was enraged and there was nothing she could do about it. She couldn't shield Cole from the hurt his family had caused him. "You should have told me."

"It's not easy to share. I was ashamed. I still feel like there's something wrong with me. Something…"

Unloveable. She pressed a kiss on his cheek. "You shouldn't be."

He looked away. "You don't know my mom's side of this."

She cupped his face and looked into his eyes. "It doesn't matter. I know who you are. I know what kind of man you've become. I will always be on your side." She touched her lips to his. "Thank you for telling me. It explains a couple of things."

Cole winced. "Like what?"

"Your interest in finding missing persons, the pictures in this office." His inability to commit, she added silently. He wanted to, but there was no way he would overcome his family's desertion.

"I don't like the sound of that," Cole said.

Angie realized that he was feeling exposed. He was a loner who felt more comfortable in the shadows. She awkwardly patted his shoulder and moved to get up. "I should go now."

"Stay." The one word sounded more like a plea than a command. His hands were still on her back but she could easily leave.

She wanted to stay. She loved him—always had, always would—but it wasn't right. She should get up and go before she got too attached again.

"Please," he whispered as he brushed his mouth against hers.

She'd stay, Angie decided as she leaned into him and kissed him. She wanted him for one night. She wanted everything and was willing to take the risk. Starting now.

As she kissed him softly, Angie felt an overwhelming need to touch him. Caress his chest and hug him. Hold his hand and take away his pain. She wanted to protect him and show him love. But a part of her knew that kind of slow intimacy would scare off Cole.

Her lips clung to his before Cole pulled way. She wasn't sure what she'd expected when he opened his eyes. His vulnerability tore at her. She knew he was wary of her. He was unsure of what her kiss meant.

She kissed him again, pouring everything she felt into it. She wanted to tell him how much she loved him. That she wanted to be with him, share the good and the bad. But he wasn't ready to hear that. He may never be.

Cole moaned and broke off the kiss. "Wait a second," he said as he held her an arm's length away. "Just a few minutes ago you thought this was a mistake. That *I* was a mistake."

Angie pulled at the front of his shirt and drew him closer. "I was wrong." She never should have used the word *mistake*. It brought up bad memories and deep insecurities.

"All of a sudden you're wrong?" he asked as he lowered her down on the sofa and lay on top of her.

"Because now I understand," she said as she tilted her hips, cradling Cole against her. She understood what drove him away. Now she knew he had been betrayed by his loved ones.

She also knew he was very private, but now she had a reason why he felt safer alone. She wanted him to know that not only was he safe with her, but she would also protect him and give him strength by being at his side.

Cole slid his hand over her bare leg and pulled off her shoe. He tossed it across the room and the other shoe followed. Angie wrapped her legs tightly around his waist. She held him close as she trailed a string of hard, fast kisses along his throat. She smiled when she felt the rumble of a growl against her mouth.

Cole hiked her skirt up and placed his hand between

her legs. He stilled. "Are you completely naked under this dress?" he asked hoarsely.

"Yes," she said. His touch felt incredible. She wanted more.

"It's a good thing I didn't know that until now. I wouldn't have been able to concentrate before." He stroked her and Angie shivered with delight.

She moaned as the anticipation built. Cole always knew just how to tease her, dipping his finger into her wet heat before withdrawing completely. And doing it over and over until she writhed underneath him. "Please, Cole."

He didn't follow her request. Instead, Cole slipped off the sofa and placed her feet on the floor. For a moment Angie thought he was ending this before it started. She reached out for him just as he kneeled between her legs. Her stomach tightened with excitement as he splayed her legs and placed his mouth on her sex.

Angie bucked her hips at the first flip of his tongue. She gripped the back of his head, her fingers winding through his hair, as he pleasured her. She wanted to hold on to this moment, but this night was supposed to be for him. She meant to show him love but got caught up in the sensations that only Cole could provide.

"You shouldn't," she murmured as she gently lifted her hips. Angie gasped when his tongue touched her clit.

"I want to," he said against her skin. "Let me."

She reluctantly let go of his hair. Angie gave a keening cry as he explored her with his mouth and fingertips. The hot need pulled deep in her pelvis, growing stronger.

Her climax came suddenly, pulsing hard through her body. It stole her breath as her skin went hot. Angie tightened her legs against Cole as she clutched his head. She rode out the wicked pleasure before sagging against the sofa.

She was aware of Cole taking off her clothes. She was limp and spent, her mind buzzing, as Cole tugged the snug outfit off of her. Her small breasts swung freely as he discarded the dress. She reached for him, their fingers colliding as they pulled at his shirt.

Their uneven breaths and the rustle of clothing were the only sounds in the room. The rush of blood pounded in her ears as Cole stood before her naked. She slowly licked her lips as she stared.

He was magnificently masculine, from his broad shoulders and wide chest to his powerful thighs and thick penis. Angie's core clenched as she noticed his arousal. His skin was flushed and his muscles were trembling with barely leashed restraint. Cole was ready to pounce.

He reached for her, his hands firm but urgent, and he laid her down on the floor. She felt the crumpled dress and the soft carpet underneath her spine. Cole was on his knees in front of her, his hands caressing her breasts, resting at her hips. She felt the nervous flutter of excitement as he surged into her.

"Hold on to me," he said roughly.

She pressed her body against him, acutely aware of their differences. His hard chest ground into her soft breasts. His movements were rushed and urgent while her hands lingered on his heated skin. She moved beneath him, yielding to his demanding thrusts.

Angie curled her arms and legs around Cole. She burrowed her head into his neck as he drove into her. She felt his desperation. The wildness poured through him. Cole let out a hoarse cry as he pulsed in her. He thrust one last time before he sank onto her.

Angie welcomed his weight and his heat. She welcomed him back into her heart. And this time, she wouldn't let him go.

13

ANGIE WOKE UP with a start. She looked around, her heart pounding. The room was shadowy and quiet. It took her a second to realize that she was in Cole's office. She was on the sofa with a soft fleece tucked around her.

She noticed her dress was lying still crumpled on the floor next to her heels. Cole's clothes were gone. "Cole?" she called out. She waited but there was no response.

Slowly sitting up, Angie glanced at the windows. The shades were pulled down but she could tell by the shadows that it was wet and gloomy outside. She looked at the clock in the office and saw that it was early morning.

Where was Cole? She glanced at the closed door. It felt wrong waking up alone. She was used to rising in the early morning with him. They took their time getting out of bed, unwilling to break apart.

Don't think about that. That is in the past, Angie reminded herself. And she wouldn't read in to Cole's absence, either. It wasn't a big deal.

She wiggled into the bandage dress. Great, she thought as she combed her hair with her fingers. She stayed out all night the one time she wears a dress and heels. Now she gets to do the walk of shame.

I've done nothing to be ashamed about, Angie thought as she scooped up her shoes. She made love to Cole because she wanted to. She loved him and she wanted to be with him. Last night she felt closer to him than ever before.

Damn. She was still in love with him. She had been prepared to break it off because he wouldn't let her get close. But last night gave her hope. He opened up and trusted her with his most painful secret.

Angie looked at the framed print of the family dinner and shook her head. She couldn't imagine what Cole went through. She wanted to take that pain away and carry it for him. But the only thing she could do was offer him understanding and patience.

She wasn't sure what her next move should be. Angie suspected that Cole would feel awkward with her. He'd revealed something he clearly wasn't comfortable sharing. Nothing she said to him would make him believe he wasn't responsible for his parents' desertion. He'd left her a year ago because he thought it had only been a matter of time before she was going to leave him.

And she almost did last night. He knew it, too. Otherwise he wouldn't have told her about his past. She knew she had to show him that she wasn't going to leave. Not now, not when she finally understood why he was so private and why he kept pushing her away. He was waiting for her to see him as too much trouble and break up with him.

She strode into the waiting room barefoot just as

she heard the key in the lock. Angie's heart leaped and she smiled when Cole entered the office carrying two cups of coffee.

He skidded to a stop. "You're up."

"Morning." She couldn't contain the joy inside her. She felt gloriously, vibrantly alive. She took a step forward, ready to open her arms wide and greet him with a loving embrace and a long kiss.

"Here, this is for you." He held out a coffee cup.

"Oh…" She stopped in midstep and slowly dropped her arms. Her chest tightened as she saw the hunted look in his eyes. He didn't want to be here. Correction, she thought, as the joy fizzled, he didn't want to be here with her. "Thanks."

She was the one who felt awkward as she accepted the cup. She noticed how careful Cole was not to let their hands touch. She glanced up through her lashes but he wasn't looking at her.

"Are you okay?" she asked quietly.

"Me? Yeah." He held his coffee cup with both hands. "You?"

She knew he was ready to bolt. Whatever she did next was important. She had to tread carefully.

Angie stared at the cup as she turned it in her hands. "About the wedding rehearsal tonight…"

"I'm going." His voice was harsh.

How did he know what she was going to say? "You don't have to."

"We made a deal," he reminded her. "I'll keep my side of the bargain."

"But that was when you needed to look into Heidi's accident," she said. "The whole reason we pretended to be together was so you could get behind-the-scenes access. That's no longer an issue."

He gave her a cold look, his eyes narrowed and his jaw set. Cole suddenly moved and set his coffee on the table. "Angie, do you want me to stay away from the wedding?"

"What? No!" She was making a mess out of this.

"You were ready to get rid of me last night. You're still trying. But I gave my word and I'm taking you to the rehearsal dinner and the wedding."

"I wasn't trying to get rid of you." She closed her eyes. "I thought we were getting caught up in the pretense."

Cole looked at the floor and shuffled his feet. She saw the tips of his ears turn bright red. "I know that last night was…"

Awesome. Amazing. Incredible. Take your pick. She held her breath as she waited for Cole's next words.

He exhaled and started again. "Last night you gave me comfort when I needed it."

She blinked as he said those words in a rush. "Comfort?" she repeated. "You think that was comfort?" She gave him her heart and soul. She showed him how she felt with every touch and every kiss.

"You're important to me, Angie," he continued. "Though last night I didn't know if I was out of your life or back in your bed. You obviously don't know what you want but I don't want to be pushed out and then pulled back in over and over. I've had enough of that in my life and I don't need it from you. We've finally got back to where we are friends and I don't want to risk that over last night."

She flinched as his words drove into her like a twisted knife. *Friends?* They just made love and he wanted to be *friends?* Angie swiped the tip of her tongue along her dry lips. "Do you usually have sex with your friends?"

"I've never had a friend who was a woman," he admitted. "It's different with you. I think this is all I can handle right now."

That hurt. She loved him and he didn't love her like that. He didn't love her enough. She was in the same place she was a year ago. Only this time, she thought they were getting closer. Instead, she pushed him too hard, too soon. This guy didn't want a second chance anymore. She'd scared him off. The best he could offer was friendship.

"So…" He gave her a quick look. "We're good?"

She wanted to hide. She had put herself out there and had given him everything. She was renewing her commitment to Cole but he wanted to keep her at a distance. It was like a slap in the face but she refused to show her hurt.

"Sure," she said, praying that he couldn't see she was dying inside. "You never can have enough friends."

14

"That was the longest wedding rehearsal ever," Angie muttered to Cole. They were standing at the window of the fancy restaurant in Seattle's downtown waterfront district and watching the other guests at the post-rehearsal dinner. She was glad he was there with her. She could express her real feelings with him. "I am starving. I don't think I can face another of Brittany's home videos without something in my stomach."

"That rehearsal was pretty intense," Cole said. "I'm not surprised Robin kept making mistakes. Brittany was putting a lot of pressure on her."

Angie rubbed her stomach and looked longingly at the empty table settings. "I don't know who was the worst taskmaster, the bride or the minister."

"Cheryl," Cole decided. He had sat quietly in the back of the church, thinking it would be a quick walk-through of the ceremony. An hour later he had been stunned at the focus on detail. "She is like a drill sergeant."

"How can someone that tiny be so scary?" Angie

leaned against the wall and studied Brittany's assistant. "I think the best man may be traumatized for life."

Cole looked at where Cheryl stood. At first glance the curvy blonde appeared almost sweet and nonthreatening. Maybe it was the pink leopard-print dress or the way she flirted with the men. But Cheryl was tenacious and didn't back down until she got the results she wanted.

He cast a quick glance at Angie, who wore a black pantsuit and flat shoes. The jacket was big and her shirt was buttoned all the way to the high collar. The pants had a wide leg. Last night she wore a skintight dress that showed a lot of skin. Tonight she was hiding her body. Her femininity. She was dressed similar to the groomsmen.

"What's with the suit?" he asked.

She slowly looked at him and then at her outfit. "What's wrong with it?" she asked with warning.

He shrugged. "I liked what you wore last night." The little black dress had been out of her comfort zone. She had shown a side of herself she wasn't confident about. But she had given him a glimpse and he thought it meant something.

"You made that obvious," she said. "But don't read anything into it. It wasn't like I was dressing for a date. I wore it so I would blend in at the strip club."

"And what is this?" He reached out and flipped the lapel. The fabric was surprisingly soft.

She straightened the jacket lapel. "This is what I wear when I'm hanging out with the guys." Angie glared at him. "Why the sudden interest in my outfit?"

"Why the sudden interest in hiding behind several layers of clothes?" he countered. "You weren't last night."

"I'm not hiding. You are," she accused. "We made love last night and then you turn around and say 'Hey, thanks for comforting me. Let's stay friends. No hard feelings.'"

Made love? Her choice of words intrigued him. "I was doing you a favor. My past is my burden, not yours. I knew you would see me differently and I was giving you an out."

"You weren't giving me a choice. You're pushing me away. *Again,*" Angie stressed. "Only this time you're not walking away. No, this time you're putting me in the friend zone where you know I don't want to be."

"How am I supposed to act? You were the one calling it quits last night. I tried to do better. And suddenly we're having sex because you felt sorry for me. Excuse me if I don't jump up and down with joy for getting pity sex from you."

"Pity sex?" she hissed, her eyes wide. "Cole, that wasn't pity. That was…"

"What?" he asked when she stopped and pressed her lips together. "See? This is what I get when I tell you stuff. I don't want your pity. I'm not a charity case. I'd rather have your anger than have you feel sorry for me."

"That's not how I see you," she said. "I see a man who struggled and made something of himself without the support of a family. I see a guy who tracks down the forgotten because he had once been left behind. That's not pity, Cole."

Cole stared in her eyes. She was sincere, but there was something else. Respect? Love? He couldn't be sure. His heart started to pound. "Then what—"

"Angie," Robin said as she approached them. Her cloud of perfume enveloped them when she stopped at Angie's side. She gave them both a cautious look. "Am I interrupting something?"

Angie was the first to break eye contact. "No, Robin. Not at all," she said with a polite smile. "What's up?"

How could she do that? Cole wondered. She had him off balance and desperate for answers. He wanted to drag Angie away from this party and find out if he still had a chance with her. Instead, he clenched his hands and tried to find the last of his patience.

"Did you notice that you're in every picture and video with Patrick?" Robin asked, gesturing at the television screen set up in the corner, causing her martini to slosh in the glass. "I didn't realize you two were that close."

"They've been best friends since kindergarten," Cole said. Friendships were important to Angie. Her circle of friends was small but long-lasting. She'd break up with a boyfriend but her friends were forever.

"And you never went on a date?" Robin asked as she took a sip of her drink. "Not even once?"

"What can I say?" Angie said with a shrug. "I'm always in the friend zone."

Cole stiffened. He knew that was aimed at him. "That's not true," he said as he grasped the end of her ponytail. "Becoming your basketball buddy was the last thing on my mind when I met you."

"That's because I'm better at basketball," Angie said before she turned away and faced Robin. "I've never dated those guys but they've given me lots of dating advice."

"And none of their tips worked," Cole pointed out as he gave her hair a tug, demanding her attention. Her friends had tried to make her into the kind of woman they'd date. He had wanted the real Angie. A woman who could challenge him on the field and who could bring him to his knees with a simple touch.

"Weird." Robin smacked her lips and frowned at her martini glass. "Have you tried the Britini? It's really sweet but it has a kick."

"No, thanks." Angie held her hand up as Robin offered the glass.

"It tastes a little different tonight. I'm not sure why." Robin puckered her lips. "So, tell me, Angie. Which of the groomsmen are single?"

Angie jerked her head back at the maid of honor's question. "Tim and Steven. I don't think either of them even brought dates tonight."

"Good." Robin leaned against the wall and studied the men on the other side of the room. "I haven't decided which one I want."

"For what?" Angie asked.

"A bridesmaid always hooks up at a wedding." Robin gave her a strange look. "How do you not know this?"

Angie turned to Cole. "I haven't heard of that tradition."

"It doesn't apply to you because I'm your date," he said as he wrapped his finger around her ponytail. "Don't forget it."

"How could I?" Angie said sweetly.

"Angie, you hit the jackpot and landed a stripper. It really isn't fair." Robin rubbed her forehead and looked at her martini glass. "I probably should put this down. It's stronger than I remember and it's giving me a headache."

Angie tried to step away from his hold but he wasn't letting go. He was rewarded with a glare as Robin set down her glass at her assigned seat.

"So, you know all the guys here, right?" Robin asked Angie as she tugged her pink strapless dress in place. "Which ones have you dated?"

"None of them," Angie replied.

"Seriously?" Robin studied the men and then studied Angie. "Not one of these guys made a move on you? What are you doing wrong?"

The question seemed to fluster Angie. "I…I don't…"

Cole curled his arm around her waist. "The problem with growing up with these guys," he said, "is that there's no mystery left. They know each other's secrets, embarrassing moments and questionable dating history."

"Ah, got it. Finding out is half the fun." Robin fluffed out her hair and yanked up her strapless dress. "I'm going to go flirt with the redhead. What's his name? Tim? Wish me luck."

"LET GO OF my hair," Angie told Cole as she watched Robin sashay toward the group of men. "Don't make me pull out my self-defense moves."

"You should know better than to put your hair in a ponytail. It puts you at a disadvantage." Cole said as he reluctantly let go.

She felt like Cole was the one who put her at a disadvantage. She was very aware of him and she couldn't think straight. Her skin tingled when he touched her and she wanted to lean into him when he drew near. But he didn't seem to have the same problem. He wanted to just be friends.

"I have to ask since Robin brought it up," Cole said. "Why haven't you dated any of those guys?"

"There was no mystery left," she said in a monotone. "We know each other's secret—"

He stepped closer and rested his hand on her hip. "The real reason," he whispered in her ear.

They're not you. Cole was a mix of strength and gentleness, of hard-earned wisdom and quiet humor. She was amazed at his level of curiosity and patience. He was everything she wanted in a man. In a partner. No man could compare to Cole.

Maybe that was why she was thinking of marriage when they hadn't discussed it. She saw something in Cole that he didn't see in himself. He didn't have a family but he valued the connection so much that he dedicated his life's work to reuniting relatives. When they had been together, she instinctively knew he had claimed her as his own. His way of making a commitment wasn't by living together or exchanging vows. He would protect and take care of her, even if it meant keeping his distance.

"Come on, Angie," he cajoled. "You can tell me the truth. Why haven't you dated any of the men in your life?"

"Lack of interest," she finally said. "On my part and on theirs."

"Don't be too sure about that." He gave a sidelong look at her friends. "I think Tim has always had a crush on you."

She rolled her eyes. "You weren't worried about that while we were dating. But why should you? You knew no one would notice me."

"That's because you don't want to be noticed," he accused. "It's like you want to be invisible. The day I met you in the gym you had on sweatpants and an old T-shirt. I noticed you right away. You thought you were blending in but you had no idea how smoking hot you are. You walked right by me on the treadmill and I tripped."

"I remember that part. But what did you think when you first noticed me?" she asked. "Did you think I should let my hair down? That it was a shame I didn't do anything with my appearance?"

"I liked the way you walk." Cole's eyes took on a carnal gleam. "How you moved. It was powerful and sensual. I couldn't stop watching you."

Angie felt the heat crawl up her neck. She wasn't expecting that. Most people saw what she lacked. How she could improve and what a makeover could do for her. Cole saw something else.

"What about now?" she challenged. "Do you think I'm sexy in this suit?"

"You can't hide from me, Angie." His voice was a rasp. "Not even in that jacket."

Angie shivered and she buttoned up the jacket. She wasn't sure if she liked hearing that. "It's not that bad. I like it. It's comfortable."

"Wear whatever you want," he said. "It won't stop me from remembering how you feel underneath me, hot and naked."

"Stop it. Someone might hear you." She looked around and caught Cheryl's eye.

"I know what you look like when you're going wild. For me," he said, his tone thick with satisfaction. "Go ahead and hide. But know that I'm imagining peeling those clothes off you, layer by layer."

"Cheryl is coming this way. Behave," she pleaded. "Stop looking at me like you want to pin me against this wall and have your wicked way with me."

Cole's smile was slow and sexy. "Now there's a thought...."

"Have you seen Robin?" Cheryl asked as she tapped her pen against her small clipboard. "She's supposed to make a speech before we show the video of Brittany's college years."

"She went to flirt with Tim," Cole told her. Angie could feel his gaze on her. She adjusted the high collar that suddenly felt coarse and confining.

Cheryl glanced over at the groomsmen. "No, they said they haven't seen her."

"She was complaining about a headache," Angie said. "Something about having too much to drink. I'll go see if she's in the bathroom."

"Oh, you don't have to," Cheryl said, trying to stop her. "You're a guest."

"I know but you have so many other things on your to-do list," Angie replied. "It's not a problem." It would also allow her to break the spell that Cole was weaving around her. He was too close. He saw things about her she wanted to keep hidden.

Angie hurried out of the room and looked around for the restroom. She saw the sign and turned, bumping into her friend Steven.

"Hey, Angie," he greeted, his voice loud and slightly slurred. "Can you believe Patrick is going to be married tomorrow?"

Angie watched in horror when she saw Steven's chin wobble as tears formed in his eyes. "Steven, keep it together."

"He'll be the first of us to get married." He flung his arm around her shoulders and she staggered from his weight. "I never thought that would really happen."

"I'm surprised that a woman is marrying Patrick on purpose," Angie said as she tried to push Steven to stand on his own, "but I guess we underestimated him."

"Sssh." His fingers fumbled over her mouth. "I could have sworn you would be the first to marry in our group."

"Because I'm a female and therefore dream of weddings?" she asked. She never daydreamed about a wedding ceremony. She had no interest in dresses and tiaras.

"I thought you and Cole would make it down the aisle," Steven said as he clumsily patted her head. "Angie and Cole, sitting in a tree…first comes love, then comes marriage, then comes…something…how does it go?"

Angie gritted her teeth. This was why she hated weddings. "Steven, I'm never getting married. I'm not catching the bouquet so don't try to push me into the line of fire tomorrow. And if you keep saying that I'm the next one to get married, I will put you in a head-lock."

"I should put Cole in a headlock," he grumbled.

She propped Steven against the wall. "Leave Cole alone. Promise?"

"Just one punch?" Steven wagged a finger at her. "He broke your heart last time. He's going to do it again."

Angie sighed deeply. Her friends were only protecting her. They had no idea that Cole just wanted to be friends. The anger bubbled up inside her. She was so tired of being one of the guys. "Okay, fine. One punch."

"What?" Cole's voice was right behind her.

Angie jumped and looked around to see Cole's incredulous expression. "What? You have nothing to worry about. Steven's never been in a fight in his life."

"So you don't just hate weddings," Cole said with

a look in his eyes that Angie couldn't identify. "It's marriage, too."

She wasn't ready to have this discussion. She hated being Brittany's bridesmaid and she was getting sick of this wedding, but she didn't hate the idea of weddings. Not really.

Angie believed in love and marriage. True, she never thought about it for herself until she met Cole. She wanted to make a lifelong commitment with him, but she also knew now that he would never marry or settle into a family life. Okay, he could commit to her but he still bore the scars of his childhood. Cole Foster was the only man she wanted to marry but that wasn't going to happen no matter how much she wished for it.

"Cole, can you make sure Steven gets back to the rehearsal dinner? His sense of direction isn't that great even when he's sober." She didn't stop to see if Cole would agree. "Steven, have you seen Robin? The maid of honor?" she added, given her friend's confused expression.

"Yeah, wow." Steven shook his head. "She can't hold her liquor."

"What are you talking about?" Cole asked. "We just saw her and she was fine."

"She was making a play for me. Then her face got all red and blotchy. She clutched her throat."

"Like she was choking?" Angie asked.

"No. I assumed she was going to throw up. I saw her stagger into the bathroom." Steven pointed at the door down the hall.

"I should check on her," Angie told Cole as she rushed to the bathroom. She wasn't sure why she was so worried. Robin was getting sick. It happens. No big deal.

But she couldn't suppress the alarm that was shooting through her veins. Angie mentally braced herself before she pushed open the door. "Robin? Are you doing okay?"

Angie froze when she saw Robin sprawled on the bathroom floor.

Cole stood behind Angie as they watched the paramedics wheel Robin away on a stretcher. Angie had taken care of Robin and now looked as if she were going to collapse herself. He knew how she felt.

"Are you okay?" he asked Angie softly as he put his arms around her. "You're shaking like a leaf."

"I'm fine. It's just the adrenaline." She stuffed her hands in her pockets. "It'll go away soon."

"You did great," he said. "She's going to recover."

He had been impressed in how Angie jumped into action. He had raced to her when she called out. There had been something in the way she'd called his name. It shook him to the core and all he could think about was getting to Angie. He wanted to protect her and take over.

But by the time he stepped into the bathroom, Angie had already taken an EpiPen out of Robin's small purse. Without any hesitation, she had jabbed the needle in the maid of honor's thigh. She had continued with the rescue breathing while he phoned for an ambulance. Angie was shaking now but she had been focused and thorough during the crisis. It was one of the many things he admired about her.

He heard the piercing siren start and saw the ambulance's lights as the vehicle sped away. "How did you even know she needed an epinephrine injection?" he asked.

"She said something about food allergies when she was at the hospital café." Angie rested her head against his shoulder and didn't protest when he stroked her hair. "I know Steven thought she was drunk but we had just seen her and she had complained of a headache. I figured something was off when he described the symptoms but I didn't think about an allergic reaction until I saw her on the floor."

"I wondered what was in the hors d'oeuvres," he said as they walked slowly back to the dining room. It was eerily quiet compared to the festive spirit of a mere few minutes ago. Now the video was turned off and the guests were milling aimlessly in the entryway and parking lot. "Where was Robin going to sit?"

"There." Angie pointed at the empty seat. "The maid of honor was going to sit next to the groom."

He stared at the place setting. There was a wet ring on the tablecloth from where her pink martini had been. "Where's her drink? She had set it down when she got the headache."

"She was almost finished with it," Angie said. She stepped away from him and picked up Robin's place card from the table. "I'm sure the waiting staff removed it."

Cole wasn't so sure. "Do you remember how she said it tasted differently?"

"The recipe isn't hard science." Her fingers continued to tremble as she set the card down. "The bartender here could have used a different bubble gum. I'm sure she ate an hors d'oeuvre and didn't know the ingredients."

"No, she was careful. I saw her," he said as he examined the other tables. Most of the guests still had their drinks next to their place cards.

"I can't believe this is happening," Brittany said as she stormed into the room with Cheryl and Patrick trailing behind her. Her face was mottled red and her hair was falling out of its neat twist. Cole felt the anger come off her in waves.

"What was Robin allergic to?" Cole asked Brittany.

Brittany stepped back abruptly and gave him a strange look. As if she had already forgotten about Robin's situation. "How should I know? Am I supposed to know every food restriction and allergy of every guest?"

"I'm sure she mentioned it when she had to choose her meals for the dinners."

Brittany crossed her arms and thrust out her chin. "What are you trying to say?"

"Peanuts," Cheryl interrupted. "It was on the card when she RSVP'd. She's very allergic to peanuts. There couldn't be any cross-contamination in the kitchen."

"See?" Angie told Cole. "Accidents happen."

He knew what Angie was trying to tell him. He shouldn't waste his time and pursue the incident like he did with Heidi's fall. But he couldn't let it go. "Accidents are happening a lot with this wedding."

"They certainly are," Brittany said as she stood in front of them. Her legs were braced for a fight and her hands were on her hips. Her cream lace dress was pale compared to her flushed face. "And they always seem to happen when Angie is around."

Angie rolled her shoulders back and cast a stern glare at Brittany. "Are you saying I'm bad luck?"

"I think you're trying to sabotage my wedding." The guests gasped at Brittany's suggestion and started to whisper.

Cole felt the flare of anger. He saw Angie's lips part in shock. And he saw Patrick standing behind his fiancée and saying nothing. Cole was ready to step in and fight for Angie's honor, but Angie held out her hand and stopped him.

"Why would I do that?" Angie asked coldly.

"Oh, I don't know." Brittany's eyes glittered with rage. "Because you want Patrick for yourself."

Angie looked at Brittany as if the bride had lost her mind. "He's not my type." She gave her friend a quick look of apology. "No offense, Patrick."

"Angie has never been interested in Patrick," Tim interjected. "I always thought she wasn't into men until she hooked up with Cole."

"Thanks, Tim, but I can take it from here," Angie said without looking at him.

"I know you don't like me," Brittany said in a hiss. "You're jealous because you're not the first person Patrick calls anymore. You've been downgraded and you can't stand it."

"You're wrong, Brittany. I don't care about that."

"Then it's because you hate weddings," Brittany growled. "You've made that very clear."

Cole wanted to defend Angie. Yes, she hated weddings. It took him by surprise, too. Her declaration unsettled him and he wasn't sure why. She had a traditional streak that he loved. She wasn't the type to flip through bridal magazines or cry during the exchange of rings. But she respected the vows and she upheld the values that were symbolized in weddings.

Although that didn't stop Angie from hating this wedding, it seemed, and he didn't judge her for it. She was trying to be supportive to her friend. No one noticed that she wouldn't do otherwise for a friend. She would stand up for Patrick and defend his decision in a wife, even if he were making a huge mistake in marrying this woman.

"Angie was just saying she hated weddings," Steven said. "And marriage, too."

Cole closed his eyes and reined in his temper before he reached out and silenced Angie's friend. At least the guys were sort of helping her, unlike Patrick.

"See?" Brittany crossed her arms as if to say she had proved her point. "There you go."

"I have been nothing but obliging about your wedding." Angie took a step forward but stopped when Cole placed his hand on her shoulder. He knew her emotions were all over the place and that she could react unpredictably. "I have done everything you asked of me."

"Then why do all these 'accidents,'" sputtered Brittany, who was using air quotes, "and disasters happen when you're around?"

"Because I'm required to be at every event," Angie said calmly with a hint of real bitterness. "Every meeting, every fitting and every shower."

"I wish you didn't have to be. I knew you were trouble, but I had no choice." Brittany gestured wildly at her fiancé. "Patrick wanted you in the bridal party and I certainly wasn't going to let you be the best man."

"Brittany..." Patrick said, but his warning had no

conviction. Cole knew Patrick would take Brittany's side, even if his bride tore Angie's feelings to shreds.

"Having you in my bridal party changed everything," Brittany revealed to Angie. "Heidi and Robin weren't my first choice of bridesmaids. I had to ask them so we could work around your coloring and your body type."

"That's not my fault," Angie said. "And who picks a bridesmaid based on their hair color? That's ridiculous."

Brittany wasn't listening. "And now my maid of honor is hospitalized? Again? That can't be a coincidence." She clenched her fists at her sides and stood toe-to-toe with Angie. Angie refused to back down.

"Patrick," Cole said as he watched Brittany vibrate with anger. "Get her away from Angie or I will." And he wouldn't be gentle when protecting Angie.

"Relax, Brittany," Angie said as she met the bride's hateful gaze. "I'm sure Robin will be fine for tomorrow's ceremony."

"But what if she isn't?" Brittany poked her finger against Angie's shoulder. "You've ruined everything."

"That's enough." Cole stood between Angie and Brittany. He wasn't about to allow this to escalate into a fistfight. "Angie didn't do this. I was with her."

Brittany snorted at his claim. "I'm supposed to take the word of a stripper?"

Cole's nostrils flared. He wanted to tell Brittany that he was a former police detective and a private investigator. Most people would accept him as a credible witness and a solid alibi.

"Then take the word of the groomsman," Angie said. "Take the ushers' word. They all know me. They will vouch for me."

Tim and Steven stared at each other and then looked away. "I need to use the bathroom," Tim said as he darted for the door.

"Me, too," Steven muttered as he backed away from the group.

"Seriously, guys?" Angie asked.

"And why does Brittany think Cole is a stripper? Wait up, Tim," Steven said as he sprinted after his friend.

"Come on, Brittany," Cheryl cooed in a soothing voice as she cautiously touched her boss's elbow. "Let's have you sit down and get something to drink."

Brittany gave Angie one last hateful look before she allowed her assistant to lead her to an empty table.

Cole grabbed Patrick's arm to keep him from following. "I need to talk to you."

"Dude, I'm sorry about Brittany," he said in a low voice and looked over at his fiancée. "I'll talk to her. She's upset and she doesn't know what she's saying. Angie is still in the wedding."

"No," Cole said. "I don't want her in the wedding."

"I'm right here, guys," Angie said as she stood next to them. "Rather than talking about me, try talking *to* me."

"I'm serious." Cole glanced to where Brittany and her assistant were sitting. "Someone is trying to take out the bridesmaids, one by one. Angie is next."

Patrick's mouth twisted with displeasure. "You don't know that."

"You have two injured bridesmaids," Cole pointed out. "What are the odds?"

"Maids of honor," Angie said, correcting him. She shrugged when he and Patrick looked down at her. "They got hurt when they were maids of honor."

"That's crazy," Patrick said. "Who would do something like that?"

"I don't know." But Cole had his suspicions. He hoped he was wrong.

Patrick's features tightened with anger. "Do you realize what you're saying? The only people at this party are my friends and family."

Angie glanced at Cole. "He catches on a lot faster than Brittany."

"These were accidents," Patrick whispered fiercely. "Do not share your theories with Brittany. The last thing I need is a paranoid bride."

Cole sensed that Patrick was listening. He just didn't want to hear it. Didn't want to believe it. "Keep an eye on her," Cole suggested. "I don't know if someone has it in for Brittany or if it has something to do with the bridesmaids."

"I'm not supposed to see the bride until the wedding." Patrick rubbed his hands over his face. "Stupid tradition." He paused and looked hopefully at Angie.

"Oh, no." Angie shook her head. "That is so not going to happen. I will not be the bride's babysitter. She already thinks I'm trouble."

"Besides, I'm watching Angie tonight," Cole added.

Angie gave him a look of surprise. "No, you're not."

"I'm taking you back to my apartment."

"I have to report to Brittany's after the dinner. It's some sort of final bridal send-off, although it sounds like a bait and switch. I suspect I'll be roped into making hundreds of party favors for most of the night."

"Forget it." He didn't want Angie to be around anyone from this group. She would be trapped and defenseless if someone attempted to harm her.

She put her hands on her hips. "I can't. Brittany is

already mad at me. If I skip this last event, it will send her over the edge."

"I admit she's upset," Patrick said. "But everything about this wedding is going wrong. Fine, you guys deal with this on your own, I need to take care of Brittany."

Cole nodded and waited until Patrick was some distance away from them. "Angie, listen to me."

"I'm okay," Angie insisted. "No one is targeting me."

"You don't know that for sure." She was the last bridesmaid and would probably be promoted to be maid of honor. The wedding was tomorrow and the person doing all this would have to act fast.

"Think about it, Cole. Heidi and Robin went to the same school and the same sorority. They are friends with Brittany. I have nothing in common with them."

"Other than being a bridesmaid."

She gave a huff of exasperation, refusing to agree with the obvious. "We already decided what happened to Heidi was an accident."

"But now a pattern is emerging."

Angie scoffed at him. "Two accidents do not make a pattern."

He wasn't going to wait for the third. "I want to play it safe."

"Heidi had a head injury." She splayed one hand. "Robin had an allergic reaction." She splayed out her other hand. "Each accident is different."

"But they both look like accidents."

"All right," she said through clenched teeth. "I will be extra cautious tonight and tomorrow. Okay?"

"Not good enough," Cole said. "Whoever is doing this won't take any chances. They'll make sure you can't be at the ceremony."

Angie sighed and smoothed her hands over her hair as she tried to decide what to do. "Do you still think it's Brittany?" she asked in a low voice.

"No, not anymore."

She looked around the restaurant. "Who do you think it is?"

He hesitated. He wanted to tell Angie his suspicions so she would be wary, but he knew Angie would act on any information he gave her. She would pursue instead of retreat. "I'm not sure."

Angie narrowed her eyes. "Yes, you are. Tell me."

"Cheryl."

"Cheryl?" She glanced over at where the assistant was sitting. Cheryl was huddled with Brittany and Patrick. The conversation looked serious.

"Think about it," Cole said. "She's at all the events but in the background."

"She's too loyal to her boss to sabotage Brittany's wedding."

"Maybe she's not trying to stop the wedding," he argued. "She could think she's protecting Brittany from Heidi and Robin. I'm sure she knows all about how miserable they made her in college. Or she's showing how indispensible she is to Brittany."

"That's possible." Angie bit down on her bottom lip as she considered his argument. "She's in charge of all the details."

"And she is in the perfect position to clear away any evidence." Cole motioned at Robin's place setting.

"Brittany doesn't strike me as the kind of woman who picks up after herself," Angie muttered. Her shoulders tensed. "Uh-oh."

"What?" He placed a protective hand on her arm.

"Patrick is coming this way," she said via the side

of her mouth, "and he's got that look on his face. That is not a good look."

"Angie?" Patrick looked away and nervously rubbed his hand over his mouth. "I really hate to tell you this. I'm sure it's temporary. Just until Brittany calms down."

"Just spit it out, Patrick."

Patrick took a big breath. "Brittany wants you to leave," he said in a rush.

Angie showed no emotion and gave a short nod. "I can do that. Not a problem."

"And…" Patrick's face turned bright red. "You're banned from the wedding."

16

"BANNED!" ANGIE SHOUTED as she entered her apartment. She threw her keys on the small table by the door. "Me? *I'm* banned?"

"I know," Cole said as he followed her into the loft. He closed the door and leaned against it as he watched Angie pace. "You've been chanting that since we left."

"Banned!" She ripped off her jacket and threw it on the ground. "No one bans Angela Lawson. No one!"

"Brittany has." He pointed out as he watched her kick off her shoes.

Angie balled her hands into fists. "The nerve of that woman."

"It's not just Brittany. Patrick is backing her up." He hated to mention it but he felt it was necessary. Patrick was going to take Brittany's side from now on. Angie needed to adapt or risk losing her friend.

"Can you believe it?" She furiously tugged at her ponytail and a second later her hair tumbled free. Cole noted the long tresses as they fell around her neck and shoulders. "He has known me for twenty years. And he sides with that woman."

"I'm sure everything will be cleared up and all will be forgiven," he murmured, distracted at how soft and shiny her hair looked. His stomach clenched as he remembered how it felt against his hand and how it swept down his body when Angie was on top.

"Oh, no." She pointed at Cole. "I am not forgiving her. Or Patrick. And to think I bought them a good wedding present."

"Look at the big picture," he suggested, thrusting his hands in his pockets as he watched Angie's angry strides. "You don't have to be a bridesmaid anymore."

She stopped and turned around, her hands on her hips again. "Why aren't you angry? My best friend just kicked me out of his wedding."

"I'm happy you're out of the line of fire."

"Nothing was going to happen to me," she insisted, walking up to him. "But don't you want to go find out if Cheryl is behind this?"

"I can't prove she did any of it," he said, quietly watching the emotions flicker in Angie's eyes. "I have no motive and no weapon. The woman is smart."

She didn't budge an inch. "I bet you she's been poisoning Brittany's mind about me. It's because we've been asking questions."

"Or Brittany just doesn't like you."

Angie nodded as she considered that. "Yeah, there's that, too." She clucked her tongue. "You know, she was right. I am envious."

"What?" His heart stopped as jealousy, hot and bitter, seized his rib cage.

She gave him a curious look. "Not because she has Patrick. Oh, God, no."

"Good to know." He was tempted to rub his knuckles against his chest to ease the pain. "Then what?"

"I'm envious about what she and Patrick have." She looked away as a bittersweet smile tugged at her mouth. "You and I used to have that. I miss it. I miss having you in my life."

"I'm here." He wasn't going anywhere. But would she believe that?

Angie narrowed her eyes as she looked at the door. "You know what? I'm going to crash it."

"Crash what? The ceremony?" Was she kidding? Please let her be kidding. But he saw the look in her eye and the stubborn tilt of her chin.

"That's right." She pumped her fist. "No one can keep me from my friend's wedding."

"I can," he said. His harsh tone caught her notice.

Angie watched him carefully. "You won't."

"I'm looking after you until this wedding is over." He cupped his hands on her stiff shoulders and made her face away from the door. She protested as he pushed her farther into the room. "Consider me your personal bodyguard."

"I don't need one."

She dragged her bare feet on the floor but it wasn't enough resistance to keep him from moving her. "I'll decide that."

"I'm not a bridesmaid anymore," she said, the anger evaporating from her voice. "I'll be fine."

"We're assuming this is related to the wedding," he said as he stopped next to the bed. "It could be for a different reason. I'm not taking any chances."

She sighed. "Go home, Cole."

He shook his head. "Not unless you're coming with me."

"I can take care of myself." Her voice was quiet but steady.

"I know." Angie was strong and capable. She knew it and so did he. Yet he wanted to help her. He wanted to be there for her and prove to her that she wasn't on her own. "But I want to take care of you, too. If anything happens to you…"

"Cole, I've had a bad day." She rubbed her hands over her face. "I'm tired, I'm upset and you need to go before I do something stupid. Like lose my temper. Or cry. At this moment, it could be both."

Did she not want to show that side of herself? Was she worried he would leave if she showed too much emotion? "Go ahead. Let it all out. I don't mind."

"You don't get it, do you?" She met his gaze. "My restraint is almost gone. I don't want to lean on a friend tonight. I want something more. I want everything."

He tried to squelch down the hope building inside him. "What are you saying?"

"I can't be friends with you. Not anymore."

The hope instantly transformed into panic. What did he do wrong? He had been on his best behavior. Whatever she needed, he would do it. Anything to keep her in his life. "Why not?" he asked gruffly.

"I need more from you." She flattened her hand against his chest. "I need to know that you're there for me no matter what."

He swallowed hard, not sure if he heard correctly. "I'm with you all the way." Even if she gave up on him, even if she moved on. He would be there for her whenever she needed him. She didn't have to ask.

"You have always been the most important person in my life," she said. "And I knew that I was your top priority."

"You still are." She put him above everyone else.

In some ways he knew that. She showed it in every choice she made.

"It's not enough," she said. "I want it all back. I want to share my life with you. Have a future together."

This was more than he'd ever expected. He was afraid to make a move. If he said or did something, he could break the spell.

"I get that you can't make a commitment." She slid her hands up his chest and looped them behind his neck. "After the hell you went through...I understand that now. But I don't want to be mere friends. Or friends with benefits."

He was certain that she could feel his heart beating hard. "You want another try."

She nodded. "I want what we had, Cole. I'm not going to ask for anything more, but I refuse to ask for anything less."

He cautiously wrapped his arms around her waist and drew her closer. "Are you sure?"

"I love you, Cole." Her voice was clear and full of confidence. "I haven't stopped loving you."

He couldn't look away from her eyes. "How can you? When all I've ever done is disappoint you."

She pressed her lips against his. "I asked too much of you."

"No, you haven't." His hands shook as he caressed her back. "Tell me what you want and I'll get it for you. Your happiness means everything to me."

"You know what would make me happy right now? If you took me to bed. Let me show you how much I love you."

"No, Angie," he said as he began to unbutton her shirt. "Let me show you how good we can be together."

COLE REMOVED HER clothes in record time. She stood before him naked and aroused, throbbing with desire as he reached for her. She gasped in surprise when he playfully tossed her onto the bed.

"Come here," Angie said, her arms outstretched.

"Soon," he replied as he discarded his jacket. She noticed his hands were unsteady as he undid the buttons on his cuffed sleeves.

"Let me help you," she offered as she moved to rise.

"No." Cole slipped off one shoe and then the other. "Start without me."

Her eyes widened. "What?"

His darkened expression reflected pure passion. "Touch yourself," his said in a husky voice, "and let me watch."

Her breath hitched in her throat. "Do you mean like this?" she asked as she cupped her breasts and pushed them together.

"Yeah," he said roughly as he dragged off his socks. "Just like that."

"But I like it best when you touch me like this," she said as she rubbed her palms over her nipples. "It feels so good."

"What else feels good?" he asked as he clumsily yanked off his tie.

"When you do this." She pinched her nipple and the heat, thick and addictive, scorched through her veins. She moaned and arched her spine to accommodate the flash of pleasure.

"I didn't catch that," Cole said as he unbuttoned his shirt. His teasing tone didn't match the tension vibrating in him. Or the way his skin tightened against his features. He was getting aroused, hard and fast, as he watched her.

"It was something like this." She pinched her nipples harder. Angie gasped from the tingling sensations and rolled her hips. She focused on Cole through hooded eyes and her skin prickled when she noted the raw lust in his gaze.

"What else do you like?" he asked as he tugged his shirt off.

"Hmm…" She glided her hands along her chest and neck before sinking her fingers into her long hair. The warmth had invaded her body. Her arms and legs felt heavy. Her breasts felt large and full. And her hips…

"Show me," Cole commanded. His hands on his belt buckle.

She smiled, boldly, as she skimmed her hands along her sides. One hand stayed on her pelvic bone before she splayed her fingers over her mound.

"What would you like me to do?" he asked as he slowly unbuckled his belt.

She felt a wave of shyness and hesitated. Cole seemed mesmerized by her brazenness, but she didn't want to be too aggressive. She knew better than to ask for too much.

"Angie," Cole said as he slowly unzipped his pants. "I want to know. Don't hide from me."

She didn't want to. Not anymore. Hiding caused misunderstandings and mistakes. It meant holding back when she wanted to live and love fully.

Her pulse raced as she slid one hand over the slick folds of her sex. She glided her fingers slowly as she watched Cole's reaction. And she raised her other hand over her head. She moaned, rocking her hips as the pleasure coiled tight in her belly.

"Oh, Cole." She drew out his name. "I want you deep inside me."

Without hesitation, he shoved off his remaining clothes. Angie couldn't help but be aware that he was rock hard and already breathing deeply.

"Take me now, Cole."

Instantly, he held the backs of her knees and pulled her toward him. Cole hooked her legs over his hips. Her bottom was raised and her hips tilted up. She was totally at his mercy.

He eagerly explored her body with his hands. "Like this?" he asked with a wicked smile as he palmed her breasts. She arched into his touch, enjoying the pressure and friction.

"Yes-s-s," she assured him. She bit her lip, holding back a deep groan as he teased her nipples. "More," she muttered as she moved her head from side to side.

"What about this?" He drew one hand down her abdomen and cupped her mound. Her heart skipped a beat at his possessive hold. She undulated when he pressed her swollen clit.

"I want everything," she said wildly. "I want it now."

Cole put his hands on her hips, his fingers holding tight as he surged into her welcoming heat. The breath stuttered from her throat as he filled her. Cole stilled and closed his eyes as he savored this moment.

Angie stretched her arms out, surrendering to him. Her body accepted Cole and drew him in deeper.

Cole shuddered as he tried to control his most primitive instincts. "No," he warned. "I want this to last."

"I can't help it," she said as she bucked against him. "I want you so much."

He let out a feral growl and sank into her. Heat blanketed her skin as each strong thrust went deep. She rocked against the bed, bunching the sheets in her hands as the pleasure rippled through her.

She watched Cole and saw the sweat gleam along his ruddy skin, his muscles straining each time he withdrew.

"I love you, Cole," she said as the burning, growing pressure inside her burst. She shut her eyes as the white-hot intensity of her orgasm claimed her. Again and again it came in crashing waves as Cole climaxed.

Angie kept her eyes closed. She wanted to remember this heightened moment, this all-consuming pleasure. But she couldn't ignore the fact that Cole didn't say any words of love. And while she felt protected and desired when she was with him, she knew he may never say those important words to her.

17

COLE STARED AT the small stone church as he got out of his car. It appeared quaint and picturesque but he knew danger lurked beneath bunches of white flowers and pink luminaries. Guests were already entering the building and he heard the strains of organ music from where he stood. He hoped he wasn't too late.

He fished his phone from his pocket and checked his messages. Nothing. He tried to take a deep breath but his chest was tight with worry. Cole punched the screen and redialed Angie's phone. He felt like throwing his phone when he immediately got her voice mail.

"Angie, why don't you have your phone on? Call me when you get this." He hung up and rubbed his aching head. When he found her, he was going to make sure she never left his side.

He grabbed his suit jacket and shoved his arms in the sleeves. His movements were choppy and forceful as the panic swelled inside him. Where was Angie? Why wasn't she picking up her phone? Was she hurt? Was her phone dead? Or was she ignoring his calls?

It was bad enough waking up alone in her apartment, but his stomach had made a sickening twist when he found her note explaining that she was back in the wedding.

Back as a bridesmaid, possibly as maid of honor. Either way, she was back to being a target.

His phone rang. Cole checked the screen and saw Angie's number. He felt weak, almost boneless, as the relief poured through him. He immediately answered. "Angie?"

"Hey, Cole," Angie replied cheerfully as if she didn't hear the urgency in his voice. "I'm sorry I missed your call. And your texts. All twelve of them."

"Where have you been?" he demanded.

"Didn't you get my note? I put it where I was sure you'd see it. I didn't want you to worry but I had to leave quickly this morning."

"Yes, I got the note," he said through clenched teeth as he straightened the knot of his necktie. "You should have taken me with you."

"I tried to wake you up. I really did, honest. I guess I wore you out."

He heard the smile in her voice but he wasn't amused. "What are you doing at the wedding? You were banned."

"Patrick texted me early this morning. He and Brittany want me to be in the ceremony." She lowered her voice. "I have a feeling it's really Patrick who wants me there but—"

"Why did you accept?" The frustration rang in his voice and he didn't care.

"Patrick is my friend," she reminded him, "and I know he fought hard to keep me in the wedding. What else could I say?"

"I can think of a few things just off the top of my

head. For instance, the bride has it in for you." He ignored the woman in the floppy hat who gave him a sharp look. "And her assistant is bumping off bridesmaids."

Angie scoffed. "We don't know that."

"Also, Patrick should never have allowed Brittany to speak to you in that manner," Cole continued as he took the steps to the church two at a time. "You tore up your bridesmaid dress in a fit of rage and can't possibly participate…."

"I would never destroy this dress no matter how trashy it is," Angie said breezily. "You have no idea how much it cost."

He entered the church and looked around the vestibule. He saw a few guests. The men wore dark suits while the women looked like exotic birds with their brightly colored dresses and oddly shaped hats. He didn't see Angie. "Where are you?"

"I'm outside the bridal room. We're still getting Brittany ready for the ceremony. It's not going well. The woman is on the verge of a breakdown."

Cole frowned as the phone connection crackled. "We?"

"Robin is here. The hospital released her late last night." He heard the relief in Angie's voice. "She doesn't have a lot of energy and she looks really pale, but she's determined to see this through."

"That's great," Cole said. "I'm glad she's okay."

"She must really want to be in this wedding," Angie said. "I think they want me here as backup if Robin can't perform her maid-of-honor duties."

"Where is Cheryl?" he asked as he went down a hallway, hoping it was in the direction of the bridal room.

"Handling some detail with the minister. You don't

have to worry about me. She's too busy to plot my demise."

"I will always worry about you."

"That's sweet," she declared in a soft voice. "I want you to know I wasn't ignoring you. I'm not sure why I didn't get your messages. The connection here must be weak."

"I've been looking for you everywhere. And—" He turned the corner and spotted her alone, leaning against the wall. Cole stopped as his heart gave a violent lurch. "Holy…"

Angie wore the most provocative dress. It faithfully followed every line and curve of her body. It was designed to gain a man's attention.

"Cole." Her expression brightened when she saw him and turned off her phone.

He strode toward her and gathered her close. It felt good to have her in his arms. "You are in so much trouble."

"For what?" she asked as she held on to him. "For not answering my phone?"

For the phone. For not listening to him. And definitely for the dress. He took a step back and stared at her. The dress was shiny and a strange shade of green, but it fit her perfectly. The low-cut dress hugged her pert breasts and thrust them out like an offering. The skirt clung to her hips and was perilously short. It would ride up her legs and would draw every male's attention to her bottom when she walked.

"That dress," he said slowly.

She pulled away and crossed her arms. "Trashy, isn't it."

"No." He grabbed her wrists and held her arms out

as he took a longer look. The dress emphasized her breasts and hips. "You look…wow."

"Stop teasing me." She tried to escape his hold but he wouldn't let her.

"I'm serious. Wear this dress for me some time," he asked as his gaze lingered on her long, bare legs. He saw the delicate high heels and changed his mind. "Forget that. Just wear the shoes and nothing else."

He saw a naughty gleam in her eyes before she dipped her head. "No way."

"Why not?" Cole asked as he held her hands above her head. Her breasts threatened to spill out of her dress and she tilted her hips as he leaned into her. She was soft and yielding as her body cradled his. Desire for her pulsed right through him and he grew hard as stone.

"This is not me," she insisted.

"Yes, it is." He glanced around the hallway, wondering where he could whisk her away.

"No, it's not," she said in a biting tone. "I can't pull this look off. Do you know me at all?"

"I know every side and every facet of you," he said as he lowered his arms and caressed her cheek. "This is you. It was you last night."

"I would never choose this dress. It's too revealing. Too sexy. It promises something I can't deliver."

"You are sexy." His voice was rough and low as he brushed his knuckles down her throat. "It's driving me wild."

She gave him a skeptical look. "I thought I was sexy in sweatpants and an oversize T-shirt."

"You are. Because that's when you feel confident and comfortable. Because you can hide in those clothes." He cupped her breast and shuddered as the lust whipped through him. "You can't hide in this."

"Don't tell me that," she said, smiling and thrust her breast into his hand. "That's the last thing I need to hear before I walk down the aisle."

He let go of her and gave the dress another look. "How do you get out of this?" he asked as he licked his lips with anticipation.

Angie flattened her hands against his chest. "Don't even try."

"I'm surprised Brittany is allowing you to wear this," he muttered as he crushed the skirt with his hand. "You're going to upstage the bride."

"I look like a joke."

He hooked his finger under her chin and tilted her head up, forcing her to look into his eyes. "Angie, you don't need a dress to show that you are a beautiful and sexy woman. But don't think you have to hide in sweatpants because you're afraid of being noticed."

"Cole, you don't understand." She brushed his hand away from her face. "What you see is hours of work from a team of professionals. This is as good as it gets. And I don't… It's not…"

"I see you. The real you. Behind the makeup and… what the hell is this?" He rubbed his fingers together. "Glitter?"

"Yeah." Angie said roughly as her chest rose and fell as she drew in each breath.

He bumped his forehead with hers and stared into her eyes. "Hide as much as you want, but it's a waste of time. I don't care if you are walking down a runway or limping across the finish line. I will always see you as a strong and sexy woman."

She lowered her lashes as her cheeks turned pink. "Cole…"

He didn't want her to feel shy. He wanted Angie to

feel safe with him. "Just know that you don't have to hide from me."

The loud creak of a door echoed in the empty hallway. Angie was startled at the sound and looked in the direction of the bridal room.

"Oh, my God. Really?" Robin said and planted her hands on her hips. "Cole, do not smudge her makeup or wrinkle her dress. In fact, do not touch her at all."

Cole raised his hands in surrender and took a step back. He noticed Robin wore the same dress as Angie. He didn't spare a second glance at the maid of honor. Angie was a living, breathing fantasy.

Angie sighed and turned her attention to the maid of honor. "What do you want, Robin?"

Robin pointed at the door she just exited. "I'm having trouble tying the corset in Brittany's gown. I need help. I need muscle."

"And you thought of me," she said. "I'll be right there."

"Good," she said as she returned through the same doorway. "I swear, I can't turn my back on you for a second."

"I'm sorry, Cole. I have to go." She bit her bottom lip and gave him a hopeful look beneath her lashes. "Are you going to attend the wedding?"

"Yes." He grabbed her hand and raised it to his mouth. Brushing his lips against her knuckles, he promised, "I'm here for you."

"WHY ISN'T IT fitting?" Brittany shrieked. She stretched the corset one way and then another, and pressed it to her stomach. "I swear this dress fit perfectly two days ago."

"Breathe in," Robin suggested.

"I haven't eaten solid foods for a week," Brittany swore as tears sparkled in her eyes. "I didn't cheat once. Not once! This should fit."

"It will," Robin promised. "Don't cry or we'll have to redo your makeup. Angie, how's it going back there?"

"Are you pulling as hard as you can?" Brittany asked.

"Yes," she said through gritted teeth as she pulled the pink ribbons that crisscrossed in the back of the corset. The mermaid gown was of the palest pink but there was nothing innocent about the dress. The plunging neckline and flared hips dramatically accentuated Brittany's curves. Angie didn't know how Brittany was going to breathe, let alone walk.

Angie pulled so hard she thought she would get rope burn but the corset didn't budge. "I'm afraid to pull any harder," she said. "I don't want the dress to rip."

"Rip?" Brittany whirled around and gave Angie a hateful look. "What did you do to my dress?"

"Nothing!" Angie said as she rubbed her reddened hands. "The dress is fine."

"Stay away from me." Brittany teetered on her heels as she took a cautious step back. "I don't want you touching my dress."

Angie looked at Robin. "I give up."

"Where is Cheryl?" Brittany asked as she examined the back of her dress in the mirror. "Why isn't she here helping me?"

Robin shrugged. "I haven't seen her since we arrived at the church."

"Call her," Brittany ordered. "Call her right now."

"I have." Robin flopped into a seat next to the bride

and held her head in her hands. "Constantly. I don't think we get cell reception here."

"Go find her," Brittany screamed. "She'll know what to do."

"I'll do that," Angie volunteered. She'll do anything that didn't require her to be locked in a room with Brittany.

"Hurry," Robin pleaded. She looked at the clock. "We don't have much time before the ceremony starts."

Angie hurried out of the room with Brittany's wails ringing in her ears. She took a few quick steps before she stumbled and tripped on her heels. Angie grimaced as she twisted her ankle. She pressed her lips together as the pain shot through her leg.

It didn't seem to matter that she had practiced walking in the shoes for hours, Angie decided as she limped down the hallway. It was practically guaranteed that she was going to trip as she made her way down the aisle.

No, she won't. Angie rolled her shoulders back and held up her chin. She could master these shoes. She could wear this dress. She wasn't about to be nervous over the height of her hemline or heels. All she had to do was find Cole and concentrate on him while she came down the aisle. When he looked at her with a mix of awe and desire, she would find her confidence.

Angie saw an open door that led out to the church garden. "Cheryl?" she called. "Are you out here?"

"Yes." Cheryl appeared from behind a flowering bush. "I'm getting the place ready for the photographer."

"Brittany needs you." Angie watched Cheryl and frowned when she noticed the assistant wore the same shoes as the bridesmaids. She even had the same polish on her toes. It was bubble-gum-pink. Yet Cheryl didn't get a pedicure with the rest of the bridal party.

"What seems to be the problem?" Cheryl asked as she walked up the stone steps.

"There's a problem with the dress," Angie replied. She narrowed her eyes when she noticed Cheryl's dress. The assistant wore a soft pink cardigan but her outfit was shiny and green. It was a replica of the bridesmaids' dresses.

Cheryl stopped at the top of the steps. Angie dragged her gaze up, cataloging every detail. She was belatedly aware that Cheryl was studying her closely.

"Did you forget something?" Angie asked, doing her best to seem casual as her instincts were sensing trouble.

"I only have to do one more thing…." Cheryl suddenly reached out with both hands and pushed Angie down the steps.

18

ANGIE LUNGED OUT to grab onto Cheryl, but instead, tumbled to the ground. The rough stone steps scratched her skin. Angie wasted no time, though, before she leaped to her feet where she'd landed. She felt every cut and bruise, but she tried to ignore the pain as she focused on Cheryl.

"Damn," Cheryl groaned. She stood at the top of the steps with her hands on her hips. "What are you? A ninja?"

"So, I'm next, huh?" Angie asked as she held on to the arm that had broken her fall. She rubbed it as she scanned the garden. She didn't see a way out. "I'm surprised that you're not trying to finish the job on Robin."

Cheryl's eyes widened with surprise. "You figured it out that it was me." Cheryl gave a mocking clap. "Well done, Angie. You are not the dumb jock Brittany claims you are."

"Why are you doing this to Brittany?" Angie asked. She looked at the hedges that bordered the garden. They were too tall to climb over. "I thought you cared for her."

"I *do* care." Cheryl's face turned red with anger. "I've done everything to give her the wedding she wanted. I care more than anyone in her bridal party. I probably care more than Patrick and it's his wedding."

"Okay, calm down." Angie looked around and considered her options. She didn't have her cell phone, and even if she did, it probably wouldn't work. Everyone was in the church except for Robin and Brittany. Angie's only hope was that Robin would come looking for her. But what were the chances that she'd find her in the enclosed garden? No one would see her before Cheryl attacked again. Her only plan was to keep Cheryl talking until someone became concerned for them.

"I am calm," Cheryl retorted.

"That's true," she said as she took another step back. Maybe she could rush Cheryl and tackle her. But that probably wouldn't work in her favor. "You have nerves of steel. Like when you hit Heidi at the strip club. Did you plan that or was it a spur-of-the-moment kind of thing?"

"I don't know why she asked Heidi to be maid of honor." Cheryl scoffed and rolled her eyes. "Brittany thought she would do whatever we asked, but it turns out the woman was useless. Her ineptitude was going to ruin the wedding. Heidi needed to be told what to do, how to do it and when it needed to be done. It made my job twice as hard."

"I'm sure it did." Angie nodded her head vigorously as she took another step back. "So you had to get her out of the wedding?"

"No, that was a bonus." Cheryl took the next step. "I was reminding her of her duties and she went off on me. She was complaining about how much work was involved."

"Didn't she realize that this was an honor?" Angie asked and realized Cheryl didn't hear her sarcasm.

"She made me so angry," Cheryl growled. "I have worked on this wedding for months and I wasn't paid for the extra time. I did all this while doing my regular job for Brittany. Heidi barely did anything. I don't know what came over me. I just snapped."

Angie looked quickly behind her. There had to be another way out. "And that's why you hit her with a flower vase."

"How do you know that?" Cheryl asked, her voice rising. "I was very careful putting back the arrangement."

Angie held her hands up. "You did a great job. Honest. And you did it when no one saw you. How is that possible? I admit that those strippers were distracting, but..."

"No one notices me," Cheryl said sadly. "Not even Brittany. I'm the assistant. Invisibility is my superpower."

"Are you kidding? You are an essential part of the team. This wedding wouldn't have happened without you."

"Oh, sure," Cheryl muttered as she took the last stone steps. "I'm noticeable when something goes wrong. Then everyone is looking for me."

"What's wrong with being invisible?" Angie asked. "It's comfortable. It's safe. It means you're doing something right."

"Oh, what would you know about being invisible?" she spat out. "That stripper picked you out of a crowd of women. Beautiful, glamorous women who know the difference between Prada and Pucci. And he can't keep his eyes off you."

"Brittany notices what you do. She's desperately looking for you now." Angie glanced at the small church building. What was taking Robin so long?

"And when she finds me, I will be tending to your concussion," she said sweetly as she advanced. "Everyone knows you can't walk in heels."

"That may have worked before but not this time," Angie said as she scurried back. She jumped when the prickly needles from the hedge poked her behind. "You let everyone think Heidi had too much to drink. But you didn't know that Heidi was clean and sober."

"I don't believe you. Brittany talked constantly about Heidi's wild antics. I knew the woman was going to be trouble before I met her."

"And when Heidi was out, you saw this as your chance to get into the wedding. You wanted to be a bridesmaid." Angie shook her head with disbelief. "Why?"

"Why? A bridesmaid is chosen based on how close she is to the bride. Someone who is important and part of the bride's life. Brittany hasn't seen Heidi and Robin for years. They didn't know what was going on in Brittany's life. I do. I'm with Brittany every day. I'm an important part of her life."

"I'm sure—"

"Do you know why Brittany became a personal shopper?" Cheryl asked. "Or what her goals and dreams are? Do you know what problems she had to overcome to get where she is today? I do."

"So what?" Angie said, shrugging. "I could find all that out if I wanted to. Brittany doesn't strike me as a very private person."

"*So what?* I know every intimate detail of Brittany's life. I am her closest confidante. I get rid of obstacles in her life and I protect her. I should have been a bridesmaid." Cheryl flattened her hand on her chest. "I should have been picked to be the maid of honor."

"You've definitely proven how indispensible you are in Brittany's life. If she didn't know it before, she definitely knows it now."

"She appreciates me," Cheryl shouted. "I know she does."

Angie cringed. Her instincts were to duck and take cover, but she had to keep her talking. She had to buy herself more time. "But you did your job too well," Angie decided. "She wanted you to stay in your role of assistant and she made Robin maid of honor."

"I know. I couldn't believe it." Her face twisted with anger. "Robin? Robin was worse than Heidi."

"So how did you get rid of her?" Angie asked. "You put something in her drink, didn't you?"

Cheryl suddenly stopped advancing. She took a step back and gave Angie an assessing stare.

"Oh, come on," Angie said with a tentative smile. "You know I have no proof. You got rid of the martini glass the minute Robin started to show symptoms."

"How long have you known that it was me?" Cheryl looked at her as if she were a new type of threat.

"I didn't," she admitted. But she wouldn't dare mention Cole's observations or how he had been investigating the accident. "I thought Robin hurt Heidi because she deserves the maid-of-honor role."

"Deserves? Are you kidding?" Cheryl's voice overpowered the organ music coming from the church. "Robin didn't deserve it at all. All she cared about was getting lucky at the wedding. Like being the maid of honor would give her the extra edge. Right. A little peanut oil in the martini took care of that."

Angie was amazed at Cheryl's blaze attitude. "You could have killed her."

Cheryl snorted at the suggestion. "Why do you think I asked you to look for her? You and your stripper boyfriend had jumped into action at the bachelorette party. I knew you'd find her."

"And you got me kicked out of the wedding."

Cheryl laughed. "I'm good, but I'm not that good. That was a stroke of luck and I thought I had finally protected Brittany's dream wedding. This was my chance to be the bridesmaid. It was my reward. I could be part of Brittany's special day. Everything was working in my favor." She frowned. "But Patrick talked Brittany into letting you back in the wedding."

"And now you're after me. Why?" Angie asked. She took a step to the side and was no longer trapped between the hedges and Cheryl. "Why don't you take out Robin? She's weak."

"She's extra cautious now. Not to mention everyone is fussing over her all the time. Also, Brittany wanted Robin in the wedding."

"And Brittany doesn't want me here," Angie concluded. The bride would be happy to have her out of the wedding and thus be more willing to add her assistant in at the last minute.

"Exactly." Cheryl's smile sent chills down Angie's spine. "She doesn't want you anywhere in her life. Expect to slowly fade from Patrick's social circle."

"I can't believe you did all this to be a bridesmaid." She pressed her hand against her head and discovered that half of her updo was falling out. She blew a chunk of hair out of her eyes. "It's a horrible job."

"I'm doing this because I care about Brittany," Cheryl argued. "I got rid of all of the fake friends and backstabbing bridesmaids. Brittany deserves to be sur-rounded by people who actually love and adore her."

"You have a strange way of showing friendship. And, honestly, being a bridesmaid is a test of will and patience. Think about it," Angie stressed as she took another side step. "You have to be at the bride's beck and call. You have to put your life on hold and put up with the bride's rages. Do you have any idea what that feels like? Oh, wait. Maybe you do."

"But this way everyone will know that I'm more than her employee," Cheryl said, raising her voice. "I'm her friend."

"No, she will never think that." Angie was reluctant to share this with Cheryl, but the woman had to know that Brittany would never see her as an equal. "Brit-tany said so herself. When the suggestion was made to replace you for Heidi, Brittany made it very clear that you were only the assistant."

"She wouldn't say that!" Cheryl shouted. "Brittany likes me. She likes me more than any of her brides-maids."

Angie took another step. She was almost in the clear to make a run for the stone steps. "Even if you did get rid of me, she won't add you to the ceremony."

"Yes, she will." Cheryl grabbed her arm and squeezed tight. "She'll be in a panic and she'll want me right there."

"Fine." She tried to shake off Cheryl's hold but it was no use. "You know what? You don't need to take me out of commission. You want to take my place? Go for it."

Cheryl looked at her as if she sensed a trick. "You're not going to fight it?"

"I'll be relieved. I didn't want to do this, anyway. Tell

Brittany that I twisted my ankle while I was looking for you. She won't want me hobbling down the aisle."

"True." She tightened her hold on Angie's arm. "But how do I know you won't talk?"

Angie wasn't sure if she could come up with a convincing reason not to. "You said it yourself. There is no proof. Everything you used is gone." When Cheryl nodded, Angie kept going. "It's just my word against yours. And everyone thinks I'll say anything to ruin the wedding."

"I'm glad we're in agreement. Okay, I'll take your place." She pointed at Angie's other arm. "Now hand over the bracelet."

Angie curled her hand closer to her body. "Why?"

"Brittany gave it to her bridesmaids as a gift during the bridesmaids' luncheon," Cheryl said. "I was there. I picked out the bracelet. Why shouldn't I get one?"

"You shouldn't get one because you weren't a bridesmaid," Angie muttered as an idea formed in her head.

"But I am now." She held out her other hand. "Give it to me."

Angie slid the bracelet from her wrist and threw it as Cheryl reached for it.

"What are you doing?" Cheryl asked as she watched the bracelet fall into the dirt.

Angie swung her foot out and swiped Cheryl's legs from underneath her. They both fell down. "Cheryl," she said as they wrestled for control. "I don't care about being a bridesmaid, but no one tries to hurt me and gets away with it."

COLE SAT IN the back of the church and glanced at his watch. The wedding should have already started. What was taking so long?

He looked at the entrance where the procession should be. Instead, he saw only Robin hovering by the door. She seemed worried, almost frantic, as she motioned for him to meet her in the hallway.

Cole quickly followed her. "What's going on, Robin?"

"Have you seen Angie?" she whispered.

Her words were like a kick to his system. His body was on full alert and he immediately checked his phone. "Not since you saw me with her. Why?"

"This isn't good." Robin began chewing on her fingernail. "I've checked every room and closet hoping she was with you."

"How long has it been since you've seen her?"

"I don't know. It feels like forever," Robin admitted as tears shone in her eyes. "Brittany was freaking out and I couldn't get a hold of Cheryl on my phone. Angie went to look for her and now they're both missing."

"Keep searching inside the church. I'll go outside." He broke into a run and looked around the front steps. He didn't see anyone. He thought of the parking lot and then the church grounds. His instinct was to head for the grounds.

He ran to the side of the church, calling out Angie's name. He saw a thick wall of hedges and was about to go around them when he heard the sound of a struggle. "Angie?"

"Cole?" Angie called out. "I'm in the garden— Ow!"

Cole pushed his way through the thick shrubbery. It felt like it took him ages as he slapped, kicked and clawed his way in. He had to get to Angie. He would never forgive himself if something happened to her.

He heard Angie's scream and the sound of a body slamming against the ground. His heart twisted with fear. Cole let out a roar as he crashed through the last of the shrubbery and found Angie wrestling on the grass with Cheryl.

Angie struggled as she rolled back and forth with Cheryl. Her hair was flying out of her bun and a long grass stain streaked down her dress. Dirt and scratches covered her arms, legs and chest.

He rushed forward but Angie had staggered to her feet and was pointing at Cheryl. "Don't you dare move," she told the assistant, who lay limp and moaning.

"Need some help?" Cole asked as he wrapped his arm around Angie's waist. He peered into her eyes and frowned when he saw a bruise forming under one of them.

"You can call your friend, that woman who was the first police officer at the strip club. Cheryl confessed to injuring Heidi and Robin."

"You don't have any proof," Cheryl said weakly.

"You were also seen in a physical altercation with Angie," Cole said, refusing to look at Cheryl. "And you have me as a witness."

Cheryl made a face as if dismissing his claim. "Who's going to listen to a stripper?"

"Hey." Angie bumped Cheryl's hip with her shoe. "His name is Cole Foster and he's a private investigator and a former cop."

"What?" Cheryl said in a squawk. "Brittany didn't say anything about this."

Angie shook her head. "You've really got to stop using Brittany as your only source of information."

Cole saw something gold glitter in the dirt. He bent down and picked up a thin bracelet.

"That's mine," Angie said, extending her hand.

Cole held her fingers gently and slid it onto her wrist. "How did you lose this in a fight?"

"Cheryl tried to take it." She held up her wrist and let the sunshine gleam off the gold. "She thought she should have it."

"You said I could be a bridesmaid," Cheryl wailed.

"Cheryl, I may be just a close friend of the groom's and I may have a bad attitude toward weddings, but I'm wearing this bracelet because I earned it." She lowered her hand. "But don't worry, Cheryl. You're going to get a pair of metal, police-issued ones. You definitely earned those."

19

"I CAN'T BELIEVE Brittany kicked you out of the wedding again," Cole said as he carried Angie into her apartment. "After all you did for her."

"I don't mind," said Angie as she lifted her arm and allowed the bracelet to sparkle under the hallway light. "I still got a bracelet out of this deal."

"And least this time Tim and Steven argued on your behalf," he stated, shutting the door behind them. "I thought they were going to go slide in the mud in solidarity with you."

Angie smiled. "I think they wanted to blow off some steam. It had nothing to do with me."

Cole wasn't so sure. He knew Angie's friends were impressed by her taking down Cheryl and finding out the real reason behind the accidents. They were very vocal in their displeasure when Brittany refused to have Angie continue being a bridesmaid based on her scruffy appearance.

"Cole, you can put me down now," Angie told him as he brushed past the sofa and went straight to the bed.

"My ankle is just twisted. And that wasn't from Cheryl. That was from hurrying in these heels."

"Obviously the only safe place for you to wear these shoes is in bed with me." He laid her down. He took off his jacket and wrenched off his tie. Cole felt the anger and fear roll through him again as he cupped her jaw and studied her scratched-up face. "That is some black eye."

She shrugged. "It'll heal."

He caressed her cheek. "I never should have left you alone in the church. I knew Cheryl was behind all this. I knew she was out to get you."

"Don't blame yourself, please. We had no proof. And I had everything under control. But I was glad I had you as backup."

"I will always be there for you." He leaned down and kissed her gently. "I, too, argued to keep you in the wedding."

"Oh, I heard. The whole church heard. At least I got to see Patrick get married. That's all I really wanted." She pulled at the frayed hem of her dress. "The minute I saw these stains down the front of me, I knew there was no way Brittany would let me walk down the aisle."

Cole couldn't believe the bride's ingratitude. "Like I said, after all you did for her."

"I know, right?" Angie's eyes twinkled. "It's okay. I saved the day and the wedding went on. Patrick knows I did it for him. And I uncovered how crazy Cheryl really is. I wonder what will happen to her."

"She was saying a lot when they took her away." Cheryl's excuses and explanations were not going to help her case.

"She felt invisible because the most important person in her life didn't share her feelings. I thought I understood how she felt but I was wrong. You see me, even when I try to hide."

"It's pointless to hide from me."

"It is," Angie agreed as she pulled Cole down on top of her.

"Angie," he warned as she rolled over so she was on top. "Forget it. You need to rest."

"Later," she promised as she placed a sweet kiss on his lips. "Right now, I need to be with you."

And he needed to be with her. He realized that days ago but had been slow to act on it. Her pseudo-accident changed that.

"Angie, when I was trying to get to you, I had this one thought going through my mind the whole time." He felt almost queasy as he remembered the bitter taste of fear. "I was worried that if something happened, I would never have the chance to tell you that I love you."

He felt the tension in Angie's body before she lifted her head and looked into his eyes. "Now's your chance."

He frowned. "Weren't you listening? I just did."

"Cole," urged Angie, "tell me exactly how you feel."

Cole didn't feel nervous as he held her gaze. He wanted her to know. He wanted the world to know how he felt about this woman. "I love you, Angie. At first I thought it made me weak. Vulnerable. I didn't want to show how much you meant to me because I would give you power over me."

"What changed?"

"You've always had power over me, whether or not I told you how I feel. From the second I met you. But you didn't use it against me."

"Cole, I'm going to let you in on a little secret." She

leaned forward until her mouth was a kiss away from his. "I'm not powerful but you make me feel that way. Like right now. I'm excited and anxious. I feel safe but adventurous. When you look at me like that, I want to be everything to you."

"You are," he insisted. "And I was lost and miserable after I left you. I believed I was doing the right thing but I wished every day that I hadn't ended things. And it was a mistake that I waited so long to see you again."

"I won't lie, Cole, it hurt when you took off," she said, her eyes darkening as she recalled the pain. "I tried to get over you but I couldn't."

"Yeah, I remember your face when you saw me on stage." She had been confused and angry. It gave him a little bit of hope that she still had feelings for him.

Angie sat up straight and tightened her legs around his hips. "That reminds me, no more undercover work, especially in a strip club."

"Don't worry. I'm never doing that again." The only woman he wanted tearing his clothes off was Angie. "The one good thing that came out of that is that you owe me a lap dance."

Her mouth dropped open. "Says who?"

He moved restlessly underneath her as he imagined her performance wearing nothing but those impractical heels. "Come on, Angie. Let me watch you."

She hesitated as if she were actually considering his suggestion. "How much cash do you have?"

"That depends," he said as his gaze traveled down her body. "What are you offering to do?"

ANGIE SUDDENLY FELT shy. Shy, but intrigued. She nervously licked her lips. "There's no music."

"Doesn't matter." His voice sounded gravelly as

she saw the lust sharpen his features. "I just want to watch you."

Angie liked the idea but it would be so revealing. She wanted to seduce Cole and make him go wild underneath her. Show him how she felt. Get pleasure from his pleasure. She wanted to be as bold as she used to be.

But she wanted him to do more than just watch. "Guide me through it."

"You don't need any help," he said with a smile. Slowly, he slid his hands under his head and shifted to find a comfortable spot on the bed. "Go for it."

Angie stared at him and her heart did a strange little flip. His rumpled white shirt was pulled tight against his broad chest. His position was almost casual, but his expression was serious. He was giving her all the power. And showing her he was open to anything, while still encouraging her. She could do whatever she wanted and he would enjoy the ride.

She tentatively rolled her hips for him and then raised her short skirt. The fabric was slick and silky against her bare legs. She ran her hands along her thighs, imagining how Cole would often touch her that way when he was overcome with desire. She splayed her fingers over her breasts before skimming them along her throat and cheeks.

"Stop teasing," Cole said hoarsely. "Give me all you got."

She smiled and dragged down his zipper, then pulled his belt free. "Take off your clothes," she requested.

Cole did so, his actions quick and impatient. When his underwear hit the floor, he settled back on the bed, his penis thick and proudly erect. Heavy anticipation crashed through Angie as she grasped the base of his cock. Cole hissed between clenched teeth and bucked into her hand.

Angie bit her lip as she watched Cole's reaction. Yes, she was giving him pleasure, but he was giving her his trust. Cole was tough, he could take control again any time he wanted, but what he wanted was for her to have it.

"Take off your dress," he said, mimicking her earlier request of him. "Keep the shoes on." He grinned playfully.

Angie reached behind her. She couldn't wait to lie with Cole, skin on skin. "I need your help."

Cole rose and sat up. Angie watched him intensely, her sex clenching as her peaked nipples rasped against the tight material. She couldn't hide her shiver as Cole lowered the zipper. His hands were large and strong against the simple, fragile dress. She wanted him to rip off the fabric. Instead he peeled it off her gradually. She stretched, exaggerating each move as the intense arousal soared through her. She arched her back and thrust her breasts.

Once he removed her dress, Angie slowly exhaled, her breath echoing in the charged silence. She laid her hands on Cole's shoulders, her fingers digging into his muscles. She could feel his hot gaze on her breasts. Her skin tingled as Cole licked his lips. She waited for him to take her into his mouth.

"Keep dancing, Angie. Show off your body."

Angie held back a frustrated cry. Dancing wasn't on her mind. There was no music, except for the thrumming beat of her heart. His mouth was right at the tips of her breasts. She wanted to feel his tongue on her. She wanted him to tease her everywhere until she was begging for mercy.

She would have *him* begging for mercy, she decided. Angie caught his eye and fondled her breasts, moaning from the unreal pleasure. She felt Cole's burning passion when she gasped while pinching her nipples. She pinched harder, tilting her head back and calling out his name.

Angie slid her hands down her flat stomach before cupping her sex. She held his gaze. She no longer felt shy. She felt powerful. Naughty. Demanding. She dipped one hand into her panties and stroked the slick folds of her sex.

Cole drew her hands to her sides and held her hips. He slid something cold and metallic along her skin. She looked down and stilled. "I-is that…"

"This is the key to my apartment," he said softly. "I want you to have it."

She stared at the silver key chain. It was simple and elegant with just one key. He had made a key for her. And bought the key chain with her in mind. Excitement pulsed through her, but she was afraid she was misreading his gesture. "Why?" she asked and caution fought with elation.

"I want you to move in with me." His voice was a whisper as he stripped her panties down her legs. The key chain slipped from his fingers and fell on the bed.

"Are you sure?" she asked, helping him remove the last item of clothing. Her legs wobbled as she straddled him again. She didn't want to push him into anything.

"Yes, this is just the beginning," he said as he placed his hands on her hips and guided her down. "One of these days I'm going to convince you to marry me."

Angie groaned as Cole stretched and filled her. His words reverberated in her head. She leaned into him, sinking deeper as she wrapped her arms around his shoulders.

"I'm all for marriage," Angie said as she vibrated with need. "I said I wasn't going to marry. But that was because I thought you didn't want marriage."

Cole threaded his fingers through her hair and held her tight. She couldn't look away from him even if she wanted to. "I'm going to marry you, Angie."

"Yes." She rocked forward and back, setting a wild pace, chasing the pleasure. Cole held on to her, surging against her pressing hips. His thrusts were hard, relentless until he found his release. He kept her tightly in his arms as he pulsed into her and she climaxed.

Cole fell back onto the bed, taking Angie with him. She sank against Cole as she tried to catch her breath. The blood pounded in her ears and her heart beat against her ribs. Her skin was hot and sticky with sweat but she didn't want to move. She could stay curled against Cole forever.

"I'm going to ask you again," Cole said roughly as he held her beside him. She noticed his hand trembled as he stroked her damp hair. "I don't want you to think I said it in the heat of the moment."

"The answer will always be the same," Angie said before she kissed his neck, his cheek and mouth. "Today, tomorrow, or on our golden anniversary. I love you, Cole. And the answer will always be yes."

Epilogue

Six months later

BEST. BACHELORETTE. PARTY. EVER. Angie whooped with delight at the thought. She pumped her hands up in the air as she watched the men posture and swing their sticks for the crowd. Despite their thick and powerful legs, these men were agile. Poetry in motion. She couldn't tear her gaze away.

"Angie, what are you doing?" Brittany asked with a sigh of disapproval.

"Having the time of my life," Angie replied, staring at the macho display in front of her. "Are you still having trouble understanding what's going on? Do you want me to explain it to you again?"

"No, once was enough," Brittany declared. "But this is supposed to be your bachelorette party. We should be staring at strippers instead of hockey players."

Angie disagreed. She rarely got the chance to watch the local hockey team play and this was the first time she'd attended the game in the comfort of the sky box. It offered her the best view of the action.

"I don't need strippers," Angie told Brittany as she bit back a naughty smile. "I have my own at home."

"Spare me the details. I don't want to know. But you should realize that you broke the golden rule for bachelorette parties. You invited the guys!" She gestured at the window, where Patrick and Cole cheered loudly for their team.

"I wanted all my friends here." Angie paid attention to the goalie defending the net with a blocked shot. She cheered and looked around the sky box. Tim and Steven were flirting with every unattached woman at the party and her brothers were enjoying the game with their girlfriends. It had taken a while before her brothers and her basketball buddies accepted Cole, but now they'd gladly given their collective blessing since they could see how happy he made her. Next week at this time her friends and family would be present when she married Cole in a casual yet intimate wedding.

Brittany picked at the hem of Angie's oversize hockey jersey and shook her head. "Couldn't you have at least worn a tiara?"

"I don't need to." She waved her ring finger in front of the woman's face. "I have all the glitter I need."

Brittany grasped Angie's finger and studied the engagement ring. She clucked her tongue at the lack of manicure but lowered her head in defeat. "Okay, I admit Cole did well in choosing diamonds."

"No, Brittany," Cole said, slipping his arm around Angie's waist and gathering her close. "I did well in choosing a bride."

"Oh, please," Brittany lamented as she watched Cole capture Angie's earlobe with the edge of his teeth. "Can you save that for the honeymoon?"

"I can't help it," Angie said as she turned and looked

up at Cole. She cupped his cheek with her hand and his features softened. Her breath caught in her throat when she saw the love and desire in his eyes. "When I'm with Cole, there's no holding back."

* * * * *

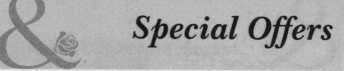

Join the Mills & Boon Book Club

Want to read more **Blaze®** books?
We're offering you **2 more** absolutely **FREE!**

We'll also treat you to these fabulous extras:

- 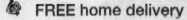 Exclusive offers and much more!

- FREE home delivery

- FREE books and gifts with our special rewards scheme

Get your free books now!

visit www.millsandboon.co.uk/bookclub
or call Customer Relations on 020 8288 2888

Her only weakness, his deepest desire

Nora has been kidnapped by Marie-Laure, Kingsley's
sister and Søren's wife, whom everyone had presumed
dead thirty years ago. Betrayed by her brother and
the husband she once madly loved, now she is
out for revenge.

Kingsley, Søren and Wes—all foes to some degree—
must work together to figure out how to save Nora.

Are you ready for Book 4?

Welcome to the world of the #OriginalSinners…
The Siren • The Angel • The Prince • The Mistress

ELECTRIFYING. EROTIC.
Are you ready to be shocked?

Have you ever craved someone's touch?

Even when you know it's wrong?

I have.

I knew.

And I did it anyway.

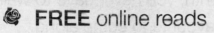

The World of
Mills & Boon®

There's a Mills & Boon® series that's perfect for you. We publish ten series and, with new titles every month, you never have to wait long for your favourite to come along.

Blaze.
Scorching hot, sexy reads
4 new stories every month

By Request
Relive the romance with the best of the best
9 new stories every month

Cherish™
Romance to melt the heart every time
12 new stories every month

Desire™
Passionate and dramatic love stories
8 new stories every month

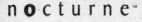